ASSASSIN'S
—C R E E D®—
HERESY

UBISOFT®

625 3rd St, San Francisco,
CA 94107, U.S.A.

Published by Ubisoft.
The publisher does not have any control over and does not assume any responsibility for author or third-party websites or their content.

Special thanks :
Yves Guillemot, Laurent Detoc, Alain Core, Geoffroy Sardin, Yannis Mallat, Etienne Allonier, Aymar Azaïzia, Antoine Ceszynski, Anouk Bachman, Maxime Durand, Richard Farrese, Arin Murphy-Hiscock, Jose Holder, Raphaël Lacoste, Yves Lançon, Misha Benjamin, Virginie Gringarten, Marc Muraccini, Cécile Russeil, Faceout Studio, Bryan Longoria, Jeff Miller, Paul Nielsen, Torrey Sharp, Michael Beadle, Heather Pond, Joanie Simms, Megan Beatie, Andrien Gbinigie, Stephanie Pecaoco, Sain Sain Thao, Michael Kwan, Clémence Deleuze, François Tallec.

ISBN 978-1-945210-02-0

10 9 8 7 6 5 4 3 2 1 16 17 18 19 20

First printing 2016. Printed in the U.S.A.

Book design by Faceout Studio, Jell Miller and Paul Nielsen

ASSASSIN'S CREED®

HERESY

CHRISTIE GOLDEN

ABOUT CHRISTIE GOLDEN

Award-winning and eight-time *New York Times* bestselling author Christie Golden has written fifty novels and several short stories in the fields of science fiction, fantasy, and horror. She has earned wide critical acclaim and a devoted fan base for both her original work and her authentic and skillful literary treatment of many beloved film, television, and gaming franchises.

Golden has written more than a dozen Star Trek novels, and about the same number of World of Warcraft and StarCraft novels. She has written three books in the Star Wars series Fate of the Jedi, which she co-wrote with Troy Denning and the late and greatly missed Aaron Allston, as well as *Star Wars: Dark Disciple*, the novelization of the unaired episodes of *Star Wars: The Clone Wars*, cited as one of the best of the new canon novels.

Golden has been an aficionado of the Assassin's Creed universe since 2014, and has already written two books for the franchise: *Black-beard: The Lost Journal*, a companion book to the video game *Assassin's Creed IV: Black Flag*; and *Assassin's Creed Unity: The Abstergo Employee Handbook*. *Assassin's Creed: Heresy* is the newest addition to this list.

Christie Golden has been publishing books for twenty-five years. The TSR Ravenloft line in 1991 was launched with her first novel, the bestselling *Vampire of the Mists*, which introduced elven vampire Jander Sunstar. To the best of her knowledge, she is the creator of the elven vampire archetype in fantasy fiction. Among her original fantasy novels are *On Fire's Wings*, *In Stone's Clasp*, and *Under Sea's Shadow*, the first three in her multi-book fantasy series The Final Dance. Her very first original novels, *Instrument of Fate* and *In Stone's Clasp*, are currently available in digital form nearly fifteen years after their original publication.

Born in Atlanta, Georgia, Christie Golden currently lives in Virginia. You can find her online at christiegolden.com, on Facebook as Christie Golden, and on Twitter @ChristieGolden.

This, my fiftieth novel, is dedicated to every reader
who has ever picked up a copy of my work and found delight,
wonder, poignancy, excitement, food for thought,
or just plain fun within its covers—and also to all of those
who will (I hope!) find the same in the next fifty.

PROLOGUE

The autumnal night's chill sliced through the man's thin shirt as he fled, feet flying over first the concrete pathway, then the manicured grass of the rooftop's park. *Why did I come up here?* he thought, wildly and far too late. *I'm a bloody rat in a trap.*

The Templars were behind him.

They knew where he had fled. And they knew, as he did, that other than the lift and the two stairways from which they now emerged with grim and silent purpose, there was no way off this roof.

Think. Think!

Thinking had saved him before, many a time. He'd always relied on logic, on rationality, on analysis, to solve every predicament that life in all its sadistic whimsy had thrown him, but now it was of no use to him at all.

The deadly percussion of gunfire exploded behind him. *Trees,* his rational mind shouted, and the logic saved him. He altered his path, zigzagging to make himself an unpredictable target, careening erratically like a drunken man toward the trees and shrubberies, statuary and now-vacant ice cream and beverage stalls that would shield him from the hail of bullets.

But it would only delay the inevitable.

He knew very well what the Templars were capable of. And he knew what they wanted. They were not coming to question him, or capture him. They were intent on killing him, and therefore, very, very soon, he would be dead.

He was not without a weapon himself, one that was ancient and powerful. A Sword of Eden, which had known the grip of both Templars and Assassins through the centuries. He had used it earlier. It was strapped to his back, its weight calming and reassuring, and he would leave it there. It would not serve him now.

The Templars were single-minded of purpose, dedicated only to dominance and death—his. There was only one way out, and it would be a bloody miracle if it worked.

His heart was slamming against his chest, his lungs heaving, his body taxed to its limit because in the end, he was only human, wasn't he, no matter what kind of training he had, no matter what sort of DNA was floating about in his blood. And he didn't slow, *couldn't* slow, couldn't allow that logical, analytical, rational brain of his to interrupt the signals from the deep primal instinct of survival. Couldn't let his brain overrule his body.

Because his body knew what was called for. And it knew how to do it.

A tree branch exploded right beside him. Splinters grazed his face, drawing blood.

The fate offered by the Templars behind him was one of heartless certainty. The stone roof that encircled the edge of the rooftop garden of the London office of Abstergo Industries offered a wild, desperate chance.

If he had the faith to take it.

He didn't slow. As he approached the wall, he surged forward, clearing it like runner would a hurdle, his long legs pedaling in the air as he arched his back, spread his arms—

—and leaped.

CHAPTER ONE

Torchlight capered over the stone walls of the chamber, casting grotesquely distorted shadows over the iron-banded wooden door and the life-sized portrait of the greatest Templar Grand Master who had ever lived. The Postulate, clad in a white vestment with a second, heavier outer red robe, gazed up at the image of the white-bearded face that regarded him, the eyes kind, the pose strong.

A voice spoke in the silence, rich and smooth and deep. "Jacques de Molay was the last public Grand Master of the Order of the Knights Templar. He was falsely accused of heresy by unscrupulous men. Men interested not in the betterment of humanity, but only in their own selfish desires. The best of us confessed to the worst of crimes; crimes he did not commit. His enemies, and history, believed the Order had died with him. It did not."

The Master Templar stepped into the chamber to stand beside the Postulate. "Jacques de Molay died, in agony, so that the Order might live— safely, in secret, known only to those who also would gladly die for it."

The Postulate looked into the Master's dark eyes. "Be humble as dust and still as stone," the Master said. He stretched out a gloved hand, and pointed toward the marble floor. The Postulate lowered himself so he lay face down on the cold stone, arms stretched out to either side, in the form of a cross.

"You will pass through the shadows of the night alone with the Father of Understanding. May he strip from you all that does not strengthen the Order, and clothe you with certainty. May he empty you, and refill you with purpose. Sleep not, dream not. As the day breaks, we will come for you. If we find you worthy, we shall elevate you. If we find you lacking, we shall turn our backs upon you. May the Father of Understanding guide you."

The Postulate heard the soft sounds of slippered feet and the creak, slam, and click of the door as it was closed and locked.

He was alone, with only one way out—through that door, as a Member of the Inner Sanctum.

If he failed.... No. He would not consider the option.

There was no danger of sleep. The torches provided light, but no warmth, and the marble leeched his body heat despite his double layer of ritual clothing. Time, aloof and leisurely, stretched out, unmoved by one man's discomfort. After what seemed like an eternity, the welcome rattle of the skeleton key in the door came at last. The Postulate was hoisted by his arms and bit back a hiss of pain; lying motionless for several hours on the merciless stone had taken its toll.

He followed the pair that had lifted him to his feet in silence. The Postulate still strode upon stone, but now, it was hard slate. They passed beneath an arched gateway of brick and rock. The large tree trunks flanking it stretched upward, disappearing into the darkness, extending past the reach of the faint light of torches flickering in their sconces.

Robed, cowled figures awaited him. Although each held a beeswax candle, their faces remained swathed in darkness, save for the glint of eyes caught by firelight.

"The human body has its heart," the Master Templar intoned. "The earth has its core. All things have a center, whence comes their deepest strength. The Templar Order, too, has its Inner Sanctum. Nine there must be, three times three; the ninth you shall become, if you are worthy. Speak now of three true things you learned about the order during your Vigil."

The question caught the Postulate off guard. His mind went blank for a moment, then he spoke.

"I have learned that genuine knowledge only comes to those who truly hunger for it. I have learned that power must be wielded by those above the fray, for only they can see the interweaving of the pattern. And I have learned that wisdom is the execution of power guided by knowledge and understanding."

There were no words spoken, but some of the Inner Sanctum members exchanged glances.

The Master Templar continued. "As all members of the Order are rare in this world, rarer still are those chosen to join the Inner Sanctum. You have already vowed to uphold the principles of our Order, and all that for which we stand. Will you travel deeper still into our core, and stand shoulder to shoulder beside the handful who will shape the world to its proper form? Do you swear to stay forever silent regarding what transpires here, to share what you know fully and completely with the Inner Sanctum, and never act against the heart of all it means to be a Templar?"

"The Father of Understanding guide me in this, as I so swear," the Postulate replied.

For a long moment, the Master remained silent. Then he nodded. In unison, the others brought the candles up to their faces, allowing him to see them.

"You are now a member of the Inner Sanctum." The Master Templar stepped forward, fastening a pin to the front of the Postulate's robe. The long, silver needle was crafted to look like a sword, while a squat cross with a ruby in its center was affixed atop the sword's hilt.

More than an ornament, the pin's sharp tip was coated in a toxin. It was to be used against an enemy if attacked... and used against oneself, if need be. When the pin was in place, the Templars blew out their candles' flames.

"Turn and greet your brethren, Simon Hathaway."

The torches, cunningly wrought holograms of fire, were instantly "extinguished" and the sconces retracted smoothly into alcoves in the gray slate walls. Small doors snicked shut to hide them. The lights came on, dim at first so their eyes could adjust. The stone structure on the left wall slowly slid aside with a slight humming sound, revealing a map of the world with small, twinkling lights. Each color represented a different area of activity for Abstergo Industries—and the Templar order.

Hoods were flipped back and ritual robes shrugged out of as the Inner Sanctum welcomed their newest member. Simon took a moment to run a hand along the heavy fabric of his ritual garb. It had been made by hand—complete with the sheep being hand-sheared and the wool carded, spun, and dyed by human labor, not machines. And the embroidery... Simon shook his head, amazed at the effort that had gone into ensuring the robe, which he would one day wear again at the induction of another new Inner Sanctum member, was as much like those worn by Templars in centuries past as possible. As a historian, he more than most valued the effort put toward authenticity.

He reluctantly traded his robe for his suit jacket, turning to his new comrades. All of them he knew to a greater or lesser extent: Laetitia England, a high-ranking executive in the Operations division. Despite her felicitous name, Laetitia was actually an American operating out of Philadelphia. Mitsuko Nakamura, Director of Lineage Research and Acquisition, divided her time between the Philadelphia office and the Abstergo Campus in Rome. Simon envied her fiercely for that. At Abstergo, "acquisition" had a rather different meaning than at other companies. The term referred to test subjects who would be appropriate for the Animus, a glory of technology Simon had yet to experience.

Simon was more familiar with the artificially jovial Álvaro Gramática, of the Future Technologies division, and the thuggish Juhani Otso Berg. Both were presently on assignment in another part of the globe. Unable to be physically present, they had nonetheless witnessed Simon's induction, and their faces now gazed down at the room from a pair of large screens.

The two men had worked with Simon's predecessor and boss, the late Isabelle Ardant. Isabelle had been killed by an Assassin a little over a year prior. Simon hadn't particularly liked her; he didn't particularly like or dislike *anybody*, really, but they'd attended Cambridge together, and a fellow Cantabrigian Templar shouldn't die stabbed in the back by someone too cowardly to face her. He harbored some resentment toward Berg, who had been acting as Isabelle's security the night she had died, and who really ought to have prevented her murder.

Also present were David Kilkerman, who had replaced the late and (to Simon at least) unlamented Warren Vidic as head of the Animus Project, and Alfred Stearns. Kilkerman was tall and heavyset, and laughed loudly and often, but his softness around the middle in no way indicated a soft nature. Stearns was the eldest member of the group of nine. He had been responsible for nearly eradicating the Assassin threat at the turn of the century in a Templar action that had been dubbed the "Great Purge." He had retired, and Laetitia had replaced him as Head of Operations, but he was still a highly valued member of the Inner Sanctum. They shook hands politely. Though Stearns was well into his eighties, balding, with a short snow-white beard, Simon thought the man as dangerous as any he'd ever met.

Agneta Reider, Chief Executive Officer of the Abstergo Financial Group, was someone else Simon was meeting for the first time. She was cool and pleasant, exactly the sort of person one would like to see at the helm of so vital an arm of Abstergo.

And of course, there was Alan Rikkin, CEO of Abstergo Industries, and the most important Templar Simon knew. Well, *knew* that he knew, at least. One was never certain about such things when it came to the Order.

Rikkin was the public face of Abstergo Industries. Simon would be hard-pressed to think of one better. Fiercely intelligent, presenting an utterly controlled demeanor, Rikkin commanded, and got, the world's attention when he spoke.

The door opened and two carts were wheeled in. The mystique of ages past retreated before pleasant, ordinary chitchat and the clatter of cups, saucers, knives, and forks as the Inner Sanctum settled in for a traditional English fry-up breakfast. Within a few moments it was as if the ritual, so steeped in tradition, had indeed happened centuries ago rather than in the twenty-first.

"How do you like your new office, Hathaway?" Mitsuko Nakamura asked.

"I'm not set up yet," Simon replied. He fished in his jacket pocket for his gold wire-rimmed spectacles and settled them atop an aquiline nose. "I thought it might be wisdom to make certain I was accepted into the Sanctum first. Save myself the trouble of packing things twice."

More laughter. "Practical," Álvaro Gramática said, his too-jovial face huge on the monitor. Isabelle hadn't been able to stand him, and Simon had to admit Alvaro fell heavily on the "dislike" end of his own personal scale. Now that Simon was Head of Historical Research, he would be seeing Gramática's smug almost-sneer much more often. Joy.

"A trait I hope to bring to the fore in the department," Simon replied politely, and dipped a soldier of perfectly crisp fried bread into the golden-orange yolk of his egg.

"We went through Isabelle's files and your name came up several times," Rikkin said. "You managed to impress her—no easy feat."

"Thank you, sir. I'm flattered. Isabelle was very good at what she did, and I will try to serve the Order as well in my own fashion."

"That sounds like you don't approve of how Isabelle managed her department." Although everyone else, including the Americans, was drinking tea during so traditional an English breakfast, Simon noted that it was coffee Rikkin stirred with a gleaming silver spoon, his dark eyes never leaving Simon's face.

Simon settled his cup in its fragile saucer with a slight clink and addressed his employer. "While I respect Isabelle's approach, I'm my own person, and I have a fresh angle I'd like to implement."

"Go on."

Here we go, Simon thought. "First... I'm a historian. That's my strength and area of expertise. The division is, after all, focused on the exploration and analysis of history."

"So as to further the goals of the Order," Laetitia put in.

"Quite right. I believe that a return to the roots of the department will benefit the Order tremendously, and here's why."

Simon slid his chair back. Striding to one of the walls, he touched a button. The wall slid away to reveal a whiteboard and several colored markers.

"Simon, you're the only person I know who still uses a whiteboard for a presentation," lamented Kilkerman.

"Hush, David, or I'll request a chalkboard and ask you to clap the erasers," Simon replied. The quip was rewarded by a few chuckles, Kilkerman's laugh the loudest. Simon wrote *HISTORICAL RESEARCH DIVISION* on the board, stepped back, examined the words, and straightened out the T in *HISTORICAL*.

"Now then. Our greatest tool is the Animus." He nodded toward Kilkerman as he spoke. The current head of the project raised his marmalade toast in solidarity. "We all know what it does; accesses the genetic memory of the subjects, homes in on specific ancestors, and so forth and so on. It's my understanding that there's a shiny new one available to be used, right, David?"

"There is indeed," Kilkerman said, straightening. "A great leap forward in technology—Model number 4.35. We've virtually eliminated such side effects as nausea and headaches. Plus we've found ways to make it even more integrative."

"I'm personally quite excited to hear that, and you'll see why in just a moment," Simon said.

He turned back to the board, writing the word *ANIMUS* in bright red. He drew two arrows below it angling toward the right and the left. "Hitherto, we've used the Animus primarily to gather one specific type of information—the locations of Pieces of Eden."

The Templars had a single task—to guide humanity's development correctly—but many tools with which to do so. The Pieces of Eden were perhaps the most important. They were the relics of a civilization variously known as the Isu, the Precursors, or the First Civilization. They not only predated humanity, but actually created—and, for a time, enslaved—it. Remnants of Precursor technology had the potential to grant users a variety of abilities and power over others. Their value eclipsed ordinary classifications as "historical" or "monetary." Although the Templar Order could likely boast the largest collection in the world, even it did not possess many of the priceless artifacts, and several of the items in the collection were broken or otherwise unusable.

"Once we learned about the existence of a Piece of Eden," Simon continued, "from, say a mention in an old manuscript, or about a person associated with one—off we went on the hunt for it."

Under the left-hand arrow jutting down from the word *ANIMUS* he wrote: *INFORMATION*. Below that, he scribbled *1. Pieces of Eden* and beneath that, *a) Locate*. "That hunt consists of, among other methods, utilizing the vast network of living genetic material at our disposal—otherwise known as the valued customers and loyal employees of Abstergo Industries." Simon wrote *i. Customers & Employees* beneath *a) Locate*.

"Our secondary branch of research involved learning more of what we could about our old enemies, the Assassins. And we wanted the same sort of thing as we did with the Pieces of Eden—the ability to sniff them out in present day."

Simon wrote *2. Assassins*, and then as he had earlier, the words *a) Locate, i. Customers & Employees*.

"Now, this is all fine, absolutely super. It's been enormously helpful in increasing both the influence of the Order *and* the bottom line of our company."

"There's a 'but' in there," Reider said.

"I hope you're not suggesting we abandon this line of research?" England's voice was deceptively mild.

"Not at all," Simon assured her. "But I think there's much more the Animus can do for the Order. There's an aspect of it that we've not investigated yet. One that I believe could, over time and if carefully managed, be as advantageous to us in its own way as the acquisition of Pieces of Eden."

He now wrote on the board, beneath the second arrow, the word *Knowledge*.

"Now, you might be thinking that information *is* knowledge. But data demands context in order to be useful. For instance, say it's a fact that there is a place where there is earth, stones, wood, and water. When we realize that the water is an ocean, the earth and stones are a rocky shoreline, and the wood is spars from a seafaring vessel, we give that information context. Now what was once merely raw data has become information that leads us to realize that there is a high likelihood of a shipwreck."

"I've got a full schedule, Simon," Rikkin said. "Get to the point, or there's a high likelihood your own ship will be scuttled before its maiden voyage."

Simon's ears grew hot, but he had to acknowledge the metaphor was apt. "My point is that while computers could decipher all this, and we've certainly put technology to good use, we've also realized the value of the human touch. I'll circle back to this in just a moment. Once we start utilizing the Animus not just for data and information, but for knowledge, with all its lovely subtleties, look what opens up for us."

He went back to the board and under *Knowledge* wrote *Pieces of Eden*.

"With information, we know *what*—enough to identify the specific artifact—and *where*. But with knowledge, we'll know *what it does*, *how it was used*, and...." He wrote the last words in bold letters. "... *how to fix it*."

His fellow Inner Sanctum members were staring at the whiteboard with expressions that ranged from dubious to enthusiastic to downright hostile. Most, however, at least seemed interested, and he seized upon that.

"And let's now apply *Knowledge* to the Assassins," Simon continued. "We won't just know *who* was an Assassin in a given time period, or *where* to perhaps locate Assassins today. We'll know *who they were*—what sort of person. We'll know what matters to them, and to the Assassin Brotherhood, and make note of how that's changed over the years. We'll better know how to manipulate them. To break them. And when we start to value *knowledge* rather than just data and information, there's no telling what we can discover. We don't know what we don't know. The potential is staggering."

He stepped back, regarding what he had written. "We'll keep these goals as primary ones, of course," he said, circling the word *INFORMATION* and its attendant comments, "but once we start the ball rolling, we can use the Animus to see interweavings. Patterns. We can rediscover lost theories, ideas, inventions. Wrap up centuries-old mysteries once and for all. Discover what truths really lay behind the old myths and legends and folklore. I posit that all this and more is possible, provided we expand the purpose of the Animus and open our minds."

"We're doing this now," Kilkerman said, his hands folded over his large belly and his eyes no longer twinkling with humor. "Trust me, Simon, we're paying close attention to what we learn."

"Yes—*and* we can do so much more with not much more effort."

"We did not need this romantic, sentimental approach to virtually wipe out our enemy over fifteen years ago." The contempt in Stearns's voice made the room feel abruptly chilly.

"No, we did not. But they're getting harder to find. Cleverer, more creative. And we need to be, too, if we're to stop them."

"Time is a precious resource," Berg said pointedly.

"It is," Simon agreed, "and we must be careful how we allocate it. We presently spend a very great deal of time gallivanting about looking for Pieces of Eden, when we're already in possession of a few we either don't understand or are damaged in some manner. We could both narrow our Animus experiences and make them more general. We need to target individuals whom we know to have an abundance of Precursor DNA, and—"

"We are already doing that as well," Gramática said.

"Through Abstergo Entertainment and Dr. Nakamura's department, yes," Simon replied, "people who aren't Templars, and don't know exactly what they're looking for. How much more effective would an Animus hour be if one of us were making use of it? Our DNA is a massive and presently untapped resource.

"One hour of our time could yield solutions to things we haven't even thought of yet," said Simon. "And of course, there is also knowledge for knowledge's sake. It's impossible to put a price tag on something like that."

"Spoken like a true historian," Berg said, and somehow managed to make the word sound unsavory. Despite himself, Simon bristled.

"I'll prove it to you," he heard himself saying. Instantly he wished the words back, but they were out there now, floating about like lost balloons. *In for a penny, in for a pound,* he thought, and took a deep breath. "As I said earlier, we all know our lineages. I have an ancestor who fought in Joan of Arc's army. She is believed to have possessed one of the Swords of Eden... Piece of Eden 25, according to the inventory. I have a theory that it might well be the one that belonged to Jacques de Molay himself."

"The one in my office," purred Rikkin. He turned to the rest of the Inner Sanctum. "There's a lot of its history that's still unknown.

What we do know is that it once belonged to de Molay, and later fell into the hands of Grand Master François-Thomas Germain, during the French Revolution. The Assassin Arno Dorian took it from Germain upon killing him."

Simon nodded. "It is my intention to spend time in the Animus myself and confirm that this sword is the same that was once classified as Piece of Eden 25."

Rikkin leaned on the table, cooling cup of coffee in one hand, chin in the other. "De Molay's sword was damaged when it was in the possession of Germain. Whatever unique abilities it once displayed, it no longer seems to possess."

"I repeat—with someone of my knowledge in the chair, I may well be able to determine how to repair it if I can see it in action."

A small smile quirked Rikkin's lips. "All right," he said. "Let's call this a test run. I'll let you follow this breadcrumb trail, Hathaway, and find out where it leads. If you can give me concrete results in one week, I'll greenlight the shift in your department's direction and allocate the appropriate resources."

Simon's heart sank. A *week*? Rikkin's smile widened, as if he could read the mind of the newest member of the Templar Inner Sanctum.

"Done," Simon said, and squared his shoulders.

"Excellent." Rikkin placed his napkin on the table and rose. "You'd best be about it, then." There might have been more obvious ways to end a meeting, but Simon currently couldn't think of one. "Oh, and Simon?"

"Yes, sir?"

Rikkin and Kilkerman exchanged glances, as if they were in a secret together. "It's not really a 'chair' anymore," Rikkin said.

"Beg pardon?" asked Simon.

"You'll see."

CHAPTER TWO

It was a familiar room, but now it was his, and Simon found that made a difference.

Carrying an enormous box of books, he paused at the wide threshold to look around. To the left, the astonishing view of the London Eye, Big Ben, and the Palace of Westminster where Parliament sat took up a huge section of the wall. A second large window on the right, closer to Isabelle's—now his—desk, ensured that plenty of light filled the room. Large, comfortable leather chairs provided the option of curling up with a book, and the massive bookcases offered hundreds of titles from which to choose. The heady smell of old paper and leather bindings permeated the room; the intoxicating scent of the past.

Simon walked through the sitting area, his feet making no sound on the thick, rich red carpeting, and placed the box on the large desk. Isabelle had not overly personalized her office, but he noticed that there were some places in the cabinets where objects had obviously been removed. Gramática had a wife and children, but never mentioned them—nor apparently *saw* them, given the hours he spent at the lab. Rikkin had a daughter, Sofia, but she was an adult and a full Templar in her own right. The cool killer Berg, oddly enough, was the only high-ranking Templar of Simon's acquaintance who had a small child he genuinely seemed to love; a little girl with cystic fibrosis. Simon only knew this because treatment for her had been the main bait with which the Order had tempted Berg to join their ranks.

Simon had no child, no wife, no girlfriend, not even a cat, and he was quite content with that status.

As he trudged back and forth down the hall with his belongings, Simon thought about the deadline Rikkin had set him. Fortunately Simon had done his research before making his presentation. Joan's life was well chronicled and there was a bounty of primary sources—the meat and drink of researchers. Hopefully, it would be enough to enable Simon to make the most use of the single week.

Joan of Arc. Fascinating, that he claimed as an ancestor someone who had traveled with her. He had never experienced the Animus personally, as he had never been a field agent and so had not participated in the Animi Training Program. He was well aware that the authors of precious primary resources were hardly impartial. But he, a historian with, as the saying went, no horse in this race—he would be able to be much more objective.

He fired up the computer and logged in. The Abstergo logo appeared on the large wall screen. "Animus Room," he said aloud. He was standing in front of the desk, unpacking a glass display case containing a rare eleventh-century version of Plutarch's *Parallel Lives*, when the face of the chief Animus technician appeared. She had long, glossy black hair gathered into a bun in a professional manner, dark brown eyes, and a friendly smile.

"Good morning, Professor Hathaway, I'm Amanda Sekibo. How may I help you?"

"Hello, Ms. Sekibo, we've not properly met yet, but I'm the new—"

"Head of Historical Research, yes, sir," she replied. "Dr. Kilkerman has told us all about you. We're all looking forward to introducing our new Animus to you. What can I do for you today?"

"I was in a meeting about an hour ago with Mr. Rikkin," he said. "I'm cleared to use the Animus for a rather time-sensitive project. I had assumed you would be notified. I'd like to schedule my first session immediately, if it's quite convenient."

Sekibo's brow furrowed. "Hang on a moment, please... ah, all right, yes, you are indeed already confirmed and cleared for Animus usage, but not until you've met with Dr. Bibeau."

"Who's he when he's at home?"

"*She*, sir, and she's one of our top psychiatrists."

Simon bristled. "I've had multiple evaluations and there's never been a jot of concern. I'm certain I don't need to be wasting the good doctor's time with—"

"I'm sorry, sir, Mr. Rikkin has made it quite clear." Sekibo had the sort of apologetic look people wore when the answer was going to be "no," regardless of anything one said.

Simon knew, of course, about the various dangers of the Animus. It was nothing like the mass-marketed videogames that had won Abstergo Entertainment so many awards and had (not at all incidentally) for several years provided the Templars with an enormous stream of income in addition to information. One needed to be monitored, and he understood that with this new model one couldn't even get settled into it without assistance. Simon removed his specs and pressed his thumb and forefinger to the bridge of his nose for a moment, then sighed and nodded.

"Well, of course I respect Mr. Rikkin's decision. I'll make an appointment with Dr. Bibeau straight away."

The young woman had the grace to look uncomfortable. "Well, sir, she's flying in tonight from the States. I expect she'll be ready to see you first thing in the morning."

"Right," Simon said. Of course. "One more thing—just confirming that Mr. Rikkin did, indeed, impress upon you that I have a project due in a week?"

"Yes, sir, once you're cleared, you're mint to go."

"Cheers," Simon said, and ended the call. To himself, he muttered, "*Six* days it is." He plopped down in the comfortable leather chair where he had seen Isabelle Ardant so many times, located Bibeau's name in the company directory, and composed an e-mail to her requesting they meet for breakfast at Temp's at seven-thirty sharp.

Heaven help you if you cost me another minute in the Animus, he thought sourly, and hit "send."

DAY 2

In the end, it was Simon who was almost late. The lack of sleep during the initiation ritual had caught up with him. Victoria Bibeau was waiting for him when he arrived at seven twenty-six.

He wasn't sure what he was expecting, but it wasn't this trim, bright-eyed woman with a pixie haircut and toothy but genuine smile. He wondered how it was she did not look a bit jet-lagged. Her handshake was firm, but not crushing.

"A pleasure to meet you, Professor Hathaway," she said, and there was just a hint of a French accent in her voice.

"I hope you had a pleasant flight."

"Thank you, I did, it is nice to be in London again. Tea always tastes better to me when I and the cup are surrounded by England."

"I couldn't agree with you more," he said as they stepped inside. Abstergo had a total of three restaurants on site, ranging from the Snack Shack for quick bites, coffee, and tea, to the elaborate Bella Cibo, where important guests were wined and dined. Tempest in a Teapot, abbreviated to Temp's more often than not, served only light breakfasts, elevenses, and afternoon tea, and was Simon's favorite, mainly because he almost always found himself working through lunch and dinner, and Temp's delivered.

"Good morning, Professor Hathaway," the waiter greeted them. He bore a tray with a small teapot, two cups, milk, lemon, and honey, and set the items down between them as he spoke. "The usual for you, sir?"

"Always," Simon replied. "Poole, this is Dr. Victoria Bibeau, from the Aerie in the States. She'll be staying with us a week."

Poole's eyes sparkled. "A pleasure, Doctor. No doubt if you're working with Professor Hathaway, we'll be seeing a lot of you here at Temp's."

"I'm getting that impression," Bibeau replied.

"Will you be traveling outside of London? The leaves are turning."

"Sadly, no, all business here in the city, I'm afraid."

"Too bad. Make sure you drop in for an afternoon tea—we've got pumpkin biscuits and apple spice cake this time of year."

"I hope we can," smiled Victoria. "For now, though, I suppose I'll have the usual, too."

"*Two* racks of toast and rashers of bacon," Poole said, nodded, and headed toward the kitchen. As Bibeau poured milk into her tea, Simon decided to get right to the point.

"So, Dr. Bibeau... why you?"

She took a sip before replying. "I have extensive experience helping to integrate first-time users of the Animus," she said.

"Yes, I read about your work at Abstergo Entertainment and in the Aerie," he said. The Aerie was a unique facility currently devoted to training a small, specific group of young adults. They were unique in that their genetic memories were more important—and valuable—together than separately. "I've not seen the teenage years for some time, Doctor."

"Please, call me Victoria," she said. "And I'm quite aware of that. I had a case at Abstergo Entertainment that... well, it was life-changing in several ways, both good and bad. The bottom line is there are few in the Order who know more about what interaction with the Animus can do to the human brain than I. I don't know if you've spoken with Dr. Kilkerman yet, but the model you'll be using is a new one—a prototype, really."

He bristled. "Yes, naturally I have spoken with Dr. Kilkerman, and I understand it's an improvement."

"Even so—you're a first timer, you have only a week to do what you need to in order to prove the value of your approach, and you'll be spending a lot of time in it. Quite simply, you need me, Simon."

Poole arrived with their toast and bacon. Simon sipped his tea for a moment, then said, "Clearly, you've read about me and my own work."

"Oh yes," Victoria said. "I will be very interested in learning about your ideas as we work together. And before you say it, I also read all your psychological evaluations and find you remarkably stable. I don't anticipate many problems."

"I don't anticipate *any*."

She showed prominent white front teeth in a genuine smile. "Well, then, *commençons*."

"I don't speak French, I'm afraid."

"You might in two weeks. Well," she amended, "whatever was spoken in the fifteenth century."

"That would be Middle French... pardon?"

"Are you familiar with the Bleeding Effect?"

"Ah... of course." The Bleeding Effect was a possible side effect of spending time in the Animus. On occasion, the personality, thoughts, emotions, and sometimes physical abilities from one's ancestor "bled" into the subject. "I'm already fluent in Russian, Spanish, and Arabic, but I can't imagine where Middle French would come in handy."

"Could be fun at a party," she said, grinning, then added more seriously, "but honestly, it wouldn't be immediate, and I doubt you'll be anywhere near fluent. Sometimes, a Bleeding Effect can be positive. Learning a new skill, like martial arts, or a language. But I'd be remiss if I didn't mention the potential it has to be extremely dangerous. I'm sure you're familiar with Subjects 4 and 14, and the devastating result the Bleeding effect had on them. But I, unfortunately, had a chance to observe it personally."

Her eyes were somber and her voice quiet as she spoke. "One of our research analysts at Abstergo Entertainment got far too caught up in his subject. Eventually, he became convinced that he was the reincarnation of an Assassin named Arno Dorian, who was active during the French Revolution."

"Not the nicest time in history, certainly," Simon said. "What happened?"

"He attempted to sabotage the project. He destroyed priceless research—deleted files, smashed hard drives, burned his notes. The Order tried to contain him, but he resisted." Her lips pressed together.

Simon understood what that meant. "Ah, I see. That's too bad. All that research—just gone. Were you able to recover any of it?"

She gave him an expression he couldn't fathom. "Some," she said. "Anyway, it's my understanding that most of the problems we've experienced in the Animus have been virtually eliminated. That's the goal, at least. Which means that the main concern is the Bleeding Effect. As long as people are people, I do not think we will ever fully conquer that one."

While they finished their breakfast, Victoria questioned Simon about his hobbies. He demurred at first, saying, "I'm a Templar, we don't have hobbies," but she revealed that she herself enjoyed pottery and running marathons. "Not at the same time, though." She smiled her wide, toothy grin. "They help me get out of my head and into my body for a while. You must have something you enjoy doing."

Simon admitted that he had a fondness for the ocean. "Sailing?" Victoria asked.

"Diving, actually," he said. "Shipwrecks." He paused. "And hidden passageways. There's loads of them in London."

She looked at him with new respect. "There's more to you than meets the eye, Simon Hathaway."

He thought about it and sighed. "Actually, no, I think I'm about as dull as one would expect." He steered the direction back to their task, elaborating on what he was trying to accomplish and outlining the sword's history. "If your analyst was researching Arno Dorian, you may have even seen the sword we'll be investigating. François-Thomas Germain owned it for a while, till Dorian, ah, dispatched him."

He pulled out his tablet from his briefcase and sent her some of his notes, which included a list of incidents in Joan's life that would be the most productive for them to explore through his ancestor's memories. Victoria said this would be of great help in working up an algorithm, to make the best use of their Animus time.

"How much do you know about this time period?" he inquired, flagging Poole down for another pot of tea.

"Not much, I'm afraid. I was pulled onto this project less than twenty-four hours ago. I find that I don't have to be a good historian to be of help to research analysts, but I think an understanding of the basics would be beneficial."

Simon hid his annoyance. Although he was technically a professor he found teaching frustrating, and wasn't looking forward to walking Victoria through step by step. "Well," he said with false cheer, "let's see if we can get through everything on this fresh pot of tea.

"In 1428, when Joan of Arc stepped onto history's stage, the whole concept of who France's "rightful king" was, as was so often the case, muddied by politics, armies, marriages, and inconvenient deaths. The Hundred Years' War—which actually lasted a hundred and sixteen—had been raging for over ninety of them by this time. King Henry V, made famous by Shakespeare, had died six years previously at age thirty-five, not in glorious battle, but ignominiously felled by dysentery, a disease that was no respecter of the difference between kings and commoners. King Charles VI of France, who had gone down in history both as "the Beloved," which it seemed he had been, and "the Mad," which he most *definitely* had been, had survived his English rival by a mere two months.

"Joan's Dauphin, the future Charles VII, was actually the *fourth* of his father's sons to be named heir to the throne. He never expected to become king, and was wretchedly insecure about it. That wasn't helped by rumors spread by the English and Burgundians—those were the French who followed Philip of Burgundy and joined with the English—"

"*Oui,*" Victoria interrupted, her eyes twinkling. "I think I do know about Burgundians."

"Oh, of course, right. Sorry. Back to it. Charles's mother, Isabeau of Bavaria, was accused of taking lovers—including her husband's brother, so Charles's legitimacy was in question."

"Was she really his mother?"

"We think so. He's definitely recorded as having the Valois nose."

The topic turned to Simon's new approach for the department. While much of what he shared was a recap of his presentation to the Inner Sanctum the previous day, he added something he hadn't volunteered there.

"Joan of Arc had at least three swords that we knew about," he said. "So it's not going to be quite the walk in the park we could wish for."

"So, you fudged a little to Rikkin?"

"The merest trifle," he insisted. "I have a hunch which one it might be. I'm still quite keen on seeing what turns up along the way. The sword, for me, is only part of it."

By the time they'd finished the meal, Simon was resigned to Victoria's presence throughout this phase. If he had to have a nanny holding his hand while he poked through the past, he supposed that she was a tolerable choice.

The direct lift down to the bowels of the London offices—including the rooms where Simon had been inducted into the Order and given the Inner Sanctum his presentation—could only be accessed by certain floors. This was not one of them. They would have to ride back up to Historical Research, then transition to the lift. They left Temp's and stood in slightly awkward silence as the numbers lit up, indicating the lift's arrival. The doors slid open and Simon found himself standing face to face with a petite young woman who had a rebellious cherry-red streak in her otherwise black, shoulder-length tresses.

Her brown eyes widened slightly. "Simon," she said, "Lovely to see you. It's been a while."

"Yes, it has," he said. "Anaya, this is Dr. Victoria Bibeau. She's here for a couple of weeks to help me muddle through some things up in Historical Research. Victoria, this is Anaya Chodary. She used to be a field agent, but now she's one of our best White Hats."

For a moment, Victoria looked puzzled, then understanding dawned. "An ethical hacker," she said.

"Some people think it's a contradiction in terms, but I like the name," Anaya said as she and Victoria shook hands.

"Your contribution cannot be overestimated. I am certain you have spared Abstergo a multitude of disasters."

"Thank you," Anaya said, "I try my best. I know Simon's always in a hurry, so I'll not keep you two." Her eyes wandered back to Simon's. "I'm glad I ran into you. I found your jumper the other day. The blue one you thought you'd lost."

Simon drew a blank, then remembered. "Oh! Right."

"Shall I run it 'round for you?"

"Oh, no, don't bother. Take it to the Oxfam shop or something. I've far more than I'll ever wear." He stepped into the lift, nodding to her as the door closed. "Cheers."

He punched the button and the lift ascended with a gentle whir. Victoria was quiet for a moment, then she asked, "What happened between you two?"

Simon threw her a glance. "If you must know, nothing terribly exciting. Just the usual things. Work, responsibilities, so forth. I don't have to tell you what being a Templar asks of one."

"Especially a Master Templar and a member of the Inner Sanctum."

He was taken aback. "Know all that, do you?"

"It... was deemed a good thing for me to know, yes. And yet, Templars do manage to have spouses and families."

"I don't. And I recall from your file that you are not among that happy few."

He had thought she'd bridle at the remark, but instead she laughed. "Touché, Simon."

CHAPTER THREE

The Animus was located several stories belowground. Security at Abstergo was always a top priority. Everything from the obvious measure of key cards hung about one's neck to the unseen army of ethical hackers, of which the ferociously intelligent Anaya was a brigadier, ensured that constant vigil was kept on Abstergo's physical and technical security.

The lift opened onto a spacious two-story room. On all four sides were three-dimensional monitors, with white-coated technicians seated in front of them. Out of the corner of his eye, Simon glimpsed myriad scenes of tiny, three-dimensional images of people playing out their inevitable destinies while they were analyzed and cataloged. Elsewhere in the room priceless antiquities were on stately display. Centuries-old relics softened the gray concrete and chrome of the walls; swords, small statues of Egyptian, Greek, and Roman gods, banners, shields, chalices, and horns filled elegant display cases.

But it was the Animus that commanded his attention, and he obeyed, staring at the machine with pale blue eyes gone wide behind his spectacles.

He understood now what Rikkin had meant when he said it wasn't really a "chair" anymore. Gleaming and perfect—as of course it would be—this Animus would not seat its occupants. It would embrace them.

An exquisite amalgamation of technology and unsettling, accidental art, the jointed frame hung suspended from the ceiling, looking like a metallic human skeleton—if human skeletons had been modeled on those of snakes. It had a spine, arms, legs, everything but a head, but Simon suspected a separate helmet served that function. A large metal ring would keep the occupant standing erect, and there were a variety of extremely secure-looking straps to keep said occupant in place.

They had attracted the attention of Amanda Sekibo, who headed over to greet them. "Professor Hathaway, Dr. Bibeau," she said, "welcome to the Animus Room. So, Professor—what do you think of our new model?"

"It looks a bit like something the Inquisition might have used back in the day, doesn't it?"

Victoria stepped in quickly at Sekibo's expression. "It's actually much more sophisticated than the Aerie's Animus. You should have few, if any, headaches, and probably no vomiting at all."

"Lovely," Simon said.

"I'm hoping I'll be able to tell the kids they can have an Animus like this one soon." To Sekibo, she said, "Would you mind familiarizing me with the controls?"

"Of course, Doctor."

"Please, call me Victoria." Simon wondered if she let anybody call her by her last name. He tagged along, tuning them out when they delved into too-technical jargon and listening politely when they went over things he already knew. If he'd been sitting at a desk, his fingers would have been drumming on it. After what felt like a century, Victoria thanked Sekibo. The young woman went to her team and gently tapped them on the shoulders. They closed down their stations, the miniature avatars disappearing, and quietly entered the lift.

Simon and Victoria were alone. "Are you ready?" Victoria asked.

"For the Iron Maiden over there?"

"Oh, I wouldn't call it that," she said. "I don't think you appreciate how superior it is to the older models. This one's the Animus 4.35, derived from the technology Abstergo developed for the 4.3—the one currently in use in Madrid. I understand that while the Madrid one's more immersive, it's also supposed to be quite a lot more invasive. For instance, I won't have to perform a spinal tap on the 4.35."

"Oh. I see." He took a deep breath. "Well... as Joan of Arc herself is reputed to have said, better now than tomorrow."

They walked over to the apparatus. Simon stepped onto the two-part platform, shrugging into a harness that looked too light to be as durable as it was while Victoria fastened the large metal ring about his narrow waist. Gingerly, he put his weight on one foot, than the other. The platforms responded smoothly, like an advanced stair climber or elliptical machine.

"There's the potential for piece of brilliant exercise equipment here, you know," he deadpanned.

She laughed. "You don't know the half of it," she said. I should put a Bodyband on you to keep track of your steps." She continued fastening straps and clicking things into place as she spoke. "You'll have complete freedom of movement. In fact, the harness and the exoskeleton will support your body as it moves the same way your ancestor did. Remember, this won't be a minute-to-minute encapsulation of your ancestor's life. The time period is three to four years, but we only have one week."

We. Her casual insertion of herself into the project vexed Simon, but he brushed it aside. She would be supervising him the entire time, and likely debriefing him. He'd known he would require an assistant, but she was shaping up to be a partner.

Simon knew he did not play well with others, but there was no getting around it. Victoria double-checked all the fastenings and nodded in approval, and Simon realized just how vulnerable he was. Maybe he would be glad of a partner after all.

"Erm," he said, tugging slightly on one of the restraints, "What's the backup if you suddenly have a massive heart attack at your station?"

She laughed, a bright, free sound, and he smiled a little. "An alarm would sound, the doors would unlock, and the medical team would be here in seconds. Eventually someone would get around to letting you out."

"Brilliant."

"Abstergo is adamant that a subject must always be monitored. Now, if you'd be willing to risk severe injury, you might be able to leave the last back strap undone and get in by yourself." Her toothy smile dimmed. "I do not recommend it. One of the kids I work with uses the Animus to escape his own genuine paralysis."

"Oh. Quite. Well—are we all set?"

"All but the helmet," Victoria replied. "I'll place it on, and then we'll be able to communicate through it." She stepped behind him and lowered it over his blond head. The thing was almost like a sensory deprivation chamber, utterly black and sound-canceling. It was a peculiar sensation, and Simon actually started when he heard Victoria's voice in his ear. It was almost as if it was coming from inside his head.

Comfy? He moved experimentally, and was surprised to find that the answer was yes, and said so.

At the moment, it should be completely dark, Victoria continued. *The first thing you will see is the Memory Corridor. It's designed to ease you into the simulation. We can converse easily here, but communication will be harder when the simulation becomes active. We'll always start with the Memory Corridor, but the first time is particularly important.*

Don't worry. This ought to be an easy transition as compared to previous models.

The darkness seemed to be gradually retreating, turning from inky black to the soft, dove-gray of fog. Simon was reminded of a trip to the Scottish Highlands a few years back, when he'd been hiking up Ben Nevis and the fog had rolled in with startling speed. It was almost as if a cloud had decided to plunk itself down. The metaphor became suddenly more apt as Simon's eyes were dazzled by crackles of what seemed to be lightning. The fog/cloud pulsed and roiled slowly, and as Simon watched, fascinated, it reshaped itself here and there, as if it were trying to mold itself into a building, or a tree trunk, or, perhaps, Ben Nevis.

He reached out without thinking, and looked down at his hand. Simon had long, thin fingers, and did little in the way with them other than type or page through old tomes. Occasionally, they were ink-stained. But the hands he now regarded were strong, callused, sporting small scars and torn fingernails. They were darkly tanned, too; his own were milk-pale. Simon looked down at himself, seeing a beige woolen tunic that was oft-mended and more oft-stained. Blue hose covered what he could see of his legs, and on his feet Simon wore simple leather boots. A hood with a short cape covered his head.

He felt his lips curving in a stupid grin as he rubbed the rough fabric of the cape between his right thumb and forefinger, his left hand reaching up to touch his face and discovering there a youth's first downy wisps of beard.

"Bonjour, Gabriel Laxart," he said.

That's a strong resemblance, Victoria's voice said. *If I saw the two of you in a room together, I'd know you were family.*

"Is that unusual?"

No, but often people are shocked at how much they don't *look like an ancestor*, she replied. *I put you at seventeen or so. You help your father, Durand Laxart, with—*

"Farming, yes, I know," he said. "What's the date?"

Thursday, May Day, 1428. I thought we would start at the beginning. Go ahead and move around while the simulation finishes loading.

It was an odd sensation, wearing a body like a set of clothing. The boy was slender—all right, Simon was slender, Gabriel was skinny—but wiry, and moved easily. A threshing motion came naturally, but when Simon tried to use his wooden walking staff as a pike or a sword, he dropped it.

Clearly not a Templar yet, Victoria commented drily. *Now, this is very important to remember. You are just along for the ride. Don't resist the memories—you can't change them. Don't try to force Gabriel to do something or say something he wouldn't, or you'll desynchronize. And that is very unpleasant.*

"What, this Jaguar of an Animus hasn't got that all sorted yet?"

This isn't a time machine, Simon. You can't change the past, and if you try, the Animus lets you know in no uncertain terms. In a way, it's a violent action, with an equally violent repercussion. You told me Gabriel was illegitimate, and he's only recently come to live with his biological father. That's going to work in your favor. He's unfamiliar to almost everyone, so few will notice if you're acting out of character.

Simon nodded acknowledgement. The stigma attached to bastards was, historically speaking, a fairly recent development, so it wasn't surprising the Laxarts, a farming family, had taken in an able-bodied young man. Gabriel's parentage also explained why nothing in Simon's research had turned up any mention of him. Unless they were remarkable in a significant way, illegitimate children were seldom recorded. Family trees didn't like random branches.

While Victoria had been speaking, the roiling mists had become more substantial, clearer, their flat gray flushing to green and blue. Simon found himself facing emerald fields dotted with cattle and sheep. Behind him was a rough road and cottages that indicated he was on the outskirts of a small village.

Domrémy. Joan's birthplace. The only sounds were those of wind in the trees, birds, and the lowing of cattle. The quiet was unnerving. No cars or planes, or air conditioners, or computers, or mobile phones. For some reason, he hadn't expected that.

He stood for a moment, simply getting used to the idea that he was reliving the memories of a long-dead young man. So real; from the slight breeze brushing his face, to the smells, to the feel of the earth beneath his feet. *If Abstergo Entertainment's games provide even a fraction of this,* Simon thought, *it's no wonder they've won so many awards.*

Simon looked down at Gabriel's hands, and realized he was holding bread and cheese wrapped up in a cloth bundle. Victoria had said it was May 1... a feast day. Ah... now he had it figured out. He'd learned through his research that a long-standing tradition in Domrémy saw the town's young people visiting the nearby spring on certain feast days. They would, essentially, enjoy a picnic near what they called the Ladies' Tree, or the Fairy Tree. This rather charming custom was called "doing the fountains," and it was clear to him now that Gabriel was on his way to join in.

He began to walk, letting Gabriel find the way. The boy was tall and gangly, as Simon himself had been in his youth; he understood the motion of long legs, and Gabriel was someone accustomed to walking.

The breeze brought the sound of happy laughter, voices (some terribly off-key) raised in song, and the bright noises of small pipes. A large tree was silhouetted against the blue sky, and there was movement under its branches. Simon was no botanist. He wasn't even particularly fond of nature. But the tree was glorious. White petals dotted the green-leafed boughs. The simple color was offset with the pinks, reds, and blues of other flowers, all woven into garlands and draped over the large, lower branches.

Girls of various ages sat in a small cluster, their heads bowed together as they laughed and played with the flowers. Another group had formed a small circle, engaged in a dance that bordered on a dizzying run about the tree's thick trunk. The boys either climbed the tree or sprawled on the grass, tearing off hunks of coarse brown bread. The older ones offered some bread to the girls; the younger ones tossed small pieces at them instead.

I don't belong here, came a thought, and Simon wasn't sure if it was his or Gabriel's.

For a moment, Gabriel's long legs were rooted to the spot. One of the older youths dropped lithely from the branches and strode toward him. He had dark hair, a swarthy complexion, and an open, friendly smile.

"You must be our cousin Gabriel!" he said cheerfully. "I'm Pierre. That lout over there is my brother Jean." The lout under discussion was busily polishing off the last of the bread and brushing crumbs off his shirt. He was older and larger than Pierre, solid where the younger brother was quick and lithe.

"Hello, Pierre," Gabriel said. "Y-your mama sent me with this."

"Ha!" Pierre said. "Hey, Jean, you don't have to stop eating after all." Jean looked up at the sound of his name and got to his feet, ambling toward them.

Even as Gabriel spoke with his cousins, Simon was wondering where Joan was. "I hear your father saves the town when brigands come," Gabriel was saying. Jacques d'Arc was the town's doyen, a position that collected taxes and organized Domrémy's defenses.

"Burgundians, you mean," Pierre said darkly.

"It's the same thing," Jean said. He tore off a piece of bread and handed the loaf back to Gabriel. The bread was coarse but delicious, and the cheese was creamy and rich and gamy. "Living in Burey-en-Vaux, you're close to Vaucouleurs, so you have the king's soldiers to protect you."

"They're supposed to protect you, too," Gabriel said, but Pierre simply shrugged. Clearly, this was an uncomfortable subject in Domrémy. "So," he said, trying again, "do you fight the brigands yourselves?" Gabriel had never seen a raid, and it sounded terribly exciting.

"Oh, no. We get out of their way. Papa has rented an old fortress on an island in the river where we can all go with our animals, and as much as we can take with us. Sometimes we go to Neufchâteau, if the attack blocks our way to the island," Pierre's pleasant face hardened. "Our house is made of stone, but most aren't so lucky."

Gabriel sobered at the words. "Has... has anyone been killed?"

"Not recently. We generally get enough warning that everyone and their animals can get to shelter."

Pierre kicked his brother, who responded with a yelp muffled by a mouthful of cheese. "Gabriel, go give some to Jeannette before this pig eats it all. She's been dancing all day, when she hasn't been wandering off to go stare at the river as if it's talking to her. I'm sure she's hungry."

"Which one is she?" Excitement fluttered in Simon's chest.

"The lively one there, in the red," Pierre said, pointing. Joan was indeed the "lively one," moving with high energy, her body strong and lithe as she moved. Long, slightly wild black hair dotted with flowers fell the length of her straight back.

I am the luckiest historian who has ever lived, thought Simon, almost giddy as Gabriel strode on long, coltish legs toward Joan of Arc.

"Jeanette?" Gabriel said. His hands were shaking as they clutched the offering of bread and cheese.

Joan of Arc, La Pucelle, the Maid of Orléans, future patron saint of France, turned around.

Her eyes were large and fierce and blue and steady, and they seemed to slice through Gabriel as if piercing through body and bone to his very soul. He couldn't breathe, could only stare back, blood suddenly galloping through his veins to rush into his face and—

The world folded in on itself like a crumpled piece of paper, all its images and color and solidity retreating at a breakneck pace, bearing away that ineffable, transcendent face with them.

Simon Hathaway was left only with blackness and his own scream.

CHAPTER FOUR

S imon, what—

A tsunami of nausea crashed over Simon, as if an irate giant had gut-punched him. His throat was raw; he realized he had shouted, was still shouting, although he couldn't hear a sound. He shivered in the restraints, his body drenched in sweat, his mouth dry as cotton. Then the helm was lifted and cool air bathed his damp face. He stopped screaming and gulped in oxygen, staring at a woman's face he didn't recognize.

Not *hers*.

"I'm so sorry, Simon." The voice was familiar, and a name floated to him, piercing his panic. *Victoria*. "I wasn't expecting that sort of a reaction from this particular simulation. Do you need a bucket?"

The thought was so appalling Simon forced back the bile from sheer will and grunted something she would interpret as "no" as she unfastening him from myriad clasps and monitors that suddenly felt as if they were crawling all over him. Good, simple, rough wool was what his skin abruptly craved.

"What happened?" he asked in a hoarse voice.

She eyed him, concerned. "You desynchronized, pretty violently," she said. "That reaction was more suited to a battlefield recollection. What happened?"

"Not sure." He nodded his thanks and started to step off the platform. He was still a bit wobbly, and when Victoria slipped a hand under his elbow, he accepted her assistance. She guided him to a chair and handed him a glass of water. "You were right—desynchronization is indeed not pleasant. I feel like I've been kicked in the chest by a horse."

Victoria gave him a little smile, looking relieved at his quick recovery. "You say that like you've had firsthand experience. Have you?"

"No," Simon said, "but Gabriel has, and that's precisely what it feels like. What happened?"

"I'm not sure," she said. "It could be a couple of things. Simon—*you* deliberately pulled yourself out of it. Why?"

"I did not," he said.

"Yes," she persisted, "you did. Gabriel wasn't about to go *anywhere*."

"Nonsense. Neither was I. I'm a historian meeting Joan of Arc, for heaven's sake, why would I try to avoid that?"

"You tell me." Victoria held up a hand to forestall his protests. "I've been doing this quite a while, Simon, and I have gotten very good at determining the origins of a sudden desynchronization." Gently, she said, "Simon... you *fled*."

His face was burning.

"I can't in good conscience continue with you until I understand why. It might not be safe."

"I'll tell you what wouldn't be safe—my job, if I don't present Rikkin with something he wants to see," Simon snapped. He ran a hand through his hair, finding it damp with sweat.

Victoria continued implacably. "If it's the Bleeding Effect, a job hunt will be the least of your worries. Simon, your stats went through the roof. You began to sweat, your heart rate dramatically increased, and your brain released a flood of chemicals. As I said—had you been in battle, it would make sense, but...."

She shook her head and fell silent for a moment. Then, in a calmer voice, she continued, "I told you I have seen someone so lost in the past that he thought he actually was the Assassin whose memories he was studying. He broke up with his girlfriend, because he was in love with a girl two centuries dead. He had blackouts, and when he came out of them found letters written to him from Arno Dorian—in French. He didn't speak a word of it. It killed him, Simon, in the end. I found it extremely difficult to bear, and I've lived with guilt ever since. I should have removed him from the assignment before things got so bad for him. I refuse to make that mistake again. So tell me now—why did you desynchronize?"

Simon sighed, closing his eyes for a moment. "Something about that girl thrilled him—and terrified him."

"But not you?"

He hesitated. "I don't feel it now," he said, and that much, at least was the truth.

Victoria cocked her head and looked at him with a strange expression. Then, to his confusion, she seemed to be holding back a smile.

"One moment," she said, and went back to the computer, checking his stats. "The chemicals that were released were primarily serotonin, dopamine, and norepinephrine. Do you understand what that means?"

"I'm not a chemist."

Her smile widened. "Don't tell me you've forgotten how overwhelming first love can be," she said.

He stared at her. "Really?" he said, chagrined.

"Really."

He blew out a sigh. "Well, that's just bloody wonderful," he said. "I'm going to be tagging along in the body of a teenage boy in the grips of a massive first crush. I hope some fighting proves to be a good release for all that testosterone."

"Oh, it could be worse," Victoria said.

"No," Simon said, his voice weary and his words utterly sincere. "It really couldn't."

"If it helps any," Victoria said, "I'll remind you that Joan of Arc was supposed to be astonishingly charismatic. A teenage boy with an interest in girls probably wouldn't have stood a chance."

Calmer now, his thoughts his own, Simon recalled what he had seen, trying to view a woman who later would become France's patron saint not through the eyes of a hormone-addled youth, but through his own.

"I suppose I can accept that hypothesis. But I think... it was more than that, somehow. Something else was at play." He looked at her. "I want to go back in."

She considered it, then nodded. "All right. But let's not pick up right there." Simon was quietly grateful. Victoria's eyes flickered over her notes. "Joan went back to Burey-en-Vaux with the Laxarts for about a week." She looked up at Simon, smothering a grin. "Maybe she wanted to spend more time with Gabriel."

"Oh, perfect," Simon lamented.

"Sorry," Victoria said, in a voice that suggested that she wasn't. I'll send you back in the simulation to sometime late Monday, May 12—or maybe very early May 13. Ready?"

"Absolutely," he stated with a certainty he didn't feel.

He knew a bit about what to expect this time, so it was marginally less jarring. Even so, the Memory Corridor's fog felt alien, and he wasn't sure what effect returning to the simulation would have on him.

As the strange gray clouds reformed into shapes, Victoria asked, *So what do you, Simon, think of Joan?*

"Me? Well, she's fascinating," he said. "And if she did have a Sword of Eden, much of what was reported about her seems more plausible. She did live in a world that was much less skeptical than our own, when it comes to hearing voices from God. For them, it wasn't *if* someone heard something, it was whether what they heard was from God or Satan."

But what do you think *of her?*

"I—I haven't, really," he said. The restoration of the simulation was almost complete. "I'm a historian. I'm not really supposed to like or dislike, just observe."

That will help you resist any Bleeding Effects, Victoria approved.

The fog in the Memory Corridor had given way to a soft darkness, and a sky lit only by stars and the faintest sliver of a waning moon.

Gabriel had awoken around midnight. Ever since Joan's arrival, he had found himself restless and easily distracted, his sleep punctuated by waking at annoying and seemingly random hours. Not even the physically exhausting work of caring for his father's livestock, so different from his experience as an assistant to his merchant stepfather, sufficiently wore him out so he slept through the night. He had taken to wandering through the narrow streets, though Burey-en-Vaux was so small that the journey never lasted long. He would linger outside the Laxart house as he did now, leaning against the archway and looking up towards the heavens, before going back inside to toss and turn fitfully until the next time he woke.

All right, Simon, how are you doing?

"Fine," he said, though Gabriel's mouth was dry. What was it about Joan? Her face was not conventionally pretty; jaw a little too square, forehead a little too high. But she had looked at Gabriel with the bluest eyes Simon had ever seen—and that was the honest truth, not hyperbole—and those eyes, her tumble of hair as black as a raven's wing (all right, that part *was* hyperbole) combined with a sense of barely leashed energy made for a heady combination.

"You keep the Night Office," came a soft, musical voice.

Gabriel started. Joan stood a few steps away, fully dressed, as was he, a cloak pulled tight against the night's dampness. It should have been too dark to see her, but Gabriel took in every curve of cheeks and lips, her strong, pale hands holding the cloak closed in front of her. The glimmer of stars caught her eyes, and she seemed to him to glow as if made of starlight herself.

"The what?" he stammered.

She stepped closer to him. "That's what the monks call it. It's also called vigil, or nocturnes, or matins. You know the Hours." Of course he knew them. Everyone did. Church bells were rung eight times a day. But he had never heard matins called by the other names.

"At home, I would drop everything and go to church when I heard the hours tolled," she said, laughing a little. "I even had to chide our bell ringer from time to time when he was late. But at night, to attend matins... I had to sneak out."

Her smile widened into a mischievous grin, and Gabriel stopped breathing for a moment. She turned her face up to the stars, and her grin faded. "They tease me, you know."

"Who?"

"The boys, mostly; my brothers, even my friends. They love me, but they think it's strange, that I like going to church so much."

Hearing how others had talked about her, Gabriel himself had thought it odd. But that was before he had met her. In some ways, Joan was just a girl—she laughed, and went about her chores, and never seemed to let their teasing upset her. In fact, she'd give as good as she got, sometimes, so this admission from her surprised him.

She turned to him, her eyes brimming with starlight in the deep shadow. "Do *you* think I'm strange?" He wanted to tell her no, he didn't, but he found his tongue disobeying him. He couldn't lie to her.

"Yes, at first. But then I got to know you. I... I see how happy you are. How it makes you shine. And I think it's beautiful."

He almost blurted out *I think* you're *beautiful*, but he bit down hard on his treasonous, too-glib tongue. Her face softened in a smile.

I'm drowning, Gabriel thought, his heart racing.

"Gabriel... do you ever feel like you are different from other people?"

In the midst of the moment, the words struck him harshly. He almost winced. "I'm a bastard. I know I'm not like other people."

"It troubles you?" Her eyes were sympathetic.

He nodded. "It didn't when I was with my mama and my papa. My stepfather, I mean," he amended. "They were the only parents I knew. My stepfather was a merchant in Nancy. I didn't even know he wasn't my real father until after... after he died. He took ill with a fever."

Joan made a soft sound and took his hand. Gabriel tensed, anticipating the strange, almost painful sensations that seemed to gallop through him at the most inappropriate times. But her hand was cool, and comforting, and instead of exciting him, her touch calmed him. The tension in his body eased. The words flowed more easily.

"Mama fought it off for another month. But toward the end, she had me write a letter to Durand, asking if he would take care of me. I didn't think he would, and even if he did, I didn't know what his wife would think of me."

Joan tilted her head, still shining. *Is it the starlight, or me?* Gabriel wondered. "Your family here, the Laxarts... they are good people. That's why...." She paused abruptly, then squeezed his hand. "Jeanne seems to treat you well."

That's right... another Jeanne, thought Simon. "Joan" was an Anglicized pronunciation of the French "Jeanne," and was, apparently, also the name of Gabriel's stepmother. It seemed to be absurdly common, and Simon expected would be challenging to keep all the Jeannes— and the Jeans—straight.

"She does," Gabriel hastened to assure her. "You are right. She is good. Like her cousin." Tentatively, Gabriel squeezed her hand back. "But it's not been very long. Nancy is a much larger town. I counted coins and wrote receipts and managed inventory. Farming... is different. And I still don't know where I fit in."

"I am different, too," Joan said. "But I know what I must do in this life." She withdrew her hand. Gabriel felt suddenly hollow, and the night abruptly turned cold. "We are friends, yes?"

Inside his chest, Gabriel's heart seemed to stop beating for a moment, before it returned to its task in slow, painful lurches. The words were as ash in his mouth, but he spoke them. "Yes," he said, softly. *If there can be nothing more between us, then I will cherish this.*

"Then I must ask for your help. I do not do so lightly."

"Anything," he said, too eagerly. "Anything at all, Jeanette."

"Tomorrow, I will ask your father to do something for me. It will sound strange, and you will wonder at it. But I need you to help me persuade him."

"Can you not tell me now?"

Joan looked away, and her face grew pensive. She seemed to be staring at something over his shoulder, but Gabriel turned and saw nothing. Only a cat, pale in the darkness, perched atop a wall and licking its forepaw.

"No," she said. "Not yet. I need you to trust me. Can you do that?"

She stared at him, her strong, slender body taut, and that strange starlit glow seemed brighter than before. There was only one answer. "Of course, Jeanette. Whatever it is you ask of my father, I will make it happen."

The serious expression melted into a smile and Gabriel could have sworn he felt his heart cracking in his chest. "You're a good person, Gabriel. Good night." Then she was gone, and for a long moment Gabriel stood and wondered if he had imagined the entire thing.

Simon was confused by what Gabriel had seen when he looked at Joan. The scene began to fade, becoming misty gray, then darkening. *I'm bringing you out,* came Victoria's voice. A moment later, Simon felt a light touch on his shoulder alerting him to Victoria's presence. The air felt cool on his face as she removed the helmet, and he realized he had been sweating.

"Victoria," Simon ventured as she began unfastening the myriad clips, "did... did you see what happened? With Joan's face?"

She shot him a quick, curious glance. "What do you mean?"

"She... she...." Simon fumbled for the words. "She was—I'm not sure if it was starlight mixed with Gabriel's infatuation, but she looked—like she was *glowing*."

Her face went carefully neutral. Doubtless she was putting on her therapist's cap. "I saw, through your perception, that *Gabriel* thought she was glowing," she said noncommittally.

"I was expecting to see something of the sort when we found the sword, but... it was her. It was all *her*. And Gabriel sees it."

His right arm was free, and as she turned to liberate his left, he placed his hand on her shoulder.

"Victoria... I think we've found not one, but *two* people with an extraordinarily high percentage of Precursor DNA."

CHAPTER FIVE

Victoria had refused to discuss anything until Simon had eaten something. "Food is grounding," she said. "It brings you back into your body, and out of Gabriel's. Eat," she said, tossing him a Lion Bar. Simon was annoyed, but obeyed.

"All right, I'm following doctor's orders. So, Dr. Bibeau, please share your thoughts."

"I confess I was a little worried when you first pulled yourself out of the simulation." Simon had been so, too, but opted to keep that scrap of information to himself. "But between Gabriel's feelings for Joan, the powerful charisma she was reputed to have exerted, and the fact that it was your first time in the Animus, I'm not overly concerned. Honestly, the fact that you were able to choose to desynchronize speaks to your personal strength of will. I don't think you're in any danger of negative Bleeding Effects, at least not for the time being."

"That's a relief," he said. "But as for Joan and Gabriel—I've never heard of anything like this."

"Neither have I," Victoria admitted.

"She's exerting the same type of...." He searched for the word. "Compulsion. No, that's not it. And 'charisma' is a word far too over-used. Gabriel is reacting to her the way people usually do to one of the Apples of Eden. He's drawn to her, almost despite himself. I can literally see this—this radiance through his eyes. And her whole career—at the beginning, at least—give us example after example of how she inspired and persuaded people."

"Gabriel, maybe, but we already know there are perfectly normal hormones at work in his brain. And obviously, she didn't influence everyone. It's not as if she's a Piece of Eden given human form."

Victoria didn't mean it to be cruel, but Simon winced slightly. He'd been trying not to think about how this story was going to end. Victoria was correct. If Joan was a Piece of Eden somehow given human form, she would not have met her bitter fate. No one would have sentenced her.

"No, she's not, thank goodness. Pieces of Eden are powerful enough as inanimate objects. Living persons, even fighting for good causes, would truly be too terrifying to contemplate."

"At the same time, I have to agree that Joan and Gabriel do appear to have large concentrations of Precursor DNA. And this is important for us to find out. *Any* Precursor DNA is rare today, and becoming rarer with every generation."

Simon was well aware of that. There was, in fact, a Templar effort right this moment to track down one Charlotte de la Cruz, who is rumored to have merely a tiny bit of the precious DNA.

"Joan of Arc has always been remarkable," Simon said. "I guess we're going to find out just *how* remarkable. I know what she's going to ask Durand and Gabriel to do for her—she's going to make them take her to Vaucouleurs."

"What happens there?"

"She insists on seeing the captain, Lord Robert de Baudricourt. Joan wants him to escort her to Chinon, where the Dauphin is staying."

"Does he?"

Simon frowned. "Actually, no. Not yet, anyway. I suppose we ought to jump ahead to the next significant event. I'm not sure you appreciate how difficult it is as a historian to not experience the crucial moments. It's gutting me to bypass even *one* of them. When Joan went back to Domrémy after that first failed attempt, her whole village was forced to evacuate south to Neufchâteau. They returned to see their church burned down. A few months later, Joan was involved in a breach of contract lawsuit. How could I not want to see that?"

Victoria looked interested despite herself. "What kind of contract?"

"Marital. Her parents betrothed her, and her would-be fiancé called her to court when she refused. She said she never agreed to it. The fellow's name is lost to history, but I'm burning to find out. You can't tell me you aren't curious, too."

"No, I can't. But I do know we only have a week—correction, five days—to explore Gabriel's memories. Once you've demonstrated the value of your approach to Rikkin, you will likely have more time for your own personal curiosity."

He eyed her. "*Professional* curiosity. I'm not in any danger of waking up finding notes I wrote to myself in the guise of Gabriel."

"I'm not worried about that either," she said. But he could tell by her expression that something, indeed, was worrying her. He wondered what the next "important event," according to the algorithm Victoria had designed and implemented, would turn out to be.

WEDNESDAY, 7 JANUARY, 1429

Gabriel held Joan in his arms while she sobbed into his chest.

What the hell? Simon thought wildly.

"It is so *clear* what must happen!" Joan's voice was muffled against Gabriel's shirt. She was crying so hard, he felt the fabric growing damp. "Why will this man not see me? What am I doing wrong?"

Somewhat alarmed, Simon reached into Gabriel's knowledge for an update. Durand Laxart, at his son's suggestion, had gone back to Burey-en-Vaux to be with his wife and new baby. Joan had shared one room with Catherine Royer, and Gabriel and Henri another. At this moment, Henri was at his shop, and Catherine was in the single front room that served as kitchen, dining room, and hearth.

A short time earlier, Joan had stood outside the door to de Baudricourt's hall until she collapsed from the cold and a refusal to eat. Gabriel had brought her back, and a moment ago had been sent to tempt her with a bowl of soup. He had expected to see her exhausted but fiery, and had braced himself for an argument about returning to the castle. Instead, Joan had met him with tears pouring down her face.

Gabriel held her as he might have held a child, offering comfort and an emotion that was calm and peaceful yet left him in awe of its depth. Joan clung to him, releasing at last her tears of anger at de Baudricourt's repeated refusals and her frustration at the impasse.

"The good people of Orléans have been besieged since October. Just today, they have suffered another defeat in an effort to get food brought in. Children hunger behind those walls, and this foolish captain will not even speak with me!"

12 February, 1429—the Battle of the Herrings, Simon thought. It was a disastrous raid on an English supply convoy led by Sir John Fastolf, who would live in infamy caricatured by Shakespeare as the drunken hedonist Sir John Falstaff. The battle's name came from the large amount of salted fish being brought in for Lent. Jean Dunois, better known as the Bastard of Orléans, had barely escaped with his life. Joan would meet him soon.

But how the hell did Joan know?

Gabriel, too, was shocked at her words, but Joan uttered them as a simple fact, and he believed her.

After a time, Joan stopped sobbing and drew back. Her face was puffy and her eyes red and swollen, but her light was shining again. Gabriel felt his heart ease in his chest to see it; her light was more important to him than the sun. "Will you eat something now?" he asked. She looked at the soup and winced. "For me, Jeanette—I mean Jeanne?" Ever since her first meeting with de Baudricourt, she had taken to calling herself Jeanne the Maid, putting aside the girlish nickname.

Joan sighed. "For you," she said, reluctantly.

He smiled in relief. "Thank you. I'll bring you some bread and wine, too." Rising from where he sat beside her on the bed, he went to the door—and froze.

In the main room, he heard a man's voice... and Henri was still in his shop. Joan paused, lowering her spoon, her head cocked to one side. She placed the bowl down and rose, her movements fluid and deliberate, gently pushed Gabriel aside, pulled open the door, and walked through it boldly, as if all her strength had returned at once.

Another one of de Baudricourt's men, this one so tall that he seemed a giant in the small room, was speaking politely with Catherine. At their entrance, he turned. He was about a decade older than Gabriel, clean-shaven, his dark eyes sparkling with good humor. His was a face that seemed to want to smile often.

"Just the little vixen I have come to see," he exclaimed. "You are the infamous La Pucelle who has been tormenting my master, Captain de Baudricourt."

Before Joan could reply, most likely with something sharp, Catherine said smoothly, "Jeanne, Gabriel—this is one of Lord de Baudricourt's squires, Jean de Metz. He has come here to speak with you."

Looking uneasy, Catherine offered the stranger a seat. Joan deliberately straightened and said nothing, folding her arms and glaring at this squire, as she had glared at all the others before.

Her attitude seemed to amuse him. He leaned back in the chair, stretching his long legs to the fire, and the hint of a smile broadened into a grin. He sighed, somewhat exaggeratedly. "My dear girl... what are you doing here? Don't you think the king is doomed to be cast out of his kingdom, and the rest of us will soon be speaking English?"

Joan growled, very softly, and Gabriel smothered a smile of his own. This Jean de Metz had no idea who he was dealing with.

"I have come here, to a place that claims to love the Dauphin, to talk with Robert de Baudricourt, so that he may lead me or send me to the king. But he pays no attention to me or to my words." She said this slowly and with care, as if she were talking to a child. "And yet, before we are in mid-Lent, I *must* and will be at the king's side, even if I have to wear my legs down to my knees!"

"It's a long journey, to Chinon," de Metz continued. "Twelve days, maybe a fortnight. By day, you could be attacked by the English or their Burgundian friends, and by night, by rough men scouring the roads for coins to take and maidens like you to despoil."

He let his gaze travel up and down her body. Gabriel felt a burst of white-hot anger, but Joan didn't flinch. She strode toward de Metz, who got to his feet at her approach. He towered over her.

Joan looked him straight in the eye. "I'm not afraid. If there are soldiers or brigands in my way, God will make a safe path for me."

"My, you are confident, aren't you?"

"You have heard the prophecies," Joan stated. "The ones that say France was lost by a woman, but will be restored by a maiden from the region of Lorraine. The wicked Queen Isabeau signed the Treaty of Troyes, and gave France away to the English boy-king." Her eyes flashed. "And *I* am from Lorraine."

"You're not the first Maid of Lorraine—" de Metz began, but she would have none of it.

"I was *born* for this. There is nobody in all the world, neither king nor duke, nor *any* other, who can recover the kingdom for France. This kingdom will have no help, if not from me!"

Her voice, always melodious, was resonant now. Still, de Metz grinned insufferably down at her.

"Was it your brothers who put the idea of battle and war into your pretty little head?"

She emitted a short, bitter laugh. "I would rather stay with my poor mother in Domrémy and spin. This is not my station. But I must go, and I must do it, for God wishes me to."

Her voice and words were strong, and the light, that magnificent radiance that always lifted Gabriel's heart, blazed fiercely. The glibness faded from de Metz's handsome face, to be replaced by something else; something joyful, but deeper, and before the astonished gaze of Catherine, Gabriel, and the Maid herself, Jean de Metz went down on one knee before her.

"La Pucelle," he said, and there was no hint of humor now in his voice or his mien. "I offer you my hands as a sign of my faith in you. I will take you before Lord de Baudricourt, my master, and I pledge by my honor, I will see to it that you reach the Dauphin safely."

De Metz pressed his hands together, as if in prayer, and then raised them to Joan. Wonderingly, her face growing so bright that Gabriel could scarcely stand to look upon it, she clasped her hands around both of his. It was an age-old gesture of fealty, and the hairs on Gabriel's—and Simon's—arms lifted.

Gabriel was responding to de Metz's pledge to be Joan's liegeman. Simon was reacting to something else entirely.

Joan's beautiful face was not the only thing that was radiant. Hidden in the shadows of de Metz's sleeves, invisible to all eyes but those of a very few who could see more than ordinary men, something glinted.

Something sharp. Something deadly.

The tip of a Hidden Blade.

Jean de Metz was an Assassin.

CHAPTER SIX

"Do you see it?" Simon shouted before he could help himself. The second the words were out of his mouth he was terribly sorry, as the images twisted, contorted, faded to gray, and he felt a sharp pain in his skull as if de Metz's Hidden Blade was neatly spearing his temple.

And then he was out of the simulation, sweat sheeting his body, his eyes wide and his heart pounding. Victoria lifted off the helm and clucked her tongue reprovingly. "Simon, you are worse than my younger subjects. You get far too excited sometimes."

The comment stung Simon, who fancied himself a rather cool customer. But it was true—and surprising. As a child, he had always preferred history—true "stories"—to fairy tales, and the predilection followed him into adulthood. He realized now that part of the appeal had been how distant it was. History's lessons were to be observed and made note of, not experienced. Certainly not experienced like this, not until now, and Simon was only starting to realize how profoundly it was affecting him.

I blame Gabriel, he thought.

"So what did you see that excited you so much you had to desynchronize?" she continued, lifting his arms so she could free him from the Animus's embrace.

"Jean de Metz had a Hidden Blade," he said calmly.

Her head whipped up and her eyes widened. Joy flooded her face. "An Assassin! Oh, Simon, this is truly wonderful news!"

"I'm kicking myself for not thinking about it sooner," Simon said, working it out as he spoke. "Joan was a galvanizing figure. Of *course* both Assassins and Templars would be interested in her. They'd probably be keeping an eye out for anyone who looked to fulfill the prophecies. It appears we'll have the opportunity to increase our knowledge about Assassin activity in the fifteenth century, as well as learn about Piece of Eden 25 *and* study two fascinating individuals with traces of Precursor DNA."

"Yet another way to keep Rikkin's interest in your new approach." Victoria unfastened the last clasp and stepped away as he descended. Simon realized he was trembling, his heart still beating fast, and he let Victoria guide him to a seat and hand him a glass of water. She fetched her tablet and started looking through it.

"You look almost more pleased than I am," he observed.

"And why shouldn't I be?" She offered a smile as she drew up a chair next to him.

He craned his neck to look at the screen. "Any idea as to who might be a Templar or Assassin? We will make sure to include those encounters in our research if so."

"Well, of course, at this time in history," Victoria said, tapping and swiping as she spoke, "it has only been a bit over a century since the execution of Jacques de Molay and the disarray of the Order."

Disarray. It was an apt word choice. The Order, once so powerful, had been plunged into chaos—especially in France. The Templars had been forced to retreat. The Assassins had pressed their advantage, ruthlessly hunting their enemies down and eliminating them one by one. But nothing could keep the Templar Order from rising again, and it had been slowly clawing its way back, having retreated from Europe to Britain for a time.

"France would be an important prize for the Templars to reclaim, and the Assassins would dearly love to keep it from them," Simon said.

"We don't have many names from this time period," Victoria said. "So much was lost. The Assassins rejoiced when the Order fell and de Molay was burned as a heretic. They would not want to see France become a foothold for a strong Templar resurgence. For the Assassins, France must be French, and for the Templars, it would need to be under the control of Britain and its stronger Templar presence. The English and the Burgundians would be doing everything they could to discredit the Dauphin—and all those who supported him."

"Like our Joan."

Victoria nodded. "Now... we do know of one Templar's ancestor for certain." She showed him the image, and Simon's pleasure dimmed somewhat.

"Ah, him. Lovely chap."

He had read the file on this particular individual. The late and, as far as Simon was concerned, unlamented Warren Vidic, the cruel and clever creator of the Animus, had explored his own genetic memories as part of the technology's development. He claimed as his ancestor someone almost as unpleasant as he—Geoffroy Thérage, one of Joan's executioners.

"One of the more ghoulish rumors from those wanting miracles was that Joan's heart stubbornly refused to burn," he informed Victoria. "Some witnesses claimed it remained whole in the pile of ashes. Thérage is the fellow who gathered up the ashes—and, conveniently, the seemingly magical noncombustible heart—of the future saint and tossed them into the Seine, so there would be no rumors of relics to trouble her enemies down the line. The irony's delicious. His descendant—any Templar, really—would have been thrilled to have had some of Joan's DNA to study. Must have vexed Vidic to no end."

Thérage had been an Englishman. Simon was starting to get the uncomfortable feeling that he, as a British Templar, was coming down on the wrong side of history on this particular occasion.

Victoria interrupted his rumination with a light touch on his arm. "It's getting late."

"Not that late."

"You've done a great deal of good work today, but your brain needs to process what you've learned. The first few days in the Animus take a lot out of one."

Simon started to protest, then sighed. "I suppose that's doctor's orders, not just friendly advice?"

"Yes, I'm afraid it is. Your dreams are going to be very interesting tonight. You might want to try to remember them and jot them down when you wake up. Sometimes there's a secondary recall after sleep."

Simon tried and failed to stifle a yawn. "My body betrays me," he grumbled. "As you wish. I'll bring a Temp's Hard @ Work basket to the office. See you there first thing?"

"First thing."

In his office with the door closed, Alan Rikkin poured a small snifter of brandy. He offered it to Bibeau, but she declined.

"We have some solid progress already," she began, but he held up his hand.

"First things first," he said. "I want to know your thoughts on Hathaway. You are my eyes and ears when it comes to our new head of Historical Research—and our newest member of the Inner Sanctum. I think it's apparent that he is, shall we say, enthusiastic."

"I'm flattered by the trust you place in me in asking for my assistance," Bibeau said. "I'm honored to help. And to be honest—I would rather see an overabundance of enthusiasm than a lack of it."

He eyed her for a moment, swirling the amber beverage in the glass to release its fragrance before taking a small sip. Dr. Victoria

Bibeau sat in front of his desk, patiently awaiting his response. Rikkin returned to his seat, tapped on his keyboard, then turned the monitor so she could see it. She blanched and looked down at her folded hands.

The picture showed a man who once might have been pleasant-looking, but who now presented a picture of stark horror. His body had been riddled with bullets, and he had died with his eyes and mouth open in what might have been terror or rage—or both. His hands clutched torn pieces of paper.

"Are you quite sure about that, Dr. Bibeau?"

Bibeau took a deep breath and forced herself to regard the brutal image. "Robert Fraser was a fairly ordinary man," Rikkin continued. "A talented amateur artist, a keen observer, a loyal employee. *He* had an abundance of enthusiasm for his work, too."

"Mr. Fraser was not a Templar, let alone a member of the Inner Sanctum," Bibeau replied. "Professor Hathaway is much more mentally stable."

"Again… are you certain, Doctor? Fraser found himself too caught up in the excitement of being Arno Dorian, Assassin. And," he added, "swept away by Dorian's ill-fated romance. Now, we have a man who is already more passionate about history than most who is studying Joan of Arc through the eyes of a besotted teenager. It's… concerning."

His words made Bibeau stiffen. "I know what part I played in the tragedy that was Robert Fraser. No one wants this to happen again less than I do—particularly with someone as valuable to the Order as Simon Hathaway."

Rikkin smiled in a friendly manner, pulling back from his cool attack. "You, too, are valuable to the Order, Doctor. I wouldn't want either of you to come to harm. It's why I've instructed you to report to me—so that if anything does arise, we'll be prepared to act, quickly and efficiently, to nip it in the bud."

Her gaze was level with his. "I will of course come to you at once with any suspicions I have, sir."

He simply continued to smile. "I feel vigilance is a more... appropriate attitude, with so much at stake. Now. You mentioned the happy words 'solid progress,' I believe?"

"Of course, sir. On several fronts. First, Joan of Arc appears to have an almost excessive amount of Precursor DNA." He listened as she described Joan's charisma and her ability to influence others even without Piece of Eden 25."

"Fascinating," he said. "It's a shame she doesn't have any descendants."

"Secondly," Bibeau said, "one of her loyal followers has revealed himself to be an Assassin."

Rikkin's eyes widened slightly. "Only one? Given the political climate, I would have expected more."

"We've identified one for certain. I agree it's likely there will be more. Once I realized the potential for interacting with Assassins, I cross-referenced what we know of the political climate in France in 1429 with information gleaned from previous Animus research. If my extrapolations are correct, I think there's better than an eighty percent chance that Joan and Gabriel will encounter a Mentor at some point."

Rikkin sank back in his chair, regarding her with renewed respect. "That would be quite useful," Rikkin was forced to admit. "We know about Thomas de Carneillon in the early 1300s. We don't hear anything about another one until Ezio Auditore, two centuries later. I suppose I shouldn't be surprised one would turn up during the Hundred Years' War."

"It does support Professor Hathaway's theory of casting a wide net," she said. "All we knew going into this was that Joan of Arc possessed a Sword of Eden, which was later taken from her. We knew nothing about the Assassin connection, or Joan's own DNA."

"Duly noted. But... you still haven't even found the sword." He smiled. "You and Professor Hathaway have five days left. Make good use of them, Doctor."

Rodrigo Lima, Anaya's supervisor, poked his head in into the office she shared with two other coworkers.

"You're not high-level enough to have your own office," he said, looking meaningfully at the two empty desks. "You don't get overtime, you know."

She gave him a smile. "Look who's talking. You're here late, too."

"Ah, yes, but *I'm* leaving now. And *you're* not."

"Don't worry, I'm not after your job," she said. "You're too good a boss."

He grinned, leaning against the door. "Well, good, because I like my job. And part of my job is taking care of my staff." Rodrigo's smile faded a little. "This job can get to you, and I don't want to see you burn out. Abstergo needs you. So not too much later, okay?"

She nodded. "Okay, mother hen." He rolled his eyes and left, closing her door behind him.

Anaya had meant it. Rodrigo was the best kind of boss—he pushed his people hard, but worked right alongside them, blending Brazilian warmth with experience and a knack for understanding how to inspire his team. Abstergo needed him here.

But... did Abstergo need *her* here?

It wasn't the first time this question had occurred to her. She's looked into this before—more than once. Now, yet again, she went to the official Abstergo website, clicked on "careers," and entered her clearance code. The subset of positions specifically available to Templars popped up. She scrolled down until she found what she wanted. What had been sitting there for three whole weeks already.

Director, Information Security: Montreal.

Everyone said Abstergo Entertainment was a fun place to work. Conventional wisdom held that it was better for one's career to be at a lower level in London, Madrid, or Tokyo than a top rank at AE-Montreal, which wasn't even featured on Abstergo's main page... but Anaya wondered. There wasn't much opportunity for upward mobility here; she'd gone about as far as she could go without dethroning the capable Rodrigo, whose position she really didn't even want.

Anaya took a deep breath. She didn't want to be reactionary, but running into Simon so unexpectedly had rattled her more than she would have thought. Considering the nigh-obsessive relationship between Security and the Animus department, such encounters were sure to become much more likely. They hadn't parted badly. Anaya thought it might have been easier if they had. No, it had just... died out. Hadn't even fizzled out, really; there hadn't even been that much of a spark there. On his end, at least.

But there was still enough there on her side for her to have felt an unwelcome stab at the sight of his sharp-featured face.

Besides—she loved the idea of being able to use her French again. She'd worked in the Paris office before coming to London, and missed it.

Anaya had to smile at herself. Her entire career had been built on being daring, but when it came to doing anything outside of the job, she balked at change. What was that quote? "Fortune favors the bold," she murmured under her breath, and clicked "apply online."

CHAPTER SEVEN

DAY 3

Temp's Hard @ Work delivery basket had been designed by wiser heads than Simon's some years ago and was terribly popular with its customers. As Simon thanked the delivery person and tipped her generously, he dolefully predicted to himself that he'd polish off the whole thing before Victoria actually arrived at the office.

Victoria had told him to watch his dreams. Simon had had a very busy night, it would seem, as he woke exhausted. He remembered no specifics, but had been sufficiently unsettled to come in early, deciding to hunker down and do some work before Victoria arrived, though he did fire off a text in case she, too, was up early.

Careful to keep the Hard @ Work provisions safely away from the more fragile texts, he went over everything that might be of import, scribbling down questions like *What about Dauphin?*, *Where Templars?*, and *Which Bloody Sword???*

Victoria showed up at nine on the dot. "Despite my best efforts, I think I still have a muffin and some tea left, if you'd care for anything," he said, indicating the basket.

She sank down onto the leather couch and lifted a large takeaway cup. "I've got some coffee, thanks."

"Coffee is of the devil."

"It's the devil I know," she shrugged, and peered at him more closely. "You look exhausted," she observed.

"Busy dreams," he replied. "I'll be right as rain once we get back in the Animus." He sat down next to her on the couch and gave her a copy of his notes so they could go over them together. "All right. Here's what comes next for our Joan. De Metz does arrange a meeting with his lord. A rather clever fellow, this de Baudricourt. He—oh, what do the Americans call it—'passed the buck' to his *own* liege lord, Charles, Duke of Lorraine. The duke was fairly keen to see her."

"Do you think this duke might be an Assassin?"

"It's highly doubtful," he said as she entered the information, her fingers dancing over her tablet. "I looked into him thoroughly over the last hour. By 1429, he was sixty-five and quite ill, which is, honestly, likely the reason he agreed to meet with her. Rumors were swirling about the prophecy, so he might have thought Joan could perform some sort of miraculous healing. Unfortunately for him, all she did was request the aid of his son-in-law, René, and other men to accompany her, and then scold him for his morals and tell him to put aside his mistress and return to his wife."

"Ha! Did he?"

"No, but he *did* approve her journey to Chinon, and assigned several men to escort her. Quite frankly, if I were an old man in my last two years on this earth, if that little spitfire had come in and dared say such things to me, I'd have done exactly the same. Probably the most entertainment the old fellow had had in years."

"So Joan and her escort head off to Chinon next, yes?"

"Not quite. Before they do... we're going to get a glimpse of the first of Joan's swords."

TUESDAY, 22 FEBRUARY, 1429

Word of the Maid of Lorraine had been spreading throughout Vaucouleurs ever since Joan's first visit, back in May of 1428. While the girl with the black hair and the glorious eyes stubbornly kept vigil every day, hoping for a meeting with de Baudricourt, she had spoken freely to anyone who would listen about her purpose and calling. By the time she returned from Nancy, the townspeople had taken up a collection for clothes and supplies so she might continue safely on her journey.

Joan, de Metz, and another squire, Bertrand de Poulengy, had been in de Baudricourt's hall for some time. Now, as Joan stepped out of the audience hall, clothed in a man's tunic and hose, her black hair cropped short as a soldier's, Simon's heart skipped a beat.

Gabriel had been surprised when de Metz had suggested the clothing, but it made perfect sense. They were traveling through dangerous territory. If Joan could pass for a man at first glance, the group would draw less attention. It would be easier for her to ride as well, without the encumbrance of a dress and skirt. Now she stood, her face pink, uncomfortable with the attention as the crowd cheered for her, and she seemed to hold back tears when Gabriel made his way through the throng leading a well-groomed, obedient brown horse.

"It is from Papa," he told her, and Simon felt the boy's pride in his father. Joan sought out Durand's face in the throng, and put her hand to her mouth, overcome.

"Gabriel, your family—all these good people—you cannot afford—"

"Maid," came de Baudricourt's voice, "worry not for the generosity of your cousin and the good people of Vaucouleurs. I will reimburse them for anything they give you out of love for you and faith in your mission."

Lovely words, came Victoria's voice, *but he certainly doesn't look like he shares the sentiments.* Indeed, Simon recalled Joan dubbing him "Sourface" at one point when she was particularly upset with him, and it was particularly apt today. Jean de Metz, however, looked very pleased. He stepped forward at his lord's nod. In his outstretched arms, he bore something wrapped in the de Baudricourt colors of black and gold.

"I place you in good and careful hands, Maid," de Baudricourt said, "and I pray you come to no harm as you ride to our king. But I also give you your first weapon. May you never need it, but may it serve you well if you do."

And here it was. Simon felt his body taut as a bowstring. The sword currently in Rikkin's office was intact; a priceless antique weapon, yes, but nothing more. The only power it currently possessed was that shared by other swords. But if this was Piece of Eden 25—would it appear different from its present state? Would Simon be able to see that it was special, or did it have to be utilized to come to its rarified life?

The last corner of the fabric fell away from the sword.

Joan raised the weapon, and the crowd cheered her madly.

It was definitely *not* Piece of Eden 25. *Dammit.*

"Go, then," de Baudricourt shouted as the group mounted their horses and turned the beasts' heads toward the gate, "and let come what may!"

Let come what may, indeed, Simon thought. *My demotion, certainly, and perhaps worse.*

With the Assassin Jean de Metz at her left hand and her devoted Gabriel on her right, Joan the Maid passed through the Gate of France and took her first real steps into the pages of history. What ought to have been a powerful moment for Simon to have experienced had been spoiled by the disappointment. Gabriel, at least, was happy.

For now, at any rate.

I'm sorry, Simon, came Victoria's voice in his ear.

The scene was swallowed by the mists, and Simon was glad of it. It was too optimistic, too filled with a sweet anticipation that would turn bitter soon enough, once these two innocents had their first taste of the horrors of war and the anguish of betrayal.

The mist reformed itself into shapes; a waxing moon throwing cool light on snow-covered earth, the hunch of a building against the night sky. As the mist further solidified, Simon realized the structure was a church by the colors of its small, stained glass windows, lit from within by candles. Soon the only mist was that which formed from Joan's and Gabriel's breath as they walked. It was not the hour of the Night Office, yet both had woken almost as if summoned.

Joan's group had taken eleven days to travel from Vaucouleurs to Chinon. Although several of the towns they skirted en route were held by the enemy, and the journey was over four hundred miles, Joan's bold prediction that they would come to no harm had proved to be correct.

Tonight the group lodged safely, as the town of Sainte-Catherine-de-Fierbois was occupied by French troops. But other nights, the travelers heading for Chinon had been forced to sleep in fields and in forests. Sometimes, when Joan was not with the men, they had said crude things about her and what they would do if they hadn't vowed to guide her safely. At first, Gabriel had leaped to his feet in outrage, but Jean de Metz calmed him and steered him away.

"Watch, and wait," he had said to the younger man quietly, adding, "I swear by my life I will cut the hand off the man that lays it on her ungently."

Sure enough, Joan would arrive and settle down among them, as content and fearless as if she were with her own family, and the soldiers—all young, strong, and clearly appreciative of the curves her masculine attire could not quite hide—would seem to lose all desire for her, their expressions shifting from leers to genuine smiles of warmth and their language shifting from rude to decorous. The first time this happened, Gabriel had stared, then turned to de Metz, eyebrows raised in question.

De Metz had smiled and said, "I know because it happens to me. She is beautiful, and well formed, but... to just be around her is enough."

Gabriel had nodded, turning to watch Joan smile and laugh, completely trusting these men, and completely safe in that trust. It should not be; but it was so, and Joan alone seemed unsurprised.

The church door was unlocked and they entered. Earlier that day, the small group had been able to celebrate mass here for only the second time on their journey. Joan had dictated a letter to the future king—she always referred to him as the Dauphin, not the king, and maintained she would continue to do so until she had escorted him to Reims—and a rider had been sent on ahead.

Now, in the hush of this small hour, Joan and Gabriel seemed to have the church to themselves. Joan stared at the statue of Saint Catherine, but the living girl's rapt face sang to Gabriel's soul more than that of a carved image. They had not spoken on the walk up, and remained silent now. As they approached the altar, Simon felt his weariness drop from him, as if it were a cloak he discarded. Joan was radiant to his eyes, and his own heart felt warm and full the closer they drew. He followed Joan's example, kneeling before the saint and praying silently.

Then, quite unexpectedly, the stillness was broken by Joan's voice.

"You should know, I think," she said. Gabriel, confused, opened his eyes to discover she was gazing at him, their faces only inches away from one another. Her eyes caught the warm glow of the candlelight.

"They gave me the choice as to whether I told my family I was leaving. They have given me the same choice about you. I almost told you last May, that night when we were both called to keep the Night Office together. But I was afraid. The doubt, even the contempt, of others, I could accept. But not from you."

Gabriel knew, somehow, that what she was about to reveal to him would change him forever in ways he could not possibly anticipate. But hadn't she done so already?

Joan took a deep breath. "You have heard me say I know what God wants. Yet you have never asked how it was that I knew. You have just accepted. As I did."

The glow upon her seemed to increase, and both Gabriel and Simon were rapt, moved beyond words for utterly different reasons. Simon knew what Joan was about to reveal, and it thrilled him to his very core.

"I was thirteen when it first happened," she said, her voice taking on a hushed and reverent tone. "I was in my father's garden." She looked down at the ring on her right little finger. Gabriel knew it was a gift from her family. She had asked him to write them, begging their forgiveness for what she had to do. She had not heard back, and now she caressed the simple ring as she spoke.

"It was summer. I heard a voice, and I knew this voice was from God. It came from my right-hand side, where the church was, and there was a tremendous, almost blinding light as it spoke to me. I was terrified, but the voice was so gentle."

Gabriel's breath came in rapid, shallow sips. "What did it say?"

"At first, only to be a good child, and to do everything that was pleasing to God. To be unafraid, because He would help me. Later, I learned that it was Saint Michael who spoke to me that first time, and I—I saw him." Her eyes shone, and a smile curved her lips as she spoke. "I fell to my knees and hugged him about the legs, like a child would her parent. He told me that Saint Catherine and Saint Margaret, too, would come to me, and that God had set me a task." She turned from him, looking up at the stone figure of Saint Catherine, whose church this was, and smiled.

"Jeanne...."

"Saint Michael told me the pitiable state that the kingdom of

France was in, and that I was to help its rightful king. And to do that, I would have to leave home. I didn't want to, I was afraid, but my Voices insisted. They told me to go to Captain de Baudricourt—that he would give me people to go with me to help the king—and to not give up if he turned me away the first time. That I was to keep coming back, and not allow myself to be refused. That God would turn the captain's ear toward me."

Gabriel's mouth was dry as hay, and he swallowed with an effort. He was almost afraid to ask the question in a holy house, but he could not help himself. "How do you know they were really angels?"

A smile that swept through him curved her lips. "I knew it here," she said, and placed a hand on Gabriel's heart. "No devil would have made me feel so... so calm. So loved."

The gentle touch made him tremble and he started to speak, letting the words pour out of him. "I see a light in you, Jeanne. It must be your angels, shining through you, just as they speak through you. Do... do they speak to the rest of us, too?"

Her radiance increased. "Oh, yes," she breathed softly, her words the barest, most exquisite of whispers. "But others don't always hear them."

Joan was not the first girl who had caught Gabriel's eye. But he had known instantly that there was something different, something sweet and strange in her voice and eyes and spirit, and he knew he couldn't bear to be without it. He wondered wildly if this devotion to her was coming from his own heart, or from an angel's whisper, or if perhaps the two things were the same.

The words came from that full heart. "Don't tell me to leave your side. Ever. Please."

She turned to look at him, her blue eyes sad. "I cannot promise we will never be parted. Only God knows that. And there are other things I cannot promise." Gently, she placed her hand on his arm. "How can I be Jeanne, a wife, when I have pledged to remain Jeanne, the Maid of Lorraine as long as it should please God? I made that promise three years ago. My body, my heart... my Voices need of all of me right now."

The mark of a reckless, smitten fool, no doubt, to cling so desperately to the words "right now." But Gabriel had long since accepted that he was indeed a reckless, smitten fool. "Only let me share your journey for as long as you can."

Impulsively she leaned in and grasped both of his hands. "Dear Gabriel, that... *that*, I can promise with a full and easeful heart. My Voices are glad that I've told you. They say that you have chosen to follow me. You will bear witness, be my shadow, for as long as is necessary."

Tears filled Gabriel's eyes. Simon's own heart ached at the thought of what was to come for this blue-eyed girl, so cheerfully and almost earthily human, who felt herself guided by the divine.

This... will be difficult, Simon thought. *At the end.*

The Animus was not a time travel machine. He was a passenger, not a pilot, and he, like Gabriel, was here to bear witness.

Their hands met and clasped. Gabriel lifted his face toward the saint, and felt peace settle upon him. He wanted to be closer to the image, to stand and go right up to the altar, to—

And then, like a thunderclap, Simon knew where the Sword of Eden was.

CHAPTER EIGHT

Rikkin had initially been annoyed when Bibeau had texted him wanting a meeting. *I do not come when bidden,* he had replied.

Important. You'll be pleased.

Fifteen minutes.

He'd intended to be out the door almost at once, but instead, as he waved her inside his office and listened, he realized he'd be a bit late to the private luncheon at Hibiscus.

"So, you know where the sword is?"

"Not for certain, but Simon started acting oddly. He said there were a few things he wanted to check on before he talked to me about them."

"So, he's being secretive. Interesting."

"I think it's as innocuous as he said—he wanted to research before presenting a theory. But I think he might have sensed where the sword might be. And," she added, pleased, "I think Joan of Arc may be in contact with Consus."

That did get Rikkin's attention. Consus was the name adopted by an Isu—at least, what remained of one. While the Precursors had created (and enslaved) humanity, Consus was known as one Precursor who had instead consistently shown sympathy for humanity's desire for freedom. He was the creator of what came to be known as Shrouds of Eden; technology somehow woven into a fabric that healed and restored. No one quite understood how the technology functioned, but it was accepted that somehow, while no part of Consus existed physically any longer, some of his essence—his "spirit," if one liked so sentimental a term—had been incorporated into the Shrouds. Such Shrouds formed the basis for tales of the Golden Fleece, and Joseph's Coat of Many Colors; garments, or cloaks, or winding sheets. The most famous of these, the Shroud of Turin, had been in Gramática's possession, and the man had routinely injured himself or others to force the Consus essence to interact with him. Like all constructs of the Precursors, these Shrouds were regarded as mystical or holy by those who did not understand their true technological nature.

For a moment, Rikkin considered canceling what had been put into motion. Perhaps Hathaway really was on to something. He might be able to discover information about Consus that could prove vital. He might be able to discover...

... *uncover* certain other things. No, that couldn't be allowed to happen.

"Observing Joan has been fascinating," Bibeau was saying.

"This isn't a video game. You and Simon are not supposed to be having an interesting experience, he's supposed to be proving to me and the Order why we need to channel funds to this broader net of his. And thus far, we have no sword at all—let alone information on how to repair it."

For just an instant, Bibeau's eyes flashed. "I think perhaps you don't fully understand the import of Joan's Voices and the Assassin—"

"So far the Assassin has done absolutely nothing, the Mentor you promised hasn't shown up, and Joan may still be talking to herself."

"May, or may not be. It seems she does have a high level of Precursor DNA. And we will obviously make attempts to identify the Mentor and any other Assassins while we follow Joan to Chinon."

"Where she meets the Dauphin. Correct me if I'm wrong, Doctor, but doesn't Joan discover the sword after that incident? Quite a *while* after that incident, point of fact?"

Bibeau hesitated. "It depends on which sword turns out to be the Sword of Eden."

He stared at her for a moment. "Well, well," he said, "this is the first time I've been informed of this particular wrinkle."

Bibeau took a deep breath. "We're investigating all reasonable leads. Sir, we have five days, and now we have a Mentor to seek out. Don't you think that our discoveries—the only Mentor we're aware of in a two-century span and the possible presence of Consus—warrant granting Historical Research some extra time?"

"I'm traveling to Spain shortly, Dr. Bibeau, and I intend to see this wrapped up with a tidy bow before then. I dislike leaving HQ with something as important as a department's entire direction up in the air. Surely you understand." He smiled, thinly and without humor, and glanced at his watch. "I've a luncheon engagement. Text me with any developments, but don't expect an immediate response."

"Yes, sir."

As she left, a text from a number consisting entirely of noughts appeared on Rikkin's silenced phone. *Phase 1 of Omega-104 initiated. Awaiting instructions.*

Continue Phase 2. Initiate prep for Omega-105. Stand by.

When they had paused for lunch, Victoria had told Simon he would have to grab something on his own. Something had come up, she said.

"With the Aerie?"

"Sort of," she had replied distantly as she typed on her phone. "We'll meet around two. Try to nap if you can."

The arrangement worked for him. He had a theory he wanted to research, and rather than napping he was back in his office when his phone chimed to announce an incoming text. He raised his eyebrows as he realized it was Anaya and read: *Meet for lunch?*

Simon wanted to beg off for a variety of reasons. He had plenty of food left for lunch. He had work he could be doing. And... seeing Anaya always made him feel uncomfortable. Not that he had any reason to feel guilty. He'd given the relationship his best shot. It just hadn't worked out.

He sighed and thumbed back, *Got my basket.* She'd know what he meant; she'd seen it on his desk often enough. *Thanks though.* Thinking that would be that, he started to put the phone down, but it chimed again.

I have news. Kind of important.

Simon frowned, a little worried now. Anaya had meant a great deal to him once. He'd gone so far as to consider getting a ring. She wasn't the sort to text him out of the blue over nothing, either. It'd been months since they'd done anything together, and weeks since he'd run into her, until the day before yesterday.

Of course, he said at once. *Are you free now?*

Yes. Temp's?

Always.

KK CU soon.

Simon couldn't help but cringe at the SMS, and reminded himself that Anaya and her crew had used SMS shortcuts and leetspeak long before the proverbial "kids these days." He sighed, pocketed the phone, and headed for the lift.

Anaya was waiting for him outside the tea shop, wearing a smart navy blazer with trousers, a cream silk blouse that set off her dark skin, and conservative earrings; a professional and understated ensemble that contrasted with her impudent cherry-streaked hair.

She smiled when she saw him. He stepped forward, unsure if she were expecting a handshake, or a kiss on the cheek, or nothing at all, and the whole thing became an awkward bump-and-apologize event.

Anaya's face flushed, but then she laughed.

"Come on," she said, grinning, and he felt the knot in his belly untangle. She'd always had a light touch, and her laugh meant that her news wasn't bad. Which was a huge relief. "Let's get takeaway and head to the roof."

"The roof? Anaya, it's October."

"All your beach trips have made you too sensitive to cold," she teased.

Abstergo had transformed the entire cement rooftop into a pleasant garden. Everyone was welcome to bring takeaway or a bagged lunch and sit and enjoy the magnificent view. It was lovely in the spring and summer, and, Simon had to admit, even in the autumn. The trees were turning, and with the blue sky today it was pleasant. But Anaya was right—he found it too cold. He'd left his overcoat in his office, but at least he still had on his suit jacket.

Shivering, he cut to the chase. "So, what's your news? Everything all right, I hope?" he asked, warming his hands around the paper cup.

Anaya stared at her own cup for a moment before lifting her eyes to his. "I anticipate so, yes." She took a deep breath. "There's a director's position open at Abstergo Entertainment. I sent in my application last night. I came in this morning to a request for a video interview this afternoon. If I get the job, it'll be quite a step up for me, and I think I'll enjoy it."

"Oh. I see." Simon adjusted his spectacles with one hand. AE's response time was shockingly fast, but then again, this *was* Anaya. He gave her a genuine smile. "Anaya, you're amazing at what you do. It boggles my mind, frankly, and you'll do a smashing job in Montreal. And," he added, "I know you'll enjoy speaking French again."

Her face softened. "I will, yes," she said. "I'm surprised you remember."

"I've always wanted you to be well and happy," he said, and he realized he meant it.

"I know that," she said. "But I've not got the job just yet."

"You will. They'd be nutters not to take you. Did they, ah, say when they'd expect you to start working there?"

"Straight away, or as soon as I can manage it. Shouldn't be too long. It's just me to move, after all."

She didn't say it with any particular emphasis, but the words stung. But then again, it was nothing more than simple truth. It *was* just her. Just as it would be "just him," if he were to transfer.

So he merely nodded. "Try some of those ghastly sounding chips while you're there, eh?" She looked at him, puzzled. "You know the ones. With the gravy and the cheese."

"Oh... you mean poutine?"

"That's the stuff." There was a lot Simon could say. *I'll miss you.* And yet for months, he hadn't bothered to even shoot her a text or grab a cup of tea with her. *I'm sorry.* He was... but it hadn't been his fault, or hers.

At a loss, he reached out and squeezed her hand. "Best of luck, Anaya."

"Thanks, Simon."

The wind picked up, slicing through his jacket with almost malevolent glee. Even Anaya shivered this time. "I should be getting back," Simon said. He lifted his tea in salute, paused, nodded, more to himself then her, then left. She didn't follow, standing alone in the cool but clear morning, and he felt strangely melancholy as he turned away.

"So I have a theory about Joan's Voices," Simon said as he and Victoria rode the lift down to the Animus Room after their separate lunches.

She eyed him. "Before we get into it—is everything all right?"

He thought she looked worse than he did, and he debated telling her about Anaya, but honestly, what was there to say? *My ex-girlfriend, whom I haven't talked to in months till I ran into her at the lift, is taking a job elsewhere?* Rubbish.

"I'm fine," he said, and steered them back on topic. "Most people today, when they talk about her Voices, assume Joan had true visions from God, outright lied, or had some sort of mental illness or physical condition that caused her to hear them. Schizophrenia, for instance, or perhaps a form of epilepsy."

"For people who don't know what we do, the latter seems a reasonable theory, though as a psychiatrist I can assure you there are some definite holes in it," Victoria agreed.

"It's pretty obvious that she saw something that the fifteenth-century mind would perceive as angels. We've seen examples before of both Templar and Assassin interaction with Precursor artifacts. And individuals with high concentrations of Precursor DNA, like Charlotte de la Cruz, have been known to somehow receive messages from the Precursor past specifically targeted to them."

Victoria didn't seem too surprised by his theory. But then again, she was an intelligent woman and had likely come to the same conclusion. "I've been briefed about de la Cruz. So you think Consus somehow found a way to speak to Joan? Because of her strong percentage of Precursor DNA?"

"If there is really a 'voice' speaking to Joan, as one of the more benevolent Isu, Consus is by far the most likely candidate," Simon said. "Let's think about this. It looks as though Joan of Arc has been in contact with a remnant from the Precursors. We'll just call him or her the Voices. This started at age thirteen and continued all the way through her final day, so it's got nothing to do with the sword. I can—I mean Gabriel can-literally *see* her radiance, and I suspect that Durand can, too. So does Jean de Metz. This can help direct some of our focus as we start seeing some of the really significant events in Joan's life. Hopefully, after today, we'll have some really specific things to take to Rikkin, and he'll grant us an extension."

Simon suddenly realized how comfortable he was using the words *we* and *us*. It was odd. He'd been so opposed to having a keeper, but now he couldn't fathom progressing without Victoria. He cleared his throat and shifted uncomfortably. "And, ah... you've been tremendously useful. Thank you."

Victoria glanced up at him, surprised. "You're welcome," she said. Fortunately the door opened at that moment, sparing Simon further discomfort.

Victoria helped him into the Animus. He was growing used to it now; it felt less like he was being imprisoned in an Iron Maiden and more like he was being safely strapped into a hang glider. He frowned a little at the overly romantic metaphor. A little bit of bleeding from Gabriel, no doubt, but nothing he couldn't handle.

"Right," he said briskly. "Joan's made it to Chinon, and she's finally gotten the royal summons."

"Do you want to start with her private meeting with the Dauphin?"

"No. I'd like to see their first encounter."

"That's not exactly pertinent to the project," Victoria cautioned.

"Not directly, but I'd like Gabriel to take a gander at those the Dauphin surrounds himself with. See if we can spot any more Assassins."

She nodded and slipped the helmet on. A few moments later, the blackness in Simon's vision began to pale, turning to the by-now-familiar gray mist, and then to a night lit by torches.

SUNDAY, 6 MARCH, 1429

Chinon.

Simon knew that many nigh-legendary figures other than Joan of Arc had figured into its history. Among them were the fiery Plantagenets—Henry II, his wife and queen Eleanor of Aquitaine, their sons, Richard the Lionheart and Bad King John, and Cardinal Richelieu, of *The Three Musketeers* fame.

Jacques de Molay and several of his Templars had been imprisoned in the Coudray Tower, where, Simon knew, Joan herself would be staying—although she would not be a guest in its dungeon. The Grand Master had left graffiti on his prison walls, and Simon wondered if Gabriel would be able to get a glimpse of it.

Gabriel and Joan had had ample time to gaze up at the fortress from the town nestled at its base. Despite the letter that Joan had sent ahead, Charles had kept them waiting while two clergymen had come down from the castle to speak with her. When asked why she wanted to see the king, Joan had replied, "God has seen me safely for over a hundred leagues on my journey, and He has given me two tasks. I am to raise the siege of Orléans, which is causing so much suffering, and I am to bring the Dauphin to Rheims, where he is to be anointed and crowned King of France."

Finally, convinced by the clergy and a personal letter from Robert de Baudricourt, the king decided to grant her an audience.

Dusk had fallen as Joan, Jean de Metz, de Poulengy, and Gabriel ascended the narrow, winding path that led to the great castle. Their escorts carried torches to light their way as the shadows crept forward, emboldened by the sun's withdrawal.

A drawbridge was lowered to admit them. De Metz and de Poulengy dismounted, but two guards rode up to take the other two horses. Gabriel nodded to the man who held the reins of his mount, but the one tending to Joan's horse leered at her, licking lips that glinted wetly in the torchlight. He was large, and bulky, and his jaw disappeared in a row of doughy flesh.

"So, this is the famous Maid from Vaucouleurs?" he said, his lascivious smile widening as he looked her up and down. "Stay with me for a night, and you wouldn't be a maid on the morrow!" He turned, laughing, to his companion, but his friend did not seem to think the comment amusing.

Anger surged through Gabriel, but before he or the other men could speak, Joan held up a hand. Her face was sad and kind. "What is your name?" she asked him, softly.

He seemed a bit taken aback, but bluffly replied, "Antoine Moreau," adding with a wink, "the *Giant*."

"Antoine Moreau," Joan said as she dismounted, "your words

offend God. Make peace with him... quickly."

Even in the flickering light, Gabriel could see the man pale and his eyes widen. He started to mutter something under his breath, then he stepped back, leading Joan's horse through the gate to a stable for the night. Other men came forward now to take the rest of the horses in the ensuing uncomfortable silence.

"My apologies for my companion's rudeness, Maid," said the remaining mounted guard.

She smiled sadly. "God forgives all. Me? I just feel sorry for him."

De Metz glanced at Gabriel, raising a brow in question. Gabriel shrugged slightly. He had no idea what had passed between Joan and the guard, and wasn't sure he wanted to.

On foot, Joan's group made their way through the Fort du Coudray, a courtyard with small buildings and four towers stretching up into the inky sky, slightly silvered by the waning gibbous moon. Another bridge lay to the right of Coudray Tower, and again, they crossed it with great care. The dry moat below them was so deep, the moonlight didn't even reach the bottom.

The next courtyard area of the second, main fortress, Château du Milieu, was so vast, Simon thought it more like a small town. Part of it was a garden, with trees and statuary. Smaller buildings—perhaps smithies or barracks, it was hard to tell in the darkness—lined the left-hand wall. They were closed and dark now, with only the occasional torch throwing flickering light.

Immediately to the right was a row of structures that could only be the royal lodgings, and they were most certainly *not* closed and dark. Light blazed in the windows, and Gabriel could hear music and the laughter and chatter of a sizeable gathering. He stopped in his tracks as the full import of what was about to happen descended upon him.

He had been so captivated by Joan, so caught up in the divine beauty of her and what she wanted, that more earthly events had diminished in significance. But now... now, he was about to step into a king's hall. He, Gabriel Laxart, bastard son of a simple farmer.

A hand reached for his and he looked down to see Joan smiling serenely at him. "All will be well," she said. "God is with us."

Deep in his heart, he knew she was right. He could see it in her, her incandescence brighter to him than the torchlight. But would others see it? He had heard some of the others talking about Charles; about how indecisive he was, and how some in his court held greater sway over him than they should.

Joan was from God, of that he was certain. But it was not angels she had to impress. It was a king.

Gabriel took a deep breath and stepped forward into the court of Charles, Dauphin of France and, hopefully, its future liege.

CHAPTER NINE

Gabriel had thought Vaucouleurs magnificent, and Nancy a bustling town. Now he realized just how provincial they were compared to a royal fortress and a king's hall.

"How many people are here?" Gabriel asked de Metz.

"Oh, I'd say about... three hundred or so."

"Three hun... all to see Jeanne?"

"Some, certainly, but others of the king's court simply like a good party. They have expensive tastes, and the king wants them happy." The words were spoken in a neutral tone, and Gabriel couldn't tell if de Metz disapproved or simply didn't care.

Everything competed for Gabriel's attention: the sounds of loud laughter and talking over music, the smell of food and the beeswax candles, the riot of colors on the tapestry-covered walls and the celebrating courtiers' clothes. It was almost overwhelming, and he threw a glance to the older, more experienced de Metz and de Poulengy. They seemed, if not at home, at least unperturbed by the cacophony and the throng of well-dressed nobility.

So, too, did Joan. This was her first glimpse of such a world, too, but she did not even appear to be breathing quickly. They were starting to draw attention, now, the three travel-worn men and the girl in men's clothing, and conversation halted as small clusters caught sight of her and turned to gawk.

Gabriel shook his head to clear it and began looking around with purpose. The ceiling was high, and the timbers supporting it vanished up into the darkness. From the lower beams hung banners, presumably the coats of arms of the various nobles. Tables were piled with food, and wine and ale appeared to be flowing freely to entertain a crowd of powerful men and their wives... or mistresses. Gabriel observed several occupied benches, but only one one chair, large, ornate, and set on a dais at the far end of the room.

The king's. And it was empty.

Gabriel paled, then flushed with anger. He turned to de Metz. "Where is the king?" he demanded. "What is going on?"

De Metz didn't answer. He had an unreadable expression on his face. Joan looked at the squire for a moment, then nodded. To Gabriel, she said, "I think His Majesty has another test for me."

Oh, Joan, Simon thought, *you've just begun to be tested.*

She straightened her tunic, lifted her dark head, and began moving through the room. After a confused glance at de Metz, Gabriel darted after her, trying not to lose sight of her. Now and then she would gaze searchingly at one of the noblemen.

Then she paused for a moment, and closed her eyes. The crowd was openly staring at her now, and Gabriel realized the music had stopped. Joan turned slowly, her eyes still closed. She smiled slightly, opened them, and marched directly to a rather ordinary-looking man in garb no finer than what most others were wearing.

The courtier appeared bald beneath a large, floppy fabric hat, but Gabriel suspected that his hair was merely cut short well above the ears and nape of the neck in the current bowl-like fashion. He seemed to be about the age of de Metz—older than Gabriel but not in his middle years, and he did not display the raucous good cheer that most of the others did. His nose was his most distinctive feature—large, hooked, and slightly crooked, and he regarded Joan with a peculiar sort of wariness.

Joan pushed through the crowd toward him. Once she reached him, she gazed up at him for a moment, then fell to her knees.

The murmuring of the crowd fell almost completely silent. Gabriel stared. The man whose lower legs Joan now clasped looked down, stunned, a hint of a smile on his face.

"My Dauphin," Joan said, and her voice rang in the suddenly still hall, "you cannot hide your glory from me! I was sent by God, and I have come to bring help to you and your kingdom!"

This was the future king? Gabriel blinked. Charles looked more ordinary than many another man at the gathering. And yet he raised Joan gently and smiled at her, and everyone else seemed delighted that the girl had found him. No, Gabriel amended as he looked more closely, not everyone. Several frowned and turned away. It would seem only some welcomed the Maid.

Tears were on her face, but she was so radiant to Gabriel that she seemed to burn brighter than the torches. She clung to the Dauphin's arm, her lips parted with joy, and he had to gently extricate himself.

"Well, well," he said, and his voice was pleasant and cultured, "it seems the Maid can find the true king, even if we do not yet sit upon our throne. Not everyone thought you would."

"I told you in my letter, I am sent by God," Joan said; then, sobering, added, "and yet... I see you do not entirely believe me."

"You are not the first Maid of Lorraine to come claiming prophecy," came a gruff voice. The speaker's splendid garb of yellow and red seemed to be straining at the seams as it struggled to contain his soft, round girth. Graying hair and a short beard framed a ruddy face that bore a scowl of suspicion. His eyes were hard, almost swallowed up by the rolls of flesh around them. A beringed hand closed around the stem of an ornate goblet. "His Majesty has met many such as you."

"No," said Gabriel at once, as surprised as everyone else. "He has not."

"Peace," Joan said gently, silencing Gabriel with a gentle touch.

"This is Georges de La Trémoille, Count of Guînes, our friend and our Grand Chamberlain," the Dauphin said. "He was not entirely convinced by the reports of the clergy we sent to speak to you. But in your letter, you said you had things to tell us?"

Joan nodded, her eyes flitting from face to face as various members of the court pressed closer, eager to listen. Color came to her cheeks. "I do, but they are for your ears alone. Take me where only you will hear, and I shall speak what God has told me to tell you."

"Your Majesty," Trémoille said, "I enjoy a show as well as the next man, but if she comes from God, then surely the Almighty doesn't care who hears her little secrets."

"We all have secrets, Count," Joan said, "but I care not to uncover yours. My words are simply for his ears alone. Surely the king must always know things his court does not."

Trémoille's flushed face reddened further, but the king smiled. "The Maid speaks truly, on this at least," he said. "Come then. We will retire to a place where you may speak God's words freely to us."

The count obviously didn't like that, but he shrugged it off. "I'll make you a wager, Your Majesty, that I'll be able to tell you everything she says. We know what the holy maids say. We've heard it all before, eh?" He looked around, and some of his companions laughed along with him, but the Dauphin did not.

Nor did Joan. Her dark brows drew together. "Gambling is a sin," she said. "The Dauphin will not partake."

"Well," the Dauphin said, trying to pour oil on the waters, "only if we win." He gestured that she should follow him, and the crowd parted for the two as he turned.

Joan did not move at once. She turned to Gabriel, and smiled gently. "With me, my witness," she said, and wordlessly, hardly daring to breathe, Gabriel followed. The king glanced at him with his pale eyes, considered, then shrugged, paying no more heed to the boy than if he had been Joan's shadow.

Which he is, Simon marveled. History had forgotten Gabriel Laxart. There had been only mention of his father, Durand, who had testified at Joan's rehabilitation trial. Simon had always found it hilarious that most of those who professed belief in reincarnation always turned out to have been either Queen Elizabeth or King Arthur or some other famous personage in a previous life. In reality, all but a tiny fraction would have been peasants, living proverbial poor, nasty, brutish, and short lives and having nothing to do with anything of import. For every petty lord, there was an entire household of servants, not to mention by-blows like Gabriel.

It was not remarkable that Gabriel had been forgotten. What was remarkable was that he had been there at all.

They followed the Dauphin to a small side solar. It was a pleasant chamber, nowhere near as elaborate or gaudy as the main hall, but elegantly furnished nonetheless, with tapestries, a small table with fruit and wine, and chairs. The ceiling here was identical to that in the vast room they had just left, although the timbers fading into the shadows were undecorated. It was a room that had clearly been designed for the purpose it now served—that of providing quiet, comfortable space for private conversations.

Gabriel's palms were sweating, and there was a brazier and candles inside the room. Yet he was suddenly chilled as he stepped inside and closed the door behind them. Vast as the hall had been, there had been hundreds of warm bodies and half a hundred torches to keep it warm. He made an effort to keep from trembling, aware that most of it was not the coolness, but his own excitement.

In contrast, Joan was the epitome of calmness, standing quietly with her hands clasped behind her back as the king sat, poured himself a goblet of dark wine, and reached for an orange. He offered nothing to either of his guests, nor did he suggest they sit. He peeled the fruit idly, glancing up at Joan expectantly. "You may speak, child," he said, not unkindly. "What has God told you to tell us?"

Joan cocked her head and her face grew soft, her expression distant. "You have no cause to fear," she said softly. She closed her eyes and tilted her face heavenward, as if toward the light of a radiant sun. "I am to tell you that you are truly the son of your father, Louis, and that you are the rightful heir to the throne of France. Weep no more, noble Dauphin. God has heard you, and I am sent to dry those tears."

The orange fell from Charles's suddenly nerveless fingers, rolling about on the rushes. His hands gripped the arms of the chair. "I have prayed," he whispered, more to himself than them. "I have prayed...."

"You are to be bold, but merciful," Joan continued, "for you have God and all His angels on your side. Do not harm those who have not harmed you. Stay your blade from the flesh of the innocent."

Simon was blindsided.

Joan opened her eyes, and her soft smile suddenly melted into a sharp intake of breath. Her radiance increased and she dropped to her knees as she stared upward at something over the king's head. Gabriel followed her gaze. His mouth opened and his own legs gave way.

Radiant in the shadows, glowing golden as the sun, its face hidden by a hood, was an angel.

"I see it," Gabriel whispered. "Jeanne, I can see it, too!"

At the words, the Dauphin lifted his head. He craned his neck, but by his perplexed expression Gabriel could tell the king beheld nothing in the shadows. As Gabriel watched, the figure raised its hands, holding them out. It brought the thumbs and little fingers together to form a circle. With the other three fingers held stiffly, and the golden radiance surrounding them, it looked like—

"A crown!" Joan cried. The figure nodded its cowled head, then lifted the clasped hands to its head. "God has sent an angel with a golden crown, my Dauphin! The treasures of both Heaven and earth are to be granted to you!"

A voice whispered in the stillness, "This is the sign. The Maid will make you king."

The Dauphin gasped. He had heard the whisper, even if he could not see the angel. He reached up to the rafters, but even as Gabriel watched, the angel drew in on itself and retreated, its glow abruptly disappearing.

There was silence in the small chamber, interrupted only by the sound of rapt, nervous breathing. Gabriel turned to Joan, whose face, like the Dauphin's, doubtless like his own, wore an expression of startled joy.

Charles had seen nothing. Gabriel had seen an angel. Who knew what Joan had seen?

Simon Hathaway had seen an Assassin Mentor.

CHAPTER TEN

Simon shook his head, as if in disbelief at what he had seen, keeping his eyes glued on the radiant golden figure. After its shocking announcement, it moved nimbly along the rafters, retreating into the shadows and disappearing from view.

"It's gone," he whispered. Gabriel might have thought the angel had simply returned to Heaven, but Simon was doing his best to spot a hidden passageway. Historians had already discovered more than one such in Chinon, and Simon was willing to bet that was but the tip of the proverbial iceberg. He'd have loved to have found a new one.

The Dauphin was laughing and lifting Joan up, taking her by the arm and surging toward the door. Flinging it open, he cried, "God is with us, my friends, and has sent us the Maid of prophecy!"

Joan paused to turn back to look at Gabriel, her blue eyes brimming with tears of joy. Simon found himself reaching for her outstretched hand. His fingers closed on misty gray air as the world reshaped itself. He felt a sudden pang, but dismissed it. There were too many other things to focus on, and here, in the Memory Corridor, he could speak freely.

"I assume you saw that?" he asked Victoria.

I did—and heard it, too. It's got to be an Assassin.

"Definitely, with that kind of dexterity. And especially given the precise choice of words."

"Stay your blade from the flesh of the innocent," Victoria quoted. *The first tenet of the Assassin's Creed.*

"I'd go so far as to wager it's the Mentor. Who better to want to know what the Maid would have to say to the Dauphin in private? And that was damned quick thinking, too. This makes perfect sense, Victoria! This... this vision, this angel with a crown... Joan spoke about it differently at her trial. It's as if she didn't consider it really one of her Voices. It's been a point of contention among scholars as to whether she made the whole thing up to appease her interrogators, but if it's an actual person she saw and not an angel, of course she wouldn't see it in the same way. It appears that Assassins, and possibly Templars—most likely any of the rare individuals who have Precursor DNA—are able to understand that she's something special, to be helped—or blocked, as the case may be. Maybe it's something like the Assassins' so-called Eagle Vision. I think we should stick close to de Metz. He's an Assassin, and he seems to be genuinely devoted to Joan. Can you find their next interaction?"

One moment... yes, I've got it. It's right after Joan is whisked off to get settled into Coudray.

MONDAY, 7 MARCH, 1429

The mists began to shift once again, revealing the Château du Milieu courtyard. It looked utterly different by day; just as impressive, but far less mysterious than it had appeared when Gabriel, Joan, and their group had entered the previous night. Gabriel's attention was not on his surroundings, but on Jean de Metz bearing down on him, sword raised and shouting a battle cry. All that stood between Gabriel and the weapon was his own sword, his shield, and a harness of leather armor.

Winter sunlight glinted off steel. Gabriel barely managed to get his shield up in time to block de Metz's strike. The solid blow on the leather shield jarred Gabriel's arm all the way up to the shoulder, and he let out a gasp. He lifted his own sword to strike a blow in return. The blades clashed and de Metz brought his face in to Gabriel's, his mouth curled in a snarl. Gabriel grunted, twisting his weapon as he had been instructed, to but no avail. De Metz leaped back, then charged again, feinting for Gabriel's legs. As the boy desperately tried to turn his shield to prevent being cut off at the knees, de Metz's blade clanged against Gabriel's, and the sword went flying.

Gabriel's cheeks burned. De Metz laughed, but good-naturedly. "Don't worry. You'll get it. If she can, you can."

He gestured to where Joan was sparring with de Poulengy. They had tried to find armor suited to her smaller, shorter frame, but she was swimming in it, and her helm was so comically oversized it completely swallowed her head. The sword had to have been harder to lift for her than it had been for him, but nevertheless, Gabriel realized that she was managing to bring it up in time to block de Poulengy's blows, and was even forcing the squire back.

"Well," Gabriel said, "God obviously wants her to learn quickly."

One of the pages stepped forward with a jug of watered wine and some cups. Gabriel drank deeply, and noticed that the boy kept stealing glances at Joan.

"It is strange to see a woman fighting, I know," Gabriel told the boy. "But Jeanne is special."

The boy nodded, then said, "It is good she is from God, else after last night, some would say she is a witch."

Gabriel's blood seemed to grow cold as it pulsed through his body and he crossed himself. "*Never* say that about the Maid!" he snapped, and immediately felt remorse as the boy cringed away from him. "What could be evil about inspiring the true king to claim the throne that is his right?"

The boy blanched. He looked at de Metz and Gabriel and said, "You have not heard?" As they shook their heads, the page said, "Last night, Antoine Moreau was found drowned."

For a moment, Gabriel couldn't place the name. But de Metz did. "The Giant? The one who spoke with Jeanne?"

The boy nodded, his gaze wandering back inexorably to Joan as she sparred. "They say that she told him he would die. And an hour after she arrived... they found his body floating in the Vienne river."

A chill ran along Simon's skin. He remembered reading the testimony about this, but had thought it exaggeration if not outright fabrication. It was turning out that very little regarding the Maid was complete fiction.

"I'm so sorry," came a soft voice. How Joan had managed to approach them so silently, Gabriel didn't know, but here she stood, helm in one hand, her flushed face soft with sorrow. "I did not bring his death, my young friend. But I could see its shadow on his face. I truly hope Moreau did make peace with God before He took him."

The page looked down, nodding, and stepped away to pour for the others who were also out training. De Poulengy and the other squires helped de Metz and Gabriel out of their armor and offered thick, warm cloaks, which Gabriel gratefully accepted. De Metz looked at him for a moment, then said, "Walk with me, Gabriel."

Gabriel obeyed, falling into step beside de Metz. Quietly, after they had left most of the noise of the training behind and had entered the garden area, de Metz spoke.

"Tell me about what happened last night."

Startled, Gabriel looked around quickly. They stood beneath the shelter of a few trees whose trunks and branches provided a moderate, if not complete, barrier between them and the goings-on in the courtyard.

"What passed in that room is between those of us who heard it," he said. Immediately he could have bitten his tongue off. He hoped de Metz wouldn't catch the slip, but that was futile.

"Heard what?" The nobleman stepped forward. "Gabriel... did you hear Jeanne's Voices?" De Metz had always struck Gabriel as being laconic and unruffled, but now he looked stunned—and intense.

"I've already said too much."

"Not enough, I think. Tell me."

"Jean, you know—"

"It will help me keep her safe, Gabriel," de Metz replied, an uncharacteristic urgency creeping into his voice. "I know how you feel about her, and I know you would do anything to make sure she comes to no harm. I must know what you heard. What... you *saw*."

Gabriel's eyes widened. He had said nothing of his vision—the vision that only he and Joan had beheld.

"You pledged fealty to her," he reminded the older man, "and I believe you when you say you think this will keep her safer. But I made her a promise, Jean. You understand that."

Jean sighed and nodded. "Yes, I do. I do understand." His eyes flickered over Gabriel's shoulder and he smiled. "Jeanne!" he said.

Gabriel's heart, as always, surged happily as he whirled. He saw only the imperfect curtain of branches and tree trunks, and then the world went black.

The son of a bitch knocked me out! Simon thought, shocked.

After a few seconds, the scene changed subtly. Simon could still see only blackness, but Gabriel's blinking lashes brushed against fabric. He lay on cold, hard stone, and his head hurt fiercely. Without thinking, Gabriel attempted to touch it and discovered he was bound hand and foot. The air smelled differently than it had outside; stale, slightly tinged with the scents of leather and sweat. "He's awake," came a voice both Simon and Gabriel recognized.

Gabriel exploded into a flurry of struggling motion. "Damn you, de Metz!" he shouted. "What are you *doing*?"

"Quiet, Gabriel," de Metz said. Infuriatingly, he sounded more amused than alarmed. Gabriel's heart slammed against his ribs, fueled with anger and, yes, fear.

"You swore *fealty* to her!" he spat.

"You did?" The other voice was a whisper that somehow managed to convey a certain elegance.

"I—yes, we'll discuss that later," de Metz said. "Gabriel, I'm sorry for the necessity that forces my hand."

"Like hell you are. What are you, assassins?"

Silence. Then, a burst of muffled laughter.

"Why are you laughing? If you're here to kill Jeanne—"

"No, my boy." The second voice, still a whisper. Simon realized that the speaker was trying to conceal his identity in every way possible. The lightless room, the whispering, all was carefully calculated to keep Gabriel ignorant. "Killing the Maid is the last thing any of us want."

"Fine, then let me loose," Gabriel retorted, and started to struggle again.

"Be still and listen, and we may do so," said the second speaker. Simon was trying to gather everything he could about the man. A nobleman, most likely; a person of superior rank to de Metz. A soldier.

The Mentor? wondered Simon.

"There are things you do not yet know, Gabriel Laxart," the whisper continued. "Things you *must* know, if you want to be able to keep the Maid safe."

"You know I want that, more than anything," Gabriel said, "except for her to fulfill her charges from God."

"Ah yes," came the whisper, "from God."

"Gabriel," and it was de Metz speaking in normal tones, "when you look at Jeanne, do you sometimes see her... glow with light?"

Gabriel licked his dry lips. "Y-yes," he said. "I do. Sometimes the glow comes upon her, and... and she looks like an angel to me. But I had never seen—"

He bit down hard on his lower lip.

"You had never seen an angel until last night," finished the whispering voice. "We know what you heard, when you and Jeanne spoke to the Dauphin. We know what you saw. *Who* you saw. We know what Jeanne said to the Dauphin. Those words are precious to us. They are words we will never violate.

"You are not guilty of anything, Gabriel Laxart. And we stay our blades from the flesh of the innocent."

It's the Mentor! Simon thought, jubilant.

Questions, pleas, demands—words crowded each other out so that Gabriel found he couldn't even speak. Finally, all he could manage was, "I'm listening."

"This war—the war between England and France—has lasted for almost a century," de Metz said. "But another war has raged since before time was reckoned. A war that is not about land, or countries, or kingdoms, or even faiths. A war not about *men*, but about mankind itself—and whether it should be free to carve its own destiny, or be dominated by those who would control humanity and bend it to serve themselves."

That's not accurate, Simon thought, but he and Gabriel both stayed quiet.

"All are affected by this war, but few know it even exists," the unknown Mentor whispered. The soft, sibilant sound carried in the stone room. "We do. We are players in it, and we are the ones who champion humanity's freedom. We work in the dark, to serve the light. You asked if we were known as assassins. We are—but not quite in the way you think. We watch, we learn, we target... and we eliminate threats."

"What? You—that's cold-blooded murder!"

"Our enemies would call it such. But even they understand that through the carefully planned death of a single individual, thousands—perhaps tens of thousands—of true innocents can be saved."

"Who are your enemies? The ones you say want to—what was it—control humanity for their own purposes?" Gabriel didn't understand it.

It sounded like raving lunacy at best, calculated murder at worst—and yet something inside him seemed to understand. Enough to ask questions, at least.

"They are called the Templars," de Metz answered. "And we stand against them on behalf of those who cannot fight for themselves. Those who are not born to luxury or power. Who are helpless. The slaves, the poor, the crippled, the very young, the very old."

"The bastards," Gabriel murmured.

"Yes," and Jean de Metz's voice was kind. "In our ranks, men and women, highborn and low, dark-skinned and fair—we are all members of the Brotherhood. All are equal, who wear the Hidden Blades."

"And... the Templars? Do you mean the Knights Templar? Like Jacques de Molay? But—the Order was dissolved. They were heretics. Surely they're all dead now."

"The Order *was* dissolved... as far as the world knows," said the Mentor. "Some of its members survived. They dropped out of sight, but kept the Order alive, quietly. And now, they are striving to rebuild it. It is no longer public—but it is growing. The Templars always hunger for power."

"Which is why the war still continues," said de Metz, "and why, when we come across those who might be able to help us—with full knowledge, or unwittingly; we take aid where we can—we go to them. You can see Jeanne's radiance. So do we. Not everyone can see it in her, Gabriel. Those who do—are special. We support her mission fully, because a united France led by a French king will prevent the English Templars from regaining a foothold here, where they were once so strong."

"Jeanne won't follow you," Gabriel said promptly. "She owes obedience only to God."

"We accept that," the voice said. "We are here to serve her in her mission, and perhaps teach her things that can aid her in accomplishing it. It is not her of whom we speak. It's you."

Gabriel's gut went suddenly cold. "Me? I'm just—"

"A bastard? Jean Dunois is known openly as the Bastard of Orléans, and right this moment he is fighting to raise the siege of his home. And did you have wax in your ears when I was speaking earlier? You can see Jeanne's light! You have picked up weapons faster than anyone I have ever seen. These abilities—they are passed down in our blood. Like your father's eye color, or your mother's hair. Gabriel, you were *born* for this."

I was born for this. Joan's words about herself, and her task. Born to leave her home, and make the dangerous trek to Chinon. Born to raise a siege, and crown a king, and perhaps more. Gabriel had thought he had been born to be... nothing. He felt himself trembling; not from the bone-aching cold that permeated his skin from the stone floor, but with something else. Something that he had only ever felt when looking at Joan, her blue eyes wide with wonder and that light, that exquisite incandescence, illuminating her from within.

"You—you want me to join this... the Brotherhood?"

"No," whispered the Mentor. "We only accept those who have proven their worth and loyalty, and you are as of yet an unknown. Just train, for now. Hone your reactions. Strengthen your body. Teach your eyes how to see differently, and to make sense of what you learn. Do this to honor your heritage, and to protect the Maid. We will try to teach her, too. You may not always be there for her."

They knew him well enough to understand how to offer exactly what he wanted. Brotherhood. A place. A feeling that he was special; that he had value. But most of all, they knew Gabriel Laxart would do anything, in this world or the next, to protect Joan the Maid.

"And if I refuse?"

"Well, we obviously hope you won't," de Metz said. "You'd be free to go, as long as you hold your tongue. But we'll be watching, and if you betray us... well. Castles have many secrets; many rooms that have been forgotten. Chances are your body would never be recovered."

"You—you're joking." A beat. "Aren't you? What about 'stay your blade from the flesh of the innocent'?"

There was silence. Then, to his shock, he heard laughter. The two whispered for a moment. Then Gabriel heard the sounds of booted feet on stone steps. His gut clenched.

When de Metz spoke, relief washed through Gabriel. "You should forget about battle, and instead offer your services to the king as a member of his council," he said, mirth still in his voice. "Come, Gabriel. You're too small a fish for us to bother killing. We have made our case. Will you join us?"

CHAPTER ELEVEN

Gabriel considered for a moment. He felt a flicker of concern about what these men stood for, what they offered. But somehow, he had known all his life that he was different. And he wondered if that flicker in his chest was excitement, not fear.

"Yes," Gabriel said. "I will learn what you have to teach. But I will kill you myself if you betray Jeanne."

Simon felt physically ill. Gabriel Laxart—his own ancestor—was an Assassin? Impossible! Simon was a Master Templar, a member of the Inner Sanctum. More than that, he was what was called a "legacy." Both of his parents were Templars, and his grandmother had been one as well, working quietly in the background of Winston Churchill's war office. There were several others sprinkled throughout his line. To be forced to witness Gabriel ally with the enemy felt like Simon was spitting on their graves.

"I would expect no less," de Metz said, all traces of humor now gone from his voice. Gabriel heard an odd snick, and then he felt his bonds being cut. As soon as his hands were free, he tore off the blind-fold, squinting at the daylight coming in through narrow, vertical slits set in the curving stone walls of the room. Above him the ceiling arched in a pleasant pattern of stone rows, and he noticed that some-one had etched peculiar carvings into the rock walls. A single set of winding stairs was the only exit. He turned back to de Metz and his eye fell on a blade protruding from the underside of the young noble-man's right wrist. De Metz's lips curved in a smile. He had clearly been waiting for Gabriel to notice it, and with quick flick, the blade disappeared into his sleeve.

"This," he said quietly, "is our traditional weapon. The Hidden Blade." Another slight movement, and with a soft sound the blade slid out again. "With them quite literally immediately to hand, it makes carrying out our duties even less noticeable. Which leads to the sec-ond tenet of our Creed: Hide in plain sight."

How easy it would have been for him to kill me, while putting a hand on me in the guise of a friendly gesture, Gabriel thought. His second thought was that he, too, wanted to wear this elegant, subtle, deadly weapon, and he knew he would not hesitate to use it against anyone who meant harm to Joan.

He tore his eyes away from the blade. "Where are we?" Gabriel asked.

"Coudray's dungeon," the Assassin replied.

"Someone would have found me here," Gabriel scoffed. "I could yell out the windows."

"Well... not if I'd put this in your throat," de Metz said in a shock-ingly conversational tone. "Certainly no one would have found you in the secret passageway that leads from here to the Mill Tower." Gabriel felt himself pale. So... they had *not* been making idle threats.

"Who was the other one?" he asked, keeping his voice calm.

"You'll find out—when, or if, it's time. The fewer you know of our number, the less likely you'll betray us."

"I would never betray you, as long as you protect Jeanne."

"You don't know the gentle methods of persuasion employed by our enemies," de Metz said grimly. "Who, as a matter of fact, were here themselves, once."

"The Templars? At *Chinon*?"

"Not just at Chinon. When I say they were here, I mean right here. Their Grand Master, Jacques de Molay, and three other high-ranking Templars were imprisoned for a few months in this very dungeon." He pointed at the carvings Gabriel had noticed earlier. "I wondered if you could see or sense anything about those. Some Assassins—people like you, perhaps—seem to be able to see or sense things others don't. In our Brotherhood, we call it Eagle Vision. There's got to be some kind of message here. Templars wouldn't waste their energy just to make some entertaining drawings."

Gabriel turned his eyes to the scratching on the stones. It looked like gibberish to him. It was a messy collection of Latin phrases—he knew enough to recognize the language, but not enough to read them—and seemingly random images: crosses, reaching hands, a sun—rather lopsided; it looked like an inverted teardrop, or drop of blood rather than an orb—whose rays bathed a face in profile. There were other figures, too, some who appeared to be wearing hoods, others that might have been intended as angels.

"Well," he said lightly, "can't say these Templars are going to put any artists out of work."

"Some Templars have been great masters of the arts," de Metz said, "though admittedly it looks like Grand Master de Molay was not among their number. Anything strike you? Call your attention to it?"

Gabriel desperately wanted to give de Metz some priceless piece of information. Some clue that would make the older man glad he was training him. So he kept looking. At last, he sighed. A string of letters and symbols combined. Clearly a code, but not one he had any hope of breaking. Two six-pointed stars, three circles crisscrossed by lines. A fleur-de-lis. What looked like a heart stuck by an arrow, and another one near the reaching hand.

"Anything?"

Gabriel sighed. "Well, that one there looks like a duck."

De Metz started to frown, then looked at the carving and burst out laughing. Gabriel joined in, feeling the tension roll off him.

Gabriel was regretful and slightly embarrassed; Simon felt slightly mollified after the unpleasant revelation that he had Assassin blood in him. This was a good, long look at the graffiti, which Zachary Morgenstern over in Cryptology would be thrilled to see. Another solid reason why his approach to research worked. This was not part of the major goal—locating and observing the Sword of Eden with an eye to repairing it—but it was knowledge that was priceless to the Templars, and it would otherwise have been lost.

"I'm sorry," Gabriel said to de Metz. "Nothing made any sense to me."

"It was a stouthearted try," de Metz said. "Remind me never to leave you a message in symbols, though. Let's put this time to more productive training." Gabriel nodded and moved toward the staircase. "Not back to the courtyard. This particular skill needs to be taught in private. Usually we don't let anyone who's not a full member of the Brotherhood handle these, but... you've demonstrated some interesting abilities." He grinned. "Be appreciative, eh?"

He was pushing his sleeve back as he spoke, fully revealing the Hidden Blade strapped to his lower arm. Nimbly he unfastened it and held it out to Gabriel, who took it with something almost approaching reverence.

He'd never seen anything like this before. In addition to its unique design—and function—it was simply beautiful. The steel blade had been carved with ornate symbols and sharpened to a deadly point. It was cleverly integrated into a leather harness that fit closely enough so that the weapon was unnoticeable beneath tunic sleeves. Even the harness itself was breathtaking, a masterpiece of tooled leatherwork and brutally efficient function.

De Metz fastened it with practiced speed around Gabriel's right arm. "First thing to remember—keep your hand out of the way. In earlier centuries, Assassins removed their fourth finger as a sign of complete devotion to the Brotherhood."

"That would make you easy to spot," Gabriel observed, "especially if you believe in hiding in plain sight."

De Metz looked at him sharply. "You are not Jeanne's little lamb as much as you would like us to think, are you?"

Jeanne's little lamb. It was meant as a friendly jab, but a jab nonetheless. But the strange thing was... Joan did not make Gabriel feel like a lamb. A lamb was helpless, in need of defending. Joan made him feel like a lion, that he mattered in this world, that he could help her change it. That there was a purpose to what he did.

"I am Jeanne's," he said, simply, "but I am no lamb. Now," he said, grinning at de Metz, "show me how to use this!"

Two mounted opponents faced one another, clad in heavy protective leather armor. The shields were real enough, but the lances were blunted. Returning with de Metz, it took Gabriel a moment to realize that the smaller soldier in the mismatched armor was Joan. She clapped her heels to her horse, as did her opponent, and the two steeds cantered toward one another. Joan's shield was struck square and true. Her torso jerked backward from the force of the blow, sword and lance both tumbling from her fingers.

The horse shied. Joan's foot slipped out of the stirrup and she lurched violently, her arms flailing as she struggled for balance. For a terrible moment, it looked as though she might topple beneath the churning hooves. But then, somehow, she righted herself, regathering the reins and, to Gabriel's astonishment, wheeling her horse in the direction of her new squires, who handed her the weapons she had dropped.

The other knight had maintained his grip on the lance and brought his own horse into position. Joan settled back into the saddle and brought the horse around for a second go.

Her lance wobbled as the great beast pounded down the track

toward the mounted knight. Gabriel watched, barely breathing, as the tip of Joan's lance wavered, then suddenly seemed to click into position, as the Hidden Blade had done when he flicked his wrist. It was steady and true, and Gabriel felt a cheer gathering at the back of his throat that erupted as Joan's lance struck the knight's shield almost dead center. There was a loud *crack* and her lance snapped in two pieces, knocking the shield out of the knight's grasp as he struggled to keep his seat.

His lance, this time, had come nowhere near Joan.

"How long have they been doing this?" asked Gabriel, dumbfounded.

"We weren't gone that long, and she went to mass with the Dauphin this morning. An hour, at the most," de Metz replied. He eyed Gabriel and winked. "It's as I said. You are both unusually fast learners."

Amid the cheering, Joan removed her helm, shaking out her short, sweat-damp hair. Her face was red and she was panting, but even so... even so, Gabriel saw the by-now familiar glow coming from her.

"We already feel our crown atop our head," came the Dauphin's voice. Gabriel and de Metz bowed respectful as he approached. With Charles was a man who appeared to be twenty or so, dark-haired, slender, and graceful. His face was strong, but had its own delicacy. The fineness of his features and his ease while walking beside his king indicated that he, too, was of the nobility. He moved like one of the barn cats, Gabriel thought; smoothly, with minimal effort, but with a faint tautness to his movements as if ready to spring in an instant.

"Hello again, my lord Dauphin and my good duke!" came Joan's voice. She kneed her horse over to them. The slight wariness of the duke's bearing eased completely, his handsome face relaxing into a genuine smile as he greeted her. Joan looked for Gabriel and waved him over. He loped to where the two men stood beside the mounted Joan, bowing to both of them.

"This is my cousin Gabriel, who has been with me since the beginning. This is Jean, Duke of Alençon. We met at mass this morning. I told him that he has come at a good time. The more of the blood royal there are who stand for France, the better it will be!"

The duke laughed. "I came as soon as the English would let me," he told Gabriel. "For the last five years, I have been their extremely unwilling guest. I am free but a few days, and already my king demands my presence! But I am glad I have come."

His eyes wandered back to Joan, and she smiled at him freely, trustingly. "Never would I have expected to see a maiden tilt a lance so well. This old farm horse my friend Charles has given you will not serve you in battle, Jeanne." The horse in question, which was in fact not a farm horse but a military training mount, flicked its ears, as if offended at the duke's words. "Let me buy you one that has heard the clash of steel, and will not be spooked if a sword should fall to the ground near it. You will need one."

Even as Joan's expression turned from pleasure to sheer joy, Charles lifted his hand in a gesture of caution. "We have not yet decided whether to send the Maid into battle," he said, eyeing the duke disapprovingly, "but it is kind of our friend to offer her such a gift. We still have many more who wish to question you, Maid."

Joan's face fell, but her light still shone as she regarded the duke. "I shall be most grateful for my new horse, *when* I ride him to Orléans," she said, her voice light and happy, almost playful.

Charles looked discomfited. He glanced from Alençon to Joan, and his high brow furrowed, the fingers of one hand twisting the rings on the other. "Well, although we must still listen to what the esteemed and learned clergy tell us about you, Maid, perhaps we too can give you something to take into battle—just in case. A beautiful sword, perhaps, made just for you. That would please you better than a horse, would it not?"

To his credit, Alençon only smiled, not at all nonplussed at the fact that his liege lord was obviously striving to outdo him in winning Joan's approval.

"My Voices, the ones who have sent me to you to take you to Reims, have promised that there is already a sword waiting for me. You do not need to trouble your blacksmiths to make one."

Charles blinked, and the twisting of the rings increased. "Oh?"

"Yes!" she said eagerly. "You must ask the prelates of Sainte-Catherine-de-Fierbois to give it to me. I know exactly where it is. I can dictate a letter telling them where to find it." Her smile grew impish. "You will see."

"I'll go," Gabriel heard himself saying, feeling the heat rise to his cheeks as all eyes turned to him. "I'll go fetch it."

He recalled the sensation he had experienced in the church as he had prayed beside Joan; the pull toward the altar. He yearned to feel it again, and he could not bear the thought of someone unscrupulous finding and absconding with Joan's sword.

"I'll accompany him," said Jean de Metz. "With your permission, of course."

She turned to him, doubt flickering in her blue eyes. "You and de Poulengy will not take this chance to sneak back to Vaucouleurs, will you?"

"Of course not, my lady. I have kept the promises I made you, but I would not willingly leave your service, unless I am ordered to do so."

She nodded. "Good. I have one more charge for you then. Keep my Shadow Gabriel safe when you travel to Sainte-Catherine-de-Fierbois."

"It is done, I swear," de Metz replied. "And it is clear that I leave you in good hands while I am gone." There was a look of longing in his eyes—not of lust, or desire, but wistful. Gabriel understood. When one could see Joan's light, pulling away from it took a great act of will. *Moths to a flame, but with no such cruel ending.*

Gabriel turned to regard the newcomer. He saw on the duke's face an expression similar to that on de Metz's; doubtless, similar to Gabriel's own.

He sees *her*, Gabriel realized. And then, with a clap of understanding: *Like I do. Like de Metz does.*

Like an Assassin.

CHAPTER
TWELVE

The mists started to close in around Simon. "Victoria, no!" he shouted, but her voice in his ear cut him off.

Yes, Simon, she said. *You've been in here for several hours today, and through a few intense simulations. We can reconvene tomorrow first thing. Get an early night and rest up.*

"Wait—don't you understand? Gabriel is about to get the sword! This is what we've been working toward!"

A pause. *You're right. But I've been monitoring your stats, Simon, and I don't like what I'm seeing. Your cortisol levels are up, your blood pressure's high, and you're more than a little dehydrated.*

"Oh, come now, that sounds like I've been watching football and drinking a couple of pints at the pub. I'm *fine*." He lifted his hand to run it through his hair. It bumped against the helmet instead. He hadn't realized what a subconscious gesture it was until just now. Simon had gotten vexed with Victoria before, but for the first time, he felt a real surge of anger.

"Look," he said, keeping the desperation out of his voice with an effort. "Tomorrow will be day *four*. We can go into Rikkin's office first thing and tell him we've found the sword. I'll wager he'll give us an extension."

You said Joan had three swords. What if this isn't—

"It *is*. I—I just know it is." *Easy, Simon*, he told himself. *You can't start sounding frantic or she will march you straight out of here.* "One more simulation. Where they find the sword. I want to make sure we've got the right one."

It seemed like an eternity before she said, *All right. But if I feel you are in any danger—any at all—I will pull you out.*

Simon exhaled in relief as the mists began, once again, to shape themselves into the recognizable form of Saint Catherine's.

They had left at noon on 7 March, and had arrived perhaps an hour before sunset. Saint Catherine's looked smaller in daylight, Gabriel observed as he dismounted. The round, elderly widow who cooked and cleaned for the priest met them at the refectory door and bustled them inside to warm themselves. When they gave her Charles's private letter, and explained that they were on the Dauphin's business, her ruddy, cheerful face grew solemn and wide-eyed.

"Please," she said, "there is some bread and small beer, and a bit of cheese. I'll take this to Father Michel."

"Thank you," de Metz said, sitting down and tearing of a hunk of the bread. He offered it to Gabriel, and chewed on the thick, tough brown bread until the woman had gone. "Now that we're here," he said pleasantly, "I'm going to tell you my theory on why you were so agitated during the ride."

Gabriel winced inwardly as he dunked the hard bread in the beer and took a bite. Of course de Metz had picked up on that. He'd tried to pry it out of him, but Gabriel had managed to put him off.

"We've both been in the chapel before. I'm going to guess that you went there on your own, or perhaps with Jeanne, to pray. And I think you sensed something that leads you to believe you know where this sword is."

Gabriel nodded. "Ridiculous, I know. God doesn't speak to me, he speaks to Jeanne."

"Remember what we told you in the dungeon?" de Metz continued. "About how it's in your blood to see Jeanne's light? And in mine? And in hers, to have such light at all?" Gabriel nodded. "That's because we're descended from beings that came before man ever walked this world. Powerful beings, with great abilities and skills."

Gabriel stared. He glanced around to make sure the housekeeper was not returning before he said in a sharp whisper, "You say this in a priest's house? This is *heresy*!"

De Metz nodded. "To ordinary people, yes. To us... we know it is the truth. Would it comfort you if you thought of these beings as angels? They are not gods, certainly. You've seen too much to be afraid of this, Gabriel. You see it in Jeanne, you even see it in yourself. I'll wager you felt something here—a pull, something that tugged at you to go in a certain direction. These... beings, the Ones Who Came Before—they left behind artifacts of great power. We call them Pieces of Eden, and both Assassins and Templars have been trying to find them since the dawn of time. You've heard stories of so-called magical swords, or potions, or wands, or staffs, haven't you? These things are what inspired those stories. They're not magical, not really, but the effect is the same."

Gabriel looked into his cup, at the floating bits of soaked bread, and nodded. "About what you said earlier. I *did* feel a pull. Behind the altar. Where the statue of Saint Catherine is."

"Good boy," de Metz said. "Will you believe me if Jeanne's letter confirms this?"

"I don't see that I have a choice," Gabriel replied. They heard footfalls and rose as Father Michel entered. He was small, his wrinkled skin as thin and pale as parchment, but his eyes were warm and full of welcome.

"I have read the letter from the Dauphin," he said, "and I am not quite as surprised as you might expect at the instructions therein."

"What does he ask of you, Father?" de Metz inquired.

Father Michel turned his bright eyes on the Assassin, having to tilt his head to look up at him. "We are to dig behind the altar," he said. "And there, we shall find a sword."

"And this doesn't surprise you?" blurted Gabriel.

Father Michel chuckled gently. "For as long as there have been churches, there have been soldiers in them praying for victory. Sometimes, in thanks for God's goodness, they leave an offering of a shield, or a harness of armor, or," and he smiled, "a sword. We have no records of any such weapon being left here, but it is not so irregular as to surprise me. We shall have to wait until the morrow, though. The church has no tools for such a task. We'll ask the masons for assistance. In the meantime, allow me to offer such hospitality as I may."

On Tuesday, 8 March, they were up at first light for mass. After that was completed, those who were already in the church pitched in to clear the area, and the masons got to work. Because Sainte-Catherine-de-Fierbois was a small village, the church had an earthen floor instead of tile, limestone, or crushed stone, so the work of digging behind the altar was not as destructive as it might have been. After a while, quite a crowd had gathered to watch as the masons used their picks and chisels to tear up the area behind the altar.

Gabriel, standing to one side, longed to pitch in and help but knew it would not be welcomed. He could... there was no other word... *sense* it. The Sword of Eden, as de Metz called it. With each layer of dirt that was removed, it came closer to surfacing. Gabriel chewed at his fingernail at one point, and de Metz whispered, "What's wrong?"

"I'm terrified they're going to damage it with their tools," Gabriel murmured back.

"Don't worry, boy, these things have been in existence for millennia. A mason's pick is nothing to them."

"I hope you're right. Because if it *is* damaged, *you're* the one who gets to tell Jeanne." De Metz's snort of laughter drew a reproving look from Father Michel.

At that moment, one of the masons paused. He asked for another chisel, smaller and sharper, and began to dig carefully. The crowded church nave fell silent at the slight yet noticeable change in activity. Gabriel's breath came quickly, and for a moment he felt dizzy. De Metz's hand settled on his shoulder, the grip reassuring, but also a warning to not surrender to the sensation. The boy nodded his acknowledgement.

The outline of a sword appeared. The soil around it was hard packed, so whatever it was had been buried there for some time; at least a century, perhaps more. The masons handled it carefully, calling for one of the town's smiths, who stepped forward with a piece of fabric to receive it. As he lifted it, the dirt simply slid off as if it had not encased the sword for decades. He turned and lifted it up for everyone to see. A murmur rippled through the room as the gathered crowd stared at the sword, unearthed precisely where the girl from Domrémy had told them it would be; a sword so holy, even honest dirt seemed ashamed to sully it.

How can they not feel it? Gabriel thought, his eyes wide.

Simon was staring too, hungrily. He couldn't tell if this was the same sword he recalled seeing safely mounted behind glass in Rikkin's sleek but austere metal-and-wood office. It seemed to be the same approximate length—seventy-five, eighty centimeters—and shape. He couldn't get a good look at the pommel from here, but the crossguard was straight.

It was, without a doubt, Piece of Eden 25.

They had found the sword that had belonged to Jacques de Molay, to Thomas François Germain—to Arno Dorian—

—and to Joan of Arc.

"We've got it," Simon murmured, before the world went black.

"Simon? Simon, can you hear me?"

Slowly, he opened his eyes to see the blurry faces of Victoria, Amanda, and two other technicians whose names he didn't know peering down at him. He blinked and started to rise. "What...."

Victoria put a hand on his chest and pushed him down gently. "You passed out."

He went cold inside. This was bad, very bad. Rikkin could pull him from the project. "Ah. Thank you," he said to Amanda and the technicians. "I believe Victoria and I can handle it from here."

Victoria didn't protest, and with a couple of worried looks the others left the room. "I had no idea there was a cot here," he murmured.

"This is Abstergo," Victoria said. "Somebody is always staying too late, so there is *always* a cot in each department. Usually a shower, too." Simon supposed she was correct.

"What happened, exactly?"

"Your blood sugar dropped too low and you were hyperventilating," she said. "Nothing serious, thank goodness."

"Do—do you think it was an effect from the Animus?"

She shook her head and handed him his glasses. He slipped them on, feeling slightly more in control as the world went from fuzzy to clear. "No. Simple stress and exhaustion." She nodded at a paper cup on a table beside the cot. "Drink that—it's an electrolyte solution."

He waved off her aid as he sat up, then immediately wished he hadn't. Obediently, he drank the beverage she offered him. "So—no specific effects from the Animus?"

She shook her head and sank back in the chair, folding her arms and regarding him. "No," she said. "But I did warn you about this. You should have let me wrap up when I suggested it."

It all flooded back to him and he turned to her. "Victoria—we found it. We did it!"

"Yes, we did," she said. "*You* did."

"... there's a 'but' in there, isn't there?"

She sighed. "I'm worried, Simon. You're a healthy individual, but you're not trained for this. It's wearing you down. I think we should have a rest day."

"Absolutely not."

"Simon—"

"He's got to give us more time," Simon barreled on. His breath was quick and shallow, and the hand that held the paper cup was trembling. "We've found the bloody sword, we can—"

Her hand reached out and closed on his, stilling his shaking. "Simon." Victoria's voice was calm, professional, and Simon despaired to hear it. "*Stop.* Listen to me. Tomorrow, when you're clearer, we can send him an e-mail and explain the situation. But you can't count on anything, and I don't feel comfortable proceeding at this pace."

Then she said the words he had dreaded. "We might simply have to accept that we won't be able to follow Joan through to the end. And considering how invested you are at this point... maybe that's not such a bad idea."

He was silent.

"I'm going to give you something to help you sleep," Victoria continued. He could hear the regret in her voice. It didn't help one bit. "Order some takeaway and call one of the company cars. I don't want you driving. Eat the minute you get home and then get into bed. We'll meet tomorrow morning at nine and work up a presentation to send to Rikkin together. Promise me you won't send anything—not a text, or a call, or an e-mail, *anything*—to Rikkin before I get here tomorrow."

"Very well." That didn't mean he couldn't draft something tonight. They looked at each other for a moment.

"I'm sorry," she said.

"Don't be. None of this is your fault. It's Rikkin and his bloody deadline that's rushing everything." His words didn't seem to cheer her up, in fact she looked even more solemn.

Simon reached over and patted her arm. "Chin up. I'll be right as rain tomorrow. Rikkin won't know what hit him."

CHAPTER
THIRTEEN

"Well, that was fast," said Rodrigo. He leaned up against the door frame, arms folded, pretending to look displeased and failing. He did, however, look slightly sad.

Andrew Davies and Max Dittmar had taken off their headphones at their boss's entrance, and now they looked over at Anaya. She shrugged sadly. "What can I say," she said, "I miss speaking French."

"Wait, what?" asked Andrew. "Are you going back to the Paris branch, Ny?"

"No, she's going to the wilds of North America, to Montreal," Rodrigo said. "You're looking at the next Director of Information Security for Abstergo Entertainment. Best be nice to her. And to her new replacement."

"I didn't think it would all happen quite so fast." She'd barely had time to poke her head into his office and tell Rodrigo about the interview, let alone prepare him for losing her. "I hope I'm not putting you in a bind."

"We won't have time to miss you. I spoke with HR, and they're sending your replacement tomorrow."

Now it was Anaya's turn to be shocked. She'd anticipated at least a few days before they would find someone. But then again, positions at HQ were highly coveted and quickly snapped up.

She thought back on the series of interviews. They had gone extraordinarily well, and she reflected yet again on the fact that so many high-ranking Templars at Abstergo were women, especially in fields that were the domain of men at most other corporations. In fact, both of the people she'd interviewed with had been women: CCO Melanie Lemay, who was, frankly, adorable, and Melanie's almost complete opposite, the intimidating of all, Laetitia England. She had never met Laetitia, but she knew Simon had worked closely with her as they were both involved in Historical Research. Simon tended to be close-mouthed about most things. In a relationship, that made for bad communication, but in business, it was an excellent quality. He'd only let a single cutting comment about Laetitia escape his lips in the year he and Anaya had been together.

Still, it had been somewhat nerve-racking speaking to so many powerful executives, so when Melanie had called offering her the position a mere hour afterward, Anaya had been hard-pressed to, as the WWII poster advised, "Keep calm and carry on." She'd sent Simon a text.

"So much for me slacking off in anticipation of leaving," she said. "Who's the lucky person?"

"Name's Benjamin Clarke. He'll be arriving from New York first thing. I'm told he's a bit of a wunderkind, he'd been angling for a position there but apparently he jumped at the chance to come here."

"Americans," sighed Max. "I still think they secretly wish they'd never had their little revolution."

"Secretly?" laughed Anaya. "Talk to the BBC, it's not so secret." It was starting to hit her; the talk of training her replacement made everything real in a way the phone call of acceptance hadn't. She stole a quick glance at her mobile; Simon hadn't replied. Well, he was busy settling into a new position himself. Odd, that they'd both be moving up—and in her case, moving on—at the same time, when things so seldom seemed to coincide when they were together.

Rodrigo glanced at the clock. "What do you say the four of us knock off early so we can take Anaya out for a celebratory drink and dinner? We'll leave your surprise going-away party for the actual day before your departure."

Anaya laughed. "I'm going to miss you all," she said, "but honestly—a drink sounds absolutely brilliant right now."

"It's a weeknight, fairly early—I'll see if I can't pull rank and grab us a table at Bella Cibo."

Somewhat to Anaya's surprise, considering Bella Cibo was usually reserved for private parties or visiting CEOs and political figures, Rodrigo was indeed able to get them a table for four. It was next to the viewing window, no less. On warm summer days, the best seats in the house were on the balcony, where lucky diners had a marvelous view of the London Eye and the Palace of Westminster. Both sun and rain were held at bay by a long red-and-white striped awning. At this time of year, though, it was already starting to get dark, and the lights on the Eye formed a blue-white circle.

The interior wasn't hard on the eyes, either. Dark, polished wood and the strategic grouping of tables, small fountains, and ivy-encased pillars made the large space feel cozy. The chairs were simple, elegant, and comfortable, the tables black slate covered with white and red tablecloths.

"On me tonight," Rodrigo said to his team. "Order whatever you'd like. Well, except for the '70 Barolo." Anaya found it on the twenty-plus page wine list and her eyes widened. *A thousand pounds a bottle?* It was no wonder she'd never even thought about darkening the door.

"Oh, I think house red will do smashingly," she said, trying not to squeak.

"Well, well," Andrew said, "we're in fine company. Guess who just walked in the door?"

Anaya looked up. It was Alan Rikkin. She'd met him exactly once, when he'd come to "inspect" the workings of the team. It had consisted of him smiling and shaking their hands, listening politely to Rodrigo, and telling them in that silky voice to keep up the good work before he and Rodrigo went into an office for an hour.

Rodrigo had emerged looking about ten years older, and by close of business there had been a round of layoffs. To this day, her boss had never told her what had happened. She'd thought of Rikkin as charming but cold, and she had been just as glad that their paths hadn't crossed.

Now the head of Abstergo Industries stood in his Savile Row suit speaking politely to the maître d', who promptly ushered him and his companion off to a private room.

Anaya blinked and frowned. "What is it?" Max asked.

"Nothing. Just... one never really imagines one would be in the same restaurant as him, that's all," she said quickly. But Anaya's eyes continued to follow Rikkin and the athletic woman with the pixie haircut. She did not look happy.

Anaya turned back to her companions, making a crack about tinned spaghetti, and then the wine came and everyone forgot about the Alan Rikkin sighting.

Everyone except Anaya, who was wondering why the hell Victoria Bibeau was dining privately with Alan Rikkin.

Simon leaned against the comfortable leather upholstery of the company car, glad he'd let Victoria talk him into getting a driver, and checked his phone. Only one text, from Anaya:

GOT IT!!!! ☺

Simon found himself smiling, genuinely glad she'd found something that made her happy. She certainly hadn't been able to find it with him. He knew he should reply, but a wave of tiredness washed over him. *I'll text her in the morning,* he thought. He closed his eyes and let the driver bear him to his flat in Kensington.

The dreams were unsettling, vivid, drenched with color. At one point Simon woke up—or thought he did—to hear the driver speaking on his phone in what sounded like Latin. The symbols and the Latin carvings Gabriel had seen crowded his mind's eye, and he smiled a little to himself and then drifted back into sleep before he came to full wakefulness.

"Sir?"

Simon bolted upright, his heart pounding, only to discover the driver looking at him worriedly. He realized he had clenched his fists.

"Sorry," he mumbled, forcing his hands open. "Bad dream."

"Perhaps it's time for a holiday," the driver joked.

"Maybe so," Simon said, thinking how lovely a dive in warm Caribbean waters would be right about now. Then, feeling slightly stupid, he asked, "Don't suppose you know Latin?"

"Me, sir?" The driver laughed. "My father used to say, 'Latin is a dead language, dead as it can be. First—'"

"First it killed the Romans, now it's killing me." Simon finished the joke that was about as old as the Romans themselves. "Quite right. I don't speak the bloody language either. Part of a dream, I imagine."

"Definitely time for a holiday," the driver said, and they both laughed. The driver added apologetically, "You look a bit pale, sir, if you'll forgive me for saying so. Do you need any help getting to your flat?"

"No, no, that won't be necessary." How bad *did* he look? Food first, then a long, hot shower, and then sleep. Simon desperately hoped he wouldn't dream about hearing Latin again. He tipped the man generously, thanked him for his concern, and entered the building.

He didn't recognize the doorman who greeted him politely, but then again, he'd never been back to his flat this early before. The thought was mildly depressing. He nodded at the man and got into the lift.

Simon had a lovely flat, but he seldom saw it by daylight. It was filled with all the things he loved—books, statuary, antique furniture—along with the best in modern conveniences. He phoned his favorite Indian restaurant, placed an order, and was told it would be ready in a half hour. Plenty of time for his favorite modern convenience—a scalding hot shower.

He turned it on and let the water wash away the sweat and tension of the day, closing his eyes and letting the droplets beat against his scalp and back. Simon tried not to panic as he realized they only had five days left of Rikkin's original deadline. Mentally, he began composing the e-mail he intended to send first thing tomorrow.

He's got to give us time, Simon thought. *He's got to see how valuable this is, how I can't just barrel through it.*

The bathroom was steamy when he stepped out. Wrapping a towel around his waist, he reached for his razor and shaving mug, then wiped the mirror clean of fog.

Gabriel Laxart's face stared back at him.

Simon squeezed his eyes shut, counted to ten, and opened them. His own face, intimately familiar from over three decades of inspection, reflected back to him. It was flushed from the heat to a falsely healthy ruddiness. His cheekbones, always angular, now appeared to want to jut right through his skin, and his pale blue eyes were bloodshot with deep circles. No wonder he'd passed out earlier; no wonder, either, that he'd dreamed, ridiculously, of a chauffeur chatting comfortably in Latin.

Part of him said, *You can't keep this up much longer.* But the rest of him, the historian, the Templar, the part of Simon Hathaway that was all that was left of Gabriel Laxart, had the blunt, implacable response.

You don't have a choice.

CHAPTER
FOURTEEN

DAY 4

Benjamin Clarke was waiting for Anaya when she arrived fifteen minutes early. She shook her head mentally as she regarded him, thinking, *They just keep getting younger.* Benjamin looked about, oh, twelve, but he had worked for two years with Abstergo in addition to obtaining undergraduate and a master's degree in mathematics from MIT, although he'd done both in four years. So he wasn't really *that* much younger.

He was about average height, with straight brown hair and an open, eager face that looked even more excited-puppyish as he spotted her and stuck out his hand.

"Good morning! You're Miss Chodary, right? I'm Benjamin Clarke, but call me Ben. Unless they don't do first names here?"

Anaya had always found American accents to be oddly endearing. She thought it made them sound innocent and vulnerable, traits they likely detested given their opinion of themselves as scrappy, independent sorts. Ben's accent suited him—much more so than his tie, which he kept fidgeting with.

"Hello, Ben, it's nice to meet you." His handshake was firm, but not crushing, and just a tad bit sweaty. "And yes, we do use first names here, except when you're talking to the higher-ranking execs. So please call me Anaya."

"Call her Ny, she hates that," Andrew offered. "Hello, Ben, I'm Andrew."

"Oh, hi," Ben said. He couldn't seem to stop smiling and pumped Andrew's hand eagerly.

"Come on in," Anaya invited. "You came very highly recommended. Salutatorian at MIT, well done!"

"Tell that to my mom," Ben replied with an eye roll. "She still complains every Thanksgiving that I didn't make valedictorian."

"Ah, well, we can't always please our mums," Anaya replied. "Come on. Drop your things in the office and I'll show you 'round."

* * *

Victoria's eyebrows reached for her hairline as Simon slid into a seat opposite her at Temp's. She had already ordered a pot of tea for him and he poured it with a shaky hand.

"I thought I told you to rest," she said bluntly.

"I did. Eventually."

"Simon—"

He looked up, angry. "Don't. Just... don't. I didn't drive, I took a shower, I ate, I wrote the e-mail, and I went to bed. And obviously overslept."

She blanched. "You didn't send—"

"No, I didn't send the bloody e-mail. Again, I followed doctor's orders."

He sloshed some milk into his tea and sipped at it. The familiar metallic taste worked its magic, as it always did, although it had started to cool. He reached for some toast. Victoria remained quiet.

A tall blonde woman came over. "Is the tea quite hot enough, sir?" she asked.

"Just fine, thanks," he replied absently. When she nodded and left, he said quietly, "Sorry I bit your head off."

"I've heard worse. I'm just worried about you."

"Don't be. I'll be fine once we talk to Rikkin." Victoria looked down at her plate. Slowly, Simon lowered his toast. "Oh, what now?"

"I called his secretary to make an appointment. Unfortunately, Mr. Rikkin will not be available at all today. He's got back-to-back meetings in preparation for his trip to Spain."

Simon dropped the knife onto the plate with an annoyed gesture. It clattered. A few other customers turned to look their way. "Well, that's just *brilliant*, isn't it?"

"We can still send the e-mail. He might find a window where he'll have a few moments to look at it."

Simon removed his spectacles and pinched the bridge of his nose for a long moment. "Fair enough," he said, putting his specs back on. "Let's hurry up and eat. I'm more than ready to get to work."

"What exactly will the sword do?" Gabriel asked as he bit into a chunk of butter-slathered bread. He had wanted to leave immediately upon the discovery of the sword, but the town insisted they stay while they cleaned the sword and made a sheath for it.

"Each artifact is different. Unique. All the swords are, of course, functional weapons. Anyone can swing it in battle and it will do what a sword should do. But in the right hands...." De Metz shook his head as he cut a piece of cheese with his knife. "In Jeanne's hands... who knows?"

Gabriel's mind reeled. "It's like magic," he breathed.

"*Like* magic, but it isn't," de Metz reminded him. "To the rest of the world—yes, it is magic, or something divine. But it's no more magical than an astrolabe, or Greek fire, or gunpowder."

Jean de Metz had accepted the sword from Father Michel before it had been spirited away to be lovingly cleaned, holding it up to great cheers from those who had watched the unearthing process. While to Gabriel's eyes the sword still glowed, its radiance didn't change. De Metz had offered it to Gabriel. At first he had hesitated, but at last he reached out, folding nervous fingers about the hilt.

He had felt nothing. *It isn't for me,* he had thought. *Mine are not the right hands. Nor are de Metz's.*

"We'll make use of the days we're stuck here by continuing your training," de Metz said.

"Good," Gabriel said. "And what did you mean, you would stay with Jeanne unless you were ordered away? I thought you were supposed to take care of her. Us." It was such an odd thing to say. To even think, or feel.

De Metz hesitated. "Our Brotherhood is not like the Templars. We value individuality, and do our own thinking. But even so, we have ranks, and we have orders, and we defy them at our peril. Our leader is our Mentor, and the Mentor's task for me was to see if someone like Jeanne would cross my path—and to get her in front of the Dauphin if she did."

"You... your Mentor was expecting Jeanne?"

"Someone like her," de Metz said. "Just like so-called legendary swords exits, so too are prophecies often correct. We didn't want to miss the Maid if she came knocking. Which she did—right on de Baudricourt's door. Assassins like myself have been stationed in various places, waiting. I just happened to be the lucky one who found her. You," he said, grinning, "were a happy accident. A bonus, shall we say."

"But... if you are sent away, or if something happens to you—"

"There are others who would complete your training."

"*Who?*"

"They would find you, don't worry." Again, he hesitated. "Jeanne... is not just important politically. I hope you know that. I care very much what happens to her. And I can think of no better hands than yours for her to be in."

"She has God," Gabriel demurred, feeling his face grow hot. "She doesn't need me."

"We all need someone," de Metz said. "Even—perhaps especially—if we have God."

De Metz wasted no time in beginning the promised training. No sooner had they finished their meal than he had ordered Gabriel to change into his armor and bring his sword. This time, it was easier than it had been. By the end of the day, Jean de Metz was the one whose arms trembled as they brought up the sword and shield.

Simon was glad that he was a regular and vigorous exerciser, but just the same, he was grateful his flat had a deep soaking tub. Now that the Animus enabled the subject to move according to the memory's stipulations, he would be sore as hell.

The mists of the Memory Corridor closed in around him, and he asked Victoria, "I'm sure I'll have the body of an Adonis after all these workouts, but honestly, why am I here?"

Well, you have an idea of how the Animus works, she told him. *I've put in an algorithm for it to show us anything particularly useful about your Assassin training.*

"I can't tell you how disgusted I am to hear those three words in that order."

I... can tell you that everything is a little more gray than you think, Simon. The Assassins have done a few admirable things in their day.

"Heresy," muttered Simon, but without any real rancor. The mists reformed again, and this time he stood with de Metz in a copse of trees. Most were pines, but there was a single massive old oak. He wrapped his horse's reins around one of the pine trees and nodded that Gabriel do the same. Then he opened the saddlebag and handed Gabriel a small hand axe.

"Cut pine boughs," he said. "A lot of them. And make sure they're young and have lots of needles."

"But—"

"You'll see why soon enough. Don't question your training." De Metz grinned. He was clearly enjoying the mystery. Gabriel shrugged and began cutting off pine boughs. Every time he thought they had cut enough, de Metz just shook his head and said, "More. Trust me, you'll thank me."

Finally, they had accumulated a large collection of boughs beneath the big oak tree. De Metz inspected it, piling it up here, making it wider and longer there, then he nodded.

Then, to Gabriel's shock, he leaped up into the tree and shinnied up it like he was a squirrel. Gabriel's jaw dropped. He was fast! And brave—now and then he seemed to put his weight on a branch that seemed no wider than his finger.

And he didn't stop. He kept going, up and up and *up*, until Gabriel could barely see him.

"Now," de Metz shouted, "Watch, and learn."

He jumped.

Gabriel wasn't sure, but he thought he cried out in horror. De Metz spread his arms, as if, like the Lord and Savior, he too was on a cross, and arched his back slightly. Then he bent his head and rolled over in mid-air, so that he was on his back when he crashed down into the pile of tree branches. He emerged grinning and smelling of pine.

"You're mad!" yelped Gabriel.

"No," de Metz said, grinning, "I'm an Assassin. We're all able to do this, with a little bit of practice. We call it the Leap of Faith. It comes in very handy when you're on the roof of a tall building. Even more useful if someone's chasing you atop said roof. Much faster than climbing back down. Come on, it's your turn."

"Oh, no."

"Oh come now, it's barely seventy feet. I've made jumps from buildings two, three times this tall."

"I suppose you'll tell me it's all in the fall," Gabriel said.

"No, it's all in your blood, Gabriel. You should be flattered. We very rarely teach this to those who aren't full members of the Brotherhood. If you're that much of a coward, we can start from a lower branch."

Gabriel flushed. "No, it's fine, it's just...." He muttered under his breath and started climbing.

"Keep going," called de Metz. Gabriel found himself surprised at how comfortable he was, how he seemed to know which branch would bear his weight. He made good time, and sooner than he had expected he had arrived at the place where de Metz had stood when he leaped. Grasping the branches firmly, he risked a look down. The pile of pine boughs looked very small indeed, and he recalled de Metz saying Gabriel would be glad of every single one he'd cut. The Assassin was absolutely correct.

Gabriel took a deep breath and let go of the branches, balancing cat-like on a single straight one. De Metz had been right, as he had been about everything so far. His body somehow understood what to do. He steadied himself for a moment, then straightened, lifting his arms like wings, and fell.

It was glorious.

Instead of speeding up, his heart rate slowed, and a strange calmness descended upon him. He completely and utterly trusted that he would land safely. And as if he had done this a thousand times, his body effortlessly curled into the correct position, and almost too soon he found himself staring up at the sky.

"Well done!" de Metz exclaimed, extending a hand to pull him to his feet. "I knew you could do it. Want to go again?"

"Yes!" Gabriel exclaimed, then added as the thought occurred to him, "But... you can't always count on there being a conveniently placed pile of branches or a hay wagon to break your fall."

De Metz laughed and clapped him on the back. "And *that* is why we call it the Leap of Faith."

CHAPTER FIFTEEN

I'm going to bring you out and head into the next simulation. Simon found himself disappointed as the scene's colors bled away to gray clouds.

"That was quite a lot of fun," he said.

Don't enjoy it too much. I'd hate to see you wander over to the other side.

"Ugh. Don't even joke."

She laughed. *There's one more day of training... hang on, let me find it... ah, there we are.*

As the mists took on shape and substance, Simon realized that the Hidden Blade was strapped to his wrist.

The training for this weapon was as subtle and elegant as the sword fighting had been bold and powerful. At one point, Gabriel paused, staring at the blade.

"What is it?" de Metz asked.

"I'm thinking of how this is used," Gabriel said. "In battle—it's all out there. Nothing secret, nothing hidden. I—I think I could kill someone in battle, if I had to."

"Good, because he will certainly be happy enough about killing *you*."

"But this...." He lifted troubled eyes to de Metz. "Have you used this before?"

De Metz regarded him steadily. "Yes."

"How... how does it feel?"

"I can't tell you how you will feel," the Assassin replied. "But I slept well that night. The man whose throat I pierced deserved death—and more. Yes, a life was lost. But I know for a fact many, many other lives were saved." He gave Gabriel a forced smile. "But don't worry. You won't get yours until we think you can handle it."

"I don't know if I have it in me," Gabriel said.

"I think you will. You'll understand when the time comes."

Gabriel hoped he was right. He was not sure he liked how easily he moved with the deadly weapon; how already familiar it felt, like an extension of his body. Neither was Simon.

Gabriel was pleased when they returned to find the king's courier, Colet de Vienne, waiting for them in the rectory with letters for each of them. "Your Maid has dictated a letter for you, Gabriel," de Vienne said, grinning.

Delight surged through Gabriel, chasing away the ruminations of the past few hours. He excused himself and stepped outside, slipping his thumb beneath the wax seal and unfolding the parchment with hands that trembled.

My Witness,

I have heard the great good news that God has guided you to find my sword for me, as I knew He would, and that it was where I said it would be. I am ready to receive it from your hands upon your arrival here in Poitiers.

I grow weary of the constant questioning. I was first questioned at Vaucouleurs and as you recall was even subjected to an exorcism performed by Father Jean Fournier. Then in the town of

Chinon, while I awaited the Dauphin's pleasure, then again after I was received by him, and now yet again here!

Gabriel found himself smiling as he read. He well recalled Joan's exasperation and impatience at all of these "precautions."

There is an entire group of prelates who are heaping questions upon my head, their number close to a dozen. Each day is one more that the good people of Orléans must suffer, they who cry out to God who has sent me to aid them. My ladies tell me I must be kind and patient but I am no saint to suffer mildly.

I am told that also, it is important to know if I am truly a Maid, and that the Queen of Anjou, the mother of the Dauphin's wife, is coming here to meet me and make sure of this. For they say, if I lie about being a true Maid, then all I say is false. Queen Yolande will know soon enough that I am sent from God.

The Duke of Alençon has come to keep me company. I grow greatly fond of him, and he of me, and he will be a stout ally to our cause. But it is my Shadow that I miss. May God speed you here, for I am like to go mad if I am to be forced to endure this much longer without you.

Written this day, Wednesday, 9 March, 1429

Gabriel folded the letter and kissed it gently. He had envied the handsome Duke of Alençon for a moment, but her last words had reassured him of his own place in her esteem. And he would be by her side until she sent him away.

This boy's got it bad, Simon thought as the mists rolled in again.

Need a break? asked Victoria.

"No," Simon said. "I'm dying to see what happens when Joan finally gets this sword in her hands."

A pause. *All right, but then we should get some lunch.*

"Done."

SATURDAY, 12 MARCH, 1429

In Poitiers, Joan was staying with the family of the very respectable Jean Rabateau, an advocate for the Parliament of Paris, who had joined the king two years ago. No sooner had Gabriel and de Metz drawn up to the residence than Gabriel heard a familiar voice calling his name.

He turned in the saddle, but abruptly felt lost as he looked at the girl who was running out of the house to greet him. She wore a long red sideless surcoat trimmed in fur over a blue kirtle, lifted perhaps a trifle too far so that she could run faster. A red silk hairnet modestly gathered black curls from a high forehead. Around her slender throat hung a small pouch, about the size of a walnut.

Only Joan's face was the same, her blue eyes wide with delight, her lips parted in a smile, and radiant, so gloriously, wondrously lit from within. She reached her hands up to him, and he clasped them tightly.

"I almost didn't recognize you," he stammered. "You look—" There simply wasn't a word. *Beautiful* was woefully inadequate. She made a face and laughed, even as a rogue curl escaped its hairnet prison.

"I don't look like me," she said.

"You will always be you," Gabriel said, "however you dress."

"The Maid has missed you," came another voice, and Gabriel turned to see the Duke of Alençon approaching. He, too, was dressed more formally than he had been when they had met, and Gabriel bowed low.

"Your Grace," he said, "I'm sorry, I wasn't aware—"

"You have given no offense. Our Maid shines so bright she eclipses everyone and everything else. But I think you have come bearing something else that is bright and shiny, have you not?"

Impossibly, Gabriel had almost forgotten. "I have indeed! We were delayed because they wished to make you a sheath." He slid off, patted the horse, and unfastened the straps that secured the precious item to beast's back. Eagerly Joan reached for the long cloth bag that clearly housed the sword. He held it for her while she carefully unwrapped the fabric. The little pouch around her neck swung gently as she bent over her task.

His heart suddenly sped up to a gallop in his chest. *In Jeanne's hands... who knows?* de Metz had said.

She turned the last fold back.

The blade was coyly hidden from them by a sheath of red velvet upon which had been embroidered golden fleur-de-lis. The pommel's burnished steel glinted. It was a beautiful sword, but with most of it hidden, it looked like nothing more than that.

Joan regarded it with wide eyes. Then, without touching the hilt, she removed the velvet sheath. And gasped. Beside her, the duke's eyes widened as well at the sudden bright, golden glow. Slowly, hesitantly, Joan reached out a hand and curled her fingers around the hilt. With the speed and breathtaking power of a lightning strike, the entire sword glowed to life. Lines chased themselves around the weapon, from blade to hilt to pommel; strange images that looked like some sort of writing, or symbols. Symbols that part of Gabriel somehow realized were familiar.

"Jhesu Maria," Joan whispered, and lifted the sword high.

And suddenly, everything in the world felt possible. Everything. Victory, peace, prosperity to a beleaguered nation. Food for the hungry. Clothes for those whose own were threadbare. Gabriel felt as though he stood in front of a

hearth fire that blazed so brightly that all shadows, everywhere, were driven away like mist before a sunlit morning. Fear disappeared, for there was no longer anything *to* fear. There was nothing cold, or cruel, or sharp, or angry, or wrong. Gabriel, Joan—bright, bright as the sun beside him—the astonished and joyful duke, the Dauphin, the Laxarts, the French and the Burgundians and the English, all, all were warm, and safe, and loved, and all would be well, all would be well, and all manner of things would be well—

Then, slowly, the glow receded, but did not fully retreat, as Joan slipped the red sheath back into place. She uttered no word, but her face spoke all that words could not possibly say.

This, then, was what the Sword would do in Joan's hands. More than God was on their side, Gabriel understood. All that was good, and pure, and sweet, and calm, and healing was present when Joan held aloft the sword with the reverence it was due.

They would not fail. They *could* not.

Ever.

TO: arikkin@abstergo.com
SUBJECT: Update on current Animus simulation
CC: vbibeau@abstergo.com

Dr. Bibeau and I should like to schedule an appointment with you at your earliest convenience to discuss the tremendous strides we've already made over the last four short days.

Below I have listed several incidents that argue for an extension of the original deadline, as I believe they are firm evidence of the usefulness of my approach.

1. You are aware that Jacques de Molay was imprisoned in the Tower of Coudray in 1308. Yesterday, historical subject Gabriel Laxart spent several long moments regarding the graffiti left by de Molay and his fellow Templars. This is the only known visual we have on record until the latter part of the twentieth century, and it appears as though there are items Laxart saw that have not survived down the centuries. I know our cryptologists are eager to increase their knowledge about our finest Grand Master and, who knows, perhaps something that might lead us to find more Pieces of Eden. Dr. Bibeau has sent a recording of this to Cryptology.

We would have remained ignorant of the fact that Gabriel Laxart had been given this opportunity if we had been focused solely on the Sword of Eden.

2. We have encountered a Mentor. I expect that I will discover his identity in very short order. As with the de Molay graffiti, this is something that was entirely unexpected before I entered the Animus.

3. We have strong evidence that Joan of Arc possessed one of the highest percentages of Precursor DNA on record, and there is a strong likelihood that she was being directly influenced by the presence we know today as Consus.

4. Regarding Joan's sword: You'll be quite pleased to hear that we have initial visual confirmation that the sword Joan of Arc wore into battle with her is indeed the Sword of Eden you have in your office. I'd like very much to make a formal request to have it on hand in the office, so that I can examine it more thoroughly immediately upon coming off of a simulation.

Would appreciate hearing back from you soonest regarding this matter.

SH

Alan Rikkin, who was not at back-to-back meetings but rather enjoying an Aberfeldy Private Single Cask scotch at his favorite club, Blake's, read Simon's e-mail on his phone. It had been sent several hours earlier. He took a sip of the grassy, slightly citrusy liquid and rolled it around his mouth, staring out the wavy glass of the original 1788 glass window, before composing a text.

Yes to the sword. No to an extension. Force him to focus.

Truth be told, Rikkin was beginning to regret indulging Simon in his great idealistic crusade for "knowledge." Although, if he could get that sword activated, the idea might not have been without merit.

Thin ice, Rikkin thought. *One way or another, we're all skating on it.*

But the difference was, if Simon Hathaway fell through it, he wouldn't just drown.

He'd be eaten alive by what lurked below.

CHAPTER SIXTEEN

Your stats just spiked, came Victoria's voice. *I'm bringing you out.*

Simon resisted. He didn't want to leave, not now. All he wanted to do was look at Joan of Arc, wondrous and joy-filled, gazing at the sword that was almost—*almost*—as bright to him—

—*to Gabriel*—

—as she was.

But he could offer no resistance, after all. The scene dissolved around him. The last thing to be swallowed by the hungry mists was her face.

"That was amazing," he said when Victoria lifted the helmet off his head. "The sword. In Joan's hands."

Her eyes were wide as she nodded. "I've never seen anything quite like it."

Now that he was out of the simulation, Simon suddenly felt everything: the pain of his body from the training—and that of his spirit at no longer seeing the sword in Joan's hands. He was sweating and thirsty, and suspected he really ought to take the rest of the day off and just sleep. But he couldn't. He had to keep going, not just because of the ticking clock of Rikkin's deadline, but because he was so close to understanding the sword.

And because you are enthralled with this, part of him said. He squashed that part ruthlessly.

"I absolutely have to take a shower," he apologized, "then I'll meet you at Temp's in a half hour."

With five minutes to spare, Simon arrived at Temp's feeling somewhat better, but, as usual these days, ravenous. The same woman who had served him and Victoria earlier greeted him, and he took a moment to look around for his old friend Poole. Simon hoped he hadn't quit; Temp's wouldn't be the same without him.

"I'm waiting for someone," he said politely when the woman—her nametag said Lyndsey—ask if he'd like to be seated.

As if to completely discredit him, he heard a voice calling his name. He looked over to see Anaya waving at him. With her sat a young man who looked like he was barely out of university.

"Simon! Come join us!" she invited. The two were at a table for four, so he supposed he couldn't even get out of it by explaining that Victoria would be arriving shortly. There went any opportunity for private discussion, he thought, but smiled and sat down.

"Simon, this is Ben. He'll be taking over for me when I'm gone in a few weeks," she explained.

"You've got some big shoes to fill," Simon said. "Well, not literally. Anaya has very dainty feet."

"But I can kick hard with them if I have to," Anaya said, and for a moment they smiled at one another, and it was as if distance hadn't grown between them. But it had, and soon it would be physical distance as well.

Anaya, too, seemed to sense the shift, and turned to Ben. "Nobody knows tea like Simon," she said, "and you'd best learn to like it if you're going to be here in London for a while."

"Hey, I saw a lot of Starbucks around here," Ben said. "And you even have a coffee place on site. Nice try, Ny."

Good thing Anaya was leaving, Simon thought; she hated "Ny."

Nonetheless, he obligingly walked the American through the finer points of tea and steered him toward the better offerings on the chalkboard. Victoria arrived when Simon was explaining about Historical Research's role in the latest AE videogame, and she looked tired.

This ridiculous deadline of Rikkin's is hurting everything, Simon thought, frowning as he waved her over. She saw him, waved back and held up a finger, and typed something in her phone before dropping it in her handbag.

Simon's phone buzzed, and when he glanced at it he was surprised to see it was from her. He read: *Heard from R. N on deadline Y on S.*

Damn. His lips thinned. He was a Master Templar and a member of the Inner Sanctum. Why on earth had Rikkin replied to Victoria instead of him? Simon texted Victoria back even as she slipped into the seat across from him: *Need to tell him about J's reaction.*

The whole affair felt rather like passing notes in class, he thought, but it was better than discussing it in front of Anaya and Captain America. More than ever now Simon regretted being corralled into idle chitchat. He ordered the Temp's Big Breakfast and dove into it hungrily as they talked about the restaurants, the perks—"The gym's blinding," Anaya said, and the poor boy looked terribly confused— and all the sightseeing one ought to do while one lived here, but somehow never got around to doing. "Victoria, has Simon insisted on Temp's for every meal since you've been here?" she asked brightly.

"Not quite," Victoria smiled.

"You should see if you can wrangle dinner at Bella Cibo before you have to go, it's quite an experience. Too bad it's not summertime, it's got such a pretty balcony."

"I'll keep that in mind, thank you!"

Simon was about to say it was above his pay grade, but realized that now it wasn't. Maybe he *should* take Victoria there. He winced as the new hire put both lemon *and* milk into his tea, unaware that he was going to make the milk curdle. He wondered if this Ben from America was a Templar. He had to be, given the nature of his job, but he just seemed so... so....

I'm a snob, Simon thought ruefully. *Likely if I'd ever actually met Joan or Gabriel, I'd have turned my nose up at them.*

"Tell you what," he said impulsively, "once you're settled in, I'll show you around. Anaya is absolutely right. It would be a shame if you missed out on such a spectacular city."

Both Anaya and Victoria looked at him with surprise. He reddened. Ben saved him the effort of responding.

"Simon, that'd be awesome! There's so much history here. Insider tips from the head of Abstergo's Historical Research division would be very cool." He smiled, and Simon felt ever worse about his dismissal of the boy. "Thanks!"

"You're most welcome. But for now, I fear, duty calls." He turned to Anaya. "Don't you take off for the Great White North without saying good-bye."

"Don't worry, Ben needs at least a few more days before we give him his honorary White Hat."

Simon insisted on paying, and left a generous tip, still wondering where Poole was. As he signed the credit card slip, his phone vibrated. He pulled it out and saw it was from Anaya.

Need 2 talk 2 u

Soon, Simon texted back. It was obvious that her impending departure was stirring up old feelings in both of them, and that really wasn't a good thing.

As they headed to the lift, Victoria said, "I'm so sorry. I got Rikkin's response just as I was heading up to Temp's."

He pushed the button with unnecessary vigor. "Doesn't he *want* us to succeed? I mean, really, what's he going to do, turn off the Animus at midnight on the dot?" Simon sighed. "We've got to tell him about the sword," he stated, reaching for his phone.

Victoria laid a hand on his arm. "Let's not push him right now. You still have a few more days. Maybe you'll have something really specific to offer him. Besides," she said, "he did yield on allowing us to have it."

Simon nodded. He'd seen Piece of Eden 25 before, and at that time had felt no particular pull toward it. He wondered if he would feel any differently now.

Amanda Sekibo was waiting for them when the door opened. "There is a package for you, Professor. I was instructed not to touch it. It's waiting for you inside on the display case."

There was no secret handshake, or code word, or anything that Hollywood would salivate over between Templars. The only identifying item by which they would recognize one another was the pin, and there was an utterly innocuous replica of it available in the local gift shop. The trained eye could spot a real pin from its counterfeit, but generally one could never tell who was a Templar and who wasn't at Abstergo unless one was specifically informed. Simon had no idea if Sekibo was, so simply nodded his thanks and went into the Animus Room.

It looked like a perfectly ordinary package, even wrapped in plain brown paper. Simon was disappointed; he felt nothing in its presence, and said as much to Victoria. She shook her head; she, too, was unaffected.

They took off the brown paper, revealing a meter-long, polished wood box. There were no markings on it, and it looked contemporary, though well made. They exchanged glances. Simon took a deep breath, flicked the latches, and eased the box open.

Piece of Eden 25 lay on a bed of crushed blue velvet. This sword was most definitely the one they had seen unearthed from behind the altar at Sainte-Catherine-de-Fierbois, but it seemed even more dead now than it had to Gabriel's eyes when it was first unearthed. Simon took a breath, then reached into the box, grasped the hilt, and lifted it up.

"Anything?" Victoria asked.

"Nothing," Simon replied, and realized that they were both whispering. He cleared his throat and spoke in a normal voice. "Definitely broken, then. Would you like to try?"

Victoria's cheeks turned pink. Simon held the blade flat on his palms and extended it to her. Gingerly, she reached for the centuries-old weapon, curling her fingers around the hilt.

"Nothing," she said. They both relaxed, although they were disappointed.

"Right," Simon said, straightening. "We'll see if there is anything special that Joan does to it that we can emulate." He loosened his tie and took off his jacket, stepping onto the Animus platforms with familiarity. He fastened some of the belts himself while Victoria did up the others and settled the helmet on his blond head.

There's a good chance she'll be meeting with the Mentor soon, Victoria's voice said.

"How very 'Hero's Journey' of her," he said. "By all means, let's formally unhood him."

22 MARCH, 1429

"You. King of England," Joan snapped, her blue eyes ablaze and her body held taut and proud, "and *you*, Duke of Bedford, who call yourself Regent of the kingdom of France! You—William de la Pole, Count of Suffolk, and John, Lord Talbot; and *you*, Thomas, Lord Scales, surrender to the Maid who is sent here from God, the King of Heaven, the keys of all the good cities that you have taken and violated in France."

Gabriel watched raptly as Joan proceeded to make demands of the king of England. "She has come here from God to restore the royal blood. She is ready to make peace, if you will deal rightly by her, acknowledge the wrong done France, and pay for what you have taken."

She took a deep breath and continued, her voice low and rich with warning. "If this is not done... expect news of the Maid, who will go to see you shortly. King of England, if you do not do this, in whatever place I shall find your people in France, I will make them leave. And if they will not obey—"

Joan paused in mid-sentence, her eyes moving from Gabriel, to Alençon, to de Metz. She swallowed hard, and her voice trembled as she continued.

"I will have them all killed. I am sent here by God, the King of Heaven, to chase you out of France—every one of you! But if they will obey, I will be merciful. You will never hold the kingdom of France. If you will not believe this message from God through the Maid, then wherever we find you, we shall strike you there, and we will make an uproar greater than any made in France for a thousand years! And when the blows fall, then we shall see who has the better right from the King of Heaven. Give answer, if you wish to make peace in Orléans. And if indeed you do not, you will shortly remember it to your great sorrow."

"By God and the angels," exclaimed Alençon, leaping to his feet and applauding, "I'd surrender on the spot if I got this letter."

Joan scowled at him. "Do not swear!" she rebuked. "And it is my deep prayer that the English feel as you do."

Gabriel didn't envy the young man who had been charged with taking Joan's dictation. He had grown paler with every word that had escaped her lips, but Gabriel couldn't stop grinning. If only Joan could have given this speech in person, with her eyes sapphire flames, every line of her body tense with her passion, and that light shining, shining so that all he wanted was to soar toward it as Icarus had soared to the sun. Why did so many stories warn of going into the light? Joan's radiance was the most beautiful thing imaginable.

"My lady?" One of Madame Rabateau's servants had opened the door to the small room where Joan—properly chaperoned by another young lady—had spoken her challenge to the English. "Madame wishes to know if you are done."

Joan sighed. "Yes, for now," she said. She went to the small desk where the scribe had taken down her words and smiled at him. "I must trust you to write exactly what have said."

"I shall, Maid," he promised.

"Here. My Shadow has been teaching me something." She threw Gabriel a smile that warmed him more than the small fire, and proceeded to carefully write her name:JEHANNE.

"There!" she said. "Now the king shall know it is truly from me."

"I think," the duke said, catching de Metz's eye, "that the squire and I shall retire. Our rough presences shall do nothing but distress the ladies, I fear. Gabriel will keep you company."

Gabriel glared at them. He could have left, he knew; gone with them to a tavern, to drink or play dice. But he had no desire to leave Joan if he did not absolutely had to. As de Metz left, following Alençon, he mouthed, *Good luck*.

Rabateau's house was so lavish, there was an entire room devoted to simply sitting and having conversations. Madame Rabateau awaited them there, presiding over what seemed to Gabriel an entire herd of young women, all of whom flocked around Joan like breathless, fluttering birds. His only consolation was that Joan, despite her obviously expensive feminine garb, looked, if possible, more miserable in their company than he did. Their eyes met, and in hers he saw hidden, barely suppressed mirth. When one of the girls paused in her chatter, Joan crossed her eyes and Gabriel almost choked on his wine as he struggled to keep from laughing.

It really wasn't a funny situation. Joan had confided that the women were spies, keeping watch on her so she did not do anything scandalous. Madame Rabateau looked askance at Gabriel, who pretended to have swallowed wrong.

"Oh, the things these prelates ask of me!" Joan said, to draw attention back to herself and away from Gabriel. "One said to me, this or like enough: 'You say your Voices tell you that God wishes to deliver the people of France from its suffering. If He wishes to do so, it is not necessary to have men-at-arms.' And I said back to him, 'It is simple. The men-at-arms will do battle, and God will give them victory.' How is this difficult to understand?"

She shook her head. "He seemed a bit upset with me at that, because he then said, 'God would not want us to believe in you unless something made us think we should. We need something else.' And then... well, then, it was I who got a bit upset. I told him, 'In God's name, I did not come to Poitiers to produce signs! Lead me to Orléans, and I will show you the sign for which I was sent.'"

None of them, least of all Gabriel, could tear their eyes from her now. As she spoke of Orléans, her radiance had returned. *As God is my witness, I could do nothing but look upon her till the end of my days. I would need nothing else to keep me alive.*

At that moment, though, Madame Rabateau gave a little gasp, leaped to her feet, and dropped a curtsey. Immediately the others followed suit, including Joan. Gabriel turned, bowing, although he did not know who had entered the room.

"So you are Joan, who calls herself the Maid," said a warm, resonant woman's voice. "I have been greatly looking forward to our meeting, child."

"As have I," said Joan. "The Duke of Alençon sings your praises, Your Majesty. You will soon know that my claim is a true one."

Your Majesty! Gabriel felt almost dizzy. This had to be the Dauphin's mother-in-law, Queen Yolande of Aragon, who had come to verify that Joan was indeed true to her word. A queen. He, the bastard, son of a farmer, stepson of a merchant, had now not only been in the presence of a yet-uncrowned king, but also a *queen*.

Slowly, he straightened and permitted himself to look upon her.

All the breath went out of him.

Queen Yolande was tall, lithe, and well formed, her figure not entirely hid by the wine-colored houppelande she wore. Her hair, though, was completely concealed by a horned headdress from which fell delicate veils. Her face was still beautiful, with a strength that the wrinkles around her gray-green eyes and her high, plucked-brow forehead did not diminish. But none of this was why Gabriel stared.

He was an utter fool.

He had been so smugly certain that he had figured out the identity of the Assassin Mentor. The human behind the "angelic" presence that had spoken to him, Joan, and Charles. But that role did not belong to Joan's "noble duke."

Yolande's eyes flashed in her own recognition and she shook her head, almost imperceptibly. Gabriel needed no warning. He could not have uttered a coherent word at that moment if his life had depended upon it.

Well, well. An Assassin Mentor queen, came Victoria's voice in Simon's ear. *I believe this may be a first.*

CHAPTER SEVENTEEN

Simon was thoroughly annoyed with himself. He'd been so certain the Mentor was Alençon that the thought it might be someone else had never crossed his mind. The queen turned her attention to the assembled women. No one, it seemed, had noticed the brief connection between the bastard boy and the mother-in-law of the Dauphin.

Yolande smiled warmly at Joan. "I can see why those who have met you are so taken with you," she continued, as if nothing had happened, as if Gabriel's entire world had not just been upended. Now that Gabriel knew who and what she was, he could see it in how she moved; smoothly, with a hint of strength and speed that could be called upon instantly if needed. Jean de Metz moved like that; he, Gabriel, was starting to learn how to do so.

Yolande cupped Joan's chin in her hands, her eyes searching the younger woman's. Joan did not look away. It was only then that Gabriel realized that, while he had recognized the "angel" immediately, Joan had not. The queen nodded.

"I have brought some of my ladies with me," she said, indicating two other women who stood a few paces behind her, also clad in elaborate robes and headdresses. "Shall we retire to your room, Jeanne?"

"Please," said Madame Rabateau, "if you will follow me, Your Majesty. Ladies, feel free to amuse yourselves until supper."

"I, uh, will see where de Metz has taken himself," Gabriel stammered. He dropped a bow to his hostess, sneaked a final look at the woman who was both queen and Assassin Mentor, and hastened out as quickly as he could without actually fleeing.

De Metz was waiting for him outside. "Ah," he said. "I see you recognized her."

"Why didn't you tell—" De Metz hushed him, looking around, then took his arm and led him a bit away from the house.

"I had hoped you wouldn't," he said. "Did Jeanne?"

"No," Gabriel said. "I can't understand why."

"Jeanne believes she saw an angel," de Metz said. "You knew better. Even if Jeanne saw some similarity, she would give it no credence."

It made sense, but it also left Gabriel sad. "I don't like keeping things from her. It feels wrong."

"There may be a time when Jeanne is ready to know, but that time is not now."

Gabriel laughed weakly. "I thought the Mentor was the Duke of Alençon," he said. "I was not expecting an old woman."

"*Alençon*? No, he's barely farther along than you are. As for 'old woman,' you had best not let *her* hear you say that!"

Gabriel thought about the dexterity and strength Yolande had displayed in the rafters above their heads that night, and had to agree.

"There's so much more you need to learn about who we are, Gabriel," de Metz continued. "Age, sex, race—we understand how unimportant they really are. But that's enough for now. I spoke with her earlier, and she decided that if you recognized her, you'd have a chance to meet her."

"But I did meet her," Gabriel answered puzzled.

"You met Queen Yolande, the mother of King Charles's wife," de Metz said. "Tonight, you'll be meeting the Mentor."

De Metz's face began to soften, the colors draining away from him as the lines that defined him turned into swirls of billowing gray. Once again, Simon was in the Memory Corridor. He forced himself to inhale, realizing that he had all but forgotten to breathe as the encounter had unfolded.

"You are *not* going to bring me out," he said to Victoria.

Wouldn't dream of it. Your stats are good—other than the normal spikes due to shock. To be honest, after that, I think my *heart rate might be just as high.*

This time, the mists took the shape of the interior of a small, clean room in what was doubtless an inn. There was the single bed the two men shared; Simon knew that it was only due to de Metz's sway that the room wasn't filled with several people. Travelers almost always shared rooms, beds, floors... any space they could, unless they had the coin or clout to purchase individual rooms.

De Metz stretched out on the bed, a cup in his hand. Gabriel paced in front of the fire. "Drink some wine, Gabriel," de Metz encouraged.

Gabriel simply shook his head. His hands were damfvfvGabriel gasped.

"—way," de Metz finished.

The shutters were opened by an unseen hand. Cold night air blew into the room, and Gabriel shivered. Then a hooded figure appeared—upside down—and flipped quickly inside, closing the shutters. Even though Gabriel knew who to expect, he was still startled when the new arrival slid back the hood, revealing the face of the queen.

Gabriel stared to bow, then stopped himself, and looked helplessly at de Metz, who only laughed. The Mentor—Yolande—grinned back at him and sat down on the edge of the bed. De Metz poured her a cup of wine and she drank, grimacing.

"Such a sour face!" said de Metz.

"Such sour wine," Yolande replied.

"Sorry, we don't have your cellars."

"Soon enough, you will." Like Joan, Yolande wore men's clothing: breeches, a tunic, a belt, boots, and the hood. Her hair, dark blond with threads of silver, was braided and had been slightly mussed by the hood. She peered at Gabriel, evaluating him. "You, my young fellow, are not something we planned on. But we are glad to have you with us nonetheless."

"P-planned on?"

De Metz handed the bottle to Gabriel. "You might need this," he said. Dazed, Gabriel took it and gulped down a swallow, letting himself sink down on a bench across from the bed.

"Tell me who you think I am," the Mentor asked.

Gabriel was wary of a trap as he replied. "You're Queen Yolande of Aragon. The Dauphin is your son-in-law. And you're the Assassin Mentor. Which I understand makes you the highest-ranking Assassin."

"Accurate, as far as it goes," Yolande said. "I'm also the mother of René d'Anjou." At Gabriel's blank expression, she elaborated, "René's father-in-law is the Duke of Lorraine."

Gabriel's eyes widened and he took another swig of the wine. It was helping. "Jeanne went to see the duke before de Baudricourt agreed to send her to Chinon," he said. "She was... honestly, I'm told, rather rude to him. The duke, I mean. Even so, he approved of Jeanne."

"He did," Yolande agreed. "And guess who is Robert de Baudricourt's lord, whom he must obey?"

"... René?"

Yolande nodded. "Jeanne also asked the duke to order René to fight in her army. René is not doing so... not formally, at any rate. But we are all working with Jeanne, whether she knows it or not."

Gabriel wished there was more wine. Yolande smiled, and it was not altogether kind. She was enjoying his discomfiture, he realized.

"Rumors have been swirling about a Maid of prophecy for years," she said. "I have investigated them all. Most are liars, memorizing the story and adhering to it, hoping to get a little bit of coin and some fleeting fame. But the stories about Jeanne were different. I asked René to suggest that his father invite her to visit. My son was impressed with what he saw, and reported back to me. I told him to order de Baudricourt to send her to Chinon, along with a letter of approval that the Dauphin could not deny. And we all know what happened there."

"But you didn't think we would see you in the darkness."

"You're right. I was there to observe, not participate. I wanted to know what she had to say to him when she thought no one else was listening. That both of you saw me was indeed a surprise—but in the end, not a bad one. You may have heard that Charles is somewhat hesitant. Perhaps even heard him called weak-willed."

Gabriel blanched. He could not possibly reply.

Yolande laughed. "It's all right. It's true. There are reasons for it. He's not a bad man. I love him, and René adores him. Charles's life... it has not been a pleasant one. There has been more death and terror in it than you know. I still hold out hope that once we get him crowned, he will begin embracing his own strength. But for now...." Her eyes twinkled. "He needs a prophecy or two to convince him. Also, when both Jeanne and you saw me, I knew that the blood of the Precursors was strong in your veins. So as I say—while it was a surprising moment, it was a good one."

"Do you believe Jeanne?" Gabriel had to know.

"De Metz has told me about the sword's reaction to her," Yolande replied. "I am not prepared to say she has come from God, but she is kind, and single-minded of purpose, and has the courage of true conviction. What I *do* believe is that she can help us drive back the English and the Templars they harbor among them. And for that, she has my full support—and that of the Brotherhood. That's the best I can do, for the moment."

Gabriel nodded solemnly. "So... what now?" The wine, he realized, had made him bold.

"I have been working in my role as queen, not Mentor, to gather a convoy of food and supplies to take into Orléans. Those under siege are suffering, and those who have attempted to liberate them are despondent. They have met with failure after failure. What do you think wins a war, Gabriel?"

Abruptly Gabriel wished he had not had quite so many swigs of wine, but he tried to think. "Skilled soldiers," he said. "Greater numbers. Strong leaders. Good military strategy."

"All of these things are good," Yolande agreed. "But they are not enough. You need the simple things, too. You need food, and medicines. I will supply those. And you need one thing more. And that one thing, the thing that I believe can turn this war around and send the English scampering home with their tails between their legs—Jeanne will provide that."

Gabriel thought back to the moment when Joan had grasped the sword, to the joy and the peace he had felt washing through him. To the utter certainty that all would be well, and no one would want for anything.

And he knew what the "one thing" was.

"Hope," Gabriel said. "She'll bring them hope."

CHAPTER EIGHTEEN

The scene dissolved. *How are you doing?* Victoria asked.

"Humble pie is not very tasty," Simon confessed. "How stupid of me not to have considered Yolande as a Mentor candidate. I knew she was a remarkable individual, too, so it's not like it's completely out of the blue."

Don't be too hard on yourself. Remember, the Assassins love to hide in plain sight. If they were readily recognizable, the Templars would have wiped them out long ago. Want to take a break?

"No," he said. As soon as he left this room, he'd have to reply to Anaya, and he was not looking forward to that. And he *was* looking forward to continuing to "shadow" Joan of Arc. "Let's get her to her army," he said, and readied himself for the next simulation.

FRIDAY, 21 APRIL, 1429

As he rode beside Joan from the city of Tours to meet the rest of the army at Blois, Gabriel found himself well content. Odd, to feel like this as he was riding to his first battle, but how could he feel otherwise, considering how smoothly everything had gone thus far?

After three weeks of interrogating Joan, the prelates had informed the Dauphin that she had impressed them mightily. The king had gone from uncertain foot-dragging to swift and significant action. Joan now wore a full harness of plate armor, crafted specifically to fit her smaller, slighter frame. The Duke of Alençon had been as good as his word, and she rode on the broad back of a splendid white destrier. The sword that had awaited her at Sainte-Catherine-de-Fierbois was now strapped to her left side. It was no longer in the gorgeous velvet sheath; Joan, ever practical, had ordered a good, solid leather one made for it.

Also while in Tours, she had ordered two banners made. One was being carried by her confessor, Friar Jean Pasquerel, who marched with his fellow priests at the head of her army. The priests would plant this banner, which depicted Christ on the cross, in the earth where they would sleep during the march, and Joan had instructed all her soldiers to find the banner and make their confessions each morning.

The other banner was her standard.

She had prayed to her Voices for guidance in designing it, she told Gabriel, and commissioned an artist to paint it exactly as she instructed. It depicted Christ amidst the clouds, sitting in judgment, and a humble angel offering in his cupped hands a fleur-de-lis for the Lord's blessing. It was clear that Joan loved the standard more than the sword, and once, a perplexed Alençon had asked her why. Gabriel had wondered, too—all of them had seen the glory and the power of the Sword of Eden when Joan had touched it. The standard was nothing but paint and cloth.

"The sword is beautiful, and my Voices did lead me to it," she had told them. "But my standard... this is *mine*. The Voices told me what they wished to see, and the painter crafted it from my words. Besides, I will ride with it beside me, and all will see it and think of the Maid and the Lord she loves, who is behind them. I will inspire those who fight for France, and cast fear into the hearts of God's enemies, without having to kill anyone."

And she had smiled. Her light had shone, like a halo in the old paintings, and if Gabriel had ever doubted he loved her, he knew it then with the force of a hurricane.

But Joan had departed Tours with more than two standards and the armor and horse of a knight. She had many horses at her disposal—five coursers trained for battle, and several trotters for her everyday needs—and a full knight's retinue: the steward Jean d'Aulon; two pages, Louis and Raymond; and, most telling of all according to Alençon, two heralds, Ambleville and Guyenne.

"The other members of her household are good," the duke had said, "but heralds... they are officials, and they are granted immunity from capture when they perform their duties. They wear livery, bear messages, and deliver challenges on behalf of those the king considers to be important. This tells me that the king is convinced that our Maid should be treated with high regard."

And finally, she was at the head of several hundred men-at-arms, foot soldiers, and archers.

Unfortunately, Jean de Metz was not among them. As he had intimated, he was at the command of others than the Maid—Robert de Baudricourt, as far as the eyes of the world were concerned, and the Mentor in the shadows. Both Joan and Gabriel were sorry to see him go. To Joan, he said, "I have not forgotten my promise. Within what powers I have, I will do everything to serve you and keep you from harm." And to Gabriel, in private, he said, "There are eyes on you, whether you know them or not. Not all of our members are squires, or queens, or dukes."

"I'll miss you, Jean," Gabriel had said sincerely.

The other man had clapped him on the shoulder. "I think we will meet again, Laxart. Keep an eye on her. You're a better shadow for her than we could ever be."

Joan wore her armor nearly constantly, but tended to be more forgetful about her helm. She felt Gabriel's eyes on her and turned to smile at him. "You look happy," she said.

"I am," he replied. "You are on your way at last, to achieve what your Voices have promised you would."

"It is good that we are finally in motion. I have but a year, little more, my Voices tell me."

Gabriel felt shock crash through him, as though he'd been punched in the gut. Was she saying—could she mean—"*Jeanne...!*"

Joan cocked her head, gazing at him in confusion, then her eyes widened. "Oh! No, Gabriel, I do not see my death! That is forbidden for anyone to know but God. I may live to be a hundred, or die tomorrow from bad fish!"

The fear bled out of him so swiftly it left him feeling weak and sick. "Thank God," he said, and it was a true prayer.

"But... my Voices do tell me that I have but a year or so to do what I am meant to do. This is why I chafe so at every delay. I must make the best use of what time I have, to make sure that Orléans is free and the king is crowned. And," she added, "anything else God would have me do."

"And I will be beside you," Gabriel said immediately.

"As long as God wills," Joan reminded him, and despite her earlier comforting explanation of her words, Gabriel felt a shiver.

The singing ahead had stopped. They crested a hill and, halting their horses, stared in silence at the army spread out below them.

Blois was a safe place for French soldiers. Even so, Gabriel knew, as many of them as possible would be quartered within the gray-white walls of the huge fortress. But there were hundreds of tents and little orange dots to mark the sites of campfires in the surrounding fields.

Seemingly tiny horses cropped spring grass, and hundreds—thousands, perhaps—of French soldiers milled about.

Joan's army descended, pleased to have reached their destination. As they drew closer, it became clear that Yolande of Aragon had delivered on her promise. Gabriel's jaw dropped to see so many wagons and carts—quite literally dozens of them. Some were filled with sacks of grain. Others bore large barrels, presumably containing dried fish and meat. Most, though, were crowded with sheep, crates of chickens, and pigs, while several cows and oxen were tied to the backs.

"Jeanne!" The voice was familiar, and both Gabriel and Joan turned to see the Duke of Alençon. He cantered up to them on his horse, grinning. "Look what I have brought you!"

"My dear duke!" Joan exclaimed, overjoyed. "God is good!"

"And so is Queen Yolande," Alençon retorted, with a rather impudent grin. "The Bastard of Orléans himself has arrived to meet you. Tomorrow, your army will be marching to Orléans!"

"You will not be coming with me?" Joan's face fell. Alençon's dark gaze darted to Gabriel, then back to the Maid.

"I will be supervising these glorious foodstuffs," he said. "Think you the oxen will walk to Orléans on their own? We will have to take them up the Loire. But I have promised not to fight against the English until my ransom has been completely paid, so I cannot stand in battle with you. Yet," he added, grinning. "But I do not come alone. There are two other fellows who, I think, you will be even happier to see."

Two foot soldiers were loping toward Joan even as he spoke. Joan turned, confused. Then, suddenly, Joan went very still, her blue eyes wide. She reached and pulled out the small pouch, clutching it tightly. Then, to Gabriel's astonishment, her filled with tears even as her lips parted in a smile.

"Jean!" she shouted. "Pierre!"

Despite her armor, she was off her horse and running toward her brothers a heartbeat later. There was much laughter and tears, and being brothers, they mussed her hair and called her the prettiest boy they had ever seen.

"We got your letter," Pierre, the youngest, said. "It made Mama cry. Even Papa looked like he might weep."

Gabriel had been the one who had written the heartfelt letter Joan had sent once she had reached Chinon. She had felt very guilty about leaving her family without a word, but explained that she had to go, and that she loved them dearly.

"I keep the ring they gave me in here, always close to my heart, along with a few other things that are special to me," she told them, touching again the pouch she had begun wearing since Chinon. "Have—did they—"

"Of course they forgave you, and love you," Pierre hastened to assure her. "They even gave their blessing to us and said we could come join you."

"You're famous, Jeanne!" Jean said. "People have started to come visit, to see where the Jeanne the Maid was born. We are making a tidy amount in lodgers."

"Good! After frightening Papa and Mama so, I am... pleased...." Joan turned her head slowly in the direction of shouts of laughter.

Following her gaze, Gabriel saw a group of soldiers standing about, talking to a small group of women of various ages. The women were clothed modestly enough. But there was something about their faces—something hard and wary, even though they smiled and dandled their fingers against the men's arms or chests. One of the men tugged at the woman's lacings and bent to kiss her throat while the others cheered him, reaching for their own seemingly eager women. And abruptly Gabriel realized what was going on.

But Joan, despite her innocence, had caught on even faster than he. "In the name of God, I will have no *ribaudes*!" she shouted, and drew her sword from its scabbard.

It blazed, bright and glorious, as if white flame danced along its shining blade, so brightly that Gabriel had to squint his eyes against it. Before he could recover, Joan was running toward the cluster of lusty soldiers and the camp followers, her sword raised, her armor bright in the afternoon sun, and for a terrible moment Gabriel feared she would run the girls through in some awful display of the wrath of an offended God.

But Joan, so soft-hearted she created a standard to inspire her warriors rather than wield a sword that might harm the English enemy, would never do such a thing. She turned the blade and struck them with its flat, pulling the blow at the last moment. No one would suffer a true injury, but even so, Gabriel winced; the strike would sting, and there would be a nasty welt.

The other girls screamed and fled. One of them, a fair-haired girl about Joan's age who would have been pretty had she not been so dirty and hard-eyed, hesitated, staring openmouthed for a moment before she, too, turned, hiked up her skirts, and ran.

Gabriel's breath caught. Could it be possible for a *prostitute* to—

Joan turned her attention to the men, brandishing her sword. "And you! They are poor women who are hungry and desperate. You will not degrade them and your own bodies, which God has made in His own image! Do you understand?"

The soldiers, big, grizzled, bearded men who towered over the girl in the shiny new armor, all took steps backward and hastened to nod.

"Good. Do you see that standard?" Joan pointed to a small smudge of white several yards distant. "Wherever you see that, you will find priests. Go. Make your confession." When they didn't move, she shook the sword angrily. It still glowed, but Gabriel realized that neither these soldiers nor their women—nor, for that matter, Jean or Pierre—seemed to see its radiance, though they clearly felt something of its power. Even as he had the thought, he wondered about the blonde girl.

"*Now!*" Joan shouted. The soldiers didn't quite run, but they did move with haste.

The Duke of Alençon was trying and failing to stifle a grin. "Careful, Maid," he called, his voice bright and warm with humor, "you might break that blade on the back of one of those whores if you are not careful."

Joan scowled at him. "Do not swear!" she growled, then added, "You should go to confession, too."

The Duke of Alençon threw back his head and laughed.

But he did go to confession.

* * *

The mists closed about Simon as Victoria's voice came to his ears. *I can't believe Joan of Arc used a* Sword of Eden *to chase out camp followers!*

"It's one of the more persistent stories," Simon said, "but honestly I thought it didn't happen. I think it was Alençon who said she actually broke the sword striking one of the women."

Obviously not. And I'm glad her family reconciled with her, though now I'm going to worry for her brothers.

"Both of Joan's parents may have had some Precursor DNA, but it looks like it didn't manifest strongly in her siblings. Her mother, Isabelle Romée, was an independent woman who went on some very dangerous pilgrimages. And Joan's father had a nightmare of his daughter 'going off with soldiers.' He actually told her brothers to drown her if she did so."

What? Victoria's voice was shocked.

"He interpreted it to mean she would become a camp follower. Joan knew about the dream—and what her father had said. He was right—she *did* 'go off with soldiers,' but in quite a different manner than he feared. It may be the reason she feels so hostile to the camp followers."

I don't think she's going to have to worry about that for a while, Victoria said, *not after that display. What's next?*

Simon took a deep breath. "Orléans," he said.

CHAPTER NINETEEN

FRIDAY, 29 APRIL, 1429

"Are you the Bastard?"

The conversation stopped abruptly as all heads turned to look at Joan. Several men stood around a table, upon which was placed a large map with various markers.

One of them, older than Alençon but not yet into his middle years, smiled a little at the girl. "I am indeed Jean de Dunois, cousin to the king and called the Bastard of Orléans. I have heard much about you, Maid, and I—"

"Did you give counsel that I should come here, marching *past* the poor besieged city of Orléans on the wrong side of the river, instead of going straight there *where Talbot and the English are?*"

Dunois's generals had varying responses to this. One, handsome, well groomed, and clearly of the nobility, showed very white teeth when his short black beard parted in a grin. Another, about a decade older than the Bastard, dirtier and more weatherworn than the others and roughly the size of a mountain, scowled furiously—and then his mouth twitched in what could have been a hint of a smile.

The king's cousin blinked, then replied pleasantly, "I and my generals—Lord Baron Gilles de Rais and Lord Étienne de Vignolles—who are wiser than you in this matter, as we've been here longer, have indeed given this counsel. We believe this is the best and surest path to success."

Joan's face was bright with anger as she strode forward, almost standing on her toes to bring her face closer to that of the Bastard, who was taller than she by almost a full foot. "In the name of God, His counsel is surer and wiser than yours. I am bringing you better help than any ever came from any soldier or any city, because it is the help of the King of Heaven!"

"Little Maid," came a rumble from the barrel chest of the mountainous man. "You've stunned the king and his courtiers. I was there when you sniffed him out, like a clever dog. But you're in the battlefield now. Listen to the men who have spent years fighting. We're glad to have God's help, but He's not down here taking the blows."

Joan turned her scorching gaze upon him. "Which one are you?"

He had been leaning on the table, regarding the map, but now he straightened and his hand went to the hilt of his sword. He was easily six and a half feet tall. Gabriel swallowed. "I am Étienne de Vignolles. I am called La Hire."

"Well, La Hire, you should not blaspheme so," Joan chided. "I have brought priests, and they will be glad to hear your confession. I tell you, my counsel does not come from my own head, but from God Himself, who has pity on Orléans and would see it free. Why are we not attacking Talbot right now?"

The Bastard sighed. He threw a glance over his shoulder at his generals, then seemed to make a decision. "Come here," he said. Joan, Alençon, and Gabriel stepped to the table.

"This is a map of the area," the Bastard said. "This is the city of

Orléans. And yes, we are well to the east of it. You see these markings?" He tapped black squares of various sizes. "These are called boulevards, defenses constructed with wood and earth and stones, to protect vulnerable areas, such as walls or gates."

Gabriel counted. There were nine of them, most clustered on the western side of the city. He wasn't exactly sure why simple piles of earth and wood would pose such a problem.

"Their low height will absorb the impact of our stone and metal cannonballs," said Alençon, reading Gabriel's expression. "And they are manned by soldiers with quite a lot of guns, and the English brought their longbowmen as well."

That sobered Gabriel instantly. Agincourt had not happened so very long ago. The English longbowmen had won an almost absurdly decisive victory, and the thought of going up against them now was not a pleasant one. "We'd have to get through those to even get to the city's gates."

"All but one," La Hire said. He stepped forward, moving with a noticeable limp. He stabbed a thick forefinger down on the map. "Here. The Burgundy Gate is their one real vulnerability. The Saint-Loup boulevard guards the road, but it's the only obstacles."

"We've gotten messages and small groups of men to Orléans through that gate," the Bastard continued. "When we're ready, we'll instruct the Orléanais to cause a distraction."

"And walk right in the front gate," said the elegant nobleman, de Rais. He still seemed highly amused by the whole exchanged.

"And we are not doing that right this minute because...?"

The Bastard regarded Joan for a long moment. Then, "Come with me, Maid," he said.

Joan and Gabriel followed him out of the tent. They stood on a slight incline, and the Loire could be glimpsed a few hundred yards away, glinting in the afternoon sun. A brisk breeze stirred Joan's hair. "Our supplies are here, across the Loire from Chécy," the Bastard continued. "Orléans is about four miles to the west of us. Pray you, notice which way the wind is blowing."

"East," Joan said at once.

"Exactly. The boats with all the grain, and cattle, and chickens, and everything we need to get to Orléans are still in the water. They have the current, but the wind will slow them greatly."

Joan laughed. "Is this all?" she said.

The Bastard bristled. "We will have to wait until the wind changes, Maid. I have wise generals, stalwart men, and a city full of very brave people, but I am only a man."

"And I am only a girl," Joan said, "but we both have God on our side."

She closed her eyes, clasped her hands, and bowed her head. Her breathing slowed and her face softened. The light Gabriel so loved began to shine, as if starting from her heart and radiating outward. The Bastard did not see it, and he was clearly struggling not to interrupt her prayer.

Gabriel watched her face, the wind playing with her short, black hair, brushing it playfully to the right side of her face so that her left cheek was obscured.

And then, her hair fell on the right cheek.

Dunois gasped. He stared at Joan, at Gabriel, licking a finger and testing the wind not once, but twice.

Joan opened her blue eyes and smiled softly. "God is good," she said simply.

The Bastard swallowed, hard. "I will give the order," he said.

The mists closed in. *I can't believe what I just saw,* Victoria said. *It's no wonder they thought she was sent from God.*

"She didn't even touch the sword, though," Simon said. "The wind could have changed at any moment. A perfect example of really, really good timing." He said it because he had to, because he was starting to spook himself. And because he didn't want to even think of how radiant Joan, all by herself, with no Sword of Eden, was. "Another tall tale verified, though."

Indeed, Victoria said. *I'd never heard of La Hire, but the other—Gilles de Rais, why do I know that name?*

Simon smiled without humor. "You may know him better as the inspiration for Bluebeard," he said. "He squandered his fortune on plays recreating the events of Orléans, was accused of being involved in the occult, and... well, let's just say that brutally murdering possibly hundreds of children isn't the sort of thing one would like to be remembered for."

Really? Bluebeard? He certainly doesn't sound like someone Joan would have liked.

"He was devoted to her, actually," Simon said. "Her death devastated him."

It could have pushed him over the edge. How awful.

"Quite possibly. Recently, some scholars have suggested that he was framed regarding the murders, and was coerced into confessing. But considering a whole tourist industry has sprung up around him, the stain is unlikely to ever be washed clean."

Perhaps a mystery to investigate with your new approach?

"Ah, now you're really starting to see what I hope Rikkin will! But for now, let's keep going."

SATURDAY, 30 APRIL, 1429

The night before had been a triumph by everyone's standards but hers. While the French distracted the English in a skirmish, drawing their attention from the road, Joan the Maid, at the head of a caravan of desperately needed supplies, had ridden her prancing white destrier right through the gate into Orléans. She had been welcomed with shouts of joy and tears of relief. The Orléanais pressed in close, hungry to touch her feet, her standard, her arms, even her horse. She was in their minds a savior, and the siege was as good as completed. The city's treasurer general, Jacques Boucher, opened his pleasant brick-and-timber home to her and her retinue, and she had slept that night not in her armor on hard earth, but in a soft bed.

But Joan had felt betrayed when, shortly after the wind shift that had silenced the French generals' protests, she learned that the Bastard intended to separate her from her men. They would remain outside the city, while she, her retinue and a small handful of guards, would accompany the supply wagons inside. But as she argued with Dunois, Gabriel remembered the clean, bright gleam of the sword, and the gift it could bestow when held in her hands.

"You will give them hope, Jeanne," he said, as the Bastard shot him a look of gratitude. "Let that be enough for tonight. Because of you, the people will go to sleep with joy in their hearts and food in their bellies. They will rest well. Time for fighting on the morrow."

The morning had brought the news that Dunois refused to go on the offensive until reinforcements arrived. Gabriel understood the military logic behind Dunois's caution—the Bastard did not want a repeat of the Battle of the Herrings. But he also knew how fiercely Joan burned to act, after so very many examinations, and journeys, and refusals. And her words, *I have only a year, perhaps a little longer*, ate away at him.

"So... what now?"

"Dunois told me the English have my herald. The one I sent from Blois." Her eyes were fierce. "I want him back."

"Jeanne, you can't just march out there and—"

"Of course I won't. I just want to talk to them."

There was nothing to do but follow her. Now he stood beside her on the ramparts of the Renart Gate. Her brothers, four soldiers, and one of her pages, little Louis, had also accompanied her—as, it seemed, had half of Orléans.

One young woman in crowd the caught Gabriel's eye. She had long, fair hair and deep blue eyes that were fixed on Joan. Her face and clothes were dirty, dirtier than that of most of the Orléanais. She looked familiar to Gabriel, but of course that wasn't possible.

Beside Gabriel, Joan placed her hands on her hips and stared out—
—at the English.

Joan had been right. There were places in the city where the English army was close enough to the besieged town that one might engage in conversation with the enemy—if one was careful. And if one shouted.

She cupped her hands around her mouth. "Men of England!" she cried. "I am Jeanne the Maid, sent by God to deliver this city. I sent you my herald. By all laws and traditions, he was to return to me unharmed. Release him to me!"

"We used him for target practice!" one of the Englishman shouted back. Another man, apparently of higher rank than the others, stepped forward. His French was perfect, revealing him to be a Burgundian.

"Do you really want true men to surrender to a woman—a girl at that?" To Gabriel, Pierre, and Jean, who were standing beside Joan, he shouted, "You are worse than little dogs sitting in her lap! Worthless mackerels!"

"What?" shouted Pierre. "You whoreson!"

"Do not swear!" Joan chided. "Such things are for those whom God has abandoned."

Gabriel did not know what a worthless mackerel was, but judging by Pierre's reaction, he could hazard a pretty good guess.

But Joan was done, and turned to Gabriel, her eyes wide, grinning. "Let's go to the bridge now! Tonight they will talk of nothing else but their wounded pride."

They walked to the Bridge of Orléans, the crowd tagging after her. Gabriel found himself looking to see if the perplexingly familiar fair-haired girl was among them. She was, still raptly focused on Joan. Gabriel frowned. Why did he think he knew her?

The Bridge of Orléans was, before the siege, the major entrance into the city. It stretched across the Loire, most of it under French control, and culminated in a French fortification on the island of Belle-Croix. Beyond this point, two arches of the bridge had been destroyed by the French, to keep the English from advancing further. The English had taken and now occupied the fortified gate flanked by large towers known as Les Tourelles, on the south bank of the Loire. In front of it was the strongest boulevard in Orléans.

He could not see it from his vantage point, and was somewhat glad, as Les Tourelles itself was sobering enough. Gabriel glanced at Joan's brothers, who looked somber. All of them, himself included, were starting to fully appreciate what they were up against.

The soldiers defending the fortifications on the French side of the bridge cheered as they approached. As Joan and Gabriel climbed to stand beside them, he realized just how close they were—a mere four hundred or so yards.

"Glasdale is over there," one of the soldiers said. William Glasdale had been a fighting man for twenty years and part of the English invasion forces for six, and was not someone to be taken lightly. He had been placed in command of Les Tourelles, and Dunois had told them the man had vowed to kill everyone in the entire city.

Joan leaned forward and shouted the commander's name. "Glasdale! I am here by God's will to do what I said I would do! Surrender yourselves to God and King Charles, and we will spare your lives!"

The small figures suddenly grew very interested in the Belle-Croix fortification. Then one of them shouldered his way to the forefront. He was of middle years, large and powerful, His French was good, though heavily accented, and his voice was deep and commanding.

"Your letter made us laugh!" he shouted back. "And I am glad you are here, 'Maid,' though I doubt you are one. You won't be when we are done with you. You are nothing but a filthy cowherd!"

"Better a French cowherd than an English general!" she shouted back.

"You will die here, Maid. Along with everyone else in your city." The voice was cold, flat. "If we find you alive, we will take you and torture you for our sport. And when we are done, we shall *burn* you and dance in your ashes!"

Simon felt a shock through his system at the words. Beside him, Joan froze, going terribly pale. Then she reddened, as if the blood had rushed back to her face all at once. "I do not know the hour of my death, but know this, William Glasdale—if you do not surrender, it is *you* who will die!"

Joan turned and abruptly returned to the bridge, regaining her composure with every step. She turned to Gabriel, and once again, she was smiling. "Shadow," she said to him playfully, "do you know what your Jeanne is doing?"

"*I* do," her brother Jean said. "We've seen you do this before. You're picking a fight."

"Exactly! If the French will not attack the English, then perhaps I can be like a fly and sting enough so that the English will attack the French. We must fight them, and soon. My Voices are very clear."

Gabriel wanted to ask her if her Voices had been clear when she had predicted Glasdale's death, but as soon as he had the thought, he rejected it. He did not want to know.

He found himself looking for the blonde girl as they returned to Boucher's house. Sure enough, there she was, somehow managing to stand apart from the throng that Joan now permitted to fall step beside her. Gabriel hesitated, then told Pierre, "I will catch up to you." He nodded, and Gabriel worked his way back to where the girl was.

She didn't appear to have noticed him. As always, she was watching Joan with an expression of joy and wonder on her face. Gabriel came up behind her, then darted forward and grasped her arm firmly.

The girl gasped and turned to him, and all at once he realized where he recognized her from.

"You," he said. "You were one of the *ribaudes* Jeanne chased away at Blois!"

Pain filled her eyes and she lowered her gaze. "Say it. I'm a whore. A camp follower."

"I know," he said. "At least, you were. But you're not anymore, are you?"

Startled, she looked back at him. "No," she said. "I'm not. Not since I... since she...."

"What does she look like to you?" Gabriel pressed. He didn't want to put words in her mouth. "When you see her?"

She didn't answer at once. Then, softly, as if the words were a prayer, she said, "She burns with white fire. Like a candle does, when the flame has burned so deep inside it, you cannot see the fire itself, but only its glow through the wax. I—I want to be close to her. I have no right, I know she must despise me, but—"

"But you see her," Gabriel breathed. She had what de Metz had called Eagle Vision. This girl, this common camp follower, who had offered her body for money to more men than he might be able to count—she had the blood, just as he did. Just as Yolande did, and de Metz, and Alençon.

Some people were completely unaffected by Joan, like her brothers, de Baudricourt, and what he had seen of the English. Others responded to her. But only a few *saw* her.

How he wished an Assassin were here right now. He hoped he wasn't making a huge mistake. "Come with me."

* * *

Joan sat up on the bed as Gabriel entered, smiling. She was alone; it was likely Pierre and Jean were exploring more of the city on their own, or else talking with some of the soldiers. He was glad they could speak privately.

"There you are, Gabriel! I thought I had lost my Shadow."

He smiled. "Ah, never that, Jeanne." Sobering slightly, he said, "I have never asked anything from you, other than to stay with you as long as you would have me."

She smiled at him. "This is truth," she said. "My witness. I would be lost without you. Is there something you wish of me now? If God will let me grant it, I will."

He nodded. "Yes," he said. "There is someone you should talk to. I... well, you may recognize her, but please do not be angry with her."

Jeanne cocked her head, confused. "Such mystery! If you think I should meet her, then bring her in."

He ducked back outside the room, closing the door. The former camp follower stood at the foot of the stairs, twisting her hands together nervously.

"She'll see you," Gabriel said quietly. "Tell her what you told me. She won't hurt you, I promise." *If she tries, I will stop her.*

"I trust you," the girl said, although her voice quivered. Joan stood awaiting them, peering curiously at the newcomer as they stepped inside. Her welcoming smile faded slowly.

"Jeanne," Gabriel began, "This is—" He broke off, realizing he hadn't even thought to get the girl's name.

"Oh, I know who she is," Joan said, her voice soft and angry. "Or rather, *what* she is. You were at Blois—tempting good Christian men to sin! Where is my sword? You must want a good beating!"

"Jeanne, no!" Gabriel put himself between the girl and the furious Joan. "She *sees* you! She has put aside her old ways and wants to travel with us."

"Follow the camp, you mean!"

"No, just—tell her what you told me," he pleaded with the girl. For a long moment, she hesitated, then she stepped out from behind him.

"Maid," she said, her voice a whisper, "it is true, I have sinned. But God forgives those who truly repent, and I do with all my heart. Even Jesus forgave the woman who committed adultery, did He not?"

"I am not God or Jesus," Joan warned, but Gabriel could tell something was happening. Her voice had grown less harsh, and her fists were no longer clenched.

"I will gladly make confession, whether you will take me with you or not. But please... w-when I see you, I want to be near you. To help you in any way I can. You have already made me better. I want to be better still. I see your face, and I can tell that God is working through you."

"Ask your Voices, Jeanne," Gabriel pleaded. "Please."

For a long moment Joan looked from one to the other, her body held taut as a bowstring. "They are my best and finest counsel," Jeanne agreed at last. "I will do ask they ask me, as I always do. But if they say go, then you will leave forever. *After* you have made your confession."

The girl nodded. "I'll stay with her," Gabriel said. "We will be outside, by the gate."

Joan didn't answer, but she gave him a withering glance and turned her back on him. Gabriel felt sick, his heart aching with every lurching beat. *He* had done this; had driven a wedge between them. But he couldn't just abandon this poor girl, not when she had willingly forsworn her former life to follow Joan. *I might have to*, he thought, and fought back despair.

They walked out by the house's gate. A throng clustered by it day and night, hoping to see a glimpse of the divinely-sent Maiden who would free them. For a second, there was some excitement as Gabriel and the former prostitute walked out, but then the girl threw back her hood. At the sight of her long golden hair, though, the crowd lost interest.

"I had hoped it would go better than that," Gabriel said after an awkward silence. "I'm sorry."

"You did what you could, and I am grateful," she said. "Do—do you think her Voices will tell her to accept me?" Her eyes shimmered with tears. "I won't go back to what I was. I would rather die. But... where do I go if she sends me away?"

"We'll think of something," Gabriel answered. Perhaps the Assassins would take her, if Joan would not. "My name is Gabriel Laxart. I'm sorry—I never asked... what is yours?

"It does not matter."

They both turned to see Joan standing behind them. Her face was incandescent, and she smiled softly. The girl's hand went to her mouth. *Oh, yes, she definitely sees it*, Gabriel thought.

"It does not matter," Joan continued, walking toward them,

"because my Voices have told me to give you a new name. From this moment on, you are Fleur. Because you are a flower who has grown in the mud, and God is the light to which you now turn your face. I am sorry for my harshness. Together, we will go to confession. And then, I will get clothes for you, and when we have freed this city, you will come with me... as my friend."

Joy flooded the girl's—Fleur's—face. She swayed and would have fallen had Joan not stepped forward and caught her up in a tight hug. Fleur sobbed and clung to Joan, who smiled softly, her face radiant, and stroked the other girl's long, tangled gold hair. Her eyes met Gabriel's, who felt the icy grip around his heart release.

She mouthed a word to him: *Merci.*

CHAPTER TWENTY

Who was that? Victoria wanted to know as the Memory Corridor's soft fog closed in around Simon.

"No idea," he said. "There's no mention of a girl who traveled with Joan. Every time other women come up, it's clear that Joan had little interest in them. Most of them wanted to be prophetesses, too, and because of course she was the only one really quote-unquote sent from God, she despised them. I can't imagine her befriending one of the prostitutes she chased off, but... well, there it is."

Well, I'm rather glad. I like this Fleur.

So did Simon, but since he had absolutely no idea what would happen to this girl who had apparently escaped mention for over five centuries, he didn't want to get overly fond of her. It would be bad enough when Joan—

"The Bastard went to Blois for more troops on May first," Simon said briskly. "While he was gone, Joan rode about, met with the citizens, and so on. She also scouted outside the city, to see for herself what her troops were up against. The people threw a sort of procession for her, offering gifts and such, essentially thanking her in advance for liberating them. The Bastard came back on the fourth with reinforcements. I think we should start there."

Are you certain you're up for it? You've seen several simulations today already, and we're heading towards evening.

"Time's not our friend, Victoria." He felt like Joan, wanting to move forward with the raising of the siege and being thwarted by so-called wiser heads. "Let's keep going."

1 MAY, 1429

"I hear you have been stirring up the English," the Bastard said as he, Joan, Gabriel, and La Hire ate at Boucher's table. The meal was simple and had been prepared quickly—cheese, bread, hardboiled eggs from the chickens the convoy had brought in a few nights ago.

"I have, and I have made my own examinations of their defenses, too," Joan said. "Once we have eaten and I have shared that with you, we can finally attack!"

"Sounds good to me," La Hire said. "I'm with the Maid. I'm ready for battle."

Joan threw him a pleased smile. "And did you see?" she said. "You, the Bastard, and all your men—you came right through the Burgundy Gate, and the English didn't even try to stop you!"

"There is news you don't yet know," said the Bastard, giving La Hire a dirty look. "We have heard rumors of an approaching English army led by John Fastolf. It's supposed to be coming from the north."

"All the more reason to fight! We now have the reinforcements you were so insistent on getting. The people are with us, and they are so very ready to be freed! Bastard, in the name of God, I command you that as soon as you hear of Fastolf's coming, you will let me know. For if he gets through without my knowing it, I swear that I will have your head cut off!" Joan said, gesticulating with her knife.

Everyone laughed, even the Bastard. "Maid, I do not doubt *that* for a moment! I will certainly let you know."

"Gabriel!"

He had fallen asleep in a chair downstairs, but bolted up as Fleur shook him. "What is it?"

"It's the Maid," she said. "She—she woke up shouting that her Voices say the blood of France is being spilled right at this moment! Madame Boucher and her daughter are upstairs with her now, helping her dress."

"I'll help with the armor," Gabriel said, and both of them raced upstairs.

Poor Louis stood in the door, looking utterly miserable as usual.

"I will have his *head*!" Joan's voice rang through the house. "He promised me he would tell me! And Louis, you wicked boy! Why did you not wake me?"

"Louis," Gabriel said, "tell the squires to get the Maid's horse ready for her. Have them saddle mine, too. Jeanne, let me help!"

A few moments later, Joan was in her armor and hastening downstairs. Gabriel struggled into his own armor with Louis helping him. Fleur, wearing some of Joan's masculine garb, watched with sharp eyes and lent a hand where she could. Once Gabriel was ready, he went to the gate, where Joan, her brothers, and several of her men were waiting. The streets were crowded and noisy; Joan might well have been the last person to have heard of this skirmish.

Suddenly she gasped in horror. "Louis!" she called up. "My standard!"

"Here!" the boy cried, lowering it down to her from the window. Joan grasped it, clung to it for an instant, then inserted it into the cylinder near her stirrup. Calm visibly descended on her.

"Where's the fighting?" Gabriel demanded.

"The Saint-Loup boulevard," came a rumbling voice. It was La Hire, and he wore his usual expression of annoyance. Gabriel wasn't sure with whom—with the Bastard, for not notifying Jeanne, or for the Maid herself. It was clear that many of the generals were not expecting Joan to take such an active role. "It's not Fastolf, don't worry—you didn't miss that. It's a show of our determination to end the siege. The Bastard thought if we took this smaller boulevard, it would weaken the English morale without too much of a cost to us. But they're giving us more of a fight than we expected."

Gabriel knew what he didn't say—that if this French surprise attack failed, it was the English who would be heartened and the French again plunged into despair.

"I need hear no more," Joan said. She rose in her stirrups and drew her sword.

Again Gabriel almost forgot to breathe as the sword leaped to glowing life at Joan's touch. How was it possible that only a few could see the radiance—in both the Sword of Eden, and the girl who held it? Even if they did not see it, though, they felt something. The crowd had been noisy and anxious, milling about, eager to do something, anything. Now they gazed, mouths slightly open, listening with their whole hearts. She was their savior, and they loved her.

"People of Orléans!" Joan cried. "I promised you I had come to raise the siege, and today, at last, I will begin to do so. Know that I am only part of God's plan. You, the good people of this city, you have consistently offered the English resistance and determination. Now, we will act! Gather your weapons. Mount your horses, and ride with me!"

The hair on Simon's arms lifted and his heart swelled at the cheer that rose up. It was deafening, and exciting, and powerful. Joan's face shone like a beacon, and when Joan kicked her horse forward, she, her brothers, Gabriel, La Hire, and the other soldiers were at the head of their own little army.

The excited flow bore them swiftly toward the Burgundy Gate. But before they reached it and could head east along the road to the Saint-Loup boulevard, the flow suddenly changed.

The wounded and the dead were returning from the first hour of battle.

Men limped in, supported by their comrades, slung over their horses, or borne in litters as they passed through the gate. Gabriel looked past the gate to see that several bodies, some writhing in agony, some ominously still, had simply been placed on the ground until they could be attended. The cheers and shouts of victory and defiance in the distance were now joined by the more immediate moans, and sometimes agonized shrieks, of the wounded. There was a smell that seemed somehow familiar, and Gabriel realized what it was. He had often been forced to pass the butcher's shop and its adjoining abattoir when he lived in Nancy.

It was the metallic reek of blood.

La Hire grunted. "Most of them are English," he said. "Come along, Maid, you're needed at the boulevard."

But Joan shook her head and slipped off her horse. "No," she said, looking around slowly, "I am needed here."

La Hire stared at her, then at Gabriel, who had also dismounted, and then nodded. "Perhaps you are, at that," he said. "When you're ready, those men still fighting will welcome you."

"I will come," Joan said. She moved to the side and out the gate, going straight to those who had been forgotten or abandoned, and dropped down beside the first wounded soldier she saw.

He lay on his back. His helmet had been removed or knocked off. A sword had sliced along his face, but that was not his gravest wound. Blood seeped out beneath him, even though he was still fully armored, the red pool revealing the true extent of the wound. Joan removed her gloves and helm and touched his bloodied forehead, careful to avoid the bleeding gash. Her other hand went to her breastplate, over the pouch hidden beneath it; over her heart.

"I am sorry it has come to this, my foe and my brother," she whispered, and it was only then that Gabriel realized that the man was indeed clad in English livery. He had been so horrifically mesmerized by his first glimpse of war wounds that he hadn't even noticed. "I would gladly have sent you home, had your commander surrendered.

God grieves, and so do I."

Her eyes were, indeed, filled with tears, rolling down her soft cheeks unheeded. The man opened his eyes, seeking her out. Her light was shining, soft and warm and comforting, and Gabriel hoped the dying man could see it.

"P-Pucelle," he said. His mouth was filled with blood, which splattered as he spoke her name and trickled down the side of his face like red tears.

"Yes," and she covered his hand with hers. "You will not die alone, and I will pray with you."

He didn't seem to understand. Gabriel wasn't sure if it was because he did not speak French, or because he was too far gone to comprehend. Joan's lips moved softly, and the man's tension seemed to ease. He sighed, deeply, his body relaxing. A smile curved his blood-reddened lips, and then he closed his eyes.

Joan stroked his paling forehead, and moved on to the next.

French or English, it made no difference to her. How long Gabriel followed her, standing protectively over her while she prayed with dying men, he did not know, but at last, she rose and wiped at her wet face.

"None of this had to happen," she murmured, reaching for her helm and settling it back on her head. "I begged them to surrender. But for now, let us ride to the boulevard!"

They cantered down the Burgundy road. Joan's face was covered by the helm, so Gabriel could not see her light, but he knew it was shining. Her standard snapped beside her in the wind. They heard the sounds of gunfire and cannon blasts, the clash of steel on steel.

Joan drew her sword. "Here I am!" she cried, and her voice seemed to carry farther than it should have in that cacophony. "Here I am, you men of France! Here is Jeanne the Maid, you English! In the name of God, the tide is turning, and you shall be swept away!"

The blade gleamed, bright and hot. Lightning crackled along its length. Gabriel abruptly realized that his throat was raw as he, along with the rest of Joan's army, began cheering madly. He kicked his horse and plunged forward, his sword feeling like an extension of his arm, his arm an extension of his heart and soul, as he charged to the relief of a surrounded group of unhorsed French soldiers.

They were outnumbered, but fought like men possessed. The English, who by all rights should have pressed their advantage, were oddly hesitant. One of them even looked away from the fight, mesmerized by the billow of Joan's white standard. The soldier fighting him took advantage of his enemy's distraction and plunged the tip of his sword into the Englishman's neck at the vulnerable spot between gorget and helm.

The soldier next to him screamed and fled, racing back to the safety of the boulevard. Gabriel kicked his horse and rode him down. The English soldier fell, the horse's hooves crushing his armor. He was still alive when Gabriel wheeled his mount back and, bending low over its neck, speared down with his sword through the thin eye slits in the Englishman's helm.

They were falling like flies, now; falling, or attempting to flee. The roaring French followed them, like Joan's predicted wave. Some still fought, frantically but uselessly, but most surrendered at once, pleading for mercy.

Gabriel looked down at his bloodied sword, and felt slightly dizzy. *He ran away*, he thought. *He should have surrendered. I would have spared him.*

He hoped the words were true.

Uneasily he turned back to where Joan was still riding, her banner flying. Her helm was off, so her men could see her face, and she was radiant.

"For France!" she cried. "For France! I tell you, in five days, the siege will be raised, and the English will be driven from our gates!"

And Gabriel believed her.

CHAPTER
TWENTY-ONE

That was unbelievable, Victoria said as Simon returned to the Memory Corridor. *The sword took the fight right out of them. She's completely undefeatable with it.*

"But she doesn't understand that," Simon said. "She once said she loved the standard forty times as much as she loved the sword. So she's not using it to the best advantage. A Templar or an Assassin would be undefeatable, yes. But not Joan."

That's absolutely tragic, Victoria replied. *She had such a powerful weapon, and wielded it so well... but didn't make full use of it. I wonder why the Assassins never fully brought her in.*

"We don't know yet that they didn't," Simon reminded her. "That's something we may want to keep an eye out for. Also, I don't think we should be too upset that she never became an official Assassin, considering the Templars were supporting the British side during the Hundred Years' War."

We can be Templars, and still empathize with others. All right. I call this a good day's work, she said, and he realized she had decided they were done.

"Wait," he said. "We're starting to get to the actual battles."

"I know," Victoria interrupted him, removing the helmet. "And I don't like your stats. Gabriel's had his first battle, and unless you've had some military experience I don't know about, it was your first battle, too. You should eat something, then go directly to bed. It's been a very long day."

He bristled and pulled his arm back as she reached to unbuckle the straps. "Don't address me like a child," he said, stiffly. "I'm fine, and I'd like to continue." In actuality, he was famished, but he didn't want to break for dinner just yet. If they had dinner, then he'd have to reply to Anaya, and he was definitely avoiding that as long as possible. Which, honestly, actually *was* rather childish.

"Tomorrow will be day five," he protested. His heart sped up as he thought how much ground they had yet to cover. He started to tick off all that loomed ahead. "We've got to finish Orléans, and then the battles to clear the road so the king can get crowned, and then Paris, and then—"

"Not another word." Her voice was strong, sharper than he'd ever heard it. "I'm tired of arguing with you at every turn. We've done so much in such a short period of time, and I think we'll be able to determine where she lost the sword. That's your job, Simon. And you'll be no good at it if you're too exhausted to notice what you need to."

He blinked, then stepped out of the Animus and regarded her. "*Our* job," he said, coolly and precisely, "is to demonstrate to Alan Rikkin why my approach is so valuable."

"By figuring out how to get *that sword*," and she pointed to the wooden box, "functioning as something other than a glorified filet knife. I've seen it in action now. Rikkin will see it in action. It's amazing. It's astonishing. And if you can find out how to fix it, your case will be ironclad."

She was right, of course. She also looked like she was under a lot of strain. Simon suddenly wondered what it took out of someone to be on the other end—watching, monitoring several different things, always ready to pull him out in a heartbeat if need be.

But none of that excused her anger. "You're behaving in a very unprofessional manner, Doctor," he said, pointedly using her title. "Might I suggest that you follow your own advice and make it an early night. We'll meet at Temp's at eight tomorrow morning."

A muscle twitched near her eye, but she nodded. "I apologize," she said. "I shouldn't have spoken like that to you. Sometimes the doctor does need to take her own advice."

Despite his annoyance, he patted her awkwardly on the shoulder. "Let's blame Rikkin and his absurd deadline and not be cross with one another, hmm?"

"Deal," she said, and gave him a wan smile.

They said good night at the lift and Victoria headed for the parking garage. Simon decided to stop off in his office. He wanted the comforting smell of books for a moment to settle his mind. On an impulse, he took his Joan of Arc books from the shelves, stacking them on a pile. He'd made extensive notes on his tablet, but books were his favorite choice for research.

He looked at his phone and was both chagrined and annoyed to see several texts from Anaya, all of them brief, all of them reiterating that she wanted to talk to him.

Simon ran up the white flag. *In lobby. Come down*, he replied, gave the books a last caress, and went to get on the lift.

She was there within a few minutes, smiling cheerfully at him, but for some reason the smile didn't reach her eyes. "Have you had dinner yet?" she asked.

"No, and what—"

"I'm starving," she said. "I'd love to have some good old-fashioned fish and chips before I have to leave London. Oh! And it's Oktoberfest. We can see what the local pubs are featuring."

"Well, let's do that, shall we?" Simon was hardly in the mood to go pub crawling, but fish and chips did sound good. They took a taxi to

Marylebone to one of their favorite chip shops. Simon ordered a pint and found himself relaxing, which surprised him.

As they finished their meal, he said, "So... what did you want to talk about? Or was this just about getting me to buy you fish and chips?"

"Oh, so you *are* paying, brilliant," Anaya said. She still had that odd look on her face. She waved a hand airily. "Let's chat while we walk." Obviously Simon was not going to escape being dragged from pub to pub to try the autumnal specials.

They stepped out of the warm darkness of the pub into the icy night outside. She slipped her arm through his as they started walking, and he stopped, giving her a confused look. "What, a girl can't keep her hands warm?"

The edges that the beer had taken off returned with new sharpness. This wasn't like Anaya; she was an excellent respecter of boundaries. Something wasn't right. He forced himself to smile as they strolled down Thayer, past the overly precious antique stores, cute boutiques, and smart men's tailor shops.

Anaya leaned against him and murmured, softly, "Victoria is a liar."

Simon stopped dead in his tracks. "Come on," she hissed, tugging him along. Her eyes darted about nervously.

"All right," he said, thinking he'd play along. "What makes you say that?"

"She lied about Bella Cibo," Anaya said. "I saw her there the other night."

"That does seem a queer thing to lie about, but—"

"I saw her with Alan Rikkin." That almost made him come to another complete halt, but he forced himself to keep going. His heart started a slow hammering in his chest.

"She's one of the key people at the Aerie," Simon said. Now he, too, was starting to look around at passersby: families with babes in arms or in prams; couples, old and young, holding hands; a group of teenage girls clustered at the windows of one of the popular boutiques. "It's entirely possible she was discussing something about that. Or something I don't need to know about."

Even as he said the words, he thought about Victoria's increasing stress levels. The fact that Rikkin had replied to her, not him. And just tonight, the out-and-out unprofessionalism of their tiff. He suddenly felt the cold air knife through the sturdy wool of his overcoat.

"People do that all the time at Abstergo," Anaya murmured, "we're bloody Templars. What we *don't* do is lie about being spotted in a restaurant."

They kept walking while thoughts raced through Simon's head. Finally he said, "I trust your instincts. You were the field agent, not me. What should we do?"

"I think we're safe enough out here. We're not bugged, I checked before we left the taxi."

Of course she had. Simon suddenly wished he hadn't ordered the large fish and chips. His stomach felt like he'd swallowed lead. "Well, I suppose that's good."

"Can you tell me anything about what you're working on?"

It was a high-level project, so he hadn't volunteered information, but he trusted Anaya and saw no reason why he shouldn't tell her. He gave her the short version about his approach, Victoria's expertise and assistance, Piece of Eden 25, and, of course, the ludicrous deadline. "Rikkin appointed her himself, and thus far, it's been a good partnership."

"Except for the lying."

"Except for the lying. I have to keep working with her if I'm going to have any hope of making the deadline. And I do want to make it, dammit. I just don't know why there would be any deception involved in this. If my approach works, everyone stands to benefit."

"Everyone?" pressed Anaya.

Simon thought about it. The Templars? Yes. Abstergo? Possibly, but this sort of behavior didn't reflect a concern with a corporate bottom-line. Rikkin? Definitely. "Everyone," he said firmly.

Unless my approach and Joan of Arc somehow aren't really what this is all about. But what the hell else could it be?

It was time to go all in with Anaya. "I've been noticing things. They sound so stupid, but... well, one night I dozed off in a car that was bringing me home. I dreamed I heard the driver speaking in Latin."

She snorted. "Only you, Simon."

"You know I don't know it, and thank you *so* much for making me feel even more foolish."

"Sorry, go ahead."

He told her about the doorman he didn't recognize. Then about how he hadn't seen Poole at Temp's for a couple of days. "I mean—all of these things have explanations. Latin had been involved as part of the project I'm working on. I could have simply caught another man's shift at the flat. And Poole could be on holiday—he certainly deserves it, the man's a fixture."

"True," she agreed, "but we're Templars. That means we can't afford to make assumptions." She forced a grin, belied by the worry in her eyes. "I think," she said quietly, "I'd like to go back to your flat."

They took a taxi back to Abstergo, and Simon drove them to his flat in his two-year-old Jaguar sedan. They were silent the whole way. Simon had no idea what to say, what to think, and dreaded what might be about to happen. Once they were inside, Anaya looked around.

"You always did keep a tidy place, Simon," she said.

"It's much easier when you're never home. Nightcap?" he asked. He hoped he didn't sound as tense as he felt. "I think I have some of that nasty American bourbon you're so fond of."

"Lovely, thanks."

He poured her two fingers, trying to keep the bottle's neck from clattering against the glass, and poured himself a Macallan. He had to fight to not down it in a gulp.

Anaya wandered around, taking in the beautiful antique furniture, running a finger along the spines of the old leather books, stepping into the study. "Are you ever going to finish your novel?" she asked, looking at the comfortable leather chair and the state-of-the-art computer.

"One of these days."

She placed her glass down on a coaster and said, "Let me just duck into the loo," and winked at him.

What are we getting ourselves into? he wondered.

Anaya emerged a few minutes later, looked at him for a moment, then slowly draped her arms around his neck. His hands went to her waist, tentatively, and he closed his eyes as she nuzzled his ear.

"I've spotted two bugs already," she said. "No need for me to go into the bedroom. Your car has one, too. Act as if you've no idea... and watch what you say and write."

"The computer too?" he murmured.

"Most likely." What was the old joke? That it wasn't paranoia if they really were out to get you? Impulsively, he slid his arms around her and held her tightly.

"Thank you," he whispered. She nodded ever so slightly, then as they had agreed, she pulled back.

"Simon," she said, in a slightly louder voice, "I—I don't think...."

"Of course," he said, making sure he sounded understanding but slightly disappointed. Which, curiously enough, wasn't difficult. "This would be a very bad idea, with you being a short-timer."

She stepped back, then planted a quick kiss on his cheek. "You're a good man, Simon Hathaway. I'm glad we're friends."

"Always, Anaya," he said. "Montreal has no idea what a gem they're getting." He fetched her coat and helped her into it, opened the door for her, and said good night.

Alone in his apartment, he poured out Anaya's unfinished bourbon—anyone observing would know he never drank the stuff—sipping his scotch as he wondered how the hell was he going to pretend he didn't know that both his flat and car were bugged, that a trusted colleague had betrayed him, and that his fellow Inner Sanctum member was behind all of it.

CHAPTER
TWENTY-TWO

DAY 5

Simon had barely been able to sleep, and what dreams he'd had had been fraught with symbols so odd that Carl Jung would have rubbed his hands in glee: Jacques de Molay climbing out of the portrait during Simon's initiation ritual, brandishing the Sword of Eden as Simon lay prostrate on the cold floor. The teardrop-shaped sun etched into the stone wall of the Coudray dungeon. And worst of all, Joan, bound to a stake, flames licking at her feet and an enormous hole in her chest, screaming in agony.

After jolting out of sleep a second time drenched in sweat, he glanced at the clock and decided that 5:16 was indeed not too early to go to his office. He trudged into his kitchen, made some tea, and poured it in a travel mug. Somehow, though he believed that his office as well as his flat was bugged, if he were going to be watched, he'd rather it be there than here.

A strange peace settled over him as he sat down with the pile of books he'd assembled last night. Last night, in all ignorance, he'd done exactly the right thing. Over the next few hours, Simon, with old-fashioned pen and paper, jotted down notes from his collection of tomes. He had a plan, and he was fairly certain he could convince Victoria to go along with it.

Simon was also fairly certain he'd give himself away the moment he showed up at Temp's. Lyndsey greeted him with a smile. He knew he shouldn't, but he asked, "I'm just wondering—where's Poole?"

"On holiday," she said, shrugging. "Getting it in before the Christmas season hits, I imagine."

He forced a polite smile. He wondered if she was just a regular employee, or if she was a Templar field agent, or if Lyndsey was even her real name. He wondered if the teapots were outfitted with recording devices. But that way lay madness.

He ordered tea for himself and Victoria, wondering if Anaya and the American would show up. He thought not; it would be safest if they weren't seen together. *Don't panic,* Anaya had said last night as they bought burner phones before going to his flat.

Rather late for that, he'd muttered.

I mean it. It could just be Abstergo being Abstergo. They watch us a lot more often than you think.

Also not comforting.

No, really, it should be business as usual at Abstergo. It's Victoria who's the wild card as far as I'm concerned. Something about whatever it is you're doing has gotten someone's attention. So don't volunteer anything, don't do anything out of the ordinary, and we'll see what happens.

The new mobile was in his jacket pocket, next to his heart. He resisted the impulse to pat it, and was absurdly and horrifyingly reminded of the peculiar gaping hole in Joan's chest.

"Simon?"

He started. "Oh, sorry. Woolgathering."

"You look like the sheep trampled you," Victoria said, and he smiled faintly.

"I've looked better, I'm sure. But I have tea, and I shall soon have bacon, so I anticipate rapid improvement."

"Good." Victoria poured milk into her tea and was silent for a moment, then said, "I want to apologize again for last night. There was no call for me to behave that way."

Twelve hours ago, he'd have believed her. Now, he wished he knew whether any of her concern for him had ever been genuine. *Focus, Simon.*

"We've both been a bit off our game," he said. "I'm not proud my own behavior, so let's just move on."

Her brow furrowed, but she nodded. "Of course," she said. Then, with something approaching her usual warmth, she added, "So, what's next?"

"Well," he said, "Orléans is pivotal for Joan, of course—I mean, it was after this that she became known as the Maid of Orléans, rather than simply the Maid."

Victoria nodded. "I do know how much, as a historian, you want to see everything."

"She has back to back battles on the seventh and eighth of May. Both vital, both long—all day affairs—and both, ah, terrifically bloody." He paused for a moment and let his hand shake, just a trifle, as he refilled his tea.

Victoria didn't miss the motion. "Simon... I'm not sure how much of that you really need to see," she said. "There's a reason Abstergo Entertainment alters the memories they use for their games. Otherwise, most would be too traumatic for ordinary people to handle. You're not watching a film or playing a game. You're experiencing the memories as if they are actually happening to you. And with this model, you are physically moving along with the simulation, so there's a kinetic aspect to the experience that further locks it into your mind.

You don't need to live every minute of a battle. You simply don't."

What made his ploy work, Simon thought, is that she was right. He hadn't been prepared for Gabriel's memory of jabbing a sword into a fallen foe's eye. Or the smells and the sounds of battle, of ruptured bowels and blood and high-pitched screams of torment. A movie or a game, it most assuredly wasn't.

He sighed as if in resignation. "So how do we cherry-pick times when Joan is going to be carrying the Sword of Eden?"

"Let me know where you think she'd be likely to utilize the sword's abilities. I'll enter that information into the simulation parameters, and we should be able to identify the most important moments. If it's too intense, don't worry, I'll bring you out. And for pity's sake, Simon, be honest with me about how much you can handle. I can't have another Robert Fraser. I won't."

She handed him her tablet. For a moment, her eyes glinted as if with unshed tears, but perhaps it was just the light. His heart lurched. Right now, she looked as though she really did care about him.

Simon muttered a protest to keep up the pretense, but entered this morning's notes into Victoria's tablet. "If we like how this works, I think this is how we should move forward," he said. "Plus, eventually we'll come to a place where Gabriel and she are separated. He's not likely to have seen much of.... Well."

He didn't want to go down that path, not now, not when everything inside him was raw with disillusionment and suspicion and his nerves were bowstring-taut.

"On May seventh, the French achieve a major victory. They take the boulevard of the Augustins—the old friary that sits in front of the Les Tourelles. It's all military tactics; they made a bridge of boats to get to one of the islands in the Loire, then crossed to the boulevard of Saint-Jean-le-Blanc. They found it deserted and took the attack to the Augustins. There, well, they pretty much simply threw four thousand men against it in a very fierce fight. While that's impressive, it isn't one of the great moments I want to see. I mean—that I think we should see. And... we do have to witness Les Tourelles. We must. However rough it is."

THURSDAY, 5 MAY, 1429
ORLÉANS
ASCENSION DAY

"You, Englishmen, who have no right to this kingdom of France, the King of Heaven orders and commands you through me, Jeanne the Maid, to leave your fortresses and return to your country. I write to you for the third and last time. I will write no further. Thus signed, Jhesus-Maria, Jeanne the Maid."

A subdued Gabriel dutifully wrote down everything as Joan spoke it. She had changed since yesterday. They both had. Gabriel had a newfound respect for those who had repeatedly, willingly, gone forward into such scenes of chaos and kept their heads even as they faced death and dealt it. Joan's radiance was still there, but it was different: tempered by a true awareness of the terrible duty she had been charged with.

As she took the pen and shakily, carefully wrote her name, Louis appeared at the door. As ever, the boy looked worried and perplexed.

"My lady," he said, "Madame Boucher has sent the red thread you asked for."

"Thank you, Louis!" she said, smiling warmly at him, and the boy relaxed.

When the ink had dried, Joan rolled up the parchment in a tight scroll. "Come with me. You too, Fleur."

Joan had hoped to have some new clothes made for Fleur, but there had been little time for such things, so Fleur simply wore some of Joan's masculine clothing. They were of a height, and though Fleur's slenderness was a contrast to Joan's healthy, muscular build, that only meant that the blonde girl needed to tighten her belts.

Now Fleur, who had been sitting patiently, hopped up eagerly, her eyes filled with adoration. Gabriel wondered if he, too, looked at Joan in such a manner, and was forced to admit that he probably did. It was no matter. There was no shame in adoring a messenger of God.

After their taste of battle, Pierre and Jean had opted to stay with their fellow soldiers instead of lodging with their sister. Thus it was only Gabriel and Fleur who followed Joan out from the gate, where the throng had, as always, gathered to catch a glimpse of the Maid. After the victory at the Saint-Loup boulevard, their fervor had only increased.

Again, they headed toward the Bridge of Orléans. Gabriel glanced back at Fleur. She was completely new to riding, but he was impressed to see that that she gamely kept up with them, although she clutched the reins so tightly her knuckles were white.

"Come to insult Glasdale again?" one of the soldiers grinned.

"Not today," Joan replied. She held up the parchment and thread. "Will one of your archers give me an arrow?"

Gabriel started laughing as he watched Joan roll the parchment tightly around the arrow shaft, and held it securely for her while she tied it on with the red thread.

She handed it back to the archer, climbed up the fortification to where she could see and yelled, "Glasdale! Read, this is news!"

The archer stepped up and, careful to aim it true and not injure anyone—he certainly did not want to be the one to accidentally start a fight when the Maid simply wanted to deliver a note—let the arrow fly.

"News from the Armagnac whore!" one of the English soldiers called back.

Gabriel heard a swift intake of breath beside him, and turned to see that Fleur had gone scarlet. She looked down, blinking back tears. Joan, too, looked upset for a moment, then she turned away.

"Many of those who say such things will be dead within days," Joan said. "Their breaths have numbers. Let them waste them on ugly words if they choose."

FRIDAY, 6 MAY, 1429

Joan, Gabriel, and Fleur left the church together after morning mass. Gabriel was used to the routine by now; confession, then mass, then whatever Joan's Voices called her to do. But Fleur was still awkward when entering a holy house. Even so, Gabriel thought her aptly named, for she was blossoming beneath Joan's kindness.

As they walked back to the Boucher's home, Gabriel noticed the governor of Orléans, the elderly, dignified old soldier Raoul de Gaucourt, arguing with La Hire. The two stepped back at Joan's approach, behaving almost like guilty children.

"Is the Bastard finally willing to attack the English today?" Joan asked them.

The mountain frowned and stayed silent. De Gaucourt said, "As it happens, Maid, I have been specifically asked by the Bastard to guard this gate from those who might be too eager to leap into battle. There will be no fighting today."

La Hire and Joan exchanged a long look. Then Joan turned back to de Gaucourt. "I am weary of not being included in decisions that affect the very city that God has sent me to help," she said coldly. "You, La Hire, and your generals were in your council, and I in mine, and you ought to believe that the counsel of my Lord will be done and will endure, and any other counsel will perish."

"But—this is the order of the man who is in charge of the army," began de Gaucourt.

"You are the governor of Orléans! Do you not wish to see her free? I think the soldiers should depart, along with any of those in town who wish to fight alongside them. They should make a charge against the Augustins boulevard, south of Les Tourelles, and you are an evil man to want to stop it!"

Something was happening to La Hire's scarred face. It took Gabriel a moment to realize the big man was trying not to laugh. "Like it or not," Joan warned the governor, "the soldiers will come, and they will obtain what they have obtained elsewhere."

She spun, addressing the crowd that always seemed to be gathered near her. Drawing her sword, she cried out to them, "My soldiers! You know what we should be doing! People of Orléans—will you join us!"

The now familiar swell of a response drowned out the governor's voice as he tried to plead for reason. Gabriel knew that the Assassins believed that Joan's appeal, her power to inspire others, was not sent from God, but was rather something that was in her blood.

He didn't know who was right, and he didn't care. All he knew was that she believed in her mission, and she would succeed in it.

The scene dissolved into the mists of the Memory Corridor. Simon was relieved when they did not next solidify into screaming soldiers, thundering hooves, and blood and mud, but into a painting of a dark night, the silhouettes of soldiers weary but alive, and the little flowers of campfires.

"You should return to Orléans to rest," Gabriel said to Joan as they sat by their own campfire. They were out of their armor, and Joan's squires were hard at work cleaning off the blood and mud with vinegar, sand from the riverbank, and vigor. "You have done so much."

Joan smiled at him and touched his cheek gently. Fire and calmness made a strange union in his body and his heart. "I will be here, with the men who have fought so bravely. We are so close, my Shadow; so close to victory."

"Because of you," Gabriel said.

"Because of God," she corrected, and he nodded, smiling. *God, and you, and your Precursor blood, and the beautiful Sword of Eden. How can anyone hope to stand against you?*

She sobered slightly, and said, "I need you to wake me early tomorrow, and keep close to me. Tomorrow, I will have much to do, more than I have ever done before." She paused, one hand creeping up to touch the pouch that hung over her heart for a moment, then trail along the skin of her neck, chest, and shoulder. "Tomorrow, blood will leave my body... here, perhaps; above my breast."

Cold fear seized him. "Did your Voices—"

"Jeanne?" The voice was sweet, feminine, and familiar. They both looked up to see Fleur smiling down at them. She carried an enormous basket weighed down with bottles of wine, loaves of bread, and what appeared to be cheese wrapped in cloth. An abruptly-silenced *squawk* from a nearby campfire informed them that there would be chicken shortly as well.

"Fleur!" Joan exclaimed, smiling. "What are you doing here?"

Fleur gestured to the other Orléanais who were bringing gifts to other campfires. "They are so grateful! They know you all fought so hard, all day, and you must be hungry and tired." She waved someone else over, who was bearing thick blankets. "We all came over in small boats, very quietly. Of course I had to come."

She sat down between them. Her eyes were bright, and she couldn't seem to stop smiling, even here, so close to a battleground. Glad as he was that Fleur had made the trip to help reprovision them safely, Gabriel was still reeling from Joan's words. *Blood will leave my body.* A bullet? A sword? An arrow? *What weapon is evil enough to harm my Jeanne?* he thought.

And... will she live?

As the mists closed in, Simon knew what Gabriel did not: that the boy would have wished that Joan had died in the forthcoming battle, rather than meet the end she would little over two years from now.

Les Tourelles? Victoria asked.

Simon took a breath. "Les Tourelles," he said.

CHAPTER
TWENTY-THREE

SATURDAY, 7 MAY, 1429
LES TOURELLES

Simon was grateful for the Memory Corridor's slow, methodical rendering of the world. It helped him to remember that while what he was bearing witness to was real—had happened, exactly as he saw it—it also was not *his* reality, *his* present.

Les Tourelles.

He had seen it from the back, across the gap of water where once parts of the Bridge of Orléans had connected it to the city. Now, the drawbridge in the front linking it to the southern shore of the Loire was all that kept it from being its own island tower.

And before it, at the other end of that drawbridge, loomed its massive boulevard. Dunois had called it one of the most imposing fortifications ever built, and he should know: he had ordered it constructed to augment the initial masonry fortifications, in order to protect Les

Tourelles from being taken by the besieging English. That plan had failed abysmally, and the English had fortified the boulevard even beyond its original construction. Dunois estimated that the boulevard and Les Tourelles contained between them almost a thousand English soldiers—and the majority of the English guns.

A palisade of sharpened tree trunks was the first line of defense, angled outward toward the enemy. On the other side of this wall of wood was a soft earthen ditch, ten feet wide and twenty feet deep. The softness of the ground was in itself a defense—anyone who fell in would struggle even harder to escape. The wall of the boulevard itself was sixty-five feet long and eighty-five feet wide and surrounded a sort of courtyard, where the English could, at their will, fire guns, arrows, small cannon balls, spears, and axes. The boulevard was connected to Les Tourelles by a drawbridge; beneath it was a moat, through which flowed Loire river water.

Simon knew that, despite their "council," all of the French generals had shown up to camp with Joan the previous night. Starting at eight that morning, the French had been firing artillery at the barriers, beginning with the palisades. The very earth now seemed to tremble from the sounds of the bombards disgorging their round metal contents at the wooden wall. Arrows set aflame hummed like furious hornets, and small, quick, orange tongues of fire licked hungrily as archers took aim into the boulevard courtyard. No horses, not here, not this time, only the brutal simplicity of armored soldiers on foot.

"Cease firing!" came the order from Dunois, barely audible over the thunder. "*Cease firing!*" The French artillery went silent.

"Forward, my brave soldiers!" came Joan's voice, clear and strong. Like the rest of them, she was on foot, her standard in her hand. "Fill the ditch so we may cross the boulevard!"

There was a great roar as the men surged forward now. Some of them shoved blasted pieces of wood down into the ten-foot ditch. What had once been a barrier to them would now be a bridge. Others, including Gabriel, raced forward clutching bundles of twigs prepared the night before for just this purpose. He tossed his pile into the gulf, and headed back for more.

Gabriel knew he was an exposed target. The only way into the courtyard area was over the boulevard wall, and the only way over the wall was to scale it with ladders. Wooden tree trunks and bundles of twigs were not the only things filling the ditch. Bodies lay where they had fallen, sprawled at unnatural angles, and Gabriel's gut twisted as he saw them. But there was no thought of hauling them out to a respectful place far from battle. They had fallen here, and the ditch needed to be filled, and they would serve the French cause in death as they had in life. Even as he turned back from another run, he heard one of the soldiers screaming in agony, begging for help. An archer took pity on the wounded man, and his screams stopped.

The ditch was almost filled now, with wood and men dead or dying, and a cry went up: "Scale! Scale!"

Cheering soldiers now clutched scaling ladders, planting them in the filled ditch and placing them against the sides of the boulevard. As Gabriel turned to help bring one to the wall, he realized that Joan had beaten them all it. She had been the first to place her scaling ladder against the boulevard, and was now almost halfway up. A cheer tore from his throat as she nimbly ascended.

It turned into a scream.

The world slowed to a crawl, growing deathly silent to him as Joan arched backward and then let go of the ladder, her arms spread out like wings, falling in full armor into the sea of men below her as if she had taken her Leap of Faith and failed.

"No!" cried Gabriel. "Jeanne! *Jeanne!*"

He dropped the ladder, careless of the arrows and gunfire, focused only on Joan as he fought through his own people to get to her side. He clutched her arm as he and two others rushed her to the rear of the battlefield. The arrow was embedded at an angle, a good six inches into her upper chest on the right hand side, halfway between her collarbone and her shoulder.

Tomorrow, blood will leave my body... here, perhaps; above my breast....

They carried her as carefully as possible, but even so the jouncing caused her face to contort in pain and she shrieked. The sound almost tore out Gabriel's heart.

"My Voices," she said, "they... they did not say how much it would *hurt*...." She sobbed, tears making trails through the dirt and sweat on her beautiful face. There was no light shining from her, not now, and a terrible fear seized Gabriel.

They laid her down in the grass. "Stay still, Jeanne," Gabriel urged.

"This is not good," murmured La Hire. God alone knew where he had come from; he had been directing the flank on the left.

"I have a charm," one of the soldiers said. "Here—press it against the wound, it will—"

"No!" Joan's voice was surprisingly strong. "I would rather die than use something against the will of God!"

"Jeanne," Gabriel said, and her bloodshot eyes moved slowly to meet his gaze, "Jeanne... you're not going to die. God won't let you. You haven't lifted the siege."

"But you will," she said, smiling softly.

No, no... "But what about the king? You have to take him to Reims!" Gabriel looked up to see La Hire looking at him, almost pleading with him, to convince Joan to stay with them.

Joan closed her eyes for an awful moment. Then they snapped open. She clenched her teeth and growled, low and deep, then reached up her left hand, grasped the arrow, and began to pull it out herself. Her face suddenly grew luminous, even as she screamed in startlement at the depth of the agony as the point ripped more muscle and skin on its way out and Joan's blood started pumping freely.

God would not take her. She wouldn't die. Not today.

The scene began to swirl and fade, enveloped by the churning grayness of the Memory Corridor.

You all right?

He nodded and licked his lips. "I know she didn't die," he said.

But Gabriel hadn't known. *Do you need a break?*

"No," he said. "Let's push on." He had traveled so far with Joan, he had to witness this legendary military victory, the triumph the city of Orléans celebrated to this day with a ten-day festival in her honor.

The mists again solidified. They again revealed Les Tourelles, but this time, there was no battle taking place. "I am sorry, Jeanne," the Bastard was saying. "The men are so tired and hungry."

Joan was again in her armor, which covered her bandaged chest. She was pale and drawn, but otherwise, one would never have known she was wounded. "I understand," she said, surprising the generals, who exchanged glances. "I will return shortly."

She rose and went off into the gathering dusk, toward what remained of a neglected vineyard. Gabriel got to his feet to accompany her, but she lifted a hand and passed him her standard. "Not this time," she said, and walked away into the lengthening shadows.

He watched her, then went to join the generals. The mood was somber, and they ate and drank in silence. Fighting had been going on since early morning. Cannons had done damage to some parts of the boulevard, but the English had fought with heart as well. Ladder upon ladder had been laid against the walls, but the English had shoved them and the soldiers climbing them off. Or else, they waited until the intruders were nearly at the top, and attacked with lances and polearms, axes and hammers.

Morale flagged during the hours Joan had spent away from the battle due to her injury. The men were now exhausted, Gabriel among them, and dusk was approaching.

The Bastard looked at La Hire, de Rais, and Gabriel, then said quietly, "It will soon be dark. We have to retreat. I'll send a signal to the Orléanais that they should halt as well."

"Orléanais?" Gabriel asked.

De Rais shot him one of his manic grins. "We don't fight alone, Laxart," he said. "We have other plans afoot. There are attacks being prepared from other sides of Les Tourelles."

Still confused, Gabriel repeated, "Other *sides*?" From the bridge, he understood, but from where else?

"You'll see," de Rais said. "It will be beautiful!"

"We will lose all the ground we have gained today!" La Hire argued.

"Some, but not all," Dunois insisted. "But without Jeanne, the men—"

"The men will not need to be without Jeanne." They turned to see her approach. Although there were hollows around her eyes from the pain she endured, her face was alight and her lips curved in a soft smile. "She is here, and she is with them, and God is with all of us."

Without waiting for a response, she took her standard from Gabriel, turned, and began striding, alone, toward the boulevard.

"Jeanne, wait!" cried the Bastard. But around them, the soldiers were already scrambling to don the few pieces of armor they had permitted themselves to remove in order to eat. There was energy in the air again, almost crackling, like hints of lightning, and Gabriel too put on his gloves and helm and turned to follow the Maid.

It was the golden hour right before twilight, when the sun was low on the horizon and bathed everything as if in the light of God itself, softening the ugliness of the remains of battle. But it could not gentle the boulevard. Dotted with English soldiers, it was still massive, still ominous.

And Joan the Maid stood in front of it.

She had planted her standard, grasping it with one hand. In the other, she held the Sword of Eden. It looked to be catching the sunlight, except the sun had never struck earthly metal with such dazzling brilliance.

"Glasdale!" Joan shouted. Her voice seemed to reverberate inside Gabriel's chest, and he put his hand to it for a moment. He couldn't tear his eyes from the image of the young woman, straight as the standard she bore, bright as the sword she lifted. "Glasdale, give in! Give in to the King of Heaven! You, who called me a whore—I have great pity for you and your men's souls. Yield, or go to God this day!"

There was no jeering this time. The English soldiers stared, shocked. Doubtless, they had thought the Armagnac whore slain by the arrow, but here she was, as if she had never been wounded, asking—practically begging—them to yield.

But it was too late.

A terrible sound rent the evening air: a tremendous explosion mingled with the terrified screams of the injured and the dying. Black smoke and orange flame billowed upward, from behind the boulevard.

Joan whirled, her face brighter than the fire. "The people of Orléans have crossed the bridge to fight with us! Fire burns in Les Tourelles! Follow me!"

She sheathed the sword, planted the standard firmly in the sandy soil of the riverbank, and ran forward. Gabriel shouted with joy and hastened to place a ladder against the wall himself. This time, as the soldiers climbed, they faced no resistance. The English in the boulevard courtyard were too busy trying to stay alive. He cleared the top and slid down to behold absolute chaos.

The drawbridge between Les Tourelles and the boulevard was gone. The moat below was filled with burning debris, splinters of wood, and drowning Englishmen, their heavy armor donned as protection now dooming them. Even so, rather than be burned alive, soldiers were shucking what armor they could and leaping into the water. Those lucky enough to have been in the boulevard courtyard during the explosion found themselves with a wall of fire to their back and a flood of French soldiers slipping over the wall in ever-increasing numbers.

"We surrender!" cried the English in their thick and ugly accents, dropping their weapons and lifting their hands. "We surrender!"

And from the top of the boulevard wall, that wall that had appeared to be so impregnable mere hours earlier, Joan the Maid shouted, "Soldiers of France! *This city is ours!*"

***

Later, much later, Gabriel and Joan returned to the Boucher house. There, Joan had her injury cleaned and rebandaged in soft linen, and she and her retinue dined on roast beef soaked in wine. Joan's two heralds feasted alongside her; they had been freed from Les Tourelles, along with many other French prisoners.

Gabriel had learned that while the army was attacking Les Tourelles from the boulevard, the courageous people of Orléans had been laying a primitive walkway of narrow boards and gutter pipe between the broken bridge and the north side of Les Tourelles. Some of the horrified English swore they had seen Saint Michael and a host of angels approaching, but when asked, Joan had casually replied that no, Saint Michael had not made an appearance, though it was certainly clear that God was with them.

It was on Joan's orders that others had loaded up a fire barge and sent it beneath the drawbridge, where it had exploded into a fiery hell for the English. William Glasdale had been on the drawbridge, and had been among those who had sunk to their deaths, weighted down by their own armor, just as Joan had warned.

While there had been much cheering—Joan herself had crossed into Orléans that night over the makeshift bridge—there was also death, and fire, and the smell of burned bodies, and the screaming of men in torment silenced only by quick deaths by sword or arrow.

Gabriel caught Joan in a moment of somberness similar to his own. She picked at her meal, then, feeling his gaze, looked up at him. Her face, drawn and tired, softened. Even a little of her light came into it.

"War is a cruel thing, even when fought for God," she said quietly. "My heart is heavy with sorrow for all those who died today. If only they had yielded, but..." Her voice trailed off. "We have won Les Tourelles, but the siege is not yet lifted. We will see what is in store for us on the morrow.

Joan looked like an ordinary girl when she slept.

Her face was neither luminous nor drawn in righteous anger, not laughing, or weeping for the fallen. Just a girl, appearing younger than her seventeen or so years, sleeping.

Yesterday had been a great victory, but it had drained Joan on many levels, and as Gabriel regarded her for a moment, he was loath to wake her. *One day,* he thought, *God will ask no more of you, and you can be this girl again. No Sword of Eden, no standard, no armor or battle cries or blood. Just you.*

"Jeanne," he said, gently, "the English are on the move."

They had been spotted a few moments ago, seemingly all of them, flowing in marching formation from the various boulevards that were still unassailed by the French.

She awoke instantly, her blue eyes flying open, calm and alert and yet, as always, subtly shocking Gabriel with their pure intensity and rich sapphire hue. Beside her, Fleur murmured and blinked sleepily.

"Where?" Joan demanded. He told her. She called for her squires and she and Gabriel armored up quickly.

Fleur stood by, a helpless expression on her pretty features as she regarded both of them with concern, twisting her fingers. "I am useless," she murmured. "If only I could face the danger with you!" Then, impulsively, she kissed each one of them on the cheek. "I know God will be with you both," was all she said.

They crossed the Bridge of Orléans on foot. When they entered the general's tent on the other side of the Loire, they found the Bastard, La Hire, Gilles de Rais and the others deep in conversation. "What is going on?" Joan demanded.

"Damned if we know," La Hire said.

"Don't swear," Joan said, but almost absently. Her blue eyes were on Dunois.

"They're lining up to the west," Dunois said. "It could be they're planning one massive attack... all of them against all of us."

Both sides had lost a lot of men over the past two days, Gabriel knew. A single assault would kill hundreds more. And the English just might win.

"It is Sunday," Joan said. "I say, we will not be the first to attack."

"What?" exclaimed de Rais. "If we went after them now—"

"No!" snapped Joan. "Bastard—you said they are marching in formation?"

At that moment, one of Dunois's men poked his head in the tent. "My lord," he said, "they are here, but they're not attacking."

As one, the generals, Joan, and Gabriel rushed out of the tent to see for themselves. The knight had spoken the truth. There they were, close enough to make out individual faces, lining up to face their adversary as more and more soldiers assembled to swell their number.

"Battle formation," La Hire murmured, and of all of them, La Hire would know it when he saw it.

"Let us greet them in the same way," Joan said. "Bastard, line the men up. Exactly as the English are. All of us. We will not make the first move, but tell your men this: If we are attacked by the English on a Sunday, we will fight with God's blessing. And if the English choose to leave, they may go with the same."

It was eerie, Gabriel thought, to see so many of the enemy so close, and yet so still. His heart was racing as he mounted up and trotted out to the open field beside Joan. They sat atop their restless horses as the rest of the French army and the Orléanais militia fell in line behind them.

For almost an hour they waited, the only sound the creak of armor and the stamp of horses' feet. Then one of the English leaders broke formation, easing his horse into a walk and moving forward.

"It's Talbot," murmured Dunois, gathering the reins to head out to meet the English commander.

"No, Bastard," Joan said. "I will go." She looked at Gabriel and shook her head. Even he was not to accompany her, it would seem. Agonized, he nodded, watching with his heart in his mouth as she rode out alone to meet the near-legendary English general.

Slowly but deliberately, John Talbot unsheathed his sword, but did not lift it. Gabriel could sense the sudden leap in tension among the French soldiers, and the English clattered to active attention. Should their commander order it, they would be ready to charge the French army in one great line.

But oddly, Gabriel was not worried. Instead, he watched as Joan responded in kind—drawing the Sword of Eden. It blazed to brilliant life, its shape obscured by the power of its own aura, almost as if Joan held a little sun. Behind him, he could hear soft exhalations, as the French army released its tension, and he saw the English army shift uneasily. He wondered if Talbot could *see* Joan, could see how this sword shone for her.

If he did, Talbot resisted for several long minutes. Then, slowly, he nodded, and sheathed his sword. The commander raised his empty hand and kicked his horse, wheeling it roughly about and cantering back to the English line.

They turned, not quite as one but close enough, and began to trudge away from the battlefield.

Joan now turned her horse so that she faced her troops. Her face shone nearly as bright as the sword she still held, still not lifting it for concern some would take it as a signal to attack. She sheathed it and instead took her banner, grasping it as she galloped to and fro before her army, before the Orléans militia, who raised their voices in cheers to God and the Maid of Orléans.

The siege had been going on for almost seven months.

Joan, the Maid, had ended it in ten days.

CHAPTER
TWENTY-FOUR

How are you doing? Victoria's voice sounded so concerned.

Simon didn't know how much longer he could keep up the façade that everything was fine between them. Fortunately, Victoria seemed to think it was Animus-related battle fatigue, and that worked fine for him. "I think I'd like to take a break."

I think that's the first time I've heard you ask for one.

"Well, there's a first time for everything," he said.

It's lunchtime, would you like to get something to eat? This is a big moment for Joan and Gabriel—and Simon Hathaway.

He forced a chuckle. "I think I'll just get something and go back to my office for a bit. Streamlining those notes for you, as we discussed."

She lifted the helmet off. "I think that's very wise of you, Simon," she said. "Do you have any theories about how Joan is using the sword so far?"

"Not really, not yet," he said. "We can discuss that later, after I've had some time to focus."

Victoria helped him unfasten the bindings and smiled a little as she did so. "I feel a little bit like I'm your squire, getting you in and out of your Animus armor."

"You're getting very good at it, I must say, though I haven't gotten this as bloody as Gabriel has gotten his armor."

It was meant as a joke, but as soon as the words left his mouth Simon wished them back. He knew how zealous the Templars were in pursuit of what they considered the goals of the Order. He wasn't sure what the hell he'd done—or was about to do—to warrant the present amount of scrutiny, but if he came down on the wrong side of things, his own bloodshed was a very real possibility.

He thought back to his initiation ritual, about how, well, charming he'd found it; quaint, almost, with its remarkable attention to historic authenticity. He shouldn't have. It was real, it was an oath, and he wasn't safely enveloped in his happy bubble of theoretical research.

Simon stepped off the Animus platform and strode toward the display case atop which the open sword box rested. He gazed at it, willing it to give up its secrets.

"Simon?"

"Hm?"

"... you know I'm on your side in this, right?"

He almost broke down and demanded an explanation right then. Almost. Because he really, truly, did want to believe her, but he also really, truly believed Anaya, whom he'd known much longer. All he could hope was that somehow Victoria wasn't an active part of... whatever was going on.

Nonchalantly, he closed the latches on the box and picked it up. "I'll take this with me to the office. If I happen across something I might have missed regarding it, I'll have it right to hand." He patted the box and started to walk out of the room.

"Simon, I don't think you're supposed to be doing that," Victoria said, somewhat worriedly.

He paused and turned to look at her. "Victoria, I'm the head of

Historical Research. I'm *completely* supposed to be doing this. What, did you think I'd head straight to Sotheby's or the British Museum? I'll bring it back tomorrow." He gave her a reassuring smile and a perfectly casual jerk of his head in the direction of the lift.

As he strode into his office, carrying the priceless Sword of Eden as if it was a particularly elaborate box of long-stemmed roses, Simon realized something.

He was done with being afraid.

He, Simon Hathaway, was the child and grand-child of high-ranking Templars. He was a Legacy. He had been a Master Templar for several years before being selected as one of the nine—*nine!*—members of the elite Inner Sanctum. It was time Simon started acting like it. What good was it to be in the Inner Sanctum if he was going to be spied upon? It was like the line from George Orwell's *Animal Farm: Some animals are more equal than others.*

Something about what he was doing had put someone in the Templar Order—perhaps Rikkin, perhaps someone Rikkin answered to—on high alert. It was more than the sword, because Simon had already pledged to do everything he could to render it functional again. It was more than information about the Assassins, because finding out things like the identities of lost Mentors was precisely what he was supposed to be doing.

No. It was something else. Something Rikkin, or whoever he was commanding, or whoever was commanding him, didn't want him to find out—or did, and wanted to beat Simon to the punch. It was major, and it was dangerous, and Simon was no longer going to be cowed by it.

Let them bug his office, or his car, or Temp's. Let them track his computer and his phone. Let them swap out actual employees for Templar field agents, or worse. It didn't matter. Simon had his books, he had his brain, and for the time being at least, he had access to the Animus.

And he was going to make the most of it.

Rikkin stretched out his legs in the back seat of the Rolls, absently watching London zip past as he spoke on the phone with his daughter, Sofia, who was preparing for his arrival in Madrid in a few days. He was interrupted in mid-sentence by the chime that indicated an incoming text. He lifted it from his ear, saw who had sent it, told Sofia, "I'll call you back," and hung up.

A smile curved his thin lips as he read Bibeau's message: *O taken. Seen S in action.*

"Finally," he murmured to himself as he texted back, *When lost?*

Unknown yet.

How soon?

Unknown.

The smile melted away. *Get where you can talk,* Rikkin texted. He called Sofia back and wrapped up the call. Afterwards, he glanced out the windows as the Phantom hummed down the streets. The sky had started to spit cold, hard drops, but people were still outside. They hunched under what seemed to be regulation black umbrellas, stole smokes under whatever overhang they could find, argued over who had been first in line for the coveted taxis. Nearly every face—male, female, old, young—wore an expression of anger, fear, or cow-like blankness.

"Behold the 'people,'" Rikkin muttered. These were the wretches the Assassins cared so much for. But these individuals and their petty needs meant nothing to him, and in his opinion should mean nothing to the Templar Order, which had sacrificed and endured so very much for an ideal of humanity that was far nobler than what these pathetic creatures represented.

A muscle in his jaw worked as he tapped on his pad, calling up some information. His dark eyes flickered over what came up, and his lips pressed together in a thoughtful frown.

Well, well, Rikkin thought. *We're going to need to tread very carefully going forward. Very carefully indeed.*

His phone chimed: Victoria, sounding the "all clear" to talk. "What the hell," he said when she answered, pausing briefly between the words to emphasize them, "did you mean by 'unknown'?"

"Just exactly that. Mr. Hathaway is insistent that we uncover events chronologically," she replied. "He's afraid we might not get the whole picture. I've only just convinced him not to play out every single simulation from start to finish."

"Professor Hathaway is not watching a film at the cinema," he said, his voice a low purr. "Do you really mean to tell me the reason you are not now briefing me on a Sword of Eden is because a stuffed shirt of a historian wants to *keep things in order*?"

"I did suggest going forward, but the entire premise of his suggested change to the division is—"

"I know what the bloody premise is, he expounded on it quite thoroughly," Rikkin snapped. He reined himself in. "Doctor," he said in a gentler tone, "why do you think I asked you to report to me privately?"

"Frankly, sir, I don't know why you asked," she said. "There's nothing about Hathaway to indicate that he is anything other than exactly what he appears to be—a loyal Templar, and the descendant of loyal Templars. A brilliant researcher and a dedicated historian who wants to maximize the potential of his department. And if I may speak freely, Mr. Rikkin, in a handful of days I think he's done a superb job of justifying his proposal. We've got the sword. We have several instances of it in action. We've found not one but two individuals with remarkable concentrations of Precursor DNA. We've uncovered highly placed Assassins, including a hitherto-unknown Mentor, and we've gotten a glimpse of graffiti carved by de Molay himself before time and who knows what or who else damaged it. We'll keep seeing the sword, we'll pay close attention to how Joan manipulates it, and we'll find out where it's lost and how it was damaged."

Rikkin was silent for so long that Victoria said uncertainly, "Sir?"

"There was fallout, you know," he said quietly.

"Fallout?"

"Around poor Fraser."

"... yes, sir. I was aware of that."

"You gave Fraser information to leak to the Assassins."

Now it was her turn to go quiet. "I did," she said at last. "And I will remind you that at the time, I knew nothing about the true nature of the conflict—or the goals of the Templar Order. I had only just learned that the two existed."

Rikkin knew this, of course. Like the vast majority of employees at Abstergo—indeed, in all the company's divisions—Victoria Bibeau had initially been as ignorant of the Order as these pathetic fools who trudged through puddles outside the car; whose lives existed of little other than sleeping, drinking, working, and sporadically trying to bury their mediocrity in fleeting pleasure. He didn't care; Bibeau's point was irrelevant.

"We were forced to terminate Aidan St. Claire because of this mess. We came close to terminating *you*. Did you know that?"

He heard a slight intake of breath on the other end. *Ah*, he thought, *no, she didn't know that*. "You had many friends over in Abstergo Entertainment who supported you, and you have since proven your loyalty to us. We're glad we got to you before the Assassins did. We'd hate to see you on their team."

"I do believe that both groups want what is best for humanity," she said. That startled him.

"Really?" The single word was pregnant with warning.

"Yes. I simply believe the Assassin approach is wrong."

Rikkin couldn't have hoped for a better segue. "But does our friend Professor Hathaway agree with you about that?"

Hathaway did, of course. The laconic researcher had never given anyone a moment's doubt. He loved order and ritual and tidiness. Hathaway had been spared the necessity of sullying his hands with some of the more unsavory aspects of Templar business, happily ensconced in his ivory tower while others, such as Berg's Sigma team or even deeper, darker branches of the Templar Order, went about clearing the garden of the world from weeds like the Assassins, and turncoats, and heretics who wanted to upend the Order.

But Rikkin had miscalculated. Far from unnerving Bibeau, the veiled accusation made her bristle audibly. "Mr. Rikkin, there are many things in this world I'm not good at. But I *am* good at reading my patients. Doubtless that's one reason you, ah... kept me on. I am interacting with him as a subject, not a colleague."

"He doesn't know that, does he?"

"He knows I examined his profile, and that I'm monitoring him carefully during his time in the Animus and afterwards."

"And yet, you are here, talking to me." He had her now, and he closed in for the kill. "What about doctor-patient confidentiality, Doctor? No?"

"You asked me to—"

"Report on his progress, with your thoughts. As a co-worker. And you did, and I, and the Order, are grateful. You can't have it both ways, Dr. Bibeau."

There was silence on the other end. He waited. Rikkin understood the power of patience. Then, quietly, Bibeau said, "I believe in what the Templar Order stands for. I also believe in what Hathaway wants to do. I believe he is of sound mind and good heart, and is approaching this simulation with a sincere desire to serve the Order and to learn the truth. Surely you cannot say those two ideals are in opposition. Can you, Mr. Rikkin?"

"Truth," he said quietly, "like beauty, is in the eye of the beholder."

"I took the oath," Bibeau said. "I swore to uphold the principles of our Order and all that for which we stand. To never share our secrets, or divulge the true nature of our Order, and to do so from now until death—whatever the cost." Her voice was sharp with contained outrage. "So did Simon. And neither of us has broken that oath. I give you my word that I will come to you the moment I feel that he is, in any way, in violation of it, and you are welcome to do as you see fit. Until then, unless you want me to step aside, allow me to do my job. *Sir.*"

The usage of Hathaway's first name did not escape Rikkin. He considered. "I want to know how to repair the sword. I want it functional again. Hathaway cannot be allowed to chase wild geese. I hope I have made myself abundantly clear on this. We'll have another one of these pleasant chats once you have anything more to report."

"Yes, sir."

He ended the call and leaned back in the seat. There was no greatness here, on the London Streets; hardly any in Parliament, or the arts. Look where the great experiment in democracy was leading the world. And this was the sort of world that the Assassins kept yipping that they wanted. A solid hand was needed to guide humanity. The hand of the Templar Order. As ever, money and power dominated, but nowadays it was rare that one possessed these and vision as well.

The founders of Abstergo did. The Grand Masters of eras past did. Jacques de Molay let his flesh be consumed by fire for the Order.

The words of the Templar oath went through his head: *Do you swear to uphold the principles of our Order and all that for which we stand?*

As Shakespeare said, he thought, *"Aye... there's the rub."*

He typed a code on his phone and waited for a response.

Omega standing by.

Update.

Phase 2 of Omega-104 nearing completion. Suggest termination and replacement of current position occupant.

Rikkin hesitated. It would permanently solve a problem... but could draw unnecessary attention. *Negative. Relocation sufficient.*

Acknowledged. Phase 1 of Omega-105 complete. Awaiting instructions.

Initiate Phase 2. Rikkin paused, thinking. He didn't have time for this. *Double Epsilon if absolutely necessary per discussed parameters.*

Acknowledged.

The texts disappeared. Rikkin sighed and tapped the phone against his knee thoughtfully.

Double epsilon. EE.

Eliminate and Erase.

He hoped Simon would not make one too many missteps.

CHAPTER
TWENTY-FIVE

Simon ordered the never-disappointing Temp's Hard @ Work basket and settled down with his books. Despite the amount of tea he imbibed and a genuine fascination with the subject he was researching, his poor night of sleep caught up with him and he nodded off. The brief rest was hardly helpful; he again was bombarded by images of Jacques de Molay, this time shouting his curse upon his murderers as he burned to death.

He bolted upright, his heart racing. Of course, he reasoned. Joan of Arc was burned as a heretic, de Molay was martyred as one, and the two had collided, if a century apart, at Coudray. It was natural he would be thinking of the great Templar leader, even if not consciously, as each simulation in the Animus took Simon closer to witnessing Joan's death in an identical fashion.

The reminder of de Molay, though, did make Simon recall that he hadn't heard back from Cryptology on the graffiti. He knew that Victoria had translated the Latin phrases they'd run across before she'd sent the simulation over—there was, after all, an app for that—but he'd been so excited about discovering the sword, and so tired, he'd forgotten to ask what she'd come up with. He removed his specs, rubbed his eyes, rose, stretched, and said aloud to his computer, "Cryptology."

He perched on his desk as the monitor went from its multicolored Abstergo logo to Zach Morgenstern's kindly visage. "Professor Morgenstern, good to see you."

"Ah, hello Professor Hathaway! Congratulations on your promotion! What can I do for you?"

The friendly greeting took Simon aback. "Actually, I was wondering how you were coming along on the de Molay graffiti from Chinon. We sent that round to you a couple of days ago."

The professor's wrinkled, affable face wrinkled further. "I'm not sure what you mean. Of course we all *know* about the graffiti. Has a simulation turned up new information about it?"

Simon went cold. "You haven't heard from Dr. Bibeau?"

"We've not heard anything for a few days, not from this Bibeau or anyone. Do you want me to follow up?"

"No, no, that's all right. I'll chat with her myself. She may want to study it further. I'm sure we'll be in touch. Cheers." He couldn't end the video call fast enough.

Simon was completely flummoxed. The de Molay graffiti was a throwaway. A happy chance encounter that likely would make the day of fellows like Morgenstern—and, truth be told, like himself—who lived for fresh revelations about ancient things, but it wouldn't have any real impact on anything. Therefore, there was no reason for Victoria to have felt it was urgent to pass along the information.

Then again... there was no reason for her *not* to have sent it.

He was suddenly acutely aware that he might be being watched. Calmly he returned to his comfortable leather chair and picked up one of the books on Chinon. He thumbed through it, pausing at different places, then flipping as if by chance to the graffiti.

One thing he had discovered about his time in the Animus was that the memories of his ancestor were almost clearer to him than his own. No doubt Victoria had a theory about it—that it was because everything was new and different, and therefore the subject paid more attention overall or some such thing—but they were crisp and vivid. Gabriel had been asked to focus on the graffiti, and he had done so. Simon hadn't paid much attention at the time, but the dream had stirred the pot.

Some things had been worn away by time—or perhaps by other parties with more immediate interests. But there was one thing that drew his eye and held it. It was perhaps the most distinctive piece of the whole lot; the profile of, presumably, a Templar gazing at a sun that looked more like an inverted teardrop—or raindrop, or drop of blood, or perhaps even a shield; Simon wasn't sure what it was meant to represent. The sun image Gabriel had seen was as two-dimensional as the other drawings; an outline, at most a bas relief, nothing more.

This one—the one photographed in the twentieth century—was hollow. He couldn't tell from the image how deep it was, but someone had spent an awful lot of time chiseling out a concavity in the stone wall of the dungeon—only to fill it back in.

Fill it back in... or overlay a veneer to conceal it?

Had something been placed in this little hidey-hole seven hundred years ago by a Templar—possibly de Molay himself—for the right person to discover? A key, a gem, a message?

A Piece of Eden?

Something else was wrong, too. He realized that one of the two phrases that Gabriel saw on the wall did not appear in the photo. It had been erased.

Simon closed the book and reached for his burner phone. It was the exact model Abstergo had issued him, so it wouldn't arouse immediate suspicion if he was being watched.

He quickly selected and installed a translation app, and typed in the Latin phrase that had surfaced in his dreams last night; the one that was no longer visible: *Si cor valet, non frangit.*

The English translation appeared: *If the heart is strong, it will not break.*

Simon didn't dare take this to Morgenstern. If the man wasn't part of this... this *conspiracy*, he supposed he needed to call it, then Simon didn't want to involve him. And if he was....

His Abstergo-issued phone, tucked away in his pocket, vibrated. Simon did not react, simply inserted the burner phone into the same pocket, rose, and sipped at his tea before reaching for the Abstergo phone, as if it had just now gone off.

It was Victoria. *How are you feeling?*

Anxious and angry and wondering what the hell is going on, he thought bitterly, but texted, *Better with a bellyful of Scotch eggs and muffins. Sending you a list, we can meet in the Animus Room and discuss in 20.*

How do you stay so fit eating like this?

Good genes, he replied. As he tucked the phone away again and slid behind the desk, Simon's gaze fell on the sword. Good genes, indeed. He began to type.

He had the sword in the case tucked under his arm as he and Victoria descended the lift. "I think this an excellent idea and a good use of our time," she was saying, peering at the list he'd sent her. "It seemed to work very well earlier, with the French-English standoff. I wouldn't have thought the sword would play any part in that, but it clearly played a very large role."

"Accounts seem to agree that she never took a life, and also that she never used it to press an attack," Simon said.

"Well, unless you count chasing prostitutes," Victoria said, and grinned.

Simon faked amusement. "Well, yes," he said. "They do say, however, she used it in a defensive capacity. When she was attacked, she did fight back."

"We've not seen that yet," Victoria said. "Something else to add to the mix. I do wish we had more time, but we've certainly accomplished a lot nonetheless."

Simon thought, with a surge of anger, how much more they could have accomplished had they been true partners. He almost wished Anaya hadn't told him, but he knew that ignorance, for a Templar, was more likely to be deadly than blissful.

"We still have a long way to go," he said briskly. "And as Joan said, better now than tomorrow. Now... after her astonishing victory at Orléans, the Dauphin was obviously pleased. So when there was a meeting of his generals and council about what the next step should be, he listened to Joan. She was determined to get him to Reims for a proper coronation, so instead of marching on, say, Paris or Normandy, the army began clearing the path for the King to travel safely to Reims. Alençon was appointed head of the Loire campaign, but honestly, he always yielded to Joan."

They stepped out of the lift and continued talking as they entered the Animus Room. Simon carefully placed the sword box down, and stepped over to the platform.

"It sounds like it was just one victory after the other," Victoria said as she helped strap him into the Animus.

"Historians have often marveled at it," Simon agreed. "We cannot underestimate the importance of morale—or the lack of it. The French, obviously, were given hope. The English heard stories about this magical, undefeatable woman performing miracles left, right, and center. One poor chap chronicles how despondent the English troops were once word of Orléans circulated. Do you remember Fastolf?"

By this time, the helmet was settled on Simon's head, and Victoria's voice came to him as the Memory Corridor's mists appeared.

Wasn't he the one coming with reinforcements to Orléans? The one Joan was afraid she had missed the chance to fight by oversleeping?

"That's the fellow. She'd get to fight him eventually. He dragged his feet and took his time reaching the Loire—largely because his army was so thoroughly demoralized. Joan may not have won the Hundred Years' War for the French, but she certainly turned the tide.

The Loire campaign consisted of five battles—all French victories. Let's find out what our algorithm wants us to see."

SATURDAY, 11 JUNE, 1429
OUTSKIRTS OF JARGEAU

It was good, Gabriel thought, to be in armor again. For nearly a month, the king and his councilors had taken their time deciding what to do next. Finally, though, many of those who had stood with Joan as she pushed and pushed and finally lifted the siege of Orléans were gathered together in the field once more. Among their number were both of Joan's brothers, Gilles de Rais, La Hire, and the Bastard of Orléans. This time, though, the leader of the army was the Duke of Alençon, not the Bastard, and Joan was well content.

Fleur, too, had insisted on accompanying them. Joan and Gabriel both had protested, but the fair-haired girl displayed a stubbornness similar to that of the girl she so admired.

"What will I do without you?" she had challenged. "None of the noble-born women would wish a camp follower to befriend their daughters. They are kind to me only because of you, Jeanne, and once you are gone, I know that I will be gone too. All I wish is to be near you and your light. Ask your Voices." Joan had done so—and Fleur had come.

They were about an hour east of the walled city of Jargeau, discussing strategy in the duke's tent, all eyes on the map spread out on the table before them.

"We are now on the other side of things," Alençon said. "Before, it was the English who had to determine how to take a fortified city."

"The English have a goodly number of weapons and gunpowder," said the Bastard. "We don't have figures for their troops, but there are a considerable lot of them."

Joan had been listening, growing more annoyed by the moment as she saw the generals hesitating. "We came to take the city," she said, "did we not?"

The Bastard turned to her. "We did, but it's a question of tactics," he said. "We may want to consider a more indirect approach, at least until we have a better idea of their numbers and weaponry."

Joan blew out a breath in exasperation. "You should not fear their numbers, whatever they may be, or any difficulty in attacking these Englishmen." One hand had fallen to the hilt of her sword, the other had crept up over her heart. Her face began to shine with her certainty, and the expressions of the other generals relaxed somewhat.

"Let us compromise," said Alençon. "We will begin by clearing the suburbs. We will give them the option of yielding to us. And once we are settled in, *then* we can attack the city."

CHAPTER TWENTY-SIX

The mists formed the walls of Jargeau, looking dramatically different from how they had appeared the day before. Hours of French bombardment had done damage, and an entire tower had slid completely off.

They had finally started to make way in the assault. A single particularly large English soldier, utilizing what seemed like a veritable armory of weapons, had made it hell for the attackers by repeatedly knocking over ladders—and the French soldiers on them—or dropping heavy balls of iron down upon them. When he had been taken out with a precise shot from one of the culverins from Orléans, the French were finally able to press the attack and gain ground.

Shouting incoherently, Gabriel charged the nearest soldier, bringing his sword up in front of him to block the other's blow, using his momentum to get his enemy off-balance and down on the ground. The soldier had caught Gabriel's sword with his own, though, and was pushing back strongly even as he struck the earth. For a moment his left arm was raised, exposing the unarmored juncture of arm and torso. Gabriel reached for the dagger at his waist, pulled it out, and jabbed it down.

Blood spurted as he tugged it free. Panting, he got to his feet and looked for Joan. She was in the middle of it, as always, never asking her soldiers to face danger she herself would not. His heart lifted when he saw her, riding among the men, her standard billowing. She drew the sword, and suddenly Gabriel's breathing came easier, and his arms felt stronger. *We cannot be defeated, not when we have her and the sword.*

Suddenly she paused, pulling her horse up to a full stop, and looked around until she found Gabriel. "Gabriel!" she cried. "Move away from there! Hurry, or that machine will kill you!" She pointed up, at a soldier firing a small bombard from atop the wall. The man was focusing his attack elsewhere, Gabriel turned and ran as fast as he could go away from the wall, to where Joan sat astride her impatient charger. She reached down to touch him, as if to make sure he was still well and whole, and she smiled in relief. Then she was gone, cantering off, toward another section of the wall. Gabriel ran after her, and at that moment, he heard a loud *boom*.

It was but one of many desperately awful sounds of the battle, but this one made him look back to where he had been standing.

Another French soldier had not heard Joan's warning, and now lay in the ditch. Where his head had once been was a puddle of crimson mud.

Gabriel stumbled backward, trembling, crossed himself, then took off after Joan.

She had reached the wall now, and was already halfway up a scaling ladder propped against it. As he watched, he saw her pause. Her right hand went to her left hip, reaching for her sword. She turned around, not drawing it yet, to speak to the attacking Frenchmen, but he was too far away and could not hear her over the cacophony. Movement caught his eye, and Gabriel froze.

One of the English atop the wall grasped a large stone in both hands. As Gabriel watched, unable to tear his eyes from the scene, the soldier lifted the stone—

—and hurled it down upon an unsuspecting Joan.

"Jeanne!"

Gabriel still could not move, still could not stop it, and her words thundered through his head: *I have but a year, little more—*

The sword came free of the scabbard and all but exploded with light. The stone stuck Joan's helmet at that precise instant. Squinting against the unearthly radiance, Gabriel could barely make out the image of the helmet cracking in a precise, perfect line; the two halves tumbling to the ground, along with the stone, along with Joan, along with the sword that fell from her hands as she toppled from the ladder.

They had caught her as she fell, and had carried her away from the immediate area of combat. Gabriel shoved his way through to her, shouting her name. "Oh, thank God," he half-sobbed as he looked down at her and saw her eyes open. She blinked, slightly dazed, and smiled.

"I am all right," she told them, and they helped her to her feet, cheering wildly. Indeed, with each moment that passed she seemed to recover more. "My sword," she cried, and one of the soldiers brought it to her. It did nothing in his grasp, but as soon as Joan curled her fingers around it, it sparked to life. She lifted it, looking around at the faces of the men who would follow her into the valley of death, should she ask them.

"My friends!" she cried, whirling to face the stone walls of the city. "Up! Up! Our Lord has condemned the English! At this hour, *they are ours!*"

It was all the soldiers needed to hear. They swarmed up the ladders so thickly that there was no more resisting them. As the mists closed in around him, Simon heard a voice crying out in English, "No! We surrender, do you hear me? *We surrender!*"

But Suffolk's cry was too little, too late, and was lost in the jubilant raw shouts of men who believed that they were doing God's will, and therefore could not fail.

Victoria, it seemed, heard it too. *Did Alençon accept his surrender?*

"He never heard it," Simon said, his heart suddenly heavy. "It was lost in the chaos. Some of the English tried to flee, but where could they go? Others were captured, but many were simply killed outright. What's worse is most of the prisoners were later executed."

Joan couldn't have ordered that!

"It looks like she never knew about it. We have no sources saying that she did."

I'm glad. That would have devastated her.

It would have, and he was devastated himself, and the words were out of his mouth before he could stop them. "Joan once said that she feared nothing—except treachery."

There was a long silence, then: *I work with children her age, perhaps a year or two younger. To know what awaits her is difficult. I can only imagine how hard it is for you.*

No, Simon thought, *I don't believe you can.*

This is odd, Victoria said. *The Animus doesn't seem to be getting a clear fix on what to show us next.*

"I suppose it's possible that the Sword of Eden doesn't play a major role in the next three battles," Simon replied. "Meung-sur-Loire, for example, was a single-day affair. Joan's troops numbered around seven thousand by this point. They completely bypassed the castle and the city and focused on assaulting the bridge fortifications. They conquered it, left a garrison to guard it so it would be of no use to the English, and moved straight on to Beaugency."

Battle number four of the Loire campaign, Victoria said.

"Right. Essentially, the French kept firing artillery at the town's defenses until they surrendered. During this time, though, Fastolf arrived outside the city, and Joan also had unexpected reinforcements. Which leads us to Patay—the complete mirror of Agincourt, and Joan of Arc's greatest success. She pushed to chase down Fastolf and Talbot as the English retreated to Patay. She promised Alençon that—oh, what was the phrase he said she used—'if they were hung in the clouds, we would get them. The king shall have the greatest victory today that he has ever had. My counsel says to me that they are ours.'"

And they were, I take it.

"Conservative reports from English primary sources say two thousand men were killed and many others—including Talbot, which must have been very satisfactory to Joan—taken prisoner."

What were the French casualties?

"Three."

Three... thousand? Hundred?

"No. Three soldiers. Un, deux, trois. The whole battle took less than an hour, but Joan likely never even saw most of it. The English had only just begun to set up an ambush, but their position was given away when a stag startled the longbowmen and they apparently gave quite a yelp."

You're joking.

"Not in the least. Major battles are sometimes decided by the littlest things. In this case, a stag—a commonly recognized symbol of Christ, by the way—was accidentally flushed, the French pinpointed the exact location of the English, and the rest is, literally, history."

A known symbol of Christ, leaping out to warn the French. Unreal.

"She was unstoppable as long as she had the sword," Simon said. "And... I think I know where she lost it."

You do?

"I have a fairly good idea. If we go on the theory that she could not be defeated as long as she had the sword, then logic dictates that her first true defeat is where she lost it. But... but I don't want to go there just yet. I'd like to see her at the coronation."

I'd like to see her happy, and proud of herself, Simon thought. *Honored and respected as she should be, at least for a little while. Before it all goes to hell for her.*

I would like to see that too, Victoria said. The mists began to clear, revealing the high ceiling and beautiful lines of Reims Cathedral, a masterpiece painted in cool white and bright splashes of color from the stained glass windows.

Gabriel stood at attention, in his armor, but not with his fellow soldiers. Today he stood with his family instead. Durand Laxart had made the trek all the way from Domrémy for the occasion, when Gabriel had sent word of the army's march toward Reims, and nearly all of Joan's family had come as well. Her father, Jacques, who had so feared his little Jeannette would "run away with soldiers," stood with his wife Isabelle. They seemed at first glance an unusual couple—Isabelle's warmth and friendly demeanor contrasted with her husband's large, imposing presence and shock of jet-black hair. But Gabriel, who had gotten to know them, knew Jacques was intelligent and big-hearted, and Isabelle could match him in both qualities. Her brothers stood here too; the only one missing was Catherine, who was too frail to make the journey.

The doors of the cathedral slammed open and the crowd cheered as four armor-clad knights, mounted on horseback, clattered in. These were the Guardians of the Holy Oil of Clovis, with which all kings of France from the year 496 on had been anointed. Legend had it that the oil had been brought to the cathedral by four angels of God. Gabriel had been told that all the other traditional regalia had been stolen by the English occupiers of the city, many of whom had fled the night before. One of them was even a holy man, the former rector of the University of Paris, Pierre Cauchon. The regalia might be gone, but the enemy could not take the cathedral, nor, it seemed, the Oil of Clovis.

Gabriel tried not to smile as he caught Gilles de Rais's eye. The young, slightly wild nobleman had been named one of the Guardians; it was amusing to think of him in the role of an angelic stand-in.

Then the chanting reached a crescendo as the Dauphin entered.

And beside him, in a place of highest honor, was La Pucelle, the Maid of Orléans.

"Jeanne," Gabriel whispered, his heart filled to bursting with joy and pride. She held her standard and stood straight and tall, struggling not to smile. And her face, oh, her face, alight with ecstasy and the sense of a divine purpose fulfilled—her face shone brighter than the light coming through the windows, brighter than the candles, brighter than anything Gabriel could ever imagine, but he could not look away. He would never be able to look away from her, he realized; if he lived to be a hundred years old, he would always hold her here, this moment forever fixed in his mind's eye and embedded in his heart, with her sapphire eyes ablaze with incandescent, wild peace.

CHAPTER TWENTY-SEVEN

Anaya had to admit, she was having fun helping Ben learn his way around the department. He was actually not that much younger than she; she was reminded, yet again, that Americans just seemed younger to her. And once she got over his overeagerness, she found him to be startlingly intelligent and very, very quick. Too quick, almost. She sent him off with some coding, thinking that would keep him occupied for at least a few hours while she finished up some of her own work. He was done by the time she returned with a latte.

"You're going to have to be careful with this lot, they're going to go mad with jealousy," she warned him.

"What? You're not saying he's better than you, are you, Ny?" said Andrew. He put his hand to his chest and looked horrified.

"Nonsense," she replied, "or else he'd be heading off to Montreal at the end of the year instead of me."

Ben didn't quite squirm like a puppy, but the tips of his ears turned pink. *Adorable*, she thought, smiling as she sat next to him and went through his work.

She was doing her best to focus, but thoughts of Simon kept creeping into her head. They'd agreed to keep their conversations to a minimum, but she had asked Simon to report anything else he learned. And she, of course, would do the same.

Simon was a brilliant, if coolly detached, man. She knew he was trained in self-defense techniques. She knew he understood some of the darker machinations of the Order. But to the best of her knowledge, he'd never had to use those techniques, or deal with those machinations. Anaya had, and she could do it again if need be. Simon could, too. But she didn't know what having to fight, or kill, or make cruel choices would do to him, and she realized she didn't want to find out.

Anaya redirected her attention to Ben's code. "Aha, prodigy," she said, "I've finally caught you in a mistake."

Incredulous, he scooted his chair over. "Huh," he said. "I could have sworn I didn't do that." Anaya pointed to the error and raised an eyebrow. He laughed. "I know, I know, I must have if it's there. It didn't make a mistake all by itself."

"Take it from the top," Anaya said, and the boy groaned.

"Why are we in the Snack Shack and not Temp's?" Victoria asked. "Not that I mind. You know I love coffee."

Because I don't want to be reminded that for Some Mysterious Reason, Poole's not around. "Because I'm not looking forward to discussing what remains of Joan's life," he said, which was also true.

"Maybe we should be discussing this over a beer," Victoria said in an attempt at dark humor.

"A bottle of scotch might be a better idea," he muttered. "All right. Here we go." They were sitting on a sofa, and he placed his tablet down on the coffee table so they both could see. "In brief. Once Charles was crowned, he very quickly wanted to settle things diplomatically, rather than in battle."

"Well, honestly, that's not a bad way to think."

"No, it isn't... unless you have Joan of Arc with a Sword of Eden in your army, and the people you're negotiating with have no intention of honoring their agreements." He winced. "I hate that I'm talking about Templars like that, but it's true. Most of the high-ranking English of this time were either Templars themselves or had Templar support. Philip of Burgundy was most certainly a Templar. Charles was, as you've doubtless gathered, a very weak-willed individual, and naturally Templars would use that to their—*our* advantage. At one point there was a rather unholy trinity of the Duke of Burgundy, Charles's chamberlain Georges de La Trémoille, and the English regent, John, Duke of Bedford. The three were working together, ostensibly for peace, but somehow it was always the English or Burgundians who came out on top."

Shortly after Charles's coronation, Simon continued, he was approached by the Duke of Burgundy. Philip proposed a two-week truce, during which time Charles would not attack Paris. At the end of the two weeks, Philip would surrender the city to Charles.

"Of course, Philip never planned to surrender Paris, and used the time to fortify the city against attack instead."

"I imagine Joan hated Philip," Victoria said, sipping her latte.

"Actually, here's what she wrote to Philip, on the day of Charles's coronation." Simon found the letter on his tablet and read, "'High and dread prince, Duke of Burgundy, the Maid calls upon you by the King of Heaven to make a firm and lasting peace with the King of France. You two must pardon one another fully, with a sincere heart... it has been three weeks since I had written to you saying you should be at the anointing of the king, to which I have heard no reply.'"

"That's... really rather sad."

Simon was uncomfortable with how all this was making him feel, and he forced a noncommittal shrug. "Charles had gotten his coronation, and now he wanted to play a diplomat. The Templars were delighted to oblige."

"But... Yolande was an Assassin Mentor—and Charles's mother-in-law."

"I'm sure she did her best to keep control of him, but I wouldn't want to be up against those Templars. From here, Charles either dragged his heels or actively worked against Joan. He never again fully supported Joan, or even supplied her properly. Once she lost the sword, she was done."

Victoria was quiet. "I've seen both sides of the Assassin/Templar conflict," she said at last. "In the Animus with the kids at the Aerie, and outside of it as well. In the end, I will always choose order over chaos. But sometimes it does seem that we Templars have been unnecessarily cruel in our methods."

"But that is the only way the Templar Order can function," Simon said, even as he internally raged against what Rikkin and Victoria were secretly doing. In the end, order won out. Whatever the cost.

"Joan was perceived as a threat," he continued. "What happened to her was decided by those Templars, with what they knew, in their era. I have no doubt that they believed they had no alternative."

"No alternative other than to burn a nineteen-year-old girl at the stake?" Victoria certainly wasn't sounding like an evil Templar conspirator determined to destroy him; but then again, maybe this was a test.

"The trial was a sham, of course. But Templars have done such things before when there was great enough need. The end justifies the means. There must be order. Humanity will never be able to ascend to its greatest heights without it. And like everything worth achieving, there are costs. Sometimes bitter ones." *Sometimes the life of a good and pure girl with sapphire eyes who shone with light—a girl who was too brave, too selfless, who fought for the right cause but the wrong man and in the wrong way.*

Damn it all to hell.

"Come on," he said, his voice icy with pain he couldn't show. "Let's see how an angel falls."

SATURDAY, 21 AUGUST, 1429
COMPIÈGNE

"I had thought when he was crowned we would see more from him, not less," grumbled Alençon.

"Every day we wait to attack Paris makes it that much harder to take," Joan agreed. "The soldiers have had victory after victory. This hesitation by the king will only sow worry in their hearts, which ought to be filled with the spirit of God and love of France."

She, Alençon, Gabriel, and Fleur were attending the pleasure of His Majesty, King Charles VII of France, in Compiègne's royal residence. They had been there for several days while the king was in close council with his advisors. Sometimes, Joan and Alençon were invited to participate in these meetings, but not always, and not today. Gabriel had a strong feeling that there were things that Trémoille, who had always spoken against Joan, was making sure the Maid did not learn.

Instead of sending his eager army to Paris, whose citizens were by all accounts shaking in their shoes at the thought of attack, Charles had dawdled, traveling from city to city and enjoying great hospitality as he accepted pledges of loyalty.

"He wants peace, Jeanne," Fleur said gently. "He is weary of bloodshed."

"I am weary of it, too!" Joan replied. "Have I not wept over fallen soldiers, both English and French? As for peace, did I not send twice to the Duke of Burgundy urging such a thing? France needs to be whole again, but she must have her rightful king recognized!" She shook her head in disgust. "The king should have told me right away about his truce with Burgundy. Fourteen days of peace—more like fourteen days for the duke to reinforce the walls of Paris!"

Alençon and Gabriel exchanged glances. Joan, with her own innate blood and the Sword of Eden always at her side, was undefeatable in the field. Her sheer force of will and intensity was no good to

France—or the Assassins—when she was closed out of negotiations and forbidden to lead inspired men into battle against the enemy.

"Well," Alençon said, speaking to Joan but looking at Gabriel, "I am tired of sitting and eating and drinking. Let us change out of these formal things and into our armor and train for a bit."

Joan brightened at once. "Yes!" she agreed. "Maybe we can even teach Fleur how to use a sword!" Fleur laughed. The more time he spent with the fair-haired girl, the more Gabriel had come to respect her quiet calmness, so different from Joan's passion about everything. She was good for Joan, but she would never be able to wield a sword alongside the Maid.

Gabriel had spoken with her once, when she despaired about how useless she felt. "I owe all I am to Joan," Fleur had said, "and to you, for being my champion with her. Without the two of you...." She looked away. "I don't even want to think about what I—"

"Then don't," Gabriel had said. "You're with us. You don't ever have to go back to that life, and you don't have to do anything to be 'worthy'. You just... are. Just for being Fleur. Just... just love God, and love Joan, and that will be enough. She looks at you, and she can see, every day, that she has changed someone's life for the better. I know that means a lot to her. Especially now," he had added. "Not everyone remembers to thank her for what she's done for them."

"I think maybe God could teach Fleur to use a sword, but I am just a mortal man," Alençon laughed. His gaze on Gabriel, he addressed Joan. "I have something fun to teach you, Jeanne. Gabriel already knows it and so do I. It may prove useful to you at some point. I have no doubt you will learn it well—it requires, shall we say, a certain leap of faith."

Gabriel grinned.

"My good duke, while I will train with you today—tomorrow or the next day, equip your men, and those of the other captains. By my standard, I want to so see Paris from closer than I have ever seen it!"

THURSDAY, 8 SEPTEMBER, 1429

Gabriel had witnessed much since he left Vaucouleurs, which for most of his life had been the example of a fortress city. He had seen Orléans, and had helped take Jargeau.

But Paris dwarfed them all.

The walls were gargantuan, the largest certainly in France, perhaps in all of western Europe. They soared twenty-five feet in the air, with even higher towers every four hundred feet or so. There were six gates into the city, and the French army opted to concentrate the assault on the Saint-Denis Gate and—in particular—the imposing Saint-Honoré Gate, which was sixty feet by twenty-five feet. The gates had gun ports, murder holes, and arrow slits from which soldiers could attack the invaders, and a portcullis and drawbridge that could keep them out. Finally, boulevards had been erected in front of the gates as well.

By now, after so many victories, the process was becoming familiar to Gabriel. Joan, mounted and carrying her standard, rode up to the Saint-Honoré Gate and offered to accept Paris's surrender. She was greeted with refusal and jeers. Gabriel noticed that she kept the sword in its scabbard, her attention focused mainly on the white standard she so loved.

He and the Assassins knew how powerful the sword was, but Joan seemed to not fully appreciate exactly what it could do. Still, she had it, and he had faith in it—and in her.

The French army had learned what worked at Jargeau. They began with concentrating fire on the two chosen gates and the wall between them. The Parisians gladly returned fire. The noise was ceaseless and deafening. Carts and wagons, bundles of sticks, anything and everything was thrown into the moat around the city.

The Duke of Alençon was not fighting alongside them. No one truly expected to capture Paris in a day, and Alençon and some of his men were preparing for tomorrow's assault by constructing a bridge across the Seine. Gabriel understood the need for this, and he was glad that de Rais and de Gaucourt were present at the walls of Paris, but wondered if more troops might yet turn the tide today.

The ground exploded near Gabriel, pattering him with dirt and blood. A small group of soldiers, fresh from the Paris garrisons and full of energy and anger, swarmed down upon him and a small cluster of Joan's men. Gabriel was barely able to get his sword up in time to block a blow from an older, heavier knight. The clash of steel jarred him to the bone, but he relaxed, letting his body take over as de Metz and Alençon had taught him. To the other man's astonishment, his blade slid harmlessly down Gabriel's, then with a seemingly effortless twist, Gabriel turned his sword. The knight's weapon went flying. He had no chance to even raise his shield before Gabriel's blade bit deep into his neck.

Gabriel turned, searching for his next foe. All at once there was a flurry of white, and then Joan was there. Her sword was raised, and she was defending herself against what looked to be a seasoned Burgundian. She leaped off her horse, which danced away, and engaged the enemy as if she had been born with a weapon in her hand.

It was but the work of a moment. The Sword of Eden gleamed as it struck the shield of her enemy. The heavy wood splintered into tiny slivers. It looked like it had simply exploded in its wielder's hand. Joan's sword crackled, striking terror and helplessness into the enemy but sending calmness and certainty through Gabriel and others who followed the Maid. The Burgundian dropped his sword and fell to his knees, hands covering his head as he cried out in stunned disbelief at what he had just seen.

Joan pointed her radiant sword at the Parisian as he trembhhled before her. She had won without so much as scratching her enemy.

So that's what they meant when they said she fought defensively, Simon realized.

Pieces of Eden were about power. The Precursors weren't exactly the nicest of beings, and most of what they had left behind were definitely weapons. This particular Sword of Eden, which had belonged to Jacques de Molay and Joan of Arc and who knew how many others, was most certainly a weapon as well. But it was different. It was being used to kill, yes; inspiring the French troops to fight while instilling fear and defeatism in the English led to a great many deaths indeed. It was, after all, a sword, not a chalice, or an orb, or even a benevolent Shroud of Eden.

And yet... and yet. It didn't inspire bloodlust—it inspired hope, that in this case manifested as battle fervor. Simon could see, in a way that Gabriel could not, that the sword was working *with* Joan, not for her. It was as if the combination of the brightness of her Precursor DNA and the sword were stronger together rather than separately. She had not spent years training with a weapon, and yet she was using it not just well, but perfectly; to disable and defeat the foe in a way that aligned with Joan's essential nature. The more he learned about the sword, the more it confounded him. If Simon could find out how to reactivate it—

"Yield, in the name of God!" Joan demanded, and the soldier did, sobbing with fear. Joan gestured to a pair of her men, who took the prisoner back behind French lines. "Take his sword," Joan said, and Simon realized he was looking at the third and final sword known to have belonged to Joan of Arc: the sword taken from a Burgundian she had captured herself.

Joan's standard had fallen during the brief conflict. She picked it up, sheathing her unbloodied sword, and strode boldly forward to the walls of Paris.

"People of Paris!" she shouted. "It grieves both God and me to see so much French blood shed! Surrender, and we will take no more lives! Do not, and so many will die who do not need to!"

"Paris will never yield to a whore!" came an angry shout, and a heartbeat later, Gabriel stared in horror at the crossbow bolt that had suddenly appeared in Joan's thigh.

For a moment, Joan still stood, rooted in place, holding her standard, then she stumbled. Her visor was up and she had gone sickly pale. She blinked, clinging to the standard as if for support, but

Gabriel was moving, diving for her, shielding her with his own body as a cry of excitement went up and more of the Parisians began to fire their deadly bolts. He rushed her off the field, shouting for aid. De Rais had left off his own attack and hastened to them. His eyes went dark with fear as he reached to help Gabriel.

"Take care of her," he said to Gabriel. "I'll send some men with you. Get her back to La Chapelle."

Joan, who had begun to sag in their arms, lifted her head. "No! Keep fighting! This is nothing, like at Orléans...." But then her head lolled and she became so much weight.

"Go!" de Rais screamed. *"Go!"*

Gabriel went.

De Rais and de Gaucourt returned to La Chappelle a few hours later. Jean d'Aulon, Joan's steward, had immediately tended to her wounds. Fleur and Gabriel had assisted him, the former camp follower displaying a calmness in the face of such ugliness that Gabriel, whose gut twisted every time Joan was wounded, could only marvel at.

As soon as her eyelids fluttered open, Joan smiled and said, "My Shadow and my Flower. Where is my duke? How goes the battle?"

Fleur and Gabriel exchanged glances. "Jeanne," Gabriel said, "We retreated for the night. We will begin again tomorrow. Alençon's bridge—"

"Is destroyed," came an angry voice as Alençon himself entered the tent. "By the order of our own king. I have just come from tearing it down with my own hands. There will be no battle tomorrow, Jeanne. Those sitting in the council of the court have won out over those of us performing exploits in the field. We are to retreat."

"What do you mean?" cried Joan, struggling to sit up. Fleur pushed her back down; Jeanne was still so weak from blood loss that the other girl could do so easily.

"There will be no further attack on Paris," Alençon continued with barely restrained rage. He looked over at her armor, still bloody; at the standard, stained with mud, propped up against it. Suddenly he grew very still.

"Jeanne," he said, his voice unnaturally calm, "where is your sword?"

"My sword?" Horror spread over her face. "*My sword!* I had it when I was shot—I don't remember...."

Alençon and Gabriel stared at each other. Then, as one, with no further word, they put on their armor, mounted their horses and rode back to the gates of Paris.

The mists of the Memory Corridor closed about them.

CHAPTER
TWENTY-EIGHT

"Wait, what? Why are you bringing me out?"

Because there are no more instances of Gabriel seeing the sword, Simon. Their search was futile. I'm sorry.

"Well. There you have it," Simon said. His voice sounded cruel and angry in his own ears. "Not with a bang, but a whimper. The sword wasn't broken, or damaged. Not taken, not won, just... lost. Some glorified pig-keeper doubtless picked it up as a souvenir. Or else the Templars got it straight away."

Simon—

"The sword is gone, bargains have been made, and Charles refuses to support Joan's military endeavors. And then she—this was where it went wrong. Now we know. Game over."

What do you mean?

Simon stared with mingled grief and fury at the image of the young man he had grown to know so well. How different Gabriel looked now. His skin, once tan from working in the open air on his father's farm, had grown pale from too much time being covered in armor or inside at councils... or, in recent months, simply waiting to be told what to do. He looked harder, his face less open, less kind. But there was still fierce devotion to Joan in his heart, Simon knew. And he suspected that would never change. Somehow, though, Gabriel would have to do something that Simon thought next to impossible: move on from Joan of Arc. Long enough, at least, to sire a child, so that one day, Simon Hathaway could be strapped in the Animus observing his long-ago ancestor with a depth of empathy he hadn't known he possessed.

"We're done here, aren't we?" he continued. "I'd like to get out of this contraption, please."

A moment, then he felt the helmet being lifted off. Victoria regarded him with a mixture of curiosity and worry as she helped him with the straps. He stepped off the platform as soon as he was free.

"Simon, can you tell me what's going on?" Victoria asked, calmly, in the voice of the professional therapist.

How ironic, Simon thought. *Why don't you tell me, Victoria?* For a moment, he gazed at the sword on its bed of crushed velvet. At last he spoke.

"Rikkin wanted to find out if we could activate the sword. We've observed what it does, at least in Joan's hands. We've seen it do things Pieces of Eden have never done. It's almost grown along with Joan, or conversely, taught her. But I've failed. I still don't know how to fix it, and now it's gone. We have a couple more days, but we've learned all we can about it."

He whirled on her, narrowing his eyes as he almost spat, "Therefore—*game over.* All done. Finished."

Victoria pressed her lips together and looked away for a moment, as if making a decision. When she returned her gaze to him, something about her had changed.

"Rikkin gave you a week," she said. "It's five P.M. on day five. We're *not* done. As far as I am concerned, we can do whatever you want. If you want to quit, we quit. If you want to go through each battle minute by minute, hoping to discover something new about the sword, we do that. And if you want to continue to bear witness to Joan as she lose her influence, her friends, and her life... I will be right there with you."

Simon blinked. This was not what he had expected, not from someone who was spying on him and reporting to—

He almost said something right then. Then he realized that, doubtless, if there were any place in London where there would be recording devices of all varieties, it would be here, in the Animus Room.

So he sighed, removing his spectacles and rubbing his eyes as if tired. "I'm sorry. How about a brisk walk in the autumn air to clear our heads? Well, mine at least."

"Let's go get our coats."

Ten minutes later, they were strolling past a Boots chemist with a display of fragrances and grooming products and a sign announcing "Gifts for Him & Her" when Simon came to a halt. They'd not been followed, as best he could tell.

"All right, Simon," Victoria said. "What is going on?"

He looked down at her, right into her eyes, and demanded, "Why are you colluding with Rikkin against me?"

His heart sank as she leaned against the shop's brick wall, her hands shoved deep into her coat pockets.

"I'm not very good at this sort of thing," she said. "I'm glad you found out, actually. But it's not collusion, not really."

"Oh, I see, well that makes it all right then. Dammit, Victoria, I *trusted* you!"

"I know. I'm so sorry. Please... let me explain. Can we go somewhere? This... might take a while."

They found a secondhand bookstore and wandered down rows filled with old paperbacks and coffee-table books. In the rear of the store, surrounded by cookbooks and mysteries, Simon listened as Victoria told him about the phone call from Rikkin, and the immediate overnight journey to London. Rikkin had said he'd reached out to her because he was concerned about the well-being of an Inner Sanctum member. He wanted someone who'd already seen what the Bleeding Effect could do, and who would be able to spot it before Simon suffered any damage.

That did make sense. Simon nodded as he pretended to thumb through an old Hercule Poirot novel.

Rikkin wanted her to come to him straight away with any suspicions of instability, Victoria said, and she had promised.

"So I was your patient," Simon said. "Not your colleague. Not your friend."

She winced at the words, but didn't deny them. "Yes. Although... I thought we had become friends." When he didn't reply, she continued. She had emphasized her high opinion of Simon's approach, and pointed out the odds that they would encounter a Mentor. And she had asked for more time.

She had initiated contact with Rikkin a second time. "He began pushing me for more concrete information on the sword," she said. "He explained he wanted this taken care of before he left for Spain. I... it was around then that I started to feel uncomfortable about what I was doing. But Rikkin is our boss. And we're Templars, and sometimes that means not telling all we know."

"I'm aware of that." He shelved the Agatha Christie novel. "I imagine, given that I was your *patient*, you had to tell him about my collapse."

"I did."

"Did you e-mail him? Text him? Send a singing telegram?"

"We met for dinner," she said quietly.

"At Bella Cibo."

"Yes."

He folded his arms and leaned against the wall. "Why did you lie about that? People *saw* you there, Victoria."

She looked completely flustered. "Like I told you, I'm not *good* at this, Simon. I'm used to observing, and helping people, and listening. I can spot liars, but I'm obviously a terrible one myself. When Anaya asked me about the restaurant, I just froze."

Something inside Simon, something hard and angry and cold, released at that moment. He felt his chest ease, felt a warmth flowing through him that had nothing to do with the old radiator humming in the corner.

"I believe you," he said quietly. Her eyes widened, and a smile softened her taut face.

"Thank you, Simon."

They smiled stupidly at one another for a moment, then Simon reached for a musty copy of *Murder Must Advertise*. "Now. I recall he texted you back and not me, even though I'm the Inner Sanctum member and the one who had sent him the e-mail. He agreed to let us have the sword, but not extra time. Did he say why he was allowing us to keep it?"

"Perhaps he thought if you saw Joan do something specific with it, you could try to recreate the action. He was keen that you not continue past the moment where Joan loses the sword. He's not interested in your approach, Simon. I'm so sorry. For what it's worth, I think it's a marvelous idea. Which is why I offered to keep working with you, despite Mr. Rikkin's obvious desire that I don't."

Simon stared at her. "But... why? When you knew he didn't want you to?"

"First of all, you're the head of Historical Research," she said. "No one—not even Alan Rikkin—has a better right than you do to find out anything you damn well choose about history. If he's that concerned about something, he should talk to you about it himself. Secondly, he brought me on to monitor your mental health during the process. And my professional opinion is that you need closure. You need to say your good-byes—and witness Gabriel see his—in whatever way you see fit. If you don't, I think it would be detrimental. And as far as I'm concerned, you still have time to do that."

He looked around and pitched his voice low. "Alan Rikkin is a very powerful and very dangerous man."

"I swore an oath to the Order, not to him," she said, "and by hiring me to safeguard your mental health, I have the authority and the responsibility to do what is best for you. I won't knowingly let any harm come to someone placed in my charge. And I don't care who I have to stand up to in order to do so."

Simon stared at her, dumbfounded. "I... you are a woman of great courage, Victoria Bibeau. I am honored to be your friend."

Anaya was in the Accessories department of Marks & Spencer, the burner phone to her ear as she looked at gloves before heading home after work. She'd lost hers on the tube a week ago and her walk with Simon had reminded her to pick up a pair soon. "Simon, you colossal, gullible wazzock—"

"I believe her," Simon's voice said stubbornly. "She's taking a great risk, Anaya, just like you are, and we could use your help."

She couldn't speak for a moment, just kept muttering variations on "idiot" until she had gotten herself calmed down. "So you not only trust her, you want me to get myself into trouble helping both of you?"

"Hear me out, then make up your own mind." She listened over the next five minutes, the gloves completely forgotten as the story unfolded. By the time he was done, she herself believed Victoria Bibeau.

"So... you want me to hack into the Animus Room servers and find out what happened to the documentation that was supposed to go to Cryptology. And while I'm poking around in there, I'm to set up a way to monitor the new information you're recording, in case someone other than me is *also* hacking into the Animus. And you want me to do all that without being caught. Is that all?"

"I'm sorry," Simon said. "You've already done so much, it's not right for me to ask you to put yourself even more at risk. If anything happens to me or Victoria, we'll completely deny that you knew anything at all. I'll keep you safe, Anaya. You know that."

She wasn't about to let him play the gallant. She'd started this whole mess, and now that Simon had found something that looked like it would be truly important—someone hacking into the bloody Animus—she had to offer what help she could.

"I do, Simon, but you wouldn't be at risk yourself if I hadn't said anything," she said. "I'll do it. I'm heading straight back to Abstergo."

She glanced at the lines; the smart cashmere gloves would have to wait. She'd pick them up sometime in the next day or two.

If she lived long enough.

CHAPTER TWENTY-NINE

As Simon and Victoria reentered the Animus Room, they made idle chitchat about focusing on the Assassins of the period. Anyone listening would hear nothing but what appeared to be perfectly sound reasoning for continuing to explore Gabriel Laxart's memories.

Simon wanted to know what the hell had happened to the Assassins' interest in—and protection of—Joan. Was it really as simple as the fact that, since she no longer had the Sword of Eden, she was of no use to them? Or was it that since Charles wasn't using her to advance their cause, turning to ineffectual diplomacy that appeared to only serve the Templars, they did not care about his erstwhile tool?

Simon was angry about a lot of things, and he wanted answers. *I fear nothing, except treachery.*

MONDAY, 21 SEPTEMBER, 1429
GIEN

The room was wood and stone, the chairs large and ornate, the plates upon which the king and his council had just dined made of silver. Autumnal sunlight slanted in through the windows, and no one was happy to be there.

Joan was still recovering from her crossbolt wound. The loss of her sword and the news that the king had called off the assault had sorely wounded her spirit as well. For the last several days she had rarely spoken, and then only with sharp words.

Alençon, too, was miserable and angry. He was such an even-tempered, even light-hearted, man that watching him brood and seethe was utterly strange to Gabriel. He himself was there, he knew, to "manage" Joan should she become further upset at whatever would happen after the lavish meal. The fifth person at the feast was Georges de La Trémoille, who could likely have eaten as much as Gabriel, Joan, and Alençon combined.

Charles sat at the head of the long table, and Gabriel could tell by his effusive attention to Joan that something very bad was to happen. Once the dishes had been cleared away by swift and silent servants, the large doors closed, and the group left alone, the king spoke.

"Jeanne," Charles said, "we know you are disappointed that we called off the attack on Paris. And we fear we are about to disappoint you further. Please know that all we do, we do for France."

He even looks like he believes this, Gabriel thought. It was hard, these days, to think about Charles with any kind of charity.

"Our army has performed courageously over the last few months. It liberated Orléans, cleared the Loire, and saw us into Reims to be anointed as king. And we are grateful."

"But," spat Joan. Her blue eyes were hard as stone.

"But," the king continued affably, "we are pursuing a path of peace now, and we do not need a standing army of so many thousands of soldiers." He looked at Alençon. "Nor do we need to trouble the duke with its leadership."

"*What?*" Alençon shouted.

"The army is dissolved, and you are to return home to your lands and wife, Your Grace," Trémoille said, reaching for an apple. "But don't worry, Maid, we saved some fighting for you."

Gabriel stared disbelievingly at the king, who was smiling peacefully as if he had not just gutted Joan, Gabriel, and Alençon and left them to bleed to death; and at Trémoille, whose small, cruel eyes glittered with something he found very humorous.

"No," Joan said softly. "You will do no such thing. God—"

"—was not much in evidence in the skirmishes around Paris, nor in the attack of the great city itself," Trémoille said casually as he bit into the fruit.

"Jeanne, please understand," the king said. "We know you wept over the fallen of both armies. Surely peace is what you want."

"We shall find no peace but at the end of a lance," Joan said, and for an instant, her face shone with the certainty of old. Gabriel's heart contracted; he had not realized how seldom he had seen that unique facet of Joan's beauty in recent months.

"If tilting lances is what you crave, Jeanne, as I said, I have a fight for you," Trémoille said. "There is a wicked fellow, a mercenary captain, in the pay of the Duke of Burgundy. His name is Perrinet Gressart. You are to lay siege to his stronghold and bring him to the king's justice. My own half-brother, d'Albret, will lead the company, and—"

At that point, Alençon did the last thing Gabriel expected. He started to laugh, great, gulping whoops of laughter that were at the same time poisoned with bitterness.

"Tell me, Trémoille," he said, when he could breathe, "is this the selfsame Perrinet Gressart who once held you prisoner? And who nearly drained your coffers in ransom? *That* Perrinet Gressart?"

Trémoille's brows drew together and he turned as red as the apple he had half-devoured. For a moment, Gabriel wondered if the man would collapse from a seizure. He hoped so.

"That is neither here nor there," the king interjected smoothly. "What is important—"

"Is that Jeanne is now not the help to you she was," spat Alençon, rising. "And you are afraid that the two of us together may somehow desire you harm, so you need to separate us."

The duke and the king stared at one another, and Gabriel wondered if he were about to witness treason. But the king merely said, "We regret how sad the two of you are to part, but we know you will understand when you are not quite so angry with us. In the meantime, we wish to speak to Jeanne privately."

Alençon remained standing just long enough to make the king's smile waver. Then he bowed exaggeratedly and left the room. Gabriel followed him. When the doors were closed behind them, the duke began swearing so colorfully that Gabriel had to smile.

"Jeanne would be so angry with you right now," he said.

Alençon looked at him, and Gabriel thought he had never seen a man so desperately unhappy. "The king is throwing it away. All of it. Burgundy and the English—" He looked down the corridor to make certain they were alone, then said, in a softer voice, "The Templars are playing him like a pipe."

"You think the Templars are behind this?" A terrible thought seized Gabriel. "Do you think they found the sword?"

"The Assassins certainly didn't, or if we did, I don't know about it. There's a lot they're not telling me these days," he added. Gabriel sympathized. Alençon had done his best to teach Gabriel about the Brotherhood, but he was not as experienced as de Metz had been.

"I was told they would protect her," Gabriel continued. "You're the only one I know of, and now you'll be gone. Has the Mentor abandoned her?"

"Unfortunately, now that Charles is officially king, Yolande has less political power. Trémoille has always been a thorn in her side. For a while, the king shunned him in favor of Jeanne, but now... now everything is harder. Even for a Mentor who is also a queen."

"Perhaps it is time that the Assassins live up to their names," Gabriel growled. "The Templars are not afraid to act, but I have heard of no assassination attempts."

Alençon looked as if he felt he should be angry with Gabriel, but somehow could not dredge up the emotion. "I can't bear to think of Jeanne languishing in castle after castle, or squandering her ability battling bandits," he said, biting off the last word. "I will see if I can sway our king when a little time has passed. Trémoille is playing him for a fool, and the only one who can't see that is Charles himself."

Alençon glanced enviously at Gabriel. "At least he is not sending you away."

"No. But now I have no teacher."

"The Assassins will find you if they need you." Alençon was clearly uncomfortable with Gabriel's words. Unspoken was the question Gabriel wanted to ask: *But what if Jeanne or I need them?* "Take care of her for me," Alençon continued. "For Dunois, and de Rais, and that old bear La Hire. Tell her we all love her, and we will always believe in her."

"You're not going to say good-bye yourself?"

"I still hope that this isn't good-bye. Charles is consistently inconsistent. I think he will come around, given time, and you and Jeanne and I will get to attack some English together again." He managed an echo of his old grin. "Say good-bye for us all, but only for now."

"You know I will."

Simon felt a pang of sorrow. Jeanne and her "noble duke" would never meet again. And later in life, Alençon... Charles was such a fool.

"And... tell Fleur, she will always have a home with my household, if she ever wishes to leave Jeanne." Alençon hesitated. "People have been kind to her because of their respect for Jeanne. If the Maid falls out of favor, Fleur will suffer for it."

"She won't leave Jeanne, ever, any more than I will."

"I do so most unwillingly, and only because to refuse would be treason."

"I know. Jeanne does, too. Now get out of here, before we both start to cry."

He said it with a laugh, but it was too late. Only now had Gabriel realized what a good friend he, the lowborn bastard, had had in the noble duke. They embraced roughly, two soldiers departing for different battles. And then Alençon was gone.

As the mists gathered about Gabriel, Victoria's voice came to Simon. *This is like watching a train wreck,* she said.

"Charles put more effort into his own ruination than Philip did."

Did Joan really serve under Tremoille's half-brother to fight against the bandit who'd kidnapped him?

"She obeyed orders," Simon said. "The siege failed after a month because Charles ignored her letters pleading for food and supplies, including gunpowder. For most of the winter of that year, she stayed with d'Albret's family. Oh, but all that's just fine, because Charles gave Joan a Christmas gift in the form of ennobling her family. He even made it clear that the title could pass down through the females of the line. A consolation prize."

I can't even think of anything to say to that.

"Meanwhile," Simon continued, waxing angrier by the moment, "by this point Philip has founded the Order of the Golden Fleece. Cities that had pledged loyalty to Charles, including Compiègne, have been given back to Philip against their will. It was a terrible betrayal of faith, and you can imagine how furious Joan was. Most cities didn't take it well—they resisted Philip when he came to claim them."

Eventually Charles and Philip did make peace, yes?

"Eventually. But not in Joan's lifetime."

The mists, it would seem, were not yet done with him. Simon braced himself for what the Animus would show him next.

Joan was sobbing during the Easter Mass.

When it was over and Fleur and Gabriel tried to coax her to leave with them, she waved them away. They walked outside the ancient city's church, silent and somber.

"It breaks me to see her like this," Gabriel said miserably. Since the Duke of Alençon had been dismissed, Gabriel and Fleur had turned to one another to help ease the confusion and worry over Joan's situation. Fleur, who asked nothing of Joan except to be in her presence as much as possible, was the only one who grasped the depth of Gabriel's pain. They had grown close; they might have become lovers, except Joan was so fully in their hearts that there was no room for anyone else.

A year ago, Jeanne was about to become the Maid of Orléans, and there, at least, she was still welcomed with honors when she came. But ever since she had lost the sword and her king had embraced the path of diplomacy rather than battle, Joan seemed to diminish. She was still beautiful to Gabriel; how could she not be? But the strain of inactivity and meaningless skirmishing was taking its toll.

Gabriel missed de Metz and Alençon more than ever. He wondered if an Assassin presence in Joan's life might have helped her keep her fighting spirit. Only in March, when Joan had learned of the continued resistance of cities like Compiègne, had the Joan Fleur and Gabriel knew returned. By now, Joan's "army" was a handful of intensely loyal men; a mere two hundred, a far cry from the ten thousand she led after the king's coronation. She had gathered them to her, and then simply left. She did not tell Charles where she was going, or what she intended, but anyone who knew Joan knew what her plan had to be.

They had been welcomed in Melun, and for a time, Joan had

seemed hopeful. To see her devastated during mass was like a knife to the heart for the two who loved her best. They stood now, hand in hand, seeking comfort from one another as they walked outside down the streets of the ancient city.

"Did she tell—" Gabriel began.

"Did Joan say—" said Fleur.

They smiled sadly at one another, then sobered. "Where do you think this will end, Gabriel?"

"I don't know," he said honestly. "Pierre is trying to get her to go home with him." Jean, the older brother, had already left, but Pierre had been with his sister every step of the way since Blois. He did not understand her as well as Fleur and Gabriel did, but he loved her, and Gabriel was glad he had stayed.

"Do... do you think her Voices have stopped talking to her?" Fleur said in a voice barely above a whisper, lifting wide blue eyes to his.

Gabriel stayed silent. He was too afraid to ask Joan himself. "It doesn't matter to me what she does, or where she goes," he said. "I'll be there with her."

"I will, too. Forever," Fleur said, her eyes filling with tears. "But I just want her to stop hurting. What the king is doing to her is so wrong!"

"The king does what he must, and so do I," came Joan's voice behind them. "As do you, my Shadow and my Flower. We all do God's will."

Her eyes were bloodshot and swollen from weeping, but were dry now. "I would speak to you both," she said, taking Fleur aside first. Gabriel looked away, given them privacy, his own heart heavy. He soon felt a feather-light brush on his arm.

As he turned to her, for the first time, he realized how small Joan was. So much about her had been so big: her light, her spirit, her warmth, her animated features. Now he saw her as a simple human woman, somber and still.

"My witness," she said, and he felt a chill. He was both that and her shadow, but he wondered why she had chosen this nickname for him at this moment. "Do you recall what you said to me, when I first told you about my Voices?"

His blood turned to water in his veins. He couldn't say the words, but he nodded. *Don't tell me to leave your side. Ever.*

"I said I couldn't promise we would never be parted," she continued.

"'Only let me share your journey for as long as you can,'" he quoted, his voice thick.

"You will bear witness, for as long as you may. But that time is coming to an end. I need you to promise... when I tell you to go, you will obey. No matter what happens."

"I can't abandon you, Jeanne! Please, don't ask that of me!" His voice cracked, and he was unashamed. He took her hands and clung to them, feeling the bones through the skin, how terribly fragile she was, in the end, despite her inner radiance.

"I did not say 'abandon me.' I said obey. If I ask it, it is not I, but God. Swear, Gabriel, or else you will follow me not one step further."

He couldn't let her see his pain. She knew how great it was; and she herself struggled with some burden he couldn't possibly comprehend. Instead, he nodded. "I swear," he said, and added, silently, *by the depth of the love I bear for you.*

Simon was deeply grateful for the mists that started rolling in. He could not bear Gabriel's pain for a moment longer.

Simon, what... what happened? Do we know?

"We know," he said, heavily. "During her trial, she testified that Saints Catherine and Margaret told her that she would be captured before Saint John's day—June 24. She—" Simon cleared his throat. "She and a few of her men, including Pierre and her steward Jean d'Aulon, were taken prisoner at Compiègne on May 23. The Burgundian troops lured her too far away from the city, then cut off her escape route as soon as she tried to retreat. The governor of Compiègne was forced to close the gates, or else risk having the enemy actually enter the city."

And Gabriel wasn't captured, because Joan ordered him to retreat before the ambush, Victoria said.

I have but a year, little more, Joan had predicted on 21 April, 1429.

She had been right.

CHAPTER THIRTY

DAY 6

Simon knew, in great, ugly detail, the horrors that awaited Joan before her death: ridicule, false accusations, beatings, terror, and the constant fear of rape. His brain had seized on them, plaguing his sleep. Even now his stomach turned at the thought as he entered the Abstergo building, nodding good morning to the security guards on duty. Gabriel was the witness, not he. Surely he did not need to endure all this. But he couldn't help but wonder, if Consus's spirit could appear to go forward into the future to connect with people like Joan, perhaps it knew about people like Gabriel... and Simon.

They still had the rest of today and tomorrow, technically. The burner phone vibrated in his pocket as he entered the lift. Simon tensed slightly, casually turning away from the lift camera to read the text. He felt the blood drain from his face as he forwarded it to the burner phone Victoria had picked up last night, after their conversation in the book shop.

He stepped into his office just long enough to check e-mails, then called Victoria on her company-issued phone.

"I've decided to take you up on your offer. Perhaps it *is* time I started getting used to the dark swill you are so fond of. I made some notes I'd like to share before we get started today. Now would be the perfect time to introduce me to that coffee shop you mentioned."

They met in the lobby, where Victoria happily and audibly extolled the virtues of her fictitious coffee shop. Once they were out of the building and had walked a block, Victoria checked her phone.

Anaya's message was brief and to the point. *A is compromised. Waterloo.*

"I do hope by that she means the Tube station," Victoria said.

"So do I," Simon replied.

They found Anaya at Waterloo Station, purchasing a muffin approximately the size of Simon's fist from one of the snack vans. Victoria got a latte, and Simon got tea. They all pretended it was a coincidence that they'd met up here, accepted a segment of muffin from Anaya, and walked through the crowds below the great arch at the station.

"You were right," Anaya said. "Someone's hacked into the Animus server. Well, someone other than me. And they've been using computers in my department to do it."

Simon swore. "Your little American friend."

"I think so," Anaya said, adding bitterly, "I should have known something was up when I got the job so fast."

"Well, I didn't think anything of it, other than that Abstergo Entertainment knew something good when they saw it," Simon said. "It made perfect sense they'd jump when they saw your resumé. Don't take this on yourself."

She gave him a wan smile. "The point is, I'm supposedly training the man who's spying on you."

"That might turn out to be a good thing. Can you misdirect him?" asked Victoria. "And find out where he's sending the information?"

Anaya nodded. "Yes to both."

"You can stop if you want, Anaya, I mean it." Simon took her hand in his and squeezed it, causing her to look up and meet his gaze. "I—well, I'd... I don't want any harm to come to you."

She raised an eyebrow and smiled a little. "Ah, so you do care," she teased.

He went red. "Well, of course," he said lightly, "Abstergo's invested a great deal of time training you."

"That's my Simon," she said, her smile broadening. He'd lifted her spirits, and he was glad. "But yes, I can do this, and I should do this, because after all—we don't *know* that this is Templar-sanctioned. And my job is to be on the lookout for just such things."

That was something that Simon hadn't considered. What if she were right? What if Rikkin's annoyance with how long Simon was taking had nothing to do with anything else that was going on? At the very least, he was suddenly grateful that Anaya had a plausible reason for her activity.

"All right." Anaya squared her shoulders. "Whatever the two of you are doing with Joan of Arc that's arousing so much interest, hurry it up. The longer I'm poking around, the sooner someone will spot me. I'm good, but everyone gets caught, eventually."

"Really?" Victoria said.

"It's the whole premise of my job," Anaya replied. "Be quick, all right? And be smart."

And then, to Simon's astonishment, she gave him a swift kiss, her lips warm against his cheek, and melted into the crowd.

He stared after her for a moment, startled, then turned to Victoria. "We need to go straight back to Abstergo. I think Gabriel has something to say to some Assassins."

FRIDAY, 7 JULY, 1430
VAUCOULEURS

"There you are." Gabriel's voice was low and cold as he spoke into Jean de Metz's ear, sliding beside him on the bench in the dimly-lit tavern.

Either he had failed to surprise the knight, or else, more likely, de Metz hid his shock well. "Laxart," he said. "I wondered when you would show up."

The man's casualness was infuriating. "We talk outside," Gabriel stated, rising. De Metz obligingly drained his ale and rose. The summer evening was only now growing dark. The heat was stifling as they walked down the street, nodding to passersby until they had entered a merchant area that was closed for the night.

"I'm sorry about Jeanne," de Metz said.

"If you were sorry—if *any* of you Assassins were sorry—she wouldn't be in the tender care of Philip's man Luxembourg," Gabriel snapped. "She almost escaped. Did you know that? She only got caught because she tried to free her brother and d'Aulon as well. Because she *cared* about what happened to them. If they'd had any kind of outside aid from the Assassins—"

"You don't know anything, Laxart," said de Metz. It wasn't an angry accusation, it was an exhausted one. "You have no idea what we have or haven't been doing—and why or why not."

"Then *tell* me!"

"You're not a member of the Brotherhood. You're not even a formal apprentice, not yet. And I don't think you ever will be one of us."

"Why? Because I'm not good enough? Because the Assassins abandoned me when it became *inconvenient*?"

Again, de Metz seemed more regretful than angry. "No. Because for you, it's not about the cause, or the Brotherhood. It's not about the war against the Templars for humanity's destiny. It's just about Jeanne."

"That's enough for me," Gabriel said. "And it should have been enough for you. For Yolande. You once told me Jeanne was not just important politically. You said you cared about what happened to her. I believed you. I thought that was the difference between the Assassins and the Templars—that you were the ones that cared about the individual. And she is no ordinary person, Jean, you *know* that!"

"I do," de Metz agreed. "*We* do. But Burgundy's already talked to Jeanne at least once. Ah," he added at Gabriel's surprised expression, "you see, you don't know everything. More things are in play at the moment than you can possibly imagine. We can't just rush in and grab her. The political strategies—"

"Mean nothing to me! *She* means everything!"

De Metz's eyes were sad. "You're too volatile to involve, Gabriel. I'm sorry. But... the truth of the matter is that without the sword, Jeanne isn't the undefeatable angel she was. She lost at Paris."

"Because Charles ordered her to retreat! The king was being duped by Burgundy, even he admits to seeing it now!"

"She's been captured. She's not infallible."

"Her Voices told her she would be taken," Gabriel said, desperately. "And I believe she hears them. Do you?"

De Metz was silent.

Gabriel took a step back. "By Christ's blood, you don't, do you? You're as fickle as Charles! I went to him, *begged* him to ransom her, but he wouldn't lift a finger. The instant she is of no use to you, you abandon her. Is *that* the Assassin's Creed? 'Find people, use them up, toss them away when they need you?' Good God, you're no different from the Templars!"

The Hidden Blade was at his throat before he'd finished uttering the last word. De Metz had seized Gabriel's tunic and his face was only an inch away from the youth's as he hissed, "For the sake of the friendship that was once between us, I won't end your angry little life right here and now."

The blade disappeared. De Metz released his grip and shoved Gabriel away, disgusted. "You want to think that? Go right ahead. It tells me that you understand *nothing*."

Gabriel's hand went to his neck, and he touched something warm and wet. The blade was so sharp, it had nicked him without his even feeling it. "I know that you abandoned an eighteen-year-old girl who did everything she ever promised. Whose will was stronger than yours, or mine, or even your precious Mentor's. If you loved her only for the sword, then I think she may be better served by those guarding her now, rather than those who guarded her on her way to Chinon. At least they aren't pretending to be her friends."

In the dim light, despite his protestations, de Metz winced. "Go. Get out of here before I change my mind."

"What about staying your blade from the flesh of the innocent?"

"You're no innocent, Laxart. You're in this up to your ears. And if you don't see that, you're more of a fool than I thought."

"I will do everything I can to free her," Gabriel warned.

"Then you may doom her. Do you understand?"

Gabriel turned on his heel. He had no angels telling him what he should do, and when he prayed, God never answered. He didn't have the Assassins, or Alençon, or anyone, now.

He and Fleur were on their own.

Simon hated seeing Gabriel like this, knowing, unlike his ancestor, that Joan was not going to be rescued, that everything Gabriel was struggling to prevent would come to pass. "De Metz was right about one thing," he said as he and Gabriel waited in the Memory Corridor. "There was a great deal at play. This war didn't last a hundred and sixteen years because it was simple."

Did Charles really do nothing to help Joan?

"Not one thing."

Do you think he had anything to do with her capture?

"No, but he was probably quietly relieved. There was a traditional way of handling noble prisoners that wasn't followed in Joan's case. They were usually treated fairly well, and eventually found their way back home when their family could cough up the ransom or someone needed to make a deal. And it looked at first like Philip was content to keep her. She was technically the prisoner of John of Luxembourg, count of Ligny, who was Philip's vassal, and by all accounts she was treated well. John's wife seemed fond of Joan, even asking her husband not to give Joan over to the English."

But he did. Or I suppose Philip did. What happened?

"There was a lot of pressure from the English, who were naturally very hostile to Joan. Many wanted her to burn." Simon remembered the angry words hurled at Joan when she spoke to the English at Orléans, and felt ill. "Others, the Templars among both Burgundian and English, wanted to discredit her in order to thoroughly discredit Charles. Seven months after her capture, the English purchased her for ten thousand pounds from the John of Luxembourg. She arrived at Rouen on Christmas Eve, 1430. The man responsible for these negotiations was Pierre Cauchon—who would later head the tribunal against her for heresy."

Why do I know that name?

"He was a Burgundian sympathizer, one of the authors of the Treaty of Troyes. Joan had essentially forced him to flee twice— once from Reims, where he was rector of the University of Paris, and once from Beauvais, where he was the bishop. Both times, those cities turned away from Burgundy and accepted Charles. Legally, he shouldn't have been able to be her judge. Neither her birthplace nor the place where her so-called heresy was committed lay within his jurisdiction. But strings were pulled. By the way, he was angling for the archbishopric of Rouen."

He sounds terribly impartial. Victoria's voice dripped sarcasm. *He was a Templar as well?*

"Almost certainly. The instant he heard about Joan's capture, he began working to get her delivered into ecclesiastical hands instead of secular."

So that they could levy a charge of witchcraft or heresy.

"Much more unsavory than just having her be a prisoner of war. Hence, worse for Charles's reputation. Who could support a king whose victories had come to him through the devil? The University of Paris had been after that outcome since Orléans. The whole thing was a legal farce, really. So many blatant instances of a complete disregard for inconvenient legalities. Joan was treated as a POW, with leg irons on at all times in her cell, but was supposedly an ecclesiastical prisoner."

I'm confused. What's the difference between the two?

"There are pros and cons for the English either way. Or at least there ought to have been. If Joan was an ecclesiastical prisoner, she could be tried for heresy or witchcraft, just as you said. But she would also be lodged with women, and not kept in chains. She'd also be allowed to request the pope's involvement. They wanted it both ways. They wanted to charge her as an ecclesiastical prisoner, but also wanted to treat her as poorly as if she were a secular prisoner."

So they just did whatever they wanted to, to get the desired result.

"Precisely. Joan was shown instruments of torture, and threatened with them. One of the torturers walked out—said he couldn't do it. She had men *in her cell* watching her constantly. They hadn't even formulated a charge when they brought her to trial, she had no advocate... I could go on, but there's no point."

Indeed, thinking about the injustice—injustices carried out by order of the highest-ranking Templars of the time—was making him feel nauseated. *This is the Templar way,* he reminded himself. *Order must obtained. The Assassin's puppet Charles had to be brought to heel.* Yet the thoughts brought him no comfort.

I'm not going to urge you to see anything more unless you want to, Victoria said.

He thought about it for a moment. "I feel that as a historian, I should take advantage of this chance. And I feel that I owe it to her—and Gabriel—to witness something of her fall."

Don't do it for history's sake, or even Gabriel's sake or Joan's. If you're going to do this, do it for Simon Hathaway.

"I think if I don't," he said, quietly, "I'd never forgive myself."

Then in we go.

CHAPTER
THIRTY-ONE

WEDNESDAY, 21 FEBRUARY, 1431
CHAPEL OF BOUVREUIL KEEP, ROUEN

News had reached Fleur and Gabriel in late December that Joan was imprisoned in a tower of Rouen's castle. Of course they had gone to Rouen immediately, finding both work and lodging in a run-down old inn. They had followed Joan's ordeal as best they could, befriending some soldiers and even some clergy who frequented the tavern and spoke when their tongues were loosened with wine. Gabriel prayed as never before that Joan's Voices would somehow touch the hearts of the men who held sway over her destiny.

The castle's chapel was crowded to capacity and beyond. Gabriel did his best to ensure that Fleur, who was of a height with five-foot-two Joan, could see. A least, in this space, they could hear.

There were around forty tribunal members, all scholars—doctors and bachelors of theology or canon law. Some were experts in civil law. One, he'd heard, was both. Seated with them were Bishop Pierre Cauchon and the promoter-general of the diocese of Bauvais, Jean d'Estivet, the two formal judges.

Gabriel had heard that Joan had not been well treated during her imprisonment. He'd heard reports of everything from men watching her as she slept to leg irons and even a cage that held her at neck, hands, and feet, lest she try to escape.

A murmur went through the crowd, followed by muttered epithets. Fleur clutched the small pouch Joan had given her at Melun, when the Maid's Voices had told her of her impending capture. Like Joan had done, she now wore it around her neck at all times. It seemed to bring her comfort.

"Gabriel? Is it her?" Fleur asked.

For a moment, Gabriel was so shocked by what he saw he couldn't answer. Joan's hands and feet were chained. She wore a dress, dirty and of common make, and her curly black hair had grown down to her shoulders. She was thin, so thin, and pale; her muscles wasted away and her healthy color leeched from her by nearly a year of imprisonment.

"It's her," he said, his mouth dry as sand. For a long time, he couldn't even focus enough to make sense of the droning voices of those describing the process. He couldn't take his eyes off Joan, thin, pale, but still lifting her chin in defiance.

At last, the questioning began. Cauchon, who looked to be in his early sixties, tall, bony, and imposing, strode to where Joan sat with her chains fastened to a bench. Towering over her, he demanded, "Swear to tell the truth concerning whatever will be asked of you."

"About my father, and mother, and everything that I have done since I took the road to come into the heart of France, I shall willingly swear." Her voice was strong and clear; prison had not dimmed her spirit. "But never have I revealed certain revelations made to me by God except to Charles, my king."

And me, Gabriel thought. But he knew to Joan, that did not "count." He was her Shadow, placed beside her to witness; her Voices had said so.

"And even if you wish to cut my head off, I will not reveal them," Joan continued. She was stubborn, and strong, and even as he watched d'Estivet's expression turn sour and Cauchon's temper rise, Gabriel was glad.

It went on for hours. Questions came not just from Cauchon, but from everyone on the tribunal. Oftentimes, several clergymen spoke at once, bombarding Joan so that she had to beg them repeatedly to ask their questions one at a time. And the queries seemed so random. One moment Cauchon was asking about the sacring of Charles at Reims. The next, he was asking if she had ever seen fairies at the Ladies' Tree.

"They're trying to trick her," Fleur whispered, and Gabriel nodded. "Trying to make her say something against herself."

"Are your Voices angels?" Cauchon inquired.

"They are saints. Saint Michael, Saint Catherine, and Saint Margaret. Saint Michael spoke to me first," Joan replied promptly.

"Tell me about Saint Michael," Cauchon said in a patronizing voice, looking out over the crowd knowingly.

"He came to me in my father's garden when I was thirteen," Joan said. Gabriel listened as she told this stranger, this enemy, what she had confided in whispers to him long ago. "I saw him with my eyes as well as I see you."

Cauchon's lips curved in a cruel smile, and again he regarded the crowd as he continued. "What did Saint Michael look like when he appeared to you? Was he... naked?"

An outraged gasp rippled through the crowd. Joan looked at Cauchon, amused. "Do you think that God doesn't have the wherewithal to give them clothes?"

And the crowd laughed. Joan's smile grew, but Cauchon's contorted into a grimace. "Did he have hair?" he persisted.

"Oh, *that's* an important point." The crowd laughed again.

"Answer the question!" Cauchon snapped.

"Why would it have been cut off?"

Cauchon paced a moment, gathering himself. "You say your Voices have told you certain things. Do you know through a revelation that you would escape?"

"Yes, indeed, they have told me that I would be delivered, but I do not know the day or the hour, and they said that I should bravely maintain a good face."

Gabriel felt Fleur squeeze his hand so tightly that he thought she might break the bones. He wouldn't have cared. Joan's Voices told her she would escape!

"Why did you jump from the tower of Beauvais?" demanded Cauchon. "It is nigh sixty feet tall. Were you attempting to commit mortal sin and give up the life God granted you?"

A Leap of Faith! Gabriel thought, almost dizzy. Joan had tried to escape using the Leap of Faith she had been taught by the Assassins. Again, he felt anger toward them.

"I did know that I was to be delivered to the English, but

I did not do it out of despair. I jumped in the hope of saving my body and of going to assist many good men who were in need. And after the jump, I went to confession and asked pardon of the Lord."

"Was any penance imposed on you because of that?"

"I bore part of the penance in the damage I did to myself by falling!" Joan retorted. Beside Gabriel, Fleur stifled a grin.

"Did your Voices tell you to come into the heart of France?"

"I did so only at God's command. Everything was done at the command of the Lord."

"Is it God who commanded you to wear men's clothes?"

The question clearly took Joan by surprise. Gabriel remembered when it had been discussed, and everyone—from de Metz to the good people of Vaucouleurs, who paid for the clothing—thought it was wisdom, to make riding on horseback easier, to not draw undue attention, and to keep Joan safe from unwanted male advances. Joan had agreed readily, and Gabriel knew if her Voices had objected, she would have refused in a heartbeat.

"The clothes are a small matter, the least of all things." Her face was furrowed in confusion. "I neither put on these clothes nor did I do anything except by the commandment of God and his angels. I was asked about this at Poitiers, where the good clergymen decided that it was—"

"Where is your mandrake?" This time, the speaker was not the looming Cauchon, but the other judge—Jean d'Estivet. He looked like he had eaten a lemon, so drawn with distaste was his expression.

Joan blinked at the abrupt change of topic, but her voice was calm as she replied, "I don't have a mandrake, and never had one."

"But clearly you know what they are." *Traps and tricks with every question*, Gabriel thought, anger again rushing into him. Mandrakes, he knew, were some kind of magical root—and associated with witchcraft.

"I have heard they are something to make money, but I don't believe it at all." Her voice was full of contempt.

On they went—pushing her again for details about the Ladies' Tree, and inquiring if she had ever seen fairies. Others chimed in, asking about her standard. Joan stated that she preferred it perhaps forty times as much as her sword. Gabriel's heart sank. *If only you had it now....*

"I preferred it because I did not wish to kill anyone."

"Did you?"

"Never." Her voice rang with inarguable truth.

"But you are no friend to Burgundy or England," pressed Cauchon.

"My greatest hope is to see my king and the Duke of Burgundy united and at peace. As for the English, all I wished was for them to leave, and I always begged them to surrender before I attacked." She looked at him, cocking her head to one side, and her blue eyes lost focus for a moment. For the first time since she had entered the chapel, her face exuded a faint radiance.

"Her Voices," whispered Fleur, and Gabriel, too grateful for what he was seeing to speak, could only nod.

Joan blinked, then looked back at Cauchon. "Before seven years are over, the English will suffer more severe losses than they did at Orléans, and they will lose everything in France. And this will be accomplished through a great victory that God will send the French."

The tribunal erupted, shouting questions at Joan, demanding she tell them what time, what day, where this would occur. She simply shook her head. "My Voices tell me not to answer you, and I am more afraid of displeasing them than I am of you."

"Do you believe you are in the grace of God?" asked Cauchon, with deceptive casualness.

The room fell quiet. There was nothing Joan could say that would not damage—or perhaps even damn—her. If she said yes, she'd be accused of heresy, for no one could know if they were in God's grace. If she said no, then she admitted that everything she had done was a lie.

Only Joan seemed completely calm. She smiled, softly, and her radiance increased as she said, "If I am not, may God put me there. And if I am, may God keep me there, for I would be the most sorrowful woman in the world if I knew that I was not in the grace of God."

The silence lasted for a long moment. The clergymen looked flabbergasted. A peasant had just beautifully, brilliantly, and humbly sidestepped a perfectly laid theological trap.

Joan added, "I do believe what my Voices have told me—that I shall be saved. I believe this as firmly as if I were already there."

The small, cruel-looking d'Estivet recovered first. "After that revelation, do you believe yourself incapable of committing mortal sins?"

Her thick hair moved with the gesture as she shook her head. "I know nothing about that, but in everything I defer to God."

"That is a very weighty response," said d'Estivet.

"And I hold it also a great treasure."

The mists erased Joan's shining face, almost sadly, swallowing it up in great gray, soft billows. Simon was almost certain it was the last time he would see Joan's face calm and at peace.

Dammit.

That prediction, came Victoria's voice, *what was it about? Did it come true?*

Simon cleared his throat. "It, ah... yes. Paris fell to the French six years later. If only she had lived to see it."

Have you seen enough? came Victoria's gentle voice.

Hadn't he? Perhaps this should be his last memory of Joan of Arc, courageous despite imprisonment, her spirit vibrant and her faith as solid as stone, her body thin and weak but whole, untouched yet by hungry flames.

"No," he said. He couldn't let her go. Not yet. Maybe not ever.

... All right, Victoria said reluctantly, and the mists churned yet again.

CHAPTER THIRTY-TWO

THURSDAY, 24 MAY, 1431
ABBEY OF SAINT-OUEN, ROUEN

Gabriel stood in a cemetery. There were several others crowded around him, all of them peering up eagerly at the platforms that had been hastily erected for the piece of cruel theater that was about to be enacted before them. Although he felt the press of dozens of spectators around him, Gabriel had never felt more alone in his nearly two decades of life.

Fleur was no longer with him.

There had been a little boy waiting for him downstairs. *Your Flower told me to tell you she cannot bear it any more. She's sorry, but she had to go,* he told a blindsided Gabriel. *She said she hopes you find peace, and are happy, and to not try to find her.*

Don't worry, Gabriel had growled to the little messenger, even as he leaned against the wall, dizzy with shock. *I won't waste another breath on that traitor.*

Treachery was the one thing Joan said she feared. Fleur had sworn, repeatedly, that she would never abandon Joan. That there was nothing for her without the Maid. But she, too, like everyone else, had turned her back on Joan. God knew it was destroying Gabriel to continue, day after day, but he was still here. He would continue to bear witness to Joan's story, even if he had to do it alone. *In the end,* he thought miserably, *we are all alone. Except for Joan, and her Voices.*

Joan's trial had been conducted in public for eleven days, then moved behind closed doors. More and more, sympathy was edging her way, and the men who interrogated her looked like the bullies they were. Gabriel was desperate for news, plying those who might have any with drinks. They spoke in slurred voices about things he didn't quite understand: how Joan was in danger for not surrendering to the Church Militant, God's representatives in this world. They spoke of the strange angel she saw holding a crown over Charles's head. This, Gabriel knew about—they were referring to Joan seeing Yolande, the Assassin Mentor, and believing the queen to be an angel. The Assassins, in addition to abandoning Joan, had also placed her in greater danger.

Then there were her clothes. Although no one, including the clergymen who had interrogated her for days at Poitiers, expressed concern about Joan's wearing of men's clothing when riding, fighting, and sleeping in the presence of men, it seemed Cauchon and d'Estivet had seized on it like a terrier worrying a rat, deeming it an act of heresy offensive to God. Gabriel had clung to these bits of news until today, when he had heard that Joan was to be presented in public in the cemetery of the Abbey of Saint-Ouen. They were coming, now; at least a dozen clergymen. Gabriel didn't know all their roles, but many he recognized from the public trial sessions.

It had been over two months since he had seen Joan, and his heart broke to behold her. She was even thinner than before, her cheeks hollow and her blue eyes dull. Her hair was longer, an unkempt and tangled mess. Her wrists were so small now that it was a wonder the manacles didn't slide right off her hands. He moved through the crowd, trying to catch her eye without drawing unwanted attention from the soldiers who marched her onto the platform.

The priest, Guillaume Erard, began to speak. Gabriel ignored the sermon, looking through the crowd, spotting possible ways to make an escape, if he could somehow manage to leap onto the platform and—

Do what? He was one man, not even a fully-trained Assassin. He couldn't hope to fight off hundreds of armed soldiers and flee the city with a young woman, wasted from hunger and perhaps beatings, whose wrists and ankles were wrapped with chains.

The priest railed against King Charles, called Joan a "monster," a "magician," "heretical," and "superstitious." Gabriel even now found it hard to believe this was truly happening to Joan. Her face, he noted, was no longer radiant as she replied, when told she needed to submit all her words and deeds to the church, "I appeal to God and our holy father the pope."

"It is impossible to go find the lord our pope at such a distance," replied Erard. He waved one of the younger clergymen, Jean Massieu, forward. The young man looked very uncomfortable with what he was doing as he handed Joan a slip of parchment.

Gabriel did not know what it was, but Simon did. It was called a cedula, and it was designed to be attached to a separate legal document. In this case, the cedula was a letter of abjuration—a statement in which Joan swore to never again cut her hair short, or don men's clothing, or take up arms. In return for forswearing these "heresies," she would be taken into ecclesiastical custody at long last, and would never be returned to secular justice.

Simon also knew that this small piece of parchment was not the one that would be attached to the final documents on the affair. That cedula was nearly five times as long as this one. Someone would later take pains to arrange that Joan's signature would be affixed to a different statement altogether.

Joan peered at the cedula and asked, "I wish the clerks to read this to me and advise me as to what it says, and if I should sign it."

Erard had obviously had enough. "Do it now!" he bellowed, "Otherwise you will end your days by fire!"

Gabriel's gut clenched. Simon's heart slammed against his chest.

Massieu seemed to reach a decision, and began to read the cedula aloud to Joan. As he did, murmuring arose from both the spectators and those who stood on the platforms. Gabriel distinctly heard Cauchon's voice say, "You will have to pay for that," to the unfortunate Massieu.

The young man didn't falter. "If you sign," Massieu said, "you will be a reformed heretic. You will be imprisoned still, but formally transferred to a place where women will tend you, and your life will be spared. You might even be freed, and could go home one day. If you refuse—you will burn."

To everyone's surprise, Joan laughed. She took the pen thrust at her and made a circle on the parchment, with the sign of the cross.

Gabriel knew that she could sign her name. Instead, Joan had made a signal he'd seen before: a cross within a circle. The signal to whomever the letter reached that Joan meant nothing she said in it.

She suspected a trap—and his brilliant, beautiful Joan was leaving herself a way out of it.

Gabriel found himself laughing, too. Joan seemed to sense him, and for a moment her head turned and he was gazing into her large blue eyes. A flicker of her glorious inner light warmed her face, and despite himself, Gabriel found himself shoving through the crowd, trying to reach her.

Beside him, unease was turning into active disapproval. "The king has spent his money very badly on you," someone with an English accent was saying to Cauchon. "It will go poorly for the king if Joan escapes us."

Cauchon said in his most confident voice, "My lord, do not worry; if she does, we will catch her again."

Gabriel's mirth faded, to be replaced by cold fear at the words and at what was happening on the platform. Someone was speaking to Joan, saying, "You have spent the day well, and, please God, you have saved your soul."

"As to that," Joan said, "some of you men in the church—take me your prison, as you promised, so that I be no longer in the hands of these Englishmen."

The cold, ugly voice of Jean d'Estivet cut through the cacophony. "Take her back to where you found her."

"No!" The word was torn from Gabriel's throat and he pushed forward with new determination, trying to reach her, foolishly, futilely. The last glimpse he had of Joan was her face, with an expression of slowly dawning horror upon it.

I fear nothing—except treachery.

Simon, what happened? I don't understand what Gabriel just saw....

Simon was sweating and trembling, his heart pounding with grief and rage that both were and weren't his own. He took a deep breath, focused on the image of Gabriel in the Memory Corridor, and tried to explain.

"They told her that she would be deemed a reformed heretic if she rejected men's clothing and other masculine behavior. They promised she'd be put in an ecclesiastical prison and not have to have leg irons or guards in her cell. Normally in such cases, the former heretic would be released in a couple of years. Joan made a sign on the paper that she could say later was not her true signature, just in case they tricked her."

And they did.

"Oh, they did a lot worse than that," Simon spat. "On Sunday morning, Joan woke to find that her guards had taken her dresses and left *only* men's clothes for her to wear."

Oh, Simon... no....

"Someone had to have ordered that. My money's on Cauchon. Joan protested that she had no choice but to put them on. On May twenty-ninth, Cauchon assembled the assessors. Thirty-nine of them thought she needed the cedula reread to her and explained better. Only three wanted to turn her over to secular justice."

And that didn't matter either.

"No. They had no real power. Joan's judges were Cauchon and d'Estivet. Her priest, who was fond of her, sent someone to ask Cauchon if she could hear mass before she was burned alive. To everyone's surprise, he said yes. Massieu—the young man who tried to help her—went to fetch a stole and a candle, so the priest could perform the rite properly. After that, Joan was turned over to the bailiff, but before he could even pronounce sentence Vidic's ancestor grabbed her arm and took her to the pyre."

I'm bringing you out.

"No, you're not."

I don't like your stats.

"I'm telling you I want... no. I don't want to. I... I have to. She still feels alive to me. To *me*, not Gabriel. That's why *I* have to see this."

Then I'll bear witness with you.

WEDNESDAY, 30 MAY, 1431
OLD MARKETPLACE, ROUEN

So many soldiers, Gabriel thought; *just for one skinny girl....*

There were hundreds of them, armed and wary. Several were in full armor. Some were sprinkled throughout the crowd. Others stood between the throngs and the scaffolding, keeping those who would try to harm—or help—Joan at bay.

She stood straight even now, her slender body draped in a thin chemise. Her thick black curls were gone; they had shaved her head to shame her. Atop her bald pate they had put a tall, pointed miter on which was written Joan's crimes: *Heretic. Idolator. Apostate.* The miter was too large, and had been shoved down almost completely over her eyes in order to stay on. Her face, what Gabriel could see of it, had been beaten bloody, so swollen he wondered if she could even see.

Jeanne... Jeanne... this can't be real... this can't be how it ends...!

As armored men shoved Joan of Arc toward the stake and the burly executioner wrapped chains around her thin body, Gabriel Laxart broke. Tears poured down his face, blurring his vision as great, wrenching sobs were torn from him.

Please, God, take me, strike me down and let her go... don't let them do this to her.... She loved You so much, she did everything You asked....

"Hurry up and do your job!" someone called out to the executioner.

"Yes, hurry, we want to get home in time for supper!" another one shouted, and there was a wave of vicious, hungry, *evil* laughter.

Gabriel's world went scarlet. He exploded into furious motion. He cried out incoherently, striking out at everyone and anyone who was in his way, pummeling his way through the crowd, trying to find the monsters who were calling for Joan to burn and scream in agony. Trying to reach the platform, to tear Joan away from it, to bear her to safety. A dozen, a hundred Assassins hidden in plain sight amongst the crowd would rise up in solidarity, avenging angels sent by God to destroy those who would harm His chosen.

But it did not happen.

There was no divine fury. There were no Assassins. There was only fire; Hell's punishment inflicted on the most heavenly woman Gabriel had ever known.

I can't take this, Simon thought. *I can't bear it.*

Heat bathed his face. Smoke filled his mouth as he kept screaming. Hands reached for his arms, pulling him back, shoving him to the ground. Before he went down, he saw Joan's priest lifting a crucifix for her to fix her eyes upon, to distract her, if even a tiny amount, from the unspeakable agony of fire licking her body and turning her to ashes.

A mailed fist filled Gabriel's vision. The last thing he heard before the world went horribly, mercifully black was Joan's voice—high, frightened but determined, not even sounding like her voice—crying out a single word: *"Jesus!"*

Simon?

His face was wet, he realized, and he had trouble breathing. "Victoria?" he said, and his voice trembled. "Did I black out?"

No, but you wouldn't answer me for a moment.

There were simply no words for how he felt. Broken, lost, devastated, furious... all of them together couldn't even scratch the surface. He swallowed and breathed deeply, willing his mind to control his body's shaking. "I need something from you."

Of course. I'll get you out right away.

"No! No, not that, not yet. I need to go forward in Gabriel's life."

Absolutely not. After what we both just saw, I think—

"I need this, Victoria." The words gushed from him, like blood from an open wound. "I need to know he's going to be all right. I want to see the mother of his child, I want to know if he lives to see Joan's retrial. To see her vindicated. I want to know—if he's ever happy again."

What if he isn't all right, Simon? Ever? What if he never knows his child? What if he drinks or fights himself to death, or takes a Leap of Faith he knows he won't survive?

Simon winced at the ugliness of the portrait she painted.

"Then I'll know. And I'll deal with that." Somehow.

Victoria swore in French. He understood almost all of it. Then, at last, she said, *All right.*

An hour later, she lifted the helmet from his sweat-soaked head. And in her eyes, Simon saw the same grim, furious determination that he knew had to be reflected in his own expression.

"You know what we need to do," he said as she helped him out of the straps with hands that trembled.

"Yes," she said firmly. "I do."

CHAPTER THIRTY-THREE

The three met in the Hyde Park in the early afternoon, each arriving from a different tube stop. Simon's senses were on high alert as he walked past families with children energetically stomping fallen leaves as they shrieked with laughter, determined individuals whose brisk stride indicated this was their workout for the day, and couples old and young simply enjoying a clear, bright day. The sky was blue, the leaves were at their peak shades of gold and red, and the indescribable but unmistakable crisp fragrance of autumn hung in the air. The Joy of Life fountain where Simon had instructed them to meet him burbled and splashed.

Simon was moved by none of it. All he could see in his mind's eye was Joan. All he could hear were the taunts of the English.

And all he could smell was fire.

Simon had no idea why he had picked this particular spot. He enjoyed a more classic style of art, and while this fountain was not offensively modern, it still quite contemporary. As he gazed at the two figurines in the center, holding hands and appearing to dance above the flowing streams of water, the four smaller shapes of children darting and playing around them, he thought of Joan. It was such a simple emotion, joy; at least he knew she had tasted it in her brief life.

After a few moments of contemplation he was joined by Anaya, and then Victoria. They could speak without fear of eavesdroppers; the splash of the water would drown out their voices. Simon said quietly to Anaya, "Victoria and I learned about something that will quite probably turn the Templar Order on its head."

Anaya inhaled swiftly. "What Rikkin was trying to prevent you away from finding out?"

"I'm absolutely certain of it."

"Simon the whistle blower," Anaya said. "Never thought I'd see the day."

"This isn't about turning against what the Templar Order stands for," Simon replied. "It's about reaffirming what it truly means to be a Templar—what it's *supposed* to have meant all along."

"Can you tell me?"

Victoria and Simon exchanged glances. "There are a few things I'm still piecing together. I'd like to protect both of you as much as possible. I wouldn't involve you at all if I didn't think this was absolutely critical." He paused and turned Anaya to face him. "I'm not exaggerating when I tell you that this could change *everything*."

"In what way?"

"In the best way possible."

"Provided we live through it," Victoria said wryly.

"There are things Templars should be willing to die for," Simon said. "This is one of them. Even so, if this goes wrong—I want you to know as little as possible."

"I was a field agent, Simon. I was ready to die every day I went to work. But you don't have to tell me anything you don't want to." She smiled at him and poked him in the chest. "You can be a stuffed shirt,

Simon Hathaway, but you have more integrity than anyone I've ever known. I believe you, and I trust you. If you feel this is something that will help the Order, I'm with you. Just tell me what you need me to do."

He found himself reaching for her hand. "I've never been more certain of anything in my life. Thank you." He released her hand and straightened. "Both of you. Right then. Here's what we're going to do."

Simon filled the day with busywork—responding to e-mails, making a list of desired hires for his department, returning phone calls... and making preparations. He took Victoria out for a late dinner, where they were able to speak quietly and solidify the plan.

It was after ten when Simon and Victoria returned to the Animus Room. "Do you really need to leave tomorrow?" Simon said. "We've spent so much time in the fifteenth century, I've not had much of a chance to show you London's twenty-first."

Victoria slid into the seat behind the monitor and began typing. "I know," she said, "and I'm sorry too. At least I got to have a lot of tea!"

Okay, this is good—I can see everything, came Anaya's voice in Simon's ear. Victoria, too, had an earbud that enabled to hear Anaya. *Just follow my directions.*

"Since I've not heard back from Morgenstern, I'll resend the simulation involving the de Molay graffiti before I go. And then I think we're all done." Anaya had explained last night that if she could be remotely "hands on" at the Animus processing computer, she could have Victoria isolate all data from a certain time stamp forward. Not only would Victoria be able to send it send it undetected to Anaya's computer—Cryptology had been mentioned to misdirect those listening in—but she would also be able to make a copy... and delete the original simulations. Simon continued making the sort of small talk people who are wrapping up time together would, all the while paying close attention to Anaya's instructions.

"Well, that's it," Victoria said as she casually pressed a key. Simon's heart lurched. They had just passed the point of no return; they had just deleted Simon's most recent session in the Animus.

Victoria rose. "I know you're not much of a hugger," she said, "but I will miss you, Simon." He embraced her with real affection, desperately hoping she'd be as unscathed as possible by what he was about to do. "Thank you," he said. "For everything. I couldn't have asked for a better companion on this adventure."

Her hand slipped the small device into his pocket. The last simulation.

Simon opened the box that held the sword and picked it up, admiring it. Victoria gazed at it too. "I think Mr. Rikkin will be very pleased with what you've learned about it," she said. *At least,* Simon thought, *if anyone's listening, that might make them pause before they shoot me.*

With seeming casualness, he replaced the sword in its box, but took care to lay it down on the blue velvet so that it rested on its opposite side, hiding the bug he'd placed. "I'll keep this in Historical Research until it's time to make my presentation."

They parted at the lift, Simon heading up to his office, Victoria down to the parking garage. He was on his own. Anaya would not be able to intervene. It was one thing for her to keep an eye out for him; Simon refused to let her become involved more deeply than she already had been. Hacking into the Animus would he bad enough, if it were discovered. Hacking into the building's security systems would be... Simon didn't even want to think about that. Still, her voice in his ear was oddly comforting.

Okay, at this hour there aren't many people in the building.

Earlier, Simon had casually moved a coat tree over one of the cameras—just enough to create a blind spot. Now he went to his computer, clicked, and the strains of Pachelbel's Canon filled the room. Taking a pair of scissors from the desk, he opened the sword box and carefully cut the velvet lining away from the box's sides. He covered the sword with the fabric and withdrew a roll of duct tape from a bag—one of several purchases he had made earlier on the way back from Hyde Park. The music concealed most of the tell-tale sound of tape being unwound as he wrapped strips securely about the sword. Then, awkwardly, Simon rose and awkwardly strapped the sword to his body with the silver tape. It wasn't comfortable, but it should work.

His long overcoat and a thick scarf should conceal the sword. The only metal detectors were located downstairs at the main doors. Victoria would be waiting at the parking garage in a blind spot Anaya had scouted out earlier. He'd climb into the boot of the car and—

Simon, you need to go.

"Hmm?" he murmured quietly, hoping no one would hear him over the music.

I've got eyes on all three stairways, Anaya continued. *People are coming in on all ground level entrances. They're plainclothes, but they have that look to them, and I think they're armed. There's activity at the parking garage exits, too.*

"I bet they're searching cars. Tell Victoria to go ahead and get out." Victoria had the second copy of the simulation. Hopefully Security would be looking for a person, not a small data chip. "Now how do *I* get out of here?"

I'm hacking the security systems.

"Don't!" he said, too loudly, then more quietly, "We can't risk you. For—for lots of reasons."

They've got every exit of the building covered, and they just now took the elevators offline. Groups of four are climbing up every stairwell. Simon, they know your last position, you've got to go!

Go where? Simon stood frozen in the doorway of his office while precious seconds ticked away. They were moving up the stairs even as he stood here, up toward his floor and—

Up.

Yes. "They're expecting me to try to come down the stairs," he said. "So I'm going up."

Up? Unless you've got a helicopter stashed up there that I don't know about—

"No, no, it's all right, I know what I'm doing." It was a lie. Simon Hathaway had no idea what he was doing. But Gabriel Laxart did.

Up.

Simon darted down the hall, eased open the stairwell door as quietly as he could, and listened. He could hear them, closer than he thought, which meant they would hear him, too. The ship of secrecy had sailed. Simon sprang forward and felt an immense wave of gratitude for his long legs and the hours each week spent at the gym. He took the stairs two, three at a time, like a hunted fox who hears the baying of the hounds behind him.

Adrenaline spurted through his veins and he thought of Gabriel's training, of his battles, of how the boy had been able to run in armor, even spring onto his horse if need be—

—*Hands here, push, up and over the railing*—

—and keep going. "Anaya, how many floors to the roof?"

To the—damn you, Simon, six more. Her voice caught. She thought he wasn't going to make it. Simon didn't say anything to comfort her. He wasn't sure himself.

"Simon Hathaway!" came a voice. Simon didn't slow. If they were yelling at him, they were squandering their breath and he wasn't. "You are in possession of Abstergo property! Hand it over and submit to judgment!"

Two more steps at a time, up and over the railing, up onto the next floor. They were making a serious clatter now, not caring who heard them. The first shot rang out, startlingly loud, echoing in the space. Simon's heart surged in shock and he increased his pace.

There are three main exit routes in the building, Anaya was saying, a calm voice in his ear. He barely heard her, his ears filled only with the sound of pursuing feet, his hammering heart, and his increasingly ragged breathing. *They're in the two that go clear up to the roof. The ones in the second stairwell are two floors below you and your friends.*

That was the worst of it. In the end, his hunters were likely Templars of an Operations team similar to Berg's. They *should* be friends, or at least comrades in arms.

But they weren't. They were enemies.   They raced up the next flight of steps. This time, Simon wasn't running. Instead, he leaped over the railing at the leader, his overcoat held out in front of him. Temporarily blinded and caught off-balance, he went down, slamming into the Templar agent a few steps behind him. Simon leaped clear of the two entangled men and drew the sword. He'd never held it as he did now, but Gabriel understood how a hand curled over the hilt of a sword, and Simon brought the weapon swinging down in a graceful arc. It struck the third agent hard across the torso. The gun clattered to the steps and fell far below.

Gabriel would have cut the man in half. Simon did what Joan would have done, and used only the flat of the blade. The agent had not been expecting a swordfight and Simon's blow was a strong one.

But the fourth agent had his hand up, and for an instant Simon saw the stairwell light glinting off the barrel of a gun. Then he was gone, up to another level as his pursuers struggled to rise and continue the hunt.

The skirmish had bought him precious time, and Simon didn't waste it. One more flight and there it was, the final door, the one that opened onto the roof. He slammed his shoulder into it, and kept going.

The cold night air was a shock to his heated face and heaving lungs. Simon kept running, his feet flying over first the concrete pathway, then the manicured grass of the rooftop's park; he was running out of rooftop.

Why did I come up here? he thought, wildly and far too late. *I'm a bloody rat in a trap.*

He had delayed the Templars, but had not stopped them, and they charged out of the stairway behind him. On the other side of the roof, a light pierced the darkness as a door was flung open. The second team of his pursuers had made it. Both groups were charging toward him, one ahead of Simon, one behind. They knew, as he did, that, other than the lift that they'd shut down and the two staircases from which they now emerged with grim and silent purpose, there was no way off this building.

Think. Think!

Thinking had saved Simon before, many a time. He'd always relied on logic, on rationality, on analysis, to solve every predicament that life in all its sadistic whimsy had thrown him, but now it was of no use to him at all.

The deadly percussion of gunfire exploded behind him. *Trees*, his rational mind shouted, and the logic saved him. He altered his path, zigzagging to make himself an unpredictable target, careening erratically like a drunken man toward the trees and shrubberies and now-shuttered snack and beverage stalls that would shield him from the hail of bullets.

But it would only delay the inevitable.

Simon knew very well what his fellow Templars were capable of. And he knew what they wanted. They were not coming to question him, or capture him. Despite the words in the stairwell, there had also been gunfire. They were intent on killing him, and therefore, very, very soon, he would be dead.

There was only one way out, and it would be a bloody miracle if it worked.

His heart was slamming against his chest, his lungs heaving, his body taxed to its limit because in the end, he was only human, wasn't he, no matter what kind of training he had, no matter what sort of DNA was floating about in his blood. And he didn't slow, *couldn't* slow, couldn't allow that logical, analytical, rational brain of his to interrupt the signals from the deep primal instinct of survival. Couldn't let his brain overrule his body.

Because his body knew what was called for. And it knew how to do it.

A tree branch exploded right beside him. Splinters grazed his face, drawing blood. Anaya's voice was in his ear, shouting something, he couldn't make out what.

The fate offered by the Templars behind him was one of heartless certainty. The stone wall that encircled the edge of the rooftop garden of the London office of Abstergo Industries offered a wild, desperate chance.

If he had the faith to take it.

Simon Hathaway didn't slow. He surged forward, summoning an extra burst of speed, clearing it like runner would a hurdle, his long legs pedaling in the air as he arched his back, spread his arms—

—and leaped.

CHAPTER
THIRTY-FOUR

"It's a shame, really," Alan Rikkin was saying as he opened the door into the Inner Sanctum's private meeting room. Less than ten days ago, Simon Hathaway had stood here, in front of a white board, talking in an earnest voice about knowledge for knowledge's sake. "To have to start the process all over again. Can't believe Simon didn't even last a week in his role."

"Do we know what happened?" asked Laetitia England.

"Yes, we do," Simon replied calmly, standing at the far end of the room. "Well, *I* do."

Rikkin froze. Simon did not think he had ever seen pure hatred in anyone's eyes before this moment, but there it was, smoldering in the depths of Alan Rikkin's dark orbs.

"Simon. What a surprise," Rikkin said. His voice was cold and flat, belying the intensity of his gaze. "I can honestly say you are the very last person I expected to discover in this room."

Simon looked around the stunned expressions of his fellow Inner Sanctum members. He wondered what they'd been told. He wondered if he'd leave this room alive. "To paraphrase Mark Twain, reports of my death have been greatly exaggerated."

Agneta Reider smiled first. "Well, I for one am glad," she said, and there was real pleasure in her voice.

"Simon, what happened to you? Where have you been?" Mitsuko Nakamura asked. Rikkin, his gaze never leaving Simon, was busy activating monitors. In a few seconds, the faces of Otso Berg and Álvaro Gramática appeared, reacting to Simon's presence with similar stunned expressions.

"How did you get past security?" asked Alfred Stearns suspiciously.

"I'll answer your questions shortly, Mitsuko. And come now, Alfred. I'm an English Templar historian in London—a city that's two thousand years old. Who better to know about long-lost underground passages?" He squared his shoulders. "Right. Now that we're all here—in one form or another—I formally present myself to the judgment of the Inner Sanctum. I have a right to a hearing."

"He does have that right," Berg said. That surprised Simon. Otso Berg wasn't someone he had expected to come to his defense.

"What, exactly, have you done that requires judgment?" England asked.

"I've stolen a priceless artifact," Simon said bluntly. "I've also stolen, and destroyed, intellectual property of the Order. But I have returned the Sword of Eden in better condition than it was when I took it, and I will reveal and replace the content of the intellectual property. All that I have done, I have done for what I believe with all my heart is the highest good of the Templar Order." His pale blue eyes met Rikkin's.

"Alan, what's he going on about?" Stearns demanded.

"I've absolutely no idea," said Rikkin.

Liar, thought Simon. "As my employer, Alan, you can fire me and press charges right now," he said. "But as a member of the Inner Sanctum, you are obliged to permit me to speak. Who will you be today? CEO or Templar?"

A muscle twitched near Rikkin's eye. "Templar. First, and always." As Simon had gambled he would, Rikkin chose the path of seeming reasonableness instead of intolerant bullying—at least while he had an audience.

"This should be good," said David Kilkerman.

"Oh, it will. And I won't ask you to clap erasers, David." This time, Kilkerman did not laugh. Simon indicated the two pieces of technology currently on display on the meeting table. One was a 3D monitor. The other was an elongated box.

"The sword's right there." Simon nodded toward the box. "Let me briefly recap what we know of its history. It was in the possession of Grand Master Jacques de Molay until the mass arrest of Templars on the thirteenth of October, 1307. It was taken to the Temple on that date for safekeeping, and was buried behind the altar at the church in Sainte-Catherine-de-Fierbois some point after that. Joan of Arc sent someone to dig it up in 1429. It was lost—"

Simon paused, cleared his throat, and resumed. "Lost at the battle for Paris on the eighth of September, 1429. It was recovered by the Templars sometime after that date and returned to the Temple, where it stayed until François-Thomas Germain located it during the French Revolution. Thenceforth, broken, it was in the possession of Assassin Arno Dorian. It had many more adventures, no doubt, before it ended up in Alan's office. I'll return to it later."

He clasped his hands behind his back and regarded them. "When I stood before you on the date of my entrance into the Inner Sanctum, I resolved to do two things. One, determine a way to repair this sword. Two, to prove the value of my approach to the tasks of my department—to show you that if you give random chance a seat at the table, it will bring gifts. On this journey, I discovered something that I found shocking, horrifying, and exciting."

He took a deep breath. *Here we go.* "I discovered that our Order has been in desperate need of a course correction for at least six centuries. Since that time, we've misunderstood or misinterpreted almost everything."

"How dare you!" Stearns was livid with fury. "You have barely been a member of the Inner Sanctum for a week and you—"

"There is nothing wrong with what we—" England began.

"Heresy."

The word shut everyone down. It was uttered, of course, by Rikkin, who doubtless thought Simon had done him the favor of shooting himself in the head without any outside aid.

"I don't believe it is," Simon replied steadily. "I intend to prove to you that we have deviated from what de Molay intended for the Order, and we've been doing a great deal wrong since he was martyred. I am allowed to present my case. If you deem me a heretic after that, then I'll submit to your judgment, as I've said."

"I am finding all this quite entertaining," exclaimed Gramática. "Simon, I thought you so dull, but clearly I was wrong."

Before Rikkin could shut him down again, Simon continued. "The intellectual properties I stole were memories of my ancestor, Gabriel Laxart. I took them because I did not wish them, ah, tampered with before I had a chance to present my findings to you. But here they are, intact."

Simon clicked the remote control. The 3D monitor, which always struck him as looking like a very technical aquarium, came to life. The roiling mists of the so-familiar Memory Corridor blossomed and swirled, like ink dropped into water.

After a moment, the swirls took form. "Right now, you're looking at carvings—graffiti—left by Jacques de Molay and some of his knights, while they were imprisoned in Chinon Castle."

Even as Simon spoke, the voice of Jean de Metz floated from the monitor. "There's got to be some kind of message. Templars wouldn't waste their energy just to make some entertaining drawings."

"These carvings are famous," scoffed Rikkin. "You're wasting time,

Simon. Morgenstern over in Cryptography could talk your ear off—"

"Interesting, then, isn't it, that Morgenstern over in Cryptography never received this when Dr. Bibeau sent it to him." Simon watched keenly as that registered with the rest of the Inner Sanctum members, but did not look directly at Rikkin. "Look in particular at this one—a sort of inverted tear-drop of a sun, shining on the upturned face of a Templar. Look at the many instances of hands reaching upward, and hearts drawn in several places. And this line in Latin. It says, 'If the heart is strong, it will not break.'"

"Why are you showing us this?" Berg, as usual, blunt.

"You'll understand later. Just remember these." The scene reverted to mist, then reformed into Joan's face.

Simon felt like he'd been punched in the gut at the sight. He gritted his teeth and forced his voice to be calm as he looked at her, holding the pouch and smiling. "I keep the ring they gave me in here, always close to my heart, along with a few other things that are special to me," she said.

Simon closed his eyes briefly, then continued. "Gabriel could sense power in the sword, but it was just as inert when he touched it as it was when you gave it to me to research, Alan. Dead. Colorless. But watch."

Again, he saw the bittersweet image of Joan's face, her blue eyes wide, the pouch around her neck slipping forward as she leaned toward the sword and slid off the red velvet sheath, gasping as she saw the golden glow.

Simon allowed himself a moment of satisfaction as more than a few of his audience inhaled swiftly when Joan grasped the sword. The golden hue of the sword increased, and the lines of ancient technology flared to life as well.

"Jhesu Maria," whispered Joan of Arc, and lifted the sword high. Her face was alight, and so was the sword, a corona of tamed, white lightning enveloping it.

"You can tell the sword is now active. What you can't tell is how

Gabriel felt right at this moment," Simon said. "He felt joy, and contentment, and peace...." Simon frowned, knowing his words were inadequate. "He felt that there was nothing to fear. That no one would suffer. Cruelty or anger no longer needed to exist. When Joan held the sword, there was only peace and calmness."

"For the Templars?" England wanted to clarify.

"For everyone." A montage of scenes appeared, showing Joan in action with the sword: holding it aloft, fighting with only the flat of the blade, defending herself with its lightning, shattering the blade of her enemy into fragments.

"Remarkable." The comment came from Berg. Emotions seemed to be warring on his face—doubt in what he saw, and a strange... wistfulness was the only word for it. Reider had her chin propped up in her hands, watching raptly.

"We saw none of this with Germain," said Gramática.

"No," Simon said. "We didn't. Remember this, too."

Now, Gabriel Laxart was in a Rouen tavern. Simon remembered his anger. The boy had come here to kill, but in the end, what he saw had so disgusted him that he had decided to let the drunken wretch live.

"Geoffroy Thérage," Simon said solemnly. "The ancestor of your predecessor, David. Warren Vidic."

Thérage looked every inch the terrifying executioner. He was over six feet tall, a giant in that era, and strongly built. He had dark hair and a thick black beard. And at the moment, he was hunched over an ale, his eyes wide, glassy, and red-rimmed as he muttered to a companion, an older man, better dressed, whose face was slack and gray with shock.

"Twenty-five years I've done this," Thérage muttered. "I've seen 'em beg, and weep, and snarl, and soil themselves, and pray to and damn God. But this...."

He took another long pull on his drink as the young man who planned on taking his life watched from another table. "It was my duty to kill them. Never thought twice about it. But I'm going to burn in hell for this one. I've killed a holy woman, and God's seen it." Thérage's huge frame shuddered. "Her heart... three times we burned her. Three damned times. Oil, sulphur, carbon I put on it. *It wouldn't burn.*" He ran a trembling hand over his face. "In the end I threw it all in the Seine."

"We've burned a saint," murmured the other man. "God have mercy on our souls."

"The insistence that her heart didn't burn is part of the folklore surrounding Joan of Arc," Simon said. "But it seems as though this tall tale is true. We have it directly from the man who tried to destroy it three times and failed."

"Thérage is drunk," said England dismissively. "He's imagining things."

"Isn't that the official line we Templars like to trot out, when ordinary people run across things they can't explain?" Simon challenged. "Remember this moment, too. It's important."

The scene changed again. "By now, you recognize Gabriel. This elegant man he's speaking with is Jean, Duke of Alençon, recorded in history as Joan of Arc's best friend. What history *doesn't* record is that, like Gabriel, Alençon was in training to become an Assassin. He was also a lifelong friend of King Charles. So why, then, would a man like this take part in a revolt *against* Charles eight years after Joan's death? Why would he become a member of the Order of the Golden Fleece, an order founded by Philip, Duke of Burgundy—a Templar?"

"He turned his coat," murmured Stearns approvingly.

"Yes," confirmed Simon, "but historians have been wondering for centuries just what drove him to do so. But *we* know... now."

CHAPTER
THIRTY-FIVE

"A Templar?" Gabriel said, in horrified tones. Alençon had looked so old to him, Simon remembered; so very worn. But Gabriel, too, was no longer a youth.

"The Assassins could have rescued Jeanne at any point," Alençon said bitterly. "They chose not to. I pressed de Metz and Yolande, but they would not tell me why."

"'I fear nothing, except treachery,' Jeanne said once."

The duke's dark eyes regarded the younger man sadly. "There's something I must tell you. You will find it difficult to believe, but— the Duke of Burgundy never wanted, let alone ordered, Joan's death."

Gabriel scoffed, both irritated and offended at the suggestion. Alençon lifted a placating hand. "Please, old friend, just hear me out. Of course he wanted to stop her. She was threatening the Templar plan. They hadn't counted on a girl with her blood showing up, let alone that she'd find a Sword of Eden. It was Philip's man, John of Luxembourg, the count of Ligny, who took her prisoner. Don't you remember how long he held her?"

"Months," Gabriel recalled. "And," he added, grudgingly, "she was well treated. But he sold her to the English!"

"The Templars had to discredit Charles," Alençon said. "Jeanne was strongly linked to him. If she were ruled a heretic, it would reflect badly on Charles. So the Templars—the Burgundians and the English—agreed to try and convict her of heresy."

"A trial," sneered Gabriel, still angry. "With the outcome predetermined."

"Yes," said Alençon, "her trial, her conviction—her chance to recant and then be freed in three, maybe four years—you're right. *That* was all planned. Gabriel... all they wanted to do, all they *needed* to do, was to defang her. Charles was already turning his back on Jeanne, and the world would have, too." Gently, he said, "She could have returned to Domrémy. Married. Had a family. *That* was the plan."

Even now, watching it as the others did, Simon remembered how this news had torn him apart. Jeanne, back home with her family. Perhaps... perhaps with him, and their child. Gabriel sagged against the stone wall beside which the two men spoke, and Alençon caught him.

"I—I don't believe you," he whispered. He didn't want to believe it, because if he did, it almost made the pain worse. For the Assassins to have failed Joan, and for the Templars to be trying to spare her life? The world had turned upside down.

"During the trial, there was another examination to prove Jeanne was still a virgin. And she was. How in the world, with men who hated her in her cell at all times, could she have stayed that way? Because Philip told the guards that if they violated Jeanne, they would be executed!"

Gabriel rubbed his temples, trying to make sense of any of this. "But what happened? What went wrong?

"Bishop Pierre Cauchon and the prosecutor, Father Jean d'Estivet. That's what went wrong. They were out to make names for themselves, strengthen their political positions. Cauchon wanted to become archbishop of Rouen, and he had a personal grudge against Jeanne. And d'Estivet...." Alençon spat. "He simply enjoys suffering."

Gabriel was still reeling, but Alençon was relentless. "Philip had concerns about them. He sent Ligny to Jeanne's cell in mid-May, two weeks before her execution, to make her an offer. Ligny would ransom her back if she would agree to never raise arms against the Burgundians or the English. But... she—"

"She thought it was a trap."

"Yes. Philip thought everything had been decided when she agreed to never wear men's clothes. But then... oh, Gabriel...." Alençon looked as if he was about to shatter. "Cauchon ordered the guards to take her dresses. They left her only with men's clothing... or none."

"That's why she relapsed," Gabriel whispered. Then, in a hard voice, "That's why she's dead."

"Jeanne was a girl who didn't understand what was going on with her. She wasn't even an Assassin. The Templars knew that. She wasn't supposed to die, Gabriel. Do you remember Jacques de Molay?"

"Wh-what? Yes...." Gabriel looked at his old friend, confused.

"He set the standard for all Templars to follow." Alencon's dark eyes burned with intensity. "We believe that Jeanne's sword was once his. And that how it worked was the way de Molay wanted it to work. He was burned as a heretic. The last—the absolute *last*—thing he would want his Order to do is burn a girl who wielded his sword with the same good heart he had, however uninformed she might have been."

"Why are you telling me this?" Gabriel half-demanded, half-sobbed.

"Because you need to know that the Templars tried, repeatedly, to prevent Jeanne's death. The Order didn't kill her—two selfish men did. Men interested not in the betterment of humanity, but only in their own desires. And that Order thinks you might be interested in helping them enact justice."

Slowly, Gabriel lifted his head. He pressed his lips tougher in a thin line, and his face hardened.

The scene shifted. An old man sat in a chair while a servant attended to him, placing a warm cloth over his eyes before taking out a small razor and soap, laying them out on a table in preparation for shaving.

A shadow moved behind him. Gabriel slipped his arm around the servant's neck, squeezing until the terrified servant passed out. As quietly as possible, Gabriel eased him to the floor. Then he stepped forward, picked up the blade, and placed it against the old man's throat.

"Étienne?" asked Pierre Cauchon, the cloth still over his eyes. His voice was thin and high; no longer that of a powerful orator who had bullied a half-starved, exhausted young woman with questions for hours on end.

"Not Étienne," Gabriel replied. "You don't know me. I'm just a shadow. A witness to what you did to Jeanne the Maid. You've been spared by your masters, but now... now they've decided it's time to kill this old dog."

Simon knew how badly Gabriel desired to do this. But before he could slice open Cauchon's throat, the elderly man spasmed and gasped, clawing at his heart, and then sprawled half-in and half out of the chair—dead.

"Gabriel was denied the satisfaction of killing Cauchon himself," Simon continued. "But Jean d'Estivet was not so fortunate. His body was found in a sewer—his throat pierced by a slender, sharp blade. The populace called it God's justice, for what he had done to Joan of Arc."

Simon paused, bracing himself for denials and attacks. But they did not come. He couldn't read their expressions; Templars had some of the best poker faces in the world. But he was being allowed to continue.

"You will recall," he said, "that when I began, I asked you to remember three things." He clicked the remote. The scene reset, illustrating each item as he discussed it. "The graffiti left by de Molay, particularly the sun image and the Latin quote. The pendant that Joan wore around her neck. And how the sword reacted to her. To these, I will add two more things: Thérage's statement that Joan's heart refused to burn; and the information that Philip of Burgundy tried, *repeatedly*, to keep Joan alive, and was furious at what amounted to betrayal of the Templar Order at the hands of Joan's two judges."

He clicked the remote again. Another image appeared, but not an Animus memory: a simple photograph of the de Molay graffiti. "Notice the sun," he said. "It's now a hollow. Something was placed there and covered up... until the right person found it. Whatever it hid when Gabriel saw it has since been removed. And I believe I know what it was."

Simon's heart was racing. All hinged on what was about to happen. Slowly, he reached into his pocket and removed a small object wrapped in a handkerchief; an object that had been there for some time, quietly exuding calm to his racing thoughts. He placed it on the table and unwrapped it.

Murmurs rose and everyone leaned forward for a better look. It was about the size of a large grape, a perfect, glowing scarlet sphere that pulsed rhythmically. Simon watched as several members of the Inner Sanctum visibly relaxed. It wasn't controlling them. But they could sense, and were responding to, its energy.

"This," he said, "is what I call the Heart. It's the heart of the sword. It's Joan's 'heart' that would not burn. It's what makes this sword one that was rightfully wielded by Jacques de Molay and Joan of Arc, but *not* by Germain."

Simon trusted the words to flow as he told the Heart's story. Once, he informed the Inner Sanctum, it had been an intrinsic part of the Sword of Eden. De Molay had kept it separate from the sword when the weapon was not being wielded in battle, so that in case of loss or betrayal, the two Pieces of Eden would not be taken together. Somehow, some way—Simon did not know exactly—de Molay had smuggled the Heart with him into the Coudray dungeon. He had carved out a hollow in the dungeon wall, placed the Heart inside it, and covered up the hiding place with plaster doubtless also smuggled in. He had even informed those who could read Latin on how the Heart should be used: "If the heart is strong, it will not break."

"He trusted that the right person would find the Heart—that it would call to them," Simon continued. "That person was Joan of Arc, over a century later. The quote would have been misleading to the wrong reader. It didn't mean, 'If your heart is strong, it—your heart—will not break.' It meant, 'If your heart is strong, it—the Sword, where the Heart belongs—will not break.' It's ironic that Joan herself was illiterate."

He was losing some of them—Sterns, Kilkerman, Rikkin, of course. But the others were leaning in, more curious than wary now.

"It was after her time at Chinon that Gabriel observed Joan wearing a pouch around her neck. She stayed in the Coudray Tower—and was called to find the Heart sealed away in the tower's dungeon. I believe that, along with her family's ring, the Heart was in that pouch. She was wearing it when she touched the sword for the first time—the sword that, until that moment, had been dormant. It was activated because the Heart—its power source—was in close proximity. And most likely because it was wielded by someone with a high concentration of Precursor DNA.

"Thus began Joan's incredible—some would say miraculous—string of victories; battles won by military strategy she couldn't logically know, and by the passion and enthusiasm of those who followed her. This sword was powered not by conquest and pain, but by faith in doing the right thing. 'If the heart is strong, it will not break.'"

Simon opened the box.

The sword was glowing—warm, beautiful, energized by its proximity to the Heart. But it was not yet complete. He reached for the pommel at the end of the sword's hilt and began to turn it. It twisted off easily in his hands. He showed it to the rapt Templars. It was hollow—and perfectly sized to hold the glowing Heart, which Simon inserted. He replaced the pommel, then removed his hands.

"Joan of Arc had the Heart around her throat when she was burned. Her executioner, unable to destroy it, threw it into the Seine. As some of you know, diving is my hobby. I went to the Seine, to where I believed the ashes had been cast.

"I'm not Joan of Arc," he said. His voice trembled. *Let it*, he thought. They were in the presence of something greater than themselves, and they were all about to bear witness to something not seen for more than half a millennia. "I'm not even Gabriel Laxart. But I do have Precursor DNA. And just as Gabriel sensed the sword, buried and forgotten behind the altar, I could sense the Heart wanting to be found at the bottom of the Seine. It took me some time... but I recovered it.

"The Heart has not been in its home for centuries. Nor has the sword been held by one who understands its true nature since then."

He looked up at his fellow Templars, hoping beyond hope that they would see, would understand, as he did. "As I said—I am no Joan of Arc. But after all I beheld, all I felt, through Gabriel's memories—all I've learned about this Order that my family has honored through so many generations, and that I myself have pledged my life to serve—that you, too, have sworn your lives to—I believe that I can say that here, in this moment, *my* heart is strong—and very, very full."

Simon Hathaway extended a hand, grasped the Sword of Eden, and held it up.

Light, bright and clean and purifying, suddenly filled the room. It bathed them all equally—from Rikkin to Simon to Reider to England—and suddenly Simon felt as if the burdens of a lifetime, perhaps many lifetimes, had fallen from his shoulders. And all were equally silent, staring in astonishment.

Its radiance was not as bright as that witnessed by Gabriel Laxart.

Simon was, indeed, no Joan.

But he believed in what the sword stood for. And the Sword knew it.

"*This* is what the Templar Order should be!" Simon cried, joy and certainty surging through his blood. "A weapon when needed, and an inspiration at all times. A light for humanity when it needs it the most. *This* was Jacques de Molay's goal. *This* was why the sword flourished at Joan's touch. And *this* is why, if you deem my words lies and my acts heresy, I will gladly perish as those who held it before did: wrongly accused, and dying for something I believe in with my whole heart."

He held the sword out, looking each member of the Templar Inner Sanctum in the eye. "This sword's blade is keen, and its powers have been restored. It is a graceful and deadly weapon. Who among you believes so firmly in my heresy, who here thinks their heart so strong, and so unsullied, that they will strike me down with it?"

Not a single member of the Inner Sanctum of the Templar Order— eight of the highest of the high—made a movement toward the sword.

"I call for any charges against Simon Hathaway to be dropped." Simon looked at the screen, shocked that the words had come from Otso Berg. The face of the man Simon had always thought of as a thug was almost soft with wonder.

"I second that," said Reider. She was composed, but blinked rapidly. "Simon, you've done all you set out to do. If you took Templar property, it was only to make it whole again. And I agree. Some of our methods have not been in alignment with what de Molay's sword represents."

Not all faces were alight with understanding. Rikkin, Stearns, Gramática, and Kilkerman said nothing, but had clearly been unmoved. At last, Rikkin stirred.

"You've given us a lot to think about, Simon. But it's hard to argue with success. You may proceed as you see fit with Historical Research, and you may have access to the Animus at your discretion. But now, if you don't mind... I'd rather like my sword back."

Chuckles around the table broke some of the sword's spell. But not all of it. Respectfully, albeit reluctantly, Simon replaced the exquisite artifact, and handed the closed box to Rikkin.

He could not help but notice that the CEO of Abstergo Industries never once touched the sword of Jacques de Molay.

CHAPTER THIRTY-SIX

Exhausted, Simon stumbled into his flat and flung himself on the sofa. He hadn't realized how drained he had become over the last—week? Ten days? He'd lost count. But the world was falling into rightness again—or, perhaps, truly for the first time.

The bugs in his office and home were gone. Poole was back at Temp's, beaming after his surprise vacation to Edinburgh as "Tempest in a Teapot Employee of The Year." Ben Clarke, the young man whom Anaya had been training as her replacement, hadn't shown up since Simon had fled with the sword. Even the doorman at Simon's building, who also had gone on a mysterious holiday, was back.

Simon had telephoned Victoria immediately after the meeting had ended and was relieved to hear that neither she nor Anaya had come under scrutiny in his absence. "I think they were waiting to find out what had happened to me," Simon told Victoria. They were chatting on his burner phone; Simon thought that perhaps some of the habits he'd picked up ought to be kept.

"I think so too," she said. "But nothing out of the ordinary has gone on. I'm back in the Aerie, and I have to say, I've missed it. But I wouldn't trade our joint Animus adventure for anything."

"Neither would I." He paused. "I... really can't thank you enough, Victoria. You had my back the entire time, even when I thought you didn't. It's been a while since I've had a really good friend. You haven't heard the last of me."

She knew all he didn't say, and her voice was full of affection when she replied, "I certainly hope not! Perhaps you can come see what we're doing here. These young people I'm working with are quite remarkable."

"Not Joan and Gabriel-level remarkable," Simon said. He realized he was smiling.

"*No* one is Joan and Gabriel-level remarkable," she said. "But do come visit."

"I will," he said, and meant it.

"Oh, and one more thing—how in the world did you escape?"

He chuckled. "I took a Leap of Faith right into the awning of Bella Cibo. It's coming out of my paycheck, I'm told."

He'd been in touch with Anaya during his absence in France; she'd been the one to somehow scrounge enough false documentation for him to complete his journey to Rouen and return unhindered, so he knew she was safe. He hadn't talked to her since he'd gotten back, and felt vaguely uncomfortable doing so now. Although Captain America had been mysteriously "let go", he knew Anaya still planned to take the job at Abstergo Entertainment—which had proven to be a genuine offer, rather to their surprise.

Weary as he was, Simon was restless. Before he knew it, he found himself driving back to Abstergo. His security card had been upgraded, as Rikkin had promised, and he was able to access the Animus with no difficulty.

It felt strange, being in this place after midnight, without Victoria. And he knew that he really shouldn't be entering the Animus alone.

But by this point, he was comfortable with his own strength of will, and familiar enough with the technical aspect of the process, that he felt could go back one final time without being monitored

He set up the Animus, keyed in the criteria, and managed to strap himself in. He recalled Victoria's comment: *If you'd be willing to risk severe injury, you might be able to leave the last back strap undone and get in by yourself.* It was true enough. With luck, the simulation wouldn't be an overly physical one. If it was, well, Simon knew how to desynch. It wouldn't be pleasant, but it would be better than the alternative.

Once again, mist swirled around him. Simon braced himself for what it would reveal.

15 MAY, 1443
BUREY-EN-VAUX

Gabriel leaned against the archway of his father's house, gazing up at a brilliant full moon. He had returned home shortly after his frustrating encounter with the late Bishop Cauchon. He had been eager to take that life; it had been justified a thousand times over. But God—or the devil—had come for Cauchon before Gabriel had been able to slit the man's throat. He had taken it as a sign, and when he met with Alençon, it had been for the last time.

The Templars had invited him to join their ranks, but Gabriel found that all he wanted to do was return to his father, stepmother, and their child. The fire for revenge, kindled at the same moment as Joan's pyre, had guttered, even as that awful flame had eventually done. He was soul-sick, and feared healing would never come.

And so, he had bidden Alençon farewell, and had vowed to take no part in either side of the Assassin/Templar conflict. He had returned to Burey-en-Vaux on Christmas Eve last year; thirteen years to the day when Joan of Arc had arrived at Rouen. He had found quiet with his family, and Joan's, but no peace; no healing.

Tonight, Gabriel had awoken around midnight, his heart pierced with pain as he remembered going outside in the early summer night and being surprised by Joan. *Fifteen years ago*, he thought; he was in his thirties, now. Twelve since she had burned. Everyone told him it would get easier, that he would grow used to the idea of her death. It didn't. He hadn't. He never would.

"You keep the Night Office."

Gabriel froze. His breathing rasped harshly in his own ears and though he squeezed his eyes tightly shut, tears still escaped. Was he going mad? Was he hearing Jeanne's Voices? He had watched her die, die as horribly as anyone ever had. So it couldn't be her, but it didn't matter. No madman would be happier than he.

"J-Jeanne?" He turned toward the voice, and opened his eyes.

Through the blur of tears, the moon was kind, shining fully upon the face he loved and had never dreamed to see again in life. He gasped, lurching forward and dropping to his knees in front of her, clinging to her dress, disbelieving the solidity of wool against his fingers.

Then her arms were around him, holding him tight as he sobbed into the crook of her neck. "It's me," she said. "It's really me."

For a long time, they clung to one another in silence, kneeling on the hard stone street. Finally, Gabriel lifted his head and stared into her moon-silvered face, clutching her hands, still terrified she might turn out to be a dream, as Jeanne-*Jeanne, Jeanne!*—told him what had happened.

The day of her execution, Jeanne had been alone with her priest, Martin Ladvenu. He had sent someone to fetch his stole, so he could give her communion properly, and had urged her to drink something thick and sweet. She had awoken the following night to find Jean de Metz smiling down at her, along with other people she did not know, all of whom wore hoods and did not wish their faces seen.

"He said he remembered his vow of fealty. He had not forgotten me. He and his friends had rescued me, but... oh, Gabriel... *Fleur....*"

For a moment, Gabriel didn't understand. Then guilt, horror, and hot shame twisted his stomach and clutched at his throat. How angry he had been with Fleur, cursing her name. Calling her a traitor, a coward, when in the end, she had been even more loyal than he—and certainly braver.

"I thought it was you," he whispered, and part of him still could not believe it. The joy would forever be tempered with the pain of knowing that her life had been bought by Fleur's sacrifice. He thought of the blonde girl's words. Joan had changed her life, and had brought her to God. She had given the rest of her life to thank Joan for a few months of true peace.

"I—I saw...." Gabriel paused. What had he seen? What he, what everyone, had expected to see: A slender, blue-eyed girl, a miter jammed onto her head concealing half of a bloody and swollen face, her skull shaved bald to humiliate her, who cried out the name of Jesus as she died—in a voice that he now realized had not been Joan's at all. But there had been one thing that Fleur, it seemed, would not sacrifice to complete the illusion. He remembered seeing Joan's pouch hanging on her slim neck, almost, but not quite, hidden by her filthy shift.

He wondered if some of the "soldiers" in the crowd in full armor had been Assassins, making sure no one got too good a view of the false Joan. Hiding in plain sight.

"They told me that I must never reveal that I had lived, or else Fleur's death would be in vain. And so I did not. I've been wandering, going from town to town, working in inns and taverns. I've not gone back to my family. Jeanne the Maid is no more. But... when I learned you had returned... I had to come see you. To tell you I would never have asked this of our Fleur—or of you."

"No," he said. "You would never do so. But Fleur chose." This, he knew; this, he could truly comfort her with. The Assassins were many things, and it was cruel of them to have asked this of the girl, but he knew they would never force or threaten her. It would not surprise Gabriel if Fleur herself had proposed the plan. He held Jeanne's shoulders and looked into her eyes. "She loved you."

Her damp eyes widened as he spoke, hearing the words he was too fearful even now to speak. Then, softly, she said, "I don't hear my Voices any more. Have I lost my angels, Gabriel? Have they forsaken me?"

Slowly, gently, Gabriel reached to thumb away a fresh tear that rolled down her cheek. She was no longer a girl, but a woman. Her face was older, less innocent and rounded, but her skin was so soft. He realized all at once that the radiance he had taken to be light from a glorious, swollen full moon was not simply from the sky.

Joan looked up at him, her beautiful, kind heart in her eyes, and she was once again shining from within.

"No," Gabriel whispered. "I don't think they have forsaken you. They've *released* you. God, through Fleur's sacrifice, has given you back your life. You now get to choose what to do with it. What will you do, Jeanne?"

Words she had spoken so long ago came back to him. *How can I be Jeanne, a wife, when I have pledged to remain Jeanne, the Maid of Lorraine, as long as it should please God? I made that promise three years ago. My body, my heart... my Voices need of all of me right now.* And his plea: *Only let me share your journey for as long as you can.*

He knew, as he felt her cheek blush against his hand, that Joan was remembering that night, too. Her radiance blossomed as she lifted her own exploring fingers to caress his face. Gabriel trembled and leaned into her hand.

"Gabriel Laxart," whispered Joan of Arc, her face so bright he could hardly bear it, "I will let you share my journey forever."

Much, much later, Simon Hathaway unsteadily lifted the Animus helm from his head. With fumbling, shaking fingers, he undid the various clasps and stumbled over to the desk, leaning against it for a moment, catching his breath. In his distraught state, it took him a moment to recall the code necessary to erase from the records what he had just beheld.

Then he picked up his phone.

"Simon? What is it, what's wrong?" Anaya's voice was sleepy but full of concern.

"I—Anaya, I need to talk to you." Simon wanted to be calm, to explain clearly how he felt, but the words rushed out of

their own accord. "Don't go to Montreal yet. Not until after we've talked. Please. Tonight—"

"Simon." Now she was the calm one. "What happened?"

"A miracle," he said, half-laughing, half-sobbing. "And I'll tell you all about it. I'll tell you everything, Anaya. All the things I should have told you before, all the things I thought weren't important, but were really the only things that mattered. I know that sometimes it's too late for second chances, but I.... Just let me talk to you. And you can tell me if—if I'm too late for one."

A long pause. As long as twelve years. Simon gripped the phone so hard his hand hurt.

"I'll always listen to you, Simon." Anaya's voice was warm. "Come on round, then, and we'll talk. I'll put on the kettle for some tea."

EPILOGUE

"As you expected, it didn't take long."

Alan Rikkin smiled to himself, leaning back in the comfortable leather chair of Abstergo's corporate Airbus A319. "What have you got for me?"

"Hathaway used the Animus just a few hours ago."

And to think I thought Hathaway the overly cautious type, Rikkin mused. "Do you have the simulation?"

"No, sir, he was able to erase it using the bypass code Chodary had given him previously. But there's evidence that a simulation used to be there."

Rikkin glanced at his watch. "I've no time to deal with this right now. Keep monitoring him and we'll discuss proper measures upon my return. Do you think anyone suspects you?"

"Negative. Clarke was an excellent red herring. He drew all the attention. Once he was gone, Chodary was satisfied that the hacking was over."

"Do be careful as you continue," Rikkin warned. "I don't know how much Hathaway told her, but she's likely to be more sensitive to future attempts on your part."

"Agreed. She'd have caught me at once if not for Clarke."

"I'll notify the rest of Omega Team to stand down for the moment. When I get back from Madrid, however, we might be implementing the Double Epsilon."

Rikkin had tried valiantly to prevent Simon from learning the truth. He really had. He couldn't be faulted for what had to happen now. The image of Simon holding aloft the Sword of Eden, as if he were some sort of twenty-first century King Arthur who'd pulled forth Excalibur from the stone, had sent severe ripples through the Inner Sanctum. Some of them were ready to abandon centuries of how the Templar Order had *actually* worked for an idealized version of how, long ago, de Molay had *wanted* it to work.

King Arthur died in disillusionment, having been betrayed by his wife, his best friend, and his son. Jacques de Molay had been burned alive.

Their idealistic view was not the best path for the Templar Order.

"For Hathaway?" The voice in his ear drew Rikkin back to the present.

"For all of them, potentially. For... others, even. We'll see how Madrid goes."

"Omega stands by," said Andrew Davies.

There were secrets within secrets in the Templar Order. Omega Team was one of the deepest of all. The last; the end. They answered when he called upon them for endings. But for now, they would wait upon his order.

He was heading to Madrid, to what he hoped would be the beginning of the greatest chapter yet of Templar History.

"Alphas and Omegas," he said quietly, and called Sofia.

ACKNOWLEDGMENTS

A book like this is never created in a vacuum. Thanks go out to my always-wonderful agent, Lucienne Diver, for her constant support and efforts on my behalf. I was also extremely fortunate to be working with a group of creative, intelligent, and enthusiastic people at Ubisoft. Their unflagging support for this book and willingness to help, from the outset throughout the entire process, is deeply appreciated.

Thanks to Caroline Lamache and Holly Rawlinson, who reached out to me in late 2015 with the initial concept. Caroline and Anthony Marcantonio helped what turned out to be a sprawling and exciting adventure stay on track.

Aymar Azaizia helped tremendously during the brainstorming sessions where Joan, Simon, and Gabriel first made appearances. Richard Farrese and Anouk Bachman stood ready at almost any hour of the day to offer suggestions, clarification, and feedback to ensure that the world of Assassin's Creed integrated smoothly with the world of the early 15th century. Maxime Durand, historian extraordinaire, did the reverse, making certain any questions or requests for specific information were accommodated, so that the France of Joan of Arc felt real.

Kevin Stallard very kindly answered quite a lot of questions I had about how White Hats go about their days; any errors regarding Anaya's skills are entirely my own.

Appreciation goes out to the late scholar and historian Regine Pernoud. The bulk of her books on Joan of Arc consist of Joan's own words, and she is wise enough to know when to expound for the reader and when to let Joan come forward. Her books are engrossing, accessible, and informative, and I cannot recommend them highly enough to anyone interested in learning about the historical Joan of Arc.

Finally, thanks to a young woman who, in real life, didn't need a Sword of Eden to astonish the world. In 1429 and nearly six hundred years later, Joan of Arc did not and does not require embellishment to captivate, inspire, and amaze. *Merci, La Pucelle*, for letting me weave a tale around your truth.

—CHRISTIE GOLDEN